THE
CALL
OF THE
WRENS

Also by Jenni L. Walsh

ADULT FICTION
A Betting Woman
Side by Side
Becoming Bonnie

MIDDLE GRADE
Over and Out
By the Light of Fireflies
I Am Defiance
Hettie and the London Blitz
She Dared: Malala Yousafzai
She Dared: Bethany Hamilton

Praise for *The Call of the Wrens*

"In *The Call of the Wrens*, Jenni L. Walsh chronicles two volunteers in the Women's Royal Navy Service during the First and Second World Wars. Spanning decades in a story that is both epic and intimate, *The Call of the Wrens* is an original and compelling tale of sisterhood and strength."

—PAM JENOFF, NEW YORK TIMES BESTSELLING AUTHOR
OF THE WOMAN WITH THE BLUE STAR

"What a lovely surprise. The heroines in Walsh's latest can be found racing around war-torn Europe on motorbikes, relaying secret messages and undertaking daring missions as part of the real-life women's branch of the Royal Navy. There's also giddy romance, family secrets, and shocking twists, making it an absolute treat for historical fiction lovers."

—FIONA DAVIS, NEW YORK TIMES BESTSELLING
AUTHOR OF THE MAGNOLIA PALACE

"The lives of two women in two different world wars collide in unexpected ways in this powerful exploration of the British Women's Royal Naval Service, commonly known as the Wrens, a daring group of real-life women who were instrumental in both World War I and World War II. Laced with triumph and tragedy, bravery and redemption, this tale of finding oneself in modern history's darkest hours will break your heart and put it back together again, all in one delightful read."

—KRISTIN HARMEL, NEW YORK TIMES BESTSELLING
AUTHOR OF THE FOREST OF VANISHING STARS

"*Call of the Wrens* by Jenni L. Walsh is a beautifully written gem of a historical novel, shedding light on a little-known group of women, the Wrens, during both world wars. Walsh skillfully entwines the stories of Evelyn and Marion as they journey to find their voices and, ultimately, their calling. I was completely captivated by this richly drawn portrait of strength, survival, and love."

—JILLIAN CANTOR, USA TODAY BESTSELLING
AUTHOR OF BEAUTIFUL LITTLE FOOLS

"In *The Call of the Wrens*, Jenni L. Walsh has woven a wonderful tale inspired by the real-life women's branch of the United Kingdom's Royal Navy. This dual-timeline novel features two courageous heroines, Marion and Evelyn, roaring around Europe on motorbikes during both world wars. Thrilling missions, family secrets, romance—it's all here. We need more books like this that show the remarkable contributions made by adventurous women during the darkest of times."

—ELISE HOOPER, AUTHOR OF *ANGELS OF THE PACIFIC*

"In *The Call of the Wrens*, Jenni L. Walsh lends her remarkable voice to the little-known, intrepid women of the Women's Royal Navy Service, women who revved up their motorcycles and risked their necks to heed Britain's call to win the world wars. Packed full of action and with a heart-wrenching twist, Marion and Evelyn's story reads like a battle cry for anyone who's had to fight against other people's expectations and find her own place, and her chosen family, in this world."

—CAROLINE WOODS, AUTHOR OF *THE LUNAR HOUSEWIFE*

"With a winning blend of adventure and romance, Walsh highlights the bravery and intrepid spirits of women destined to forge a path beyond the restrictive expectations of their era and circumstance. A winning treatise on courage and sisterhood, *The Call of the Wrens* will have fans of Kate Quinn and Erika Robuck rejoicing with each compulsively readable page."

—RACHEL MCMILLAN, AUTHOR OF *THE MOZART CODE*

THE
CALL
OF THE
WRENS

JENNI L. WALSH

HARPER MUSE

Published by Harper Muse, an imprint of HarperCollins Focus LLC.

Lyrics quoted from "If You Were the Only Girl (in the World)" written by Nat D. Ayer and Clifford Grey were first published in 1916 by B. Feldman & Co. and are in the public domain.

Any internet addresses (websites, blogs, etc.) in this book are offered as a resource. They are not intended in any way to be or imply an endorsement by HarperCollins Focus LLC, nor does HarperCollins Focus LLC vouch for the content of these sites for the life of this book.

Library of Congress Cataloging-in-Publication Data

Names: Walsh, Jenni L., author.
Title: The call of the Wrens / Jenni L. Walsh.
Description: [Nashville] : Harper Muse, [2022] | Summary: "Based on real history, The Call of the Wrens explores the bonds of sisterhood and love even when all hope seems lost"-- Provided by publisher.
Identifiers: LCCN 2022015099 (print) | LCCN 2022015100 (ebook) | ISBN 9781400233885 (paperback) | ISBN 9781400233908 (epub) | ISBN 9781400233915
Subjects: LCSH: Great Britain. Royal Navy. Women's Royal Naval Service (1917-1919)--Fiction. | Great Britain. Royal Navy. Women's Royal Naval Service (1939-1993)--Fiction. | World War, 1914-1918--Participation, Female--Fiction. | World War, 1939-1945--Participation, Female--Fiction. | LCGFT: Historical fiction. | Novels.
Classification: LCC PS3623.A446218 C35 2022 (print) | LCC PS3623.A446218 (ebook) | DDC 813/.6--dc23/eng/20220411
LC record available at https://lccn.loc.gov/2022015099
LC ebook record available at https://lccn.loc.gov/2022015100

Printed in the United States of America
22 23 24 25 26 LSC 5 4 3 2 1

To my husband, for still believing it can be done

CHAPTER 1

MARION

July 1940
West Devon

T he knock came at dusk. Marion knew the rhythm of it instantly.
Slow—quick-quick-slow—quick-quick.

The pattern had been conceived over twenty years ago after a long night of revelry at the dance hall. Eddie, Sara, and Marion had fox-trotted for hours. Cheeks flushed, Sara had hung on her current beau's arm and instructed Eddie to rap the melody on the boys' cabin door before retiring for the evening.

The knock had become a bit of an inside joke, used liberally, even on random doors.

Now it had to be Sara calling on Marion.

It wouldn't be Eddie.

Marion didn't rise from her chair, the darkness of the room all around her.

"Marion, I know you're in there." She heard Sara's pixie voice, a voice that was once as familiar to Marion as a sister's.

The bustle of the chickens outside filled the silence that followed.

Sara tried again. "The window's open. You'd close it up tight if you were working at the library."

There was another beat of fowl-filled din, until the doorknob jiggled. Marion always kept it locked. Not that anyone ever came all the way out to her small cottage. Which was the way she liked it.

"You leave me no choice," Sara called. "I'll come in through the window if I must."

Marion rolled her head from one side to the other, stiff from sitting since her afternoon tea. There was no stopping Sara, that bullheaded woman. She did this every few years, fluttering into Marion's life and checking in on her, reminding Marion of the bond they had, reminding her of Sara's betrayal, ultimately stirring up painful memories.

Even now, hearing the knocked melody, hearing Sara's voice, knowing they shared an unspoken guilt, one Marion couldn't forgive Sara or herself for, made Marion press a hand to her abdomen, as if she needed to physically hold herself together. Marion's fingertips touched the softened paper she habitually kept within her dress pocket, a reminder—a self-inflicted comeuppance—for what she once had to do.

A tightness stretched across Marion's chest. Those moments, those feelings, that angst should've been left in Marion's past. Why wouldn't Sara allow it? Why did Sara insist on inserting reminders into Marion's present? More so, why must Sara insert herself, literally, into Marion's home?

She heard a stack of books topple by the window, the window Sara had undoubtedly just climbed through. Marion kept a stack there. She kept one beside her chair. She kept stacks nearly everywhere within her four walls.

Sara's uneven footsteps maneuvered through Marion's cottage, until there she was.

A woman who'd once been a fixture in Marion's life. A heavy-handed fixture at that.

Sara had aged since she'd last visited Marion, but she still held the same lithe figure and heart-shaped face. The scar next to her eye, given to her by Marion, could easily blend with her laugh lines if Sara had a mind for laughing, though at the moment it appeared she did not.

Marion didn't use any words to greet her. She didn't stand. She remained in her chair in front of the unlit hearth, a perfectly positioned beam of light hitting the novel in her lap. That evening she'd chosen *Lolly Willowes*, a character with whom Marion felt a peculiar kinship, both middle-aged spinsters, both having suffered great losses that upended their lives.

In the novel the character Laura, or Lolly, made a pact with the devil for her freedom. *Though was she ever truly free?* Marion wondered. She released a long sigh as Sara saw to opening the heavy curtains.

"There," Sara said, dusting her hands together. "Adequate light."

Within a large cage atop a pedestal table, a pigeon cooed, as if saying hello to an old friend. Traitor.

"I hadn't expected to see your bird again," Sara said, taking on a softer tone, making her way deeper into the room. "My father's pigeons rarely lived past fifteen. But 486 is a special bird, isn't he?"

Sara stopped beside Marion, her arm raising as if she meant to stroke Marion's hair. Instead, Sara clasped her hands together at her middle.

"I'm fine," Marion said abruptly. Her voice croaked, the first she'd used it in days. Over the years, she'd become learned on her condition. Being in the midst of an uneasy social situation all but froze her tongue. Otherwise, talking or not talking was at her own discretion. She generally spoke as a means to an end. To Sara she said, "I'm eating. I walk daily. I work at the library on my appointed days. Even 486 is doing fine, as you can see. Good on you for checking on the hermit. Go home to your family, Wren Brown."

Marion had purposely spoken in a bitter tone and intentionally used Sara's more formal title. Sara glanced at 486 again and ignored Marion's attempt to put distance between them. "I am in fact coming to you as Wren Brown."

Despite herself, Marion upturned her chin to better see Sara. These days it took a lot to pique Marion's interest, usually only stories and moments written into the pages of a book, where a happy ending was nearly always promised. There was a time when she thought her own was as good as guaranteed.

Marion had once put so much stock in serving as a Wren. Being a part of the Women's Royal Naval Service had driven her, to a fault.

But that'd been a long time ago.

The war had ended.

The Wrens disbanded.

So why was Sara coming to her as Wren Brown now?

If she knew Sara, Marion only had to wait for the woman to continue. And she did, asking Marion, "Have you kept up with the happenings? There's another war on."

There's a war on.

Hadn't Marion heard that many times before? Hadn't that been the beginning of the end?

Sara stared at Marion another few beats, neither of them blinking, before Sara looked away and studied the small room, her gaze zeroing in on a stack of books beside Marion. She'd sit there, Marion knew. Nowhere else for her to do so. As predicted, Sara perched on the stack, leaned closer. "My children are safe with my parents. But I've joined up again as a Jenny. The Wrens are back on. I think you should return with me."

Sara was slow to say more. Did she suspect Marion was reliving her betrayal? Or was Sara hesitant for another reason, as if there was something she was leaving unsaid that went beyond their secrets? Again, Marion's hand ticked toward the yellowed document in her dress pocket. She had half a mind to ask Sara what she was after. The other half simply wanted to be left alone.

"Please go, Sara." Marion wanted nothing to do with a second war.

But Sara didn't take her leave. "I'll retire here for the night. It's too late to travel."

Sara pulled free the throw blanket strewn over the back of the very chair in which Marion sat and proceeded to an armchair in the corner by the bird.

By the third *thud* from Sara's removal of books from the cushion, Marion was on her feet. She retreated to her bunk, knowing her memories would travel through time until she was back in Birmingham. Back to where it all began. To Marion's desire to be wanted, the beginning of her downfall.

⸙

March 1914
Birmingham

"Did you hear me, Marion?" Sister Margaret stood in front of Marion's chair. "I said, if it's any consolation, has anyone told you that your name means 'wished-for child'?"

Wished-for child.

Hearing those words almost brought a young Marion's head up from *Jane Eyre*. But she kept on reading, without acknowledging Sister Margaret's sentiment.

Children can feel, but they cannot analyse their feelings; and if the analysis is partially effected in thought, they know not how to express the result of the process in words.

That last part. Marion read Jane's thoughts again.

. . . *they know not how to express the result of the process in words.*

Marion had never spoken to another human being, not that she could remember, in her fourteen years and her many different homes. The memory of one of her earliest so-called homes was jumbled, almost as if Marion were seeing herself instead of possessing her own body. She'd been a babbling three-year-old, her papers stated. But then Marion had been surrounded by so many new faces, too many faces, whipping in front of her. Shouting, screaming. She'd been unable to form any words, as if her facial muscles had turned to stone of their own accord. At her feet, a wetness puddled on the ground. She turned and ran. Where, Marion didn't remember. But it had been dark where she hid. Her socks had been wet.

Later, when she was found by a pleasant enough nun, Marion had chosen to continue not to speak. She'd chosen not to talk every single day since. Her mutism, as she'd heard the doctors call it, was involuntary in situations where Marion held a lack of control or was thrust into the center of attention. Otherwise, in moments where she didn't experience paralyzing fear, Marion simply had no desire to gift that part of herself to another human being, who'd soon be nothing more than another memory. Another nun, another priest, another housemother, another foundling. A carousel of faces, coming and going, gone too quickly.

Ironic, what Marion read next: *For one thing, I have no father or mother, brothers or sisters.*

Sister Margaret's words that Marion was a wished-for child might've meant something if she hadn't just told Marion she was being relocated to yet another orphanage in the morning. Sister Margaret, with her expressionless face, didn't look like she'd cry a second over

Marion leaving. It'd be one less mouth to feed, one less child to clothe, to house, to educate.

Wished-for child? Marion thought not.

But Sister Margaret had fed her, clothed her, housed her, educated her, so for those reasons Marion raised her head and smiled at this small act of kindness before she went and packed her few belongings.

———— ⚬⚬⚬ ————

"She's a mute," Marion heard whispered as she took her first steps into St. Anne's Home for Boys and Girls. Sister Margaret had just handed Marion off to Sister Florence, who now edged her deeper into the entrance hall.

Usually there was little excitement about the arrival of someone of Marion's age, not like there was with the younger kids. It made it easier. It made Marion feel less like stone when only a few children turned up with a quick hello. But now Marion's cheeks flushed and her brow hardened from the many eyes upon her. As if she were the newest act to come to Small Heath with the Sanger's Circus. She'd never actually been to the circus, but Marion had seen a troupe's arrival to London one time. They'd had a parade to announce themselves, with a menagerie, a military band, an elephant, over fifty horses, and a collection of "living human curiosities."

For the group of kids standing before Marion, peering between and over each other, Marion was one of those curiosities.

The Wordless Waif.

See the girl who has never spoken a word. Not one. Never a grunt or groan. Nor a laugh. Try as you may.

At each home she'd lived in, the other children *had* tried, making it a game to cajole something out of Marion, generally a cuss. But soon they'd see Marion was not going to give in to their antics, and they'd tire of her.

Moreover, Marion didn't intend to play with them at all, shaking her head at marbles and Kick the Wick.

Marion would read. She was a reader. Her friends were the always-present Jane Eyre, Anne Elliot, and the Dashwood sisters.

She'd made the mistake of getting close to another girl once before, silently playing dolls and cards. The girl had even enticed Marion to play tag. Marion let herself giggle softly at the girl's jokes, a first for her. One morning on the loo, Marion even whispered her name, Caroline, for only her own ears to hear.

"Caroline . . . Caroline."

But then Caroline had been adopted a few days later. Marion hadn't picked up a book the entire time they played together. But after Caroline left, Jane Eyre was still there, waiting for Marion.

In St. Anne's foyer Marion stood ramrod straight, a small chalkboard hung around her neck. As the other children looked on, she hugged her small satchel to her chest to hide the slate but also in a protective manner. She had *Jane Eyre* inside her bag. Marion had pilfered the book three orphanages ago.

Beyond her book, the bag's contents consisted of only two more articles: the gingham cloth Marion had been found in, which she'd guessed to be a portion of a woman's dress, and a cheap brooch that had been attached to the blue-and-white fabric. Marion was certain that if the jewelry had been of worth, it never would've landed in her hands. As far as the scrap of cloth, lonely days and nights had left Marion to imagine the young mother who'd torn the skirt of her dress to wrap and discard an unwanted newborn.

Perhaps the effort to keep Marion warm had meant a portion of

THE CALL OF THE WRENS

her mother once cared for her. Or perhaps the scrap of fabric was a hastily executed afterthought, motivated by guilt from the fact it'd been a cold December day. In either case, she was abandoned.

One of the older girls, probably close to Marion's age, approached her in the entrance hall of St. Anne's and said hello.

Even if Marion wanted to, which she didn't, she felt herself unable to respond to the girl. Not with all those eyes on her. Especially not with how the girl widened her eyes in a mocking manner. The others found this funny. Sister Florence tsked.

Marion locked her gaze on the tiled floor. With relief, she watched the girl's shoes backpedal to the semicircle she'd come from. Sister Florence laid pressure on Marion's back. Marion stepped forward, slightly raising her head again, including the knees of the other children in her line of sight.

A boy with a hole in his trousers stood in front of her next. He extended a hand. "I'm Edward." He waited, his hand still outstretched.

There was a time when the idea of engaging with a peer and returning the gesture would've seemed hopeless, too overwhelming. But Marion had been in this position many times, so she focused on only his face and, ignoring the others, took a deep breath and slowly shook his hand.

The others snickered, their presence flooding her again.

Marion caught the roll of Edward's eyes before he turned to show his disapproval to the others. They fell silent, with the exception of one girl who tittered behind her hand.

To Marion, he continued, as if nothing had happened, "But everyone calls me Eddie."

Marion held no plans to call him anything, let alone Eddie. Beneath a mop of red hair, he was all arms, teeth, and freckles.

At that, Sister Florence clapped her hands once, a folder with

Marion's name on it tucked beneath her arm. "Now that we've welcomed Marion, off to breakfast. It's on the table."

Marion was quickly forgotten, thank the Lord, and she felt the muscles in her face soften and become her own again.

Sister Florence reached for Marion's bag. "I'll just put this upstairs in the girls' wing. Fifth bed on the right, next to little Millie."

Marion hesitantly let go of her meager belongings.

More slowly than the others, she walked into the dining hall. It wasn't unlike her other homes. Six or so long tables. Twenty or so children at each table. There was a short line of children waiting for a free spot to sit.

Edward was in the line, joking and jostling with the others there. He saw Marion approaching and offered her a toothy smile. His friendliness made her uncomfortable. She didn't smile back, yet he seemed nonplussed by her cold reaction.

It was clear the others were drawn to him. In line waiting to eat, Edward was holding court. *Magnetic* was a word for him. But as Marion dragged her feet toward the queue, she yearned to maintain her distance, as if they were both two souths or two norths. She kept her focus on her shoes. Embarrassment coursed through her. She wished her footwear was more remarkable. Fewer holes. Tighter stitching.

His weren't much better, but still, it seemed he'd been better looked after.

Soon a seat was vacated for Edward, and he sat to eat.

Marion shuffled forward in the queue, her hands balled at her sides, until one of the sisters motioned her toward a newly vacated spot. Of course it was beside Edward.

Now Marion's porridge was the most interesting thing she'd ever laid eyes on. Fortunately Edward was caught up in the happenings around them—watching one boy use his spoon to launch his break-fast onto another boy's face—and Marion's presence went generally unnoticed. Splendid.

⸰⸰⸰

After breakfast Marion found herself in the common room, where bookshelves defined one of the corners. There were more books than most places she'd lived. She was pleased about that. Marion planted herself in the corner, right on the floor, her feet crossed at the ankles, her dress neatly draped over her legs.

Other children milled about. Marion felt their glances and some of their stares, but they otherwise paid the Wordless Waif little mind.

At random, she plucked a book from a shelf. It was a game Marion liked to play.

Emma.

She flipped to the beginning.

Emma Woodhouse, handsome, clever, and rich, with a comfortable home and happy disposition, seemed to unite some of the best blessings of existence; and had lived nearly twenty-one years in the world with very little to distress or vex her.

Marion cocked her head, thinking, *Hello, Emma. Well, aren't we strangers? I'm not certain I like you yet. It may be some time before we're good friends.*

Shoes paused just within her line of sight.

But then they were gone.

Marion flicked her gaze up to watch Edward walking toward the draughts table, then returned to her book. Marion read again the next day too. Edward paused in front of her again, this time longer. As she resumed reading, his laugh, while he kept company with the other boys, filtered into her corner. He glanced her way.

Could his interest be in her? Or was it in one of the many books she was blocking? Marion was lolling in front of the bookcases, occasionally watching the children from behind the safety of her book. In all her orphanages she'd come to recognize something: The girls generally paired off or formed tiny clusters, sometimes merging to create larger groups to engage in this or that. The boys likewise seemed to have a favorite chap, but they usually tumbled around together like a pack of wolves. Marion hadn't yet noticed with whom Edward was most chummy.

It'd be odd if he didn't have a best mate. She thought of him again as magnetic, everyone and everything pulling toward him.

Marion herself always felt more of a repellent, after the novelty of being a "living human curiosity" quickly wore off. Which it already had, it seemed, with the other children. But perhaps not yet with Edward. With so little attention paid to her, it'd been easy to settle into her corner and escape into a book, most of the novels advanced for Marion's age.

She'd been educated in the three Rs of writing, reading, and arithmetic more than most other orphans in these places on account of her mutism. Way back when, when it first became apparent she wouldn't speak, a nun had held a bamboo cane and a writing utensil mere inches from Marion's nose.

"You will communicate," she'd been told. "Only one of these needs to be used."

Marion had chosen the writing utensil. She learned to write. She learned to read. And she had learned that if she didn't want the cane, she'd use the small chalkboard she'd been given.

Now Marion saw the special consideration that'd been given to her education as a grace. Where would she have been without her books?

On the third day, Edward's shoes stopped in front of Marion. This time Edward knelt. He leaned in conspiratorially, whispering even, "Have you been getting on all right?"

She debated not looking up, but Marion placed her finger on her spot in *Emma* and met his eyes. They were green, and her mind instantly conjured the Loch Ness Monster.

Hmm, was Nessie even green? Or was that just how Marion had imagined the creature? She turned toward the shelf to her right, wondering if there was any literature on Nessie.

Then Marion realized herself and turned back to Edward. He was eyeing the slate around her neck. Did he expect Marion to answer his question?

His green eyes seemed to smile. "What are you . . . around thirteen? Fourteen?"

She nodded.

"Well, which is it? Thirteen?"

Marion shook her head.

"Fourteen then. Older than me by a year." He snapped his fingers playfully. "Well, I think I'm thirteen. No one is sure. At my first orphanage, they lined me up against some of the other boys to try to see how old I was. Two, they decided back then." He shrugged. "They must've written it all down in my papers because at a later home they told me the story as if it were a funny way to figure me out. I'm not sure it's funny, though."

Marion shook her head. It wasn't comical. It was sad not knowing where you came from or how old you truly were. She knew all too well. Her own age had also been hypothesized. As her story went, she'd been left on a hospital's doorstep in little more than her nappy at one minute after midnight on the first of January at the turn of the century. Had it been a fresh start for the woman who'd birthed her? Had she been trying to erase everything prior to 1900, including Marion's existence? Marion would never know. But since she was still jaundiced, Marion was assumed to be days old, and she had been given the birthdate of her abandonment.

She supposed she and Edward were fortunate to know at least some of their stories, though. Many didn't have papers that followed them from home to home.

Edward gave a departing pat on his knees, then stood, brushing wavy hair from his eyes. "Marion," he began. It was startling to hear her name coming from another child. Usually it was only the nuns who spoke to her. "Can I come talk to you again? I've told the others to leave you be. But would it be okay? I like talking to you."

A peculiar thing to say, as she hadn't yet said anything to him in return. But Marion found herself nodding. This exchange had been harmless enough. But then she remembered Caroline and how she'd let herself come to enjoy the girl's company. Marion's head changed directions.

Edward chuckled, then closed his eyes. "Too late. I only saw the yes." He backed away, his lids still tight.

A laugh slipped from Marion.

"Heard that too!" he said.

Marion's hand flew to her mouth. She held it there, covering a smile that surprised even her.

CHAPTER 2
EVELYN

April 1936
Weybridge

M r. Orwell sat beside Evelyn in her father's Buick. She was wary
of his brown suit. Father always said the color brown denoted
a keen sense of duty and responsibility, someone who took his obli-
gations very seriously. Evelyn's mother, on the other hand, found the
color annoyingly dull and preferred to dress Father in lighter springtime blues and grays and in handsome vertical stripes.

Evelyn hoped Mr. Orwell was neither annoyingly dull nor excessively judicious.

"You may start," he said flatly.

Evelyn pressed the accelerator and began to travel down the long
drive of her family's estate, where she'd practiced endlessly, testing
the limits of her father's automobile in preparation for this very day.

Did Mr. Orwell know her mother had originally suggested that
Evelyn take the test for drivers with a disability? Evelyn had fought
her on it, and Evelyn had won. She was undergoing the same test her
peers were taking.

Earning a driver's license was more than obtaining a piece of paper
that claimed, "Evelyn P. Fairchild is hereby licensed to drive a Motor

Car or Motor Cycle." It meant freedom. It meant having the ability to zoom across this earth, after so many years of being immobile. It meant she was *fit* to drive.

Evelyn sucked in a breath. She and Mr. Orwell were not a mile down the road and she had already grazed a curb. Mr. Orwell's hand shot to the car's ceiling for support. She quickly apologized, citing nerves, and bit back reminding him how well she'd handled the choke and ignition lever when they'd begun. Evelyn had even announced when she thought they'd reached a good operating temperature and how she'd be switching the choke to a slightly leaner mixture of air and fuel.

"I do believe that's the proper level for ideal fuel consumption," she had said. But had her *thwack* of the curb dismissed all his goodwill?

She glanced at Mr. Orwell again, not daring to take her eyes off the paved road or an approaching lorry for more than a heartbeat. Mr. Orwell wasn't holding on anymore. An improvement.

Evelyn added an even sunnier smile to her expression, taking care not to let herself look too enthusiastic. She debated small talk. Decided against it. The lorry passed. She maneuvered gracefully around a pothole before turning down a country street. It was nothing but the two of them and the open road now, stretching on and on. Trees created a canopy overtop. Evelyn found it thrilling to be traversing something other than her own gravel drive. She slid the gear lever into Neutral, released the clutch, pressed the clutch, disconnecting the power from the engine, and transitioned the lever into the next gear. The shift of gears was silky smooth.

Mr. Orwell had to be impressed.

Evelyn squeezed her fingers into the steering wheel, feeling the leather grow warmer beneath her gloves. Exhilaration coursed through her. She was driving like any other young woman her age, despite the fact she'd spent her childhood as anything but. The casting of her leg and foot had begun when Evelyn was only hours old. It ended when she was sixteen, following a final operation. But that morning as the sun rose, she also rose as an of-age seventeen-year-old who ached to move.

Swiftly.

Quickly.

Smoothly.

"Miss Fairchild," Mr. Orwell said, a note of concern in his nasally voice. "Miss Fairchild, do slow down. This is not a race car, and you are not a racer at the Brooklands."

Evelyn was caught between alarm at the reprimand and intrigue at the mention of a race car. Now, wouldn't that be thrilling? But the idea of going even faster across the earth and whipping around a track couldn't be Evelyn's focus at the moment; she needed to focus on slowing them down. More specifically, synchronizing the shaft speeds. With the gearbox in a neutral position, Evelyn blipped the throttle, increasing the rotation of the gears connected to the engine so that they'd match the speed of the gears connected to the wheels. Perfection.

Mr. Orwell seemingly agreed, Evelyn catching how his head bounced in an appraising manner.

Well done, us, Evelyn thought. That *us* was her and her father. He'd taught her well, the insides of a car endlessly fascinating to them both. Father had grown up around cars, but the Great War had happened and he'd fallen away from it all. But Evelyn realized now that her father had been holding out on her. He'd never taken her to the Brooklands. She wondered if seeing an automobile zip around a track would be as enticing as the racehorses at Lingfield.

"I've seen enough, Miss Fairchild," Mr. Orwell said. "You may drive home."

"Of course," she said agreeably.

But had Evelyn done enough? Shown enough? Proven enough?

Mr. Orwell had to be none the wiser that her left foot was two sizes smaller than her right since both of her shoes were the same size. Where most girls her age padded their bras, wishing to be a C instead of an A, Evelyn stuffed her left stocking and shoe.

Mr. Orwell was irritatingly silent as she returned them to her home. Even with him having *seen enough*, she took care with everything she did. Eventually, there was silence around them, the car's engine off. Evelyn spotted her father's expectant face in a front window. She clenched her teeth, willing Mr. Orwell to declare his decision.

Inside her head, Evelyn screamed for him to get on with it already. But he sat there, reviewing the notes he'd made for himself.

She folded her hands in her lap, squeezing until her knuckles were surely white beneath her gloves. She thought perhaps she should've vocalized to him what having a license meant to her. The freedom, yes. But obtaining this little piece of paper would be validation.

Evelyn's mother doubted that she could pass, as her mother had doubted her many times before.

"Evelyn, no, you can't climb that tree. You're not like other children."

"No, sweetie, that ground is far too uneven to walk over. You'll stumble and fall."

"Let's school at home, Evie. Other children can be so cruel."

"Sweetheart, you aren't strong enough yet."

Being born with a clubfoot had meant a childhood of lying about; of plasters, special boots, and bracings; of a left leg so stunted and fragile looking one would've thought it could've snapped; of parents who were never farther than arm's reach. Theirs, not hers.

"Miss Fairchild—" Mr. Orwell began. His face was aggravatingly unreadable.

"Yes?" Evelyn said, unable to help herself.

The man looked annoyed that she'd cut in. Evelyn pulled her bottom lip between her teeth. He stared at her three long seconds before finally—*finally*—saying, "On behalf of the Surrey County Council, I will provide my signature that deems you an able driver."

Able driver.

Able driver.

But what Evelyn also heard was *able-bodied*.

She could've hugged him. She certainly would not. But the fact of the matter was Evelyn could've with how wonderful she felt.

She was fit to drive. She had passed the driver's test—the ordinary one.

Elation and pride filled her, and she knew exactly how—or rather *where*—she wanted to celebrate.

———— ✆ ————

August 1939
Weybridge

The Brooklands.

It'd been three years since Evelyn had begun coming to the tracks, Mr. Orwell inciting the destination upon her. Upon her first time setting eyes on the grandstands and the drivers, hearing the sounds of the engines, smelling the petrol, Evelyn immediately loved everything about it—even more so than being at the horse tracks, and that was saying something, as the majestic creatures enamored her greatly.

In fact, Evelyn had once asked her mother for a horse of her own; they had the land for it. But her mother stroked Evelyn's hair and said she feared Evelyn would fall off. Evelyn had let it go, learning at a young age to pick her battles.

But the Brooklands . . . it was different. Three years ago, Evelyn came. She saw. She immediately wanted to conquer it herself. She had pleaded with her mother to let her try racing. *"There's a roof and doors to keep me inside,"* Evelyn had argued. *"I'd have to be rather reckless to fall out of that."*

Perhaps she should've left off the last part. But after a year of insistent asking, and with some cajoling from Father, Mother had finally agreed to let Evelyn circle the track. *"To get it out of your system,"* her mother had said, "temporarily," because it was "beneath" her.

Apparently her reluctance had grown to be less about Evelyn's safety and more about appearances, and lately her mother had been demanding that Evelyn "mature" from the endeavor of racing and her so-called toys so she could be taken "seriously" by society.

Her mother could barely say the word *spinster*, the term so disparaging to her, but her mother's spiel was largely the same: *"I know your childhood felt shortened, which is why your father and I have taken the questions about your interests on the chin and have allowed this escapade for these past few years instead of requiring you to pursue a husband. But, Evelyn, you're twenty years old now. I am done smiling politely at luncheons. It's time to attend a finishing school; long overdue, in fact. You must adequately learn how to run your own household, to bring up a family, to hold events for other ladies, and to get married."*

But that wasn't for Evelyn.

Right now Evelyn belonged on the tracks.

Currently she *was* on the track, in the midst of a race, in control of how fast she went, when she maneuvered, which overtaking move to complete. In part it was why she loved racing so fiercely.

She clutched tighter at the steering wheel of her V12 Delage, as if the extra force with her hands would aid in her acceleration.

First.

Evelyn was in first.

How novel. How marvelous.

Since her first go-around two years prior, this was the moment she'd been waiting for, craving. She maneuvered slightly to block Doreen, who was in second place. The Baroness was a close third. Too close. The others were right on their tails.

The smell of exhaust was everywhere. Evelyn gritted her teeth and tightened her grip even further, her eyes spending more time on the mirrors than on the finish line.

The grandstand spanned the final stretch of track. Every spectator was on their feet, their individual faces indiscernible. The trees formed a blurred green backdrop.

Evelyn was in awe. She could've pinched herself. Truly, it had been a dream to rumble down the same circuit as the likes of Gwenda Hawkes, Elsie Gleed, Kay Petre, and Doreen Evans.

Doreen.

Oh, blast it. Doreen performed an overtaking move that Evelyn hadn't seen coming. The Baroness tried now. But—aha!—Evelyn was ready for her and the finish line was too close. Evelyn claimed second. A grin remained on her face despite losing first—a position she'd yet to hold through the finish. How could she not smile, though, after moving at such a great speed, going nowhere yet everywhere?

One after another, all the remaining cars crossed the finish line. The noise of the crowd rose as the sound of the engines slowed. Evelyn made out her nickname—Dare D-Evelyn—and she knew that somewhere in the crowd her father was cheering and her mother was risking frown lines. Nothing a good cream couldn't fix.

Evelyn's mother certainly couldn't change Evelyn's mind about wanting to be at the Brooklands, despite her mother's doggedness that a young woman's interests should be elsewhere. The need to race consumed Evelyn, especially after she had learned that this very place was where her father had come when he was younger. He had never raced, but he'd been chummy with a chap who'd worked on the cars, and her father had often helped out, having to hide the grease from his own mother when he'd returned home.

Evelyn laughed freely as she killed her engine. Her goggles went on top of her head, and she unclipped the helmet straps. From around her neck she loosened a scarf.

Within moments Evelyn's mechanic approached. "Jolly good show, Miss Fairchild."

"Thank you, Wilkes. It felt marvelous. Truly so."

"I see a real future for you in racing. You could make a real name for yourself."

"Go on," she teased. It was music to her ears. If only her parents saw racing as a viable future too. But they didn't, not even Father. When the Great War had happened, he turned his focus to more practical things. Work and Mother. Eventually, he'd enlisted. Then Evelyn had come along, completing their family.

The word *family* was her mother's focus. With Evelyn of age— well past it, in her mother's eyes—marriage and a family were all she wanted for Evelyn. But the so-called marriage bar be damned; Evelyn didn't see why racing—or a woman's occupation in general—had to cease in order for a woman to have a husband and children. She often reminded her mother of the married Elsie Gleed. Although Elsie had recently divorced. Evelyn would need a new role model of a woman who kept a job and a family to persuade her mother that it was possible to do both.

Wilkes began pushing Evelyn's V12 Delage—with Evelyn at the wheel steering—toward the paddock, where she first had to pass through the crowd of press. With her free hand, she returned the spectators' waves, smiling the entire time, though wishing she were still barreling around the tracks. But there would be another day, another race. *"A real future,"* Wilkes had said, one she hoped she could eventually convince her parents to take seriously.

As they left the track, the press closed in. Evelyn heard the shouting of the nicknames of her and the other women.

"Evelyn," a reporter began, "you came close out there."

"Next time," she said joyfully. "Doreen is a worthy competitor. And it appears I must keep my eye on the Baroness as well."

"But will there be a next time?" the reporter asked, his pen poised over his notepad.

"Pardon?"

"A next time, Evelyn. Will there be one? Rumor has it that the Brooklands will cease races in the near future."

Evelyn turned toward Wilkes, who was standing by idly waiting for her to give him the sign to continue pushing her and her car toward the motoring village. He only pressed his lips together.

The reporter went on, "With talk of a second Great War, the Brooklands will be turning their efforts to aircraft production, just as they did twenty years ago. Or that's what we're hearing."

"Time will tell," was all Evelyn said. She was at a loss for anything more. She'd heard talk of another conflict with Germany. England's prime minister had traveled to Germany a year prior in an attempt to avert war. His meeting had been successful, Evelyn had thought. But then there had been the recent leaflets, one after another . . .

The first:

SOME THINGS YOU SHOULD
KNOW IF WAR SHOULD COME

The second:

YOUR GAS MASK: HOW TO KEEP
IT AND HOW TO USE IT

The third:

EVACUATION: WHY AND HOW

The fourth:

YOUR FOOD IN WARTIME

The fifth:

FIRE PRECAUTIONS IN WARTIME

Please, no more. Evelyn's mother had become fainter with each
one. She also gasped at how single boys between twenty and twenty-
two were required to undergo six months of military training. *"Thank
goodness Percy is twenty-three,"* she had said, watching for Evelyn's reaction to the name of her childhood friend. She'd given her mother
nothing. If Evelyn's mother had her way, Percy would also be un-single
in the very near future.

Evelyn offered the reporter a winning smile, politely informing
him their interview was complete, and signaled to Wilkes. They
began moving toward the motoring village again.

Evelyn's brow furrowed as she let the reporter's words sink in. *The
Brooklands. Closing to races. Aircraft production.*

She should've expected it with all the anticipated war prepara-
tions; however, she didn't know the Brooklands aided in the war all

those years ago. Her father had only spoken of not coming to the tracks any longer. Plus, truth be told, Evelyn hadn't thought of the Brooklands's existence beyond her own existence there.

But the Brooklands was everything to her. Evelyn lived for each day she flew across the earth, after being caged for so long.

Within the paddock, Wilkes stopped outside the maintenance shed.

Evelyn swung both legs from the low automobile and stood as quickly as possible, allowing her skirt to drop and cover her thinner left leg. Her mother didn't like when society glimpsed Evelyn's past.

And there Evelyn's mother was now, coming her way, with Father at her side. Evelyn grabbed a rag and knelt beside Wilkes, intent on ignoring them for as long as possible, even if it was only for a few glorious seconds longer.

The Baroness and her mechanic, Rose, pulled in beside them.

Wilkes gave a greeting nod toward Rose.

"Evelyn, sweetheart," Mother called, approaching.

Evelyn sighed, stood.

"Brava, my dear," Father cheered.

"Yes, brava," her mother said but with far less enthusiasm. "We've come to fetch you."

Evelyn fought an eye roll. "You know you're not supposed to be back here."

"Which is why we've only come to fetch you," her mother insisted, "not stay."

"But I'd like to help Wilkes look over my car and see to any—"

"Evelyn, darling, we pay Wilkes to do such things. Things that aren't becoming of a young lady, yes?"

Rose ticked her eyes toward their conversation, and Evelyn avoided meeting her gaze. Instead, Evelyn looked to her father. But

Father's attention was purposefully elsewhere. He may've pressed Mother from time to time, but he was the one who'd taught Evelyn how to pick her battles.

On the days her parents didn't follow her to the motoring village, Evelyn was regularly involved in her car's maintenance, not one bit worried about getting grease under her perfectly filed fingernails. She had no intention of giving that up and every intention of continuing to climb the leaderboard. But for now she'd give her mother this small victory. Evelyn dropped the rag and gave Wilkes a goodbye before being ushered away.

"You'll never guess who is here," her mother said. She managed to avoid touching anyone within the crowd. She also managed to avoid raising her voice while still being heard.

"Who?" Evelyn asked.

"Percy."

"Who?" she repeated impishly. Their family had known the Harrington family for eons. Generations, in fact.

Evelyn's mother ignored her. She said conspiratorially, "I told him not to move a muscle."

Evelyn felt her mother's hand on the small of her back, thrusting her forward until she had no choice but to lay a hand on Percy's arm to steady herself, drawing his attention from where he stood at a railing.

"Hello, Percy," she began. "So nice to see you again."

His smile was warm. Most girls would swoon over it. They swooned over Percy Harrington in general. He very much had the Superman look. Or the presence of a hero from the silver screen, one who'd single-handedly solve the murder while saving the beautiful but helpless damsel.

Percy's shoulders were broad. He had a thin waist and an athletic build to his legs, or at least Evelyn assumed he did beneath the widely tapered legs of his trousers. His attire was designed for work and play. When not saving women, Percy could've been a boxer or a star swimmer. In fact, she'd heard he recently won a swimming competition. Not at anything as fancy as the Olympics, but he'd swum in races in London.

Evelyn admitted to liking Percy's competitive spirit. They were alike in that way. Even during their childhoods—when Evelyn was supposed to be on the sidelines healing from a surgery—he had egged her on, carrying her to a tire swing or hoisting her onto his back. One time he even climbed aboard Evelyn's roller chair and, trying to impress her with his grand idea, sent them flying downhill. At the bottom they had toppled over, both of them whooping from the fun of it even while Evelyn skinned her knee. Percy had begged Evelyn not to tell. She never did. She didn't think her mother ever found out either.

But the camaraderie between Evelyn and Percy felt like it ended years ago, with her playmate morphing from Percy the Boy to Percy the Man, a potential suitor. Evelyn couldn't help feeling distant from him while also feeling quite pleased with that distance.

Evelyn's mother wished to eliminate the divide. Percy didn't even have a chance to greet Evelyn before Mother was saying, "Oh, Percy, the cut of your suit is simply perfect."

"Mother's doing," he said simply.

"They do know best," Evelyn's mother replied with a smile.

They talked on. Evelyn's father had excused himself to shake hands and talk business elsewhere, and Evelyn half turned her attention to a motorcycle race that was lining up. She even spotted Rose with her own motorbike. Evelyn hadn't known she raced too.

While she kept her gaze fixed on the track, Evelyn heard her mother inquire after Percy's parents, asking when they'd be coming to London next, when they'd all dine together. Evelyn's mother went on about how she'd almost narrowed down the perfect finishing school for Evelyn. That caught Evelyn's attention and she growled internally.

Evelyn would have words with her mother about *that*.

Then her mother coyly suggested that Percy and Evelyn should bowl a frame—or ten—laughing at her own quip. "Or perhaps you'd rather go to the cinema. Is there a film you've had a hankering to see?"

"I'm afraid I'm due back at the clinic shortly. But another time?" Percy shifted his focus from Evelyn's mother to Evelyn.

Evelyn smiled just as politely, not thinking the date would ever come to fruition. "That'd be lovely, Percy."

Mother beamed at the promise of a date for her daughter. "Yes, that would be lovely, Percy."

What was more likely was that Percy would romance another young woman, or two, which was no water off Evelyn's back. It wasn't that she didn't consider Percy a dish with his dark hair and eyes. But Percy the Man had recently opened his own medical practice, and it was as if a boxing bell had rung for his mother and Evelyn's mother to find him a wife, thrusting him into the land of courtship. Had there ever been a more antiquated word?

Evelyn's mother was actively trying to hurl Evelyn into his universe, where she'd be nothing more than a physician's wife, caring for his future children, hosting his dinners. Those types of wives didn't dirty their hands in the underbelly of anything but a turkey, and only if they couldn't pay someone else to do it.

Could Evelyn lead that life? Not yet. Maybe not ever. How was she to know? She'd only just begun living—and racing. The idea of stopping now caused her stomach to knot and breath to flee her lungs. But then Evelyn thought of what the reporter had said about the Brooklands closing, and she feared her mother would get her way after all, and soon Evelyn would be back in a cage, her future at a finishing school all but set.

And Evelyn knew one thing: it would be a battle she wouldn't be able to win.

CHAPTER 3

MARION

March 1914
Birmingham

A s usual, Marion found harbor in a corner at St. Anne's. She'd only been at her new orphanage a small accumulation of days, falling into her schedule of meals, class time, free time, and lights-out. But already the spot felt like it was her own. At the moment, the common room was silent, empty. The day had grown warm, and there was a break in the springtime rain so the other children had poured out into the courtyard. Marion remained inside. She was on the final pages of *Emma*. Marion liked her more than she thought she would. Emma could be charming.

With no one else around, Marion allowed herself to read aloud softly, to give herself the gift of hearing her own voice. Being shorter in height than most, Marion guessed the other children assumed her voice was pitchy and high. But there was a low tone to it, perhaps emphasized by her whispering. She only spoke when she was alone, which in a crowded orphanage happened once in a blue moon.

Today Marion was feeling anything but blue, however. She was content for the first time in a long time. She hoped to stay at St. Anne's, where the nuns weren't quick to yell, the other children were satisfied to leave her be—save for Edward, though did she mind?—and Sister Florence had even asked if she would be interested in secretarial work that involved typing.

Marion didn't yet know how to type, but she wiggled her fingers where they touched the book, playacting like she'd be doing on the typewriter, pleased that at St. Anne's she'd be more than simply a child to clothe, to house, to educate. She'd have a job to do.

She focused again on *Emma* and whispered, "'He stopped. Emma dared not attempt any immediate reply. To speak, she was sure would be to betray a most unreasonable degree of happiness. She must wait a moment, or he would think her mad. Her silence disturbed him; and—'"

"So you *can* speak."

Marion gasped, looking up to find Edward standing a few steps into the room.

Now she was unsure how to respond, beyond going statue-still. Her mind whirled with the notion of feeling exposed yet experiencing a hint of exhilaration that Edward had been the one who'd caught her.

Edward stepped closer. "Sister Florence only told us that you can't. You can." He said this *can* almost as if he were asking Marion to verify. "But if you don't *want* to talk, that's fine. I bet you have your reasons. I can't step on cracks. I mean, I physically can, but I don't want to. There are so many bad things that can happen with stepping on a crack. I don't want to risk any of it."

He shrugged, yet Marion was no closer to finding an expression to respond to this boy. She parted her lips, letting air escape in a slow, controlled exhale.

Closer Edward came, until he sat opposite her on the hardwoods. "But if you wanted to, maybe you could read to me sometime?"

Read to him?

Marion felt her brows creasing.

"I know," Edward said. "I should know how to read. But no one's ever taught me. I was shuffled around a lot, so my learnings were so stop and start. But I've been here for a while, and it looks like kids get to stay at St. Anne's. I thought they'd begin teaching me, but they never did. I think the nuns think I already know how." He sighed. "I'd really like to learn."

By the time he was done explaining, his cheeks were rosy.

Was it embarrassment?

Marion's chalkboard sat beside her. She usually reserved the board and her one-word answers for her superiors, with whom she knew she had no choice but to respond, but a question rose to the forefront of her mind. Marion took the chalk from her dress pocket. Not wishing to embarrass him further, she used only numbers instead of words and wrote, *1? 2? 3?*

The idea of someone being at a single orphanage longer than that many years was implausible, but she also added, *4? 5?*

His mouth twisted as if he was unsure of what Marion was asking. She sucked on her tooth, thinking of how to explain without using words he couldn't read and causing him more embarrassment. She waved an arm, indicating the space around them.

"The common room?"

Marion shook her head, then circled her hand more grandly.

"St. Anne's?" he asked.

She nodded enthusiastically and pointed again to the numbers. Edward opened his mouth but then reached for her chalk. He circled 3.

Wow. Marion had only spent a year at most homes. Three years at St. Anne's . . . that was a long time. Long enough to let herself hope that she could remain the same length of time. That Edward would continue to be at St. Anne's too.

THE CALL OF THE WRENS

"I'll leave you be now," he said. "Think about it? We don't need to tell the others you can talk. Reading together can be our secret."

Our secret.

After he left, Marion's mind whirled with the revelation that Edward didn't know how to read. She would quite literally be non-existent without her books and literary friends. Then she thought again about him being at St. Anne's so long.

That night after all was dark and quiet, Marion lay awake in the girls' dorm. Her mind was still on Edward. She'd never done anything spontaneous, yet she found herself kicking free from the thin sheet. She surprised herself when she slid a book from beneath her pillow and further shocked herself when she began to sneak from her dorm on the south side to Edward's on the north side.

In the boys' dormitory Marion followed the row of beds until she found his and then knelt beside him. She listened to the soft breathing of the other boys, none stirring. And in the glow of the moonlight she began to whisper ever so softly, reading from a story where a sand fairy granted children a single wish each day.

Edward had awoken at some point, for when she was done reading for the night, he said, "Thank you."

Instantly, her stomach felt heavy. Had it been a mistake to come? Edward had said he'd been there three years, yet what if letting him hear her voice would somehow trigger his being asked to leave St. Anne's? He'd be nothing more than another memory. Just like Caroline.

But the next day he was still there. And the way he smiled at her, making her feel so special, was enough for Marion to risk reading to him again. That night she returned to read the book's second half.

When she finished, Edward whispered back, "My wish for today is to hear your real voice. Non-whispered."

She twisted her lips. In the story, the more outlandish the desire, the more likely that it could cause a poor outcome. No, she wouldn't oblige him with her full voice.

However, the next night she came back to whisper-read the book again, starting at the beginning once more. Repetition was good for learning, Marion remembered. He thanked her again. Before she could stop herself, "You're welcome, Edward," slipped out, booming in the room's quiet.

She immediately regretted her words. How fitting to the story it would be if her voice had caused her to be caught in the boys' wing. She could be sent elsewhere. Edward could be sent elsewhere. Just as she had feared. The heaviness in her stomach grew and grew.

Marion heard a rustling of sheets and the squeaking of bedsprings. She scanned the dark room, but no one called out, *Hey! You shouldn't be in here!* One of the nuns didn't rush into the room.

She returned her eyes to Edward, certain she'd see his own fear on his face, but he was looking at her with a toothy grin instead.

"Call me Eddie," he insisted quietly, loud enough for only the two of them to hear.

She paused. Then ignoring her better judgment, she tried, "Eddie."

His cheeks pushed out with a wide smile.

"I like your voice."

She dropped her gaze then, feeling more exposed than scared. The sound of her full voice was largely unfamiliar even to Marion. She didn't have any particular accent, having lived all over England with other children who had lived all over England. But she liked her voice too. Marion liked that the tone of it was low and steady, even when spoken louder than a whisper. She liked that the smile Eddie gave her was as bright and special as the first star of the night.

Every day Eddie remained at St. Anne's. Every night Marion came to read to him, their little secret. More and more, he coaxed words from her, even during daylight hours.

One afternoon they sat in her corner. The room was empty except for them. Eddie asked Marion what she would wish for from the sand fairy.

"To be wanted," she told him honestly, thinking of her name's cruel meaning of "wished-for child."

"You don't think you are?"

Marion shook her head.

"I do," he said, his cheeks reddening between his freckles.

Marion answered by reading more. They'd progressed to her reading him *The Story of the Treasure Seekers*.

But as she was reading, Marion's mind had the ability to slip elsewhere. And it did, to what it would mean to be wanted by someone like thirteen-year-old Eddie from St. Anne's.

CHAPTER 4

EVELYN

September 1939.
Weybridge

E velyn narrowed her eyes, willing herself faster. If it had been an actual race, second place wouldn't have been able to catch her. If it had been an actual race, the grandstands would've been roaring. Evelyn would've heard "Dare D-Evelyn" shouted again and again.

But it wasn't a real race. It was only Evelyn on the course. She began her final practice lap.

And she wondered, *When will this all be real again?* Last week the journalist had said the Brooklands would cease racing, and now that August had come to a close, there wasn't another official race scheduled. Would his prediction of war also come to fruition, with the Brooklands providing aid for the fighting men?

Only days ago a nationwide blackout had been issued. Just yesterday, and the day before, large numbers of children had been relocated from all over Britain. From boroughs and districts in Surrey too.

Mrs. Taylor, the Fairchilds' housekeeper, had a background that wasn't quite known to Evelyn. She knew Mrs. Taylor birthed her daughter later in life, after being with Evelyn's family a few years.

She had no husband now. Evelyn wasn't sure if Mrs. Taylor ever had a husband or what had happened, but the Fairchilds called her "missus," as her role within their household required.

When the evacuations began, Mrs. Taylor sent away her daughter to safety as part of Operation Pied Piper, relocated from her home and from Mrs. Taylor. So far war had not been declared, but to think of all those children without their parents was enough to have Evelyn closing her eyes, driving blindly, faster and faster, trying to outrace all that was on the brink of happening.

It was a childish action, and her mother had said Evelyn couldn't be behaving that way any longer. She was twenty years old, after all, as her mother liked to point out.

Evelyn returned with her car to the maintenance shed. Only Rose was inside tinkering with a car. Evelyn smiled politely at her, and Rose gave Evelyn something a little less smile-like back.

The radio was on. When Rose's wrench went still, Evelyn made an effort to listen in. She recognized the cadence of Mr. Chamberlain's voice, the prime minister sounding as if he were physically incapable of delivering more than a few words at a time.

Evelyn held her breath as he addressed the country, informing the nation that Adolf Hitler had invaded Poland two days prior and that at nine that morning, an ultimatum had been given to Germany: leave Poland or Britain would declare war. Adolf Hitler had until eleven o'clock to stop his hostilities.

A similar warning had been given to Germany during the Great War, but involving Belgium, and Evelyn knew the result of the previous ultimatum. Would history repeat itself?

Evelyn looked at a grease-caked clock on a worktable. It was fifteen minutes past the eleventh hour. Fear clutched at her throat; time had run out.

"*Hitler's action,*" Mr. Chamberlain went on, "*shows convincingly that there is no chance of expecting that this man will ever give up his practice of using force to gain his will. He can only be stopped by force.*" And then he said it; the prime minister declared, "*This country is at war with Germany.*"

Evelyn's mind was abuzz, a mockingbird to the white noise of the broadcast after the prime minister concluded and the transmission transferred to others for additional announcements.

All places of entertainment were to close immediately.

Crowds were discouraged, except to attend church.

Conscription was now imposed on males between eighteen and forty-one years of age. Those medically unfit were exempted, along with others in key industries such as baking, farming, medicine, and engineering.

Everyone was cautioned to be at the ready for air-raid warnings. When a "red warning" was heard, people were to proceed immediately to a shelter. An "all clear" would sound when an attack was over.

"Here too?" Evelyn heard herself asking. Her home and the Brooklands were at a distance of well over twenty miles from London. A close proximity; however, her district within Surrey wasn't one that had been marked for evacuation.

Rose answered Evelyn, "I'd imagine so."

Rose said nothing more, and a silence stretched between the two women. Evelyn eventually filled it by saying, "My mother is likely rattled. I should go home."

Rose didn't respond, nor did she make to leave, and Evelyn wondered where home was for her. Evelyn had guessed Rose to be a few years older than herself. More often than not, she was at the Brooklands whenever Evelyn was there.

Quickly Evelyn returned her car to the lock-up garage and set for home in Father's more practical Buick. She wasn't more than a minute into the drive when the sirens began.

No. It can't be.

Already Germany was attacking? It'd been less than ten minutes since the prime minister declared war.

Evelyn halted, leaning forward to better see through the wind-screen and to the sky. The day was particularly beautiful, sunny and cloudless. But were there planes up there?

The siren's sound pitched, becoming more powerful, then soft-ened before rising again. It wasn't oppressively loud; likely it was mounted on the nearest police station.

Evelyn startled when an Austin car was suddenly beside her on the road. Its driver, who identified himself as an air-raid warden, hol-lered for her to seek shelter. Beside him, a woman more frantically called out, "Take cover!"

Evelyn raised a hand in understanding and accelerated, ducking inside her car. Like that would do any good if a bomb landed on her. Within minutes, she was turning into her family's estate, feeling asth-matic. The gates opened for her, too slowly it felt, and closed after Evelyn passed through. She parked, and as soon as her feet hit the gravel, the distant siren stopped.

Just like that.

Evelyn searched the skies again. Nothing in sight.

The gravel crunched under her feet as she hurried toward the house. Her mother disliked when Evelyn rushed. She could move quickly, despite over a decade of being unable to walk, but her gait gave away that she had once had a clubfoot. When moving at any-thing faster than a walk, she landed toward the toes of her left foot, whereas her right foot struck properly at the middle. It gave her a wobbly look. All Evelyn cared about, however, was that she could run and that it didn't cause her pain unless she was exerting herself excessively. And when had she ever had a reason for excessive running with how her mother thought Evelyn would break if she did? It was why Mother had conceded to let Evelyn race. Evelyn argued the car did the majority of the work, unaffected by her gait, endurance, or so-called fragility.

A pang hit Evelyn at the thought of her racing days being over. Her mother would be all too pleased for her to put that effort elsewhere. Such as to marriage. To Percy. He'd known of and had long accepted her medical history without a wrinkle in his nose. That was probably why her mother had fixated on him as her future husband. *"If your condition is genetic, sweetheart,"* her mother had said, *"it limits your prospects."*

Her words had stung. The medical world wasn't certain if clubfoot was inherited, environmental, or occurred randomly, yet her mother was certain only Percy would have her.

Evelyn expelled the noxious thought with a quick shake of her head and entered the hall of her home. There, she looked left into the conservatory, right into the reception room, and then found her mother in the sitting room with her body angled against the window so she could see the sky.

Her mother turned, a hand pressed firmly to her stomach. "Oh, Evelyn, there you are. I was worried."

Evelyn's mother embraced her. Mrs. Taylor entered with a harried expression and a tray of tea.

"Where's Father?" Evelyn asked.

Her mother's mouth opened, but another siren beat her to a response. This one was a single continuous note, lasting for a full minute. Evelyn and her mother did nothing more than stare at the coffered ceiling as if the siren were mounted there.

Father entered just as the siren was ending. "The all clear," he clarified.

"The danger has passed?" Evelyn asked.

Father nodded, but still Mother paced, fanning herself so fiercely with both hands that Evelyn was surprised she didn't catch flight. A dark strand had fallen from her mother's half-up, half-down hairdo, a rare occurrence. She asked, "What does it all mean, Alfred?"

"We're at war," Father said, his voice monotone. "Like before, despite that war being called 'the war to end all wars.'" He turned his back on Evelyn and her mother then, and Evelyn wondered if it was so they couldn't see his expression.

Was fear etched there?

Father served in the Great War, but only toward the end. At first, only single men had been called up. Conscription for married men wasn't enacted until the final six or seven months. They had Evelyn shortly thereafter, and Mother said she tried to put everything prior to Evelyn in the past. Evelyn had been their focus. She still was.

"We simply cannot remain here," Mother said, studying the room as if she'd never seen it before. The settees, the grandfather clock, the walls papered in scenes of birds. Evelyn's mother took quick steps toward the window overlooking their garden and extensive grounds. "We don't have a bomb shelter on our property. Others nearby have been evacuated." Evelyn's mother said this as if the poor Mrs. Taylor wasn't standing right by them, tears in her eyes at the mention of the evacuees, surely thinking of her daughter, Penelope. Mother asked, "Why not us?"

"Children," Father explained. "Children, young mothers, educators. Those are the persons who have been relocated to reception areas."

Evelyn's mother waved him off. Her face dropped. "Oh, Evelyn's finishing school! The one I've chosen is in London. She can't go there now. In fact, we should all distance ourselves from London. We have the means, and you aren't going to be called upon to serve again, Alfred."

A comfort, yes, that her father's age disqualified him. But another point of relief for Evelyn was that she wouldn't be attending finishing school. Regrettably, Evelyn knew her mother would push for it again when conditions changed, though it was completely unnecessary. Even if she decided to marry one day, she knew serving tea to her husband's friends' wives would most decidedly not be for her.

Father considered all his wife had said, his chest filling with air. "Wiltshire," he suggested. "I believe they are noted as a reception town."

"The Harringtons," Mother said, relief in her voice. "Of course. I'll make arrangements with the Harrington household at once."

"We're truly leaving?" Evelyn asked, incredulous. Yes, she was chuffed that leaving meant not having to attend finishing school. And yes, she'd been startled by the sirens. But surely her family could find a way to be safe in Weybridge. Surely Evelyn wouldn't have to leave the Brooklands, even if official races had ceased for the time being.

"We are undoubtedly leaving," Mother said. "Thank goodness Percy had the foresight to go into medicine. He won't be forced to serve. God willing, he'll evacuate too."

And God willing he'll remain in London to see to his patients. Still, Evelyn countered, "Couldn't we have a shelter built on our property?"

Mother shook her head. "No, Evelyn. If there are to be bombings as there were during the other war, I don't want to be anywhere near the city. And neither do you. That's final."

Her mother's heels clicked out of the room, no doubt toward the telephone. Mrs. Taylor followed, knowing Mother would ask her to speak to the operator on her behalf.

Father cupped Evelyn's chin but said nothing. Mother had spoken, and he was in agreement. Their family would be fleeing to Wiltshire.

CHAPTER 5

MARION

December 1917
Birmingham

There was a war on. Everyone was talking about it, and it affected every aspect of their lives.

Cook baked fewer loaves. Of-age men had been called to serve king and country. England lived in a blackout. Everyone listened for air-raid sirens while going about their days and in the night.

Marion was listening for the sirens at that very moment while she and Eddie returned to St. Anne's. Eddie had offered to deliver a parcel for Sister Florence.

Marion's eyes ticked upward. The idea of bombs falling from the skies unnerved her, though she felt that was a common human response, even if Eddie, his hands slouched in his pockets, was seemingly cool as a cucumber. A vegetable she'd not seen in a long while on account of the food shortages and with homegrown food being sent to the soldiers.

The war had begun only months after Marion's arrival at St. Anne's. Prime Minister Herbert Asquith had given Germany an ultimatum to remove their armies from Belgium. They did not. For Marion and others the declaration of war had come as a shock and as a surprise. There had been and still was fear.

Marion's own apprehension felt complicated. Her initial concerns were not for the welfare of her island but for herself—and that this war would shatter the comfortable existence she'd finally achieved at St. Anne's.

She had Eddie.

She had her many books.

She had her typewriting and secretarial work.

She even had others she'd grown comfortable with, such as Millie. The young girl slept in the bed beside Marion and always sat next to her at meals. They didn't say much to each other. It was a relationship built on a comfortable silence. And one where Marion would often share some of her meal. Millie had a surprisingly large stomach for such a little thing.

Marion couldn't fathom not being at St. Anne's. She barely remembered her life before it. Never did she think about life beyond it. But she often wrung her hands, fearing that the war, on the dawn of its fourth calendar year, was getting too close to home. That it would disrupt her home.

Already her blood had run cold twice. The first had been when a force of Zeppelins set out for Birmingham's factories, but the Germans were apparently unable to find the city and struck elsewhere, from Tipton straight up to Derby, bombing five cities. Then, only two months ago, the Germans had again struggled to find the city center. Marion had read in a discarded newspaper how all but one of their bombs had been jettisoned in the open countryside. The remaining bomb had struck a Birmingham plant that foolishly had left its lights on after darkness fell. It'd been a beacon for the Germans.

London had been targeted eight times by airships and once by an airplane. So far.

Marion knew the Germans would return. Why stop after achieving success, even minor?

On their way back to St. Anne's, Eddie took Marion's hand, as if realizing her discomfort without her having to tell him. Together they passed a food queue and turned down a gully, a shortcut. Marion didn't particularly enjoy being out and about in the streets. Bomb shelters were all over the city, but she found relief in knowing exactly where the cellar was at St. Anne's. From anywhere on the grounds Marion could get there within two minutes. She'd counted.

Eddie suddenly released her hand and dropped to a knee.

Marion startled, her eyes shooting toward the skies again, peering through laundry lines strung between the buildings, expecting to see a balloon-like airship there. But then she realized Eddie's eyes were toward the ground.

"What is it?" she asked him. "See a stray?"

"You could say that."

Marion insisted, "You'll get fleas again."

He inched forward to move aside a crate, then another. "I caught a glimpse of . . ." But then he let his discovery speak for itself. A motorcycle.

"Well, that's not ours," Marion said immediately. She saw that glimmer in Eddie's eyes. He'd like to have it for himself.

"No," Eddie said. "Not ours yet. Makes me wonder if it was stashed here by a bloke before he signed up."

"Won't he be wanting it when he gets back?" Marion posed.

"*If* he comes back."

"Eddie, don't be macabre. What if it belongs to a Peaky Blinder?"

The last thing Marion wanted was to nick a motorbike from one of them. But with the war on, spotting a male, let alone a gang member, was rare.

Eddie must've been thinking it too. He shrugged.

"We'll call it abandoned, then," she said, relinquishing her prior point. "It looks worse for the wear. I doubt it even works."

"We could fix her up, Mare."

She loved when he called her Mare. *Marion* and her last name of *Hoxton* meant little to her. But *Mare* . . . it'd been the first name given to her with any type of true meaning.

"What?" Eddie said, misinterpreting her reaction. "I've always wanted a motorbike. And just think, it'll be great fun."

Fun. She could use a dollop of that. And Marion wouldn't keep Eddie from it, even if it did involve some quick larceny. Hadn't she pilfered her copy of *Jane Eyre* from a park bench after a governess had put the book down to see to her charge? But—"Where? How? When would we even fix the motorbike?"

"So many questions," Eddie said with a smile. "First, let's get her home and hidden away."

"Another of our secrets?" she asked, unable to help feeling giddy at the thought. If she could, she'd have a limitless number of secrets with this boy.

There was that glimmer again, Eddie looking at the motorbike like Marion looked at books. "Our alley cat."

"Alley cat" was shortened to simply "Alli." That way they could discuss her around the others at St. Anne's. In such scenarios Marion's words were for Eddie's ears only, even though the other children were largely disinterested in the fact Marion could actually talk. They accepted that she used her words like Cook used salt: only when necessary.

They understood that Marion had Eddie and Eddie had Marion.

Sorry, Jane. Though Jane would be fine. She had Mr. Rochester, and Marion still found time for her beloved literary friends. Eddie, too, still palled around with the other boys.

"Tonight?" Eddie asked Marion, wrapping up a game of draughts with one of said boys.

She nodded.

Most nights after curfew they snuck outside to Alli and rolled her out from behind a stretch of thick, overrun ivy that'd grown up the courtyard's wall. The progress they'd made on her in two short weeks was astounding. It helped that Eddie had procured a Phelon & Moore manual and various other supplies from a local garage. The motorcycle they found was a Triumph, but close enough. At least Marion hoped so.

That night Eddie straddled their new motorcycle, his face imperceptible on account of England's lighting restrictions. When the blackout had been announced, the use of outside lamps ceased. No one was to light a torch or set a rubbish-bin fire. But even in the darkness, Marion knew anticipation was etched across every inch of Eddie's face. Her eyes had long adjusted, and the moon gifted her a hint of his raised cheekbone.

Eddie gripped the handlebar. "I'm going to try to turn her on."

Marion's head ticked toward St. Anne's, worried they'd be heard inside. But Birmingham had various stray noises, including from drivers who risked nighttime driving and subsequent nighttime vehicular crashes.

"Go on," she urged.

Eddie did, but Alli only sputtered. "Drat."

Marion gave Alli a once-over, mentally going through the manual in her head. She started poking around. At a squint, she realized what was wrong: the battery connector cables. She saw to it.

Eddie tried once more to get Alli started and—aha!—the motorbike's stubborn nonstart *had* been because of the cables.

Alli was louder than Marion thought she'd be. "Shh," she said, not that Eddie heard. Her breath showed in the cold air. She scanned the darkened courtyard for movement, but it was only the two of them. Marion said louder, "That's enough racket."

"But she sounds so good, Mare. Listen to her purr," Eddie said with a fetching grin, having since grown into his teeth. With the winter's chill, they were chattering within his smile.

"Our alley cat," Marion mused.

Eddie laughed and leaned forward, playacting that he was driving, turning the handlebars sharply one way and then the other. "Can you imagine the places she'll take us one day? You and me, Mare. That's our future, wherever we go after St. Anne's spits us out."

Marion switched off the engine.

"Killjoy," he said. But his lips were still curled at the sides. His green eyes were the brightest thing about the night. Without fail, they did silly things to Marion's stomach. Still, she tempered her growing feelings for him, her practical side surfacing, and warned, "We've been out here longer than usual. We'll be caught one of these times."

Yet even with the potential trouble they could be in, Marion knew she'd never not spend time with Eddie—and their Alli. The two of them, tinkering with something they'd claimed as their own. It'd be worth whatever punishment befell them.

"So you don't want a try?" he asked with that sly smile of his.

All right, she did. Once seated, she ached to turn over the engine again. Marion tightened her hands, and her breath swirled in front of her.

"You're a natural," Eddie praised.

"At sitting here?"

He snorted. "Bet at riding it too. We'll give that a whirl soon."

The thought was exhilarating. A wish for another night.

Marion sat at what she'd come to call her desk, despite it being Sister Florence's workspace. Marion's typing was rhythmic, soothing. She fancied being useful. She liked being the first to learn all of the happenings at the orphanage.

Eddie jested that Marion was his personal informant. She squinted, deciphering Sister Florence's penmanship, and typed another few words. Her eyes caught on grease stuck beneath her nail, and she remembered the thrill of getting their alley cat started the other evening. She scraped free the incriminating grease, and not a moment too soon, as Sister Florence entered the small office.

"Marion," she began. Her voice was rough but not unkind. "I have something for you."

Marion quickened her fingers to complete her original task as she tracked Sister Florence into the room. She held a pamphlet of sorts.

"Marion," she repeated.

Marion's hands went still on the keys.

"There's something of importance we must discuss," she said. "January first is right around the corner."

Marion pressed her lips together. Her assigned birthdate. It was actually only a matter of days away, another Christmas now behind her.

"And," Sister Florence continued, "you'll be eighteen. Now, we've warmed to you here at St. Anne's. However, with the war there aren't enough beds for the orphans all this fighting is creating."

Marion's body flooded with heat. *They need me to leave*, she thought simply, despite the complexity of what it meant. St. Anne's was the longest place she'd ever lived. And now she'd be leaving the closest thing she'd ever had to a real home? Marion would return to having no one constant in her life. How strange to think of herself as an adult. Marion wondered if it'd be any easier to be an adult without parents than a child without them.

Sister Florence concluded, "St. Anne's won't receive funding for you any longer."

Marion understood. She did. But her skin itched because of a single remaining thought: *Eddie.*

He'd remain at St. Anne's. Marion would go. No kicking and screaming or pleading and bargaining could change that. She had aged out.

It was not as if her outgrowing the orphanage was a big revelation. Marion knew she was almost eighteen. She knew she was a year older than Eddie. But the war had paralyzed time. There hadn't been any talk of her leaving, so Marion didn't dare press on that bruise.

A war film had even circulated, showing how their men were fighting desperately for England. The older children at St. Anne's had been allowed to attend a screening. It'd been Eddie's and her first experience in a theater, and those first exciting moments had been just that, exciting.

The reel showed men preparing for the Battle of the Somme. They marched, unloaded munition boxes from lorries, hauled cannons. They were focused yet otherwise jovial. Most men, when realizing they were being filmed, waved enthusiastically.

Marion imagined the gesture was for the benefit of the loved ones they'd left at home. It had made her smile, fancying how their family members could've proclaimed, "*Look! There's Tommy smiling!*"

But as the scenes ticked forward, Marion's stomach sank. She then pictured those same loved ones desperately scouring every frame, praying for a half-second glimpse showing their Tommy was alive.

Those men, so vividly depicted in the film, had been the focus across the country. The ongoing war clouded her judgment. Just like it continued on, Marion hadn't questioned if she'd continue on at St. Anne's, to work there, to live there, to be with Eddie there. It was foolish of her to focus on Germany destroying what she'd created at St. Anne's when her own age had been the ticking time bomb all along.

Never once had Marion truly thought through what came next or what she wanted out of life.

Besides Eddie.

He'd suggested that Alli would take them places after St. Anne's had spit them out. It'd been left ambiguous, a developing dream. A bridge to cross when the time came.

But the time had come, and it was only Marion being spit out.

"Marion," Sister Florence began again, and Marion felt annoyance at hearing her name a third time. Sister Florence's gaze jumped to and from the pamphlet she held. "You've been schooled well, and it should be quite within your skill set to find work, domestic or otherwise, until you marry. As it is, I'm told the war is requiring an endless number of men. There's a shortage, so much so that women are being asked to volunteer." Sister Florence placed what she'd been holding on the desk. "I believe this may be an ideal opportunity for you after you leave here."

Marion read the pamphlet's bold-typed words.

JOIN THE WRENS AND FREE
A MAN FOR THE FLEET

Women's Royal Naval Service? she thought, reading the thinner line at the very top. In the foreground a woman stood proudly in a cap, jacket, tie, and skirt, saluting. A battleship floated in the background.

"They call themselves the Wrens," Sister Florence offered. "I wrote the director, and she told me it's a new women's branch of the Royal Navy. They enlist women to fulfill the nonfighting tasks. Typists. Cooks. Stewards. Typists," she repeated. "Like you."

Like Marion. She palmed her throat, nerves overcoming her. To be involved in the war? It wasn't something Marion thought possible. In fact, she'd felt guiltily relieved while watching the war film that her gender disqualified her and that Eddie's age temporarily kept him from conscription.

She dropped her hand from her neck to brush the pamphlet. The pride on the woman's face was obvious. Could this be Marion's fate after leaving St. Anne's? Sister Florence covered Marion's hand with hers, and Marion startled at the touch. "I can take you down to the exchange this weekend."

Marion licked her lips.

Aid in the war.

Shouldn't she have *wanted* to do that? For all those men waving at the camera. For Eddie, who could be waving for Marion within a year if this war wasn't won by the time he turned eighteen and was eligible to fight.

And that, right there, sealed joining the Wrens for Marion. It wasn't that come January 1 she'd no longer have a place at St. Anne's. It was Eddie, and helping to end this war within the next year before he could become a part of it.

"Marion," Sister Florence pressed.

Marion nodded, agreeing to go to the employment exchange. She balled her hands within her lap and looked about the small, familiar room. The bookshelves she plucked from. The untidy desk she worked from. The Virgin Mary on the wall. It'd be hard to leave. But Marion never had a say in her coming and going from orphanages. There was no use wallowing over something she held no control over.

It was hard enough to fathom how she was going to tell Eddie, who was no doubt in the next room, playing draughts to pass the time until Marion's typing work was complete. How on earth would she tell him it was her time to go?

CHAPTER 6

EVELYN

September 1939
Wiltshire

Evelyn, her parents, and Mrs. Taylor arrived at the Harringtons' in Wiltshire within hours of the war being declared. The drive wasn't a very far one, but it felt vast with the rolling fields of the Salisbury Plain outside their windows. As Evelyn's father always did on drives to the Harringtons' country estate, he'd tapped his window as they passed through the garrison town of Larkhill. *"Stonehenge, thataway."*

As a child Evelyn had always turned, leaning over Mrs. Taylor's lap, to peer out the car's window, not that she'd actually ever been able to see the odd stone formation from the car. Larkhill was north of Stonehenge, and the walk to and from the stone circle was multiple miles long. Evelyn's family had made the trek before. Her father had pushed her in a roller chair once along the footpaths of the fields and past various monuments, the most exertion she had ever seen from him.

When Evelyn's father tapped on his window this time, she hadn't looked toward Stonehenge. Instead, she'd watched the commotion of uniformed men at her side of the car. Even with the war only having been declared that day, there was already a posted sign.

PERMISSIVE BYWAY

SUDDEN NOISE!

YOU MAY BE STOPPED OR DIVERTED

GIVE WAY TO MILITARY VEHICLES

KEEP AWAY FROM TROOPS TRAINING

A sudden spurt of gunfire punctuated her reading. Father slammed the car to a halt. Mother covered her head. Evelyn released a pip of a scream, swallowed by Mrs. Taylor's louder yelp.

But then they were moving again, a man in uniform waving their car on, and Father had said, "We're all right. *Just like the sirens earlier, it's all a drill.*"

"*The red warning earlier was only a drill?*" Evelyn's mother questioned, a firm grip on his arm.

Father had nodded. "*Yes, I spoke with a colleague on the telephone before we left who said as much. And here it's our military training, nothing more. They've likely been at it for months in preparation. That gunfire was more distant than I first realized.*"

Still, Evelyn had heard the nerves in her father's uneven voice. Mother released her grip on his arm and patted his hand. Evelyn swallowed down her own nerves. She hadn't liked how close they were allowed to the training ground.

Evelyn didn't like the idea of war.

But with the garrison town soon behind them, Evelyn had realized how easy-peasy it would be to ignore what was happening while at the Harringtons'. Upon their arrival, the Harringtons greeted the Fairchilds casually, Mrs. Harrington appearing from the arched main door with a bright smile, acting as if it were any other ordinary day and not the day war had been declared on Germany.

Behind her, Mr. Harrington and none other than Percy followed. Evelyn acknowledged his presence with a sigh. So much for him remaining in London to see to his medical practice.

The Harringtons' stately three-story stone house originally had been their country home, but Mr. and Mrs. Harrington had recently moved to Wiltshire full time, leaving Percy to freely come and go at their London townhouse.

Evelyn had her suspicions that Percy's parents wanted him in London to encourage him to marry and fill that home with children. It certainly would align with her mother's desires, which Caroline Fairchild did little to conceal, given how she looked between Percy and Evelyn with a glint of excitement in her eyes before taking the hand that helped her from the car.

Percy opened Evelyn's door, and she couldn't help the edge of annoyance she harbored despite the fact he'd done nothing wrong. It was merely the nature of feeling as if Percy the Man was being forced upon her and she upon him.

And that was when Evelyn's thoughts suddenly became confusing. She couldn't help the sense of inadequacy that swept over her. She shouldn't have felt that way, not when she didn't even wish to be with Percy. Nevertheless, when her mother spoke *only* of Percy, it was impossible not to feel somehow deficient. Meanwhile Percy had a vast number of women to choose from. He had his good looks. He had money. He had his health and always had. His future was bright.

"Evelyn," he said, a deepness to his voice. "I'm so glad to see you safe."

She took his hand. "Thank you for your hospitality."

"Don't be silly," Percy said. "There's plenty of room for three more. Thirteen more." He laughed.

Evelyn met his laugh, welcoming the idea of there being plenty of space.

Evelyn soon found herself elbow to elbow with Percy at the dining table. Under watchful eyes they made the expected pleasantries.

It quickly became clear that adult Evelyn and adult Percy had little in common and even less to talk about.

"How is your meal?"

"Delicious. Pheasant, I see. From a recent hunt?"

"Yes. I went hunting only yesterday. How have you faired since we last saw each other at the Brooklands?"

"Fine, thank you. And how is the clinic?"

"Very well, thank you. And . . ." Percy trailed off, and Evelyn sensed he didn't know what to ask her next. Did she like her food, and was she well? Check and check. What more was there to ask her beyond those surface questions? Evelyn socialized little. She didn't have her own home to maintain. She didn't have a typical job, not that a lot of women did. Those who worked outside the home were caretakers and cooks. Most well-paid work was still reserved for men. She supposed Percy could've asked her about racing, but the war had put a stop to her uncommon occupation. Perhaps he didn't want to mention the Brooklands more than he already had, fearing the subject was a sensitive one.

He would've been right. Without racing, where did that leave Evelyn? Who was she if not Dare D-Evelyn?

CHAPTER 7

MARION

December 1917
Birmingham

E ddie," Marion said.

   She received a "Hmm?"

They'd pulled their motorbike from behind their hiding place in the courtyard, and Eddie was wheeling Alli into the streets. They wagered they had an hour or two until anyone from St. Anne's began to wonder where they'd snuck off to.

Marion tugged the collar of her coat tighter against her neck and shielded her eyes from the sun. It'd been an unusually bright day. Her earlier conversation with Sister Florence still hummed in her head. She released a slow, quiet breath at the thought of leaving St. Anne's, the longest home she'd ever had. The only home that had ever possessed an Eddie. Marion reminded herself she was leaving St. Anne's and joining the Wrens in an attempt to keep him safe. He wouldn't see it that way, though.

"I have to tell you something," she said.

"Well, go on then."

Marion swallowed, then chickened out. Riding their motorbike for the first time was a big moment. They'd spent last night each standing over the bike and rehearsing the shifting of gears. They agreed that putting what they'd practiced into motion would be best in the daylight hours.

Marion ended up saying, "I don't want to go first."

Eddie's head tilted. "Are you scared?"

"Yes."

His hand was on her cheek then. She liked the feel of it, the pressure of his skin on hers. "All right, but no laughing out of you."

She promised.

But she broke the promise.

It was hard not to with the whooping sounds Eddie made, with how his balance was tested, how he was more running *with* than riding *on* the motorbike. But he soon straightened out Alli and lifted his feet. Marion was whooping right beside him, then in the dirt kicked up behind Alli.

Eddie turned his head back toward Marion, a smile on his face, and she shouted, "Eyes ahead!"

He rode the length of the street, turned a corner, and disappeared.

Marion was left standing there smiling like a goop at nothing until she heard the rumble of the engine coming from behind. Eddie stopped and sat idling. "That was brilliant," he said, gaiety dripping from his voice. "Want to try? Once there's enough speed, your balance fixes itself. Not as wobbly as a push-bike."

Marion admitted, "Which I've never ridden before either."

"At all?"

She shook her head. "You have?"

"I was a courier boy at my last house. It's why I always offer to go when Sister Florence needs someone."

"You've never told me that."

"Says the girl who never tells anybody anything."

He had her there.

A few beats of silence sat between them. Eddie smiled all the while, until he said, "You know why, right?"

"Why . . ."

"I wanted to know you."

Marion snorted at the sudden change of topic, but she'd play along. She couldn't fathom why he had wanted to know her, actually. She'd only ever been grateful to have him. She wagered, "So I'd help you read?"

"Thank you for that," he said. "But not entirely. At first I was being nice. You looked uncomfortable. But then I sought you out so I wouldn't feel alone."

"You? Alone? Everyone adores you."

"I get along with most anyone, sure. But never had a best mate. They moved me around so much. After I came to St. Anne's, it was like I was waiting for the other shoe to drop. Then you came, and whenever I saw you, you had a book within reach. Two at your feet. One in your lap." He smiled. "And I thought . . . this girl is never alone. Anytime you wanted, you opened a book and became a part of something. I couldn't do that. But then you showed me how. And while you taught me to read, you showed me *you*. Funny. Smart. Caring. You're the best mate a bloke could ever ask for."

Best mate.

Marion tried not to dwell on the platonic phrasing, but the question slipped out: "Is that all?"

Instantly Marion was mortified. She'd controlled her words her entire life, yet in that moment they got the best of her.

Eddie laughed, and Marion was eternally grateful he saw her question as her being impish and not as words that could alter their friendship in a sour way if he didn't reciprocate.

Eddie often showed her affection: taking her hand, tucking a strand of hair, touching the small of her back, putting his arm around her waist and pulling her against him. It appeared, however, that he hadn't done those things in a Mr. Rochester type of manner. Not if he thought of her as nothing more than a best mate. Still, his kind words made Marion's heart swell, just not burst. Truly, how wonderful to know he saw those qualities within her.

If only his sentiment didn't make Marion fear what lay ahead for them, knowing she was about to drop that other shoe.

"Now," he said, "want to get on?"

Marion mounted the motorbike and felt it rumble beneath her.

Marion spurted forward, nearly capsizing as she tried to keep her feet on the ground. Alli was a few sizes too large for her.

Eddie jogged to her, saying, "Whoa."

She'd never been on one of those either.

"Easy goes it. All right, Mare?"

Marion eased in this time, beginning with less of a lurch. Eddie held on, and soon her feet were on the motorbike, and she was riding. It was an exhilarating and liberating feeling. The cool air made the skin of her face tighten, and she winced. She wished she could've scooped up Eddie and rode them out of Birmingham. She clung to his past words. *"Can you imagine the places she'll take us one day? You and me, Mare."*

It was too late to imagine.

Eddie's pace quickened beside her. This wasn't the time to tell him, but she couldn't wait any longer. Marion shouted over the engine's roar, "I'm leaving St. Anne's," and then she accelerated, cowardly distancing herself from Eddie's reaction.

Straightaway, Marion hated what she'd done to Eddie. She tenderfooted Alli around to apologize for flinging those life-changing words at him, but Eddie was no longer there.

Eddie kept his distance over the next two days. In fact, he'd done more than that. He'd virtually disappeared, somehow evading Marion at every turn. St. Anne's wasn't overly large. Where could he be?

His absence was like missing a limb. Marion had never felt so lost, so adrift, not knowing how she would go about her days or spend her time. It made her doubt she'd be able to survive without him beyond St. Anne's, and now she was set to leave within the hour. She couldn't bear doing such a thing without seeing him, touching him, saying goodbye to him.

Marion had already checked the courtyard, the kitchen, the boys' dormitory, the common room, the dining hall, and even the back staircase where they'd sometimes squirreled themselves away to be alone and whisper more freely.

Eddie was nowhere to be found.

Marion retraced her steps again as she headed to the girls' dormitory for the very last time. There, she retrieved her small satchel of belongings from under her bed. The gingham cloth she'd been found in. The brooch. Jane.

She bit her bottom lip and turned away from her bed just as a red-haired girl wordlessly slunk past her, the bedsprings squeaking as she claimed it. The other girls watched Marion go down the narrow aisle between the two rows of twenty-some beds. A few offered her a quiet goodbye. Millie gave her a small, sad wave. Marion smiled for her. One of the older girls, Agatha, smirked in her direction, and she knew it was because Agatha had been eyeing up her typing position. Marion gave her a smile too—because she knew if she did anything but, the tears would come. Not for these girls, nor for the sisters. Not really. But for her life at St. Anne's. And mostly for Eddie. The only person she'd ever truly cared for wasn't here to see her off.

Before heading downstairs Marion stopped at the entrance to the boys' dormitory.

"A note for Eddie," she said to young Peter, who was closest to the door.

He accepted the letter, his head cocking curiously at hearing Marion's voice, and he scurried off toward Eddie's bed.

The letter didn't say much, only that she'd write to him after she was settled. *I'll see you soon*, Marion insisted, even though she didn't know how much truth was in that *soon*. She had no idea where she'd be sent or even where the naval bases were located.

Downstairs, the sisters were lined up at the door.

"May God be with you always," they said, their voices overlapping, the words sounding rehearsed.

Sister Florence stepped closer. "A letter recommending you be assigned a typist position. The Wrens' director informed me that women are placed according to their existing skills." She extended the envelope, which Marion accepted with a nod of her head. She added it to her other papers that had traveled with her from orphanage to orphanage. "Are you certain you don't need help finding the employment exchange?"

Marion shook her head. She'd communicated the previous day how she wanted to go on her own. She stepped to go but then stopped. "Thank you," Marion said. They startled at her rarely heard voice.

Having said all she had to say, Marion left.

The employment agency wasn't far, a simple two-story brick building. A notice quickly caught her eye.

WOMEN URGENTLY WANTED

COOKS, WAITRESSES, CLERKS,
DRIVERS, TYPISTS, MECHANICS

AND WOMEN IN MANY OTHER CAPACITIES
TO TAKE THE PLACE OF MEN

GOOD WAGES, UNIFORMS, CABINS, RATIONS

Marion raised her chin, ready to embrace this future, feeling a slight thrill at this something new, at having a defined path forward for the first time, at doing something important and not letting other feelings worm their way inside her thoughts.

Marion would do this for Eddie, to do her part to help end this war before he came of enlistment age.

She'd write to him.

She'd see him again.

She'd only be angry with him for a short time for not saying goodbye.

She'd survive. She'd survived on far less.

"Going somewhere?" Marion heard.

Her head whipped backward toward his voice. Eddie sat straddling their alley cat, Alli's engine off.

"Eddie!" Marion's heart fluttered and tears immediately pricked her eyes. She was hurt he'd evaded her, abandoned her, but he'd come back. He was here now. She soldiered herself with a breath. "I'm sorry I surprised you with my news, but you knew I would have to go."

"It shouldn't have been a surprise to me," Eddie said, running a hand over his forehead. "But I never thought they'd ask you to leave in the middle of a war. I put it out of mind. Avoiding it, perhaps."

"Me too," Marion said. "But I have no choice."

"I know." Eddie swung a leg over the motorbike and took long, deliberate steps toward her. "Which is why I'm coming too."

"No . . . ," Marion began. "You're not old enough."

"Says who? Some sister who only guessed at my age?"

"They'll turn you away."

A sly smile spread across his face. "I happen to have my registry of birth right here"—he tapped his breast pocket—"that gives me a birth date in 1899. This very day, in fact."

"You doctored your papers?" she whispered.

"I doctored them well." He laughed. And, Lord, was she happy to be hearing his laughter again. But . . . "No, you can't enlist. I won't let you. The war could end before you're eighteen."

"I *am* eighteen, Mare."

"Be serious."

"I am."

"You know good and well it's dangerous. You saw the war film."

"I did, but, Marion, where you go, I go."

She shook her head. "No, Eddie. Sister Florence said the Wrens don't fight. I'll be a boring typist. But *you* could very well be in the next film."

"I heard there are dances. That'll be us, Mare." He wagged his brows.

Marion rubbed hers. "Who's to say we'd even be stationed in the same location?"

"I'll move heaven and earth."

But it didn't work that way, and he wasn't listening. He wasn't thinking clearly.

Eddie took her hands, pulled them to his chest. She felt his heartbeat in her palms. She felt her own heartbeat seemingly everywhere.

Eddie repeated in a soft voice, "Where you go, I go."

As a best mate? Marion questioned silently. *As more one day?* she hoped. The moment felt intimate. His intonation felt romantic. But then his tone shifted, more adamant, as he said, "I'll get the door."

She stared into his green eyes. There was affection there. Love, if only of friendship. Maybe one day he could see her differently. But for now it was enough that a boy stood before her who cared enough to enlist to be with her. Whether she approved or not. He was going to do it.

Jaw held tight, she walked ahead of him. His arm reached around her for the door's handle, but he paused, his mouth at Marion's ear. "I woke up today with a single wish. To stay with you."

Marion eased as warmth and possibilities rushed through her, but she also couldn't help a nagging sense of worry at his wish. She remembered in the book—the book she'd first read to him—how the children were granted a wish a day. The more outlandish a desire, the more likely it was for a disastrous result to follow.

Marion should heed the fairy tale, but right then she couldn't think of a greater desire than remaining with Eddie too.

CHAPTER 8

EVELYN

September 1939
Wiltshire

The Harringtons' country house was fine and dandy, but already Evelyn disliked feeling displaced from her home, even though she'd only been gone for a day. Likewise, she felt displaced from who she was, not having anything for herself. Both disturbances felt equally lousy.

It was somehow made better, and worse, by the fact that Percy would return to London the next day.

"You're leaving?" Evelyn's mother asked him. "Surely we must think of your safety," she added, though Evelyn wagered her mother was also thinking of something else: she needed Percy there, preferably smack-dab next to Evelyn. Finishing school may've been put on hold, but her pursuit of a husband for Evelyn was still full steam ahead, even if Evelyn hadn't yet been properly trained in being a wife.

"War's been declared, yes," Percy said respectfully. "But my clinic is still open. I'm needed there. Besides, there's been no action since the prime minister's address."

"It's been less than forty-eight hours," his mother protested with a mixture of exasperation and fear in her voice.

But Percy left anyway. And no action did come. For days, weeks, and even months.

Regardless, in October Mr. Churchill proclaimed that the war would go on for at least three years. Evelyn dreaded the thought. Already time passed slowly, treacle moving more quickly. When restrictions eventually loosened and she dined in town or saw a matinee by her lonesome, not knowing anyone her own age in Wiltshire, Evelyn heard people talk of the war as a "phony war."

By January word was that the majority of the children who'd been evacuated in September had already come back to London. When Mrs. Taylor learned her daughter would be returning, she asked for a leave so she could go and be with Penelope.

"Should we go home?" Evelyn asked her mother one chilly afternoon during their twice-weekly sewing circle. Really her question was *could* they.

Her mother seemed aghast at Evelyn's question. She responded not to her daughter but to the other women in the sewing circle—Mrs. Harrington and two women from church. "Please forgive Evelyn. She, fortunately, did not experience the other war as we all did."

They nodded solemnly, one woman making a soft, agreeable noise.

Evelyn swallowed a sigh. Her thoughts turned to the Brooklands as she idly stitched. Her car was still there, locked safely away. Had they resumed aircraft production, as they did in the first war? They must have by now, she mused.

She imagined the slew of movement and activity at the Brooklands. Whereas Evelyn was doing nothing more than sitting with women twice her age. But if this was to be her lot in life, she didn't see why Mother couldn't start a sewing circle back home, where it seemed just as safe as it did here in Wiltshire.

—❦—

And for another few months, London seemed to remain safe too. It remained that way, in fact, throughout the springtime and into the summer. However, during the summer months, the tides began to swiftly change and the war didn't seem so phony anymore. Germany bombed Paris. Then Germany began invading France.

Percy arrived shortly after with other updates. "They're evacuating London again," he told the Fairchilds and his parents over tea.

How horrible, Evelyn thought, her mind going to Mrs. Taylor and her daughter, Penelope.

What wasn't horrible, Evelyn hated to admit, was another visit from Percy. She hadn't had a cuppa—or even interacted—with anyone close to her age in months, not since Percy's previous visit for the holidays. During that visit Percy had surprised her with a gift.

"An elephant?"

A miniature porcelain figurine. The elephant sat on its bum, its torso raised, its trunk even higher.

"Tell me you remember?" Percy had asked, his head tilted toward her expectantly.

Evelyn twisted her lips. *"I remember?"*

"Well, there we go," Percy said, throwing up his hands in jest. *"The gift has lost all sentimental value."*

Evelyn laughed. *"Don't be a spoilsport. I can't be expected to remember everything."*

"Fine, I shall tell you. One time at the circus, you declared to your mother you'd train elephants for a living one day. I think you only said it to get a rise out of her." He'd leaned closer conspiratorially. *"It worked. Anyway, I saw this in a window shop and I immediately thought of you.*

It's actually a good luck elephant, I'm told. It signifies the coming of good things in a person's life. So I present this to you, Evelyn Fairchild, along with forthcoming good fortune."

Evelyn kept the elephant in her pocket, touched by the sentiment. She was still waiting for its effects to kick in.

"Evacuating London again?" Mrs. Harrington asked Percy now. "Is that necessary? You said the fighting is in France. There's a body of water between us."

Percy raised a brow. "Only twenty-one miles of it, swarming with German U-boats. You don't think the Luftwaffe's planes can't cross it?"

Evelyn's father opened his mouth, but Evelyn was quick to ask, "What about Mrs. Taylor and her daughter?"

Mother politely swallowed her bite of sandwich, then said, "I do miss her."

Evelyn wondered out loud, "Will Penelope be sent away again?"

"I'd imagine so," Evelyn's mother said. "Perhaps Mrs. Taylor can return to us then."

Evelyn ignored her mother's careless comment. "But won't it be hard for Mrs. Taylor to be away from her daughter a second time?"

A second time . . .

How horrible to have her daughter back, only for Penelope to be evacuated once more. She absently fingered the elephant in her pocket, the porcelain smooth and cold.

"It would be very difficult, I'd imagine," Evelyn's mother said. "You've never been away from me for more than a few hours."

Evelyn was well aware of that. Her eyes passed over Percy and onto his mother. "Could we help this time?" Such a question was presumptuous, but Mrs. Harrington was a kind, godly woman. And frankly, Evelyn was disappointed in herself that she hadn't thought beyond her own nose to consider helping Mrs. Taylor before.

"In what way?" Evelyn's mother asked.

Evelyn's nerves showed as she cleared her throat. "Please forgive my forwardness, but perhaps we could ask Mrs. Taylor to return here . . . with Penelope, instead of the child being evacuated to a random family again."

"Evelyn—" Mother began.

But Mrs. Harrington palmed Mother's hand atop the table. "It's a lovely suggestion and gesture, especially during these precarious times. Caroline, will you extend the invitation on my behalf?"

Evelyn's mother put on a counterfeit smile, but there was nothing put-on about what Evelyn was feeling.

She beamed at Percy, hoping he'd be smiling back. Like how he'd return her grin after she did something impressive on her own when they were children. Convincing the cook to sneak them a second helping of dessert was one such example.

And in this moment Percy was indeed smiling at her, and Evelyn felt even more emboldened by this small act of helping. She slipped outside to the garden, wanting to add the heat of the summer sun to her skin.

"That was good of you," she heard.

"Percy," Evelyn said, turning to face him. He had the same round, dark eyes as his mother. Caring eyes. "It's the least I can do," Evelyn went on. "There's very little else I'm doing to be helpful. Can I be frank with you?"

"Only if I can be Frannie."

Evelyn rolled her eyes. "That was a horrendous joke."

Percy dropped his head in mock shame. "I know." He walked to the shade of a nearby tree.

Evelyn joined him. "But you've had worse."

His head snapped up, one eyebrow higher than the other. "Excuse me?"

A hand went to Evelyn's hip. "It's true. You've had worse jokes."

"That's not possible," Percy said.

"When you were, oh, ten or eleven, maybe older, you once had a punch line about a bald man and rabbits. It stuck with me since my father has always been a bit lacking in hair. Now, I want to get the joke correct. Let me think." She plucked a dandelion that'd turned to seed, twirling the stem between her fingers. A few seeds slipped free. "Aha, I think I've got it. Why did the bald man paint rabbits on his head?"

Percy scrunched an eye. "I don't remember telling this one."

"Yet you remember me wanting to train elephants?"

He shrugged.

"Well, you did tell this one."

"Very well, what was it then?" Percy motioned for her to go on. "Why *did* the bald man paint rabbits on his head?"

"Because from a distance they look like hares."

He laughed. "As it turns out, I'm hilarious."

Evelyn's mouth curved into a smile. He was. He *still* was. In moments like this she could see how Percy the Boy had grown into Percy the Man. "Okay," she admitted, "maybe your joke telling isn't horrible."

His gift giving either.

She felt the weight of the elephant in her pocket, despite its small size.

Percy bumped her with his shoulder, and they stood there in silence, both watching a fleet of ducklings follow their mother across a pond, until Percy broke the quiet. "What is it you wanted to be frank about?"

Now that the moment had passed, Evelyn was hesitant to admit her feelings, but Percy's attention remained trained on her with genuine interest, and she said, "It felt wonderful to help Mrs. Taylor and Penelope in that small way. Around here, I sew. I sew some more. Did

I mention I sew? Oh, the highlight of my spring and summer was that we'd begun a victory garden."

"I saw," Percy said. "Our mothers mentioned their importance during the first war."

"'Dig for victory,'" Evelyn said with a raise of her fist, reciting the slogan. "Although, my mother already detests rationing. Do you think Mr. Churchill is correct, that this war will be on for years? Do you think it'll truly worsen?"

The questions felt so out of place in their countryside, where there was nothing in the sky but the shining sun and where ducklings glided peacefully atop the pond's water. Evelyn could only imagine the scene in the French countryside was vastly different.

"I'm no expert in war, Evie."

Few people called her by that nickname anymore. She liked that Percy still did.

"Will you enlist?" she asked.

"If I'm required," Percy responded smoothly.

Evelyn only asked her next question in her head: *But you won't volunteer to go?* She said out loud, "I wish I could do more."

"Dear Evelyn," he began in good fun, "do you only say that because you are bored stiff here? If it's any consolation, I heard your mother telling mine that she's spoken with a headmistress of a nearby finishing school."

"No, I'd first run away," Evelyn all but whined. "How can one woman be so tireless?" And lack any respect for her daughter? There was never a conversation with Evelyn about attending a finishing school, whether it be in London or in Wiltshire. Instead, her mother treated Evelyn as if she were still a child. "I'm twenty-one. Practically an old maid. You'd think she'd give up on such things. You'd think she'd realize that I am capable of making my own plans." Percy shook his head, but Evelyn continued, "Besides, haven't you heard there's a war on? Why is finishing school even a concern?" She twisted her lips. "Have you any word of the Brooklands? Have they begun manufacturing again?"

"You should see it, Evie. Your father asked me to check on your estate, and I stopped by the Brooklands, too, out of curiosity. They've built hangars on the tracks and even planted trees within the concrete to try to disguise it from the air. Can't imagine they'll be able to hide the railway tracks, though."

"Trees on the racetrack? I should like to see that. Truthfully, I'd love to go there and help in some way."

Percy watched her thoughtfully, and Evelyn worried she'd said the wrong thing. She still felt like she was navigating who he was as an adult, now that pretenses of marriage had been forced between them. But what he'd shown her recently felt reminiscent of the friend she'd grown up with.

Percy began walking, motioning for her to follow. He stopped at an outbuilding, one Evelyn had never been inside before, but not for lack of trying. It was padlocked. Percy fished a ring of keys from his breast pocket. "My mother and yours alike will have my head if they know I'm showing you this."

"Do go on."

He did, unlocking the door. "I'm only doing this because you seem unbearably cooped up. That is, until you decide to run away."

He winked, and Evelyn swatted at his arm.

It was dark inside, the building having no windows, but the door's opening let in enough sunlight to see various petrol cans, spare tires, a bicycle that looked worse for wear, and . . . "A motorcycle. How grand!" Evelyn went toward it and ran a hand over the handlebar. "Does it work?"

"I'm afraid to answer that."

"It does!"

Percy laughed. "If the excitement in your voice is any indicator, I may've made a grave mistake by bringing you here."

"Never," she teased.

"I heard about you racing around town in your father's Buick."

Evelyn shrugged, not taking her eyes off the motorbike. She *had* gone a touch over the speed limit, and the news had gotten back to the Harringtons and thus to her parents. Rules and warnings had been doled out as a result. Evelyn flung a leg over the bike. "This would be easier in trousers."

Percy crossed his arms, leaning against the door's frame. He was clearly amused. "You look like one of the women riders I see about London."

Her attention flicked to Percy. "Women riders?"

"Female motorcycle dispatch riders, I believe."

"For what purpose?"

"They hand-deliver sensitive information, such as intelligence briefs, that we can't risk the Germans intercepting if sent through a wireless."

"Fascinating," Evelyn said.

Percy smirked, no doubt enjoying how she hung on his every word. "They only just formed. Or re-formed? I think they disbanded after the Great War. But now they're at it again."

"Do they have a name?" she pressed.

Percy snapped his fingers. "They call themselves the Wrens."

Evelyn tightly grasped the motorcycle's handlebars. On either side of the bike, her feet were ground into the dirt floor of the outbuilding. "Tell me everything you know about these Wrens."

CHAPTER 9

MARION

December 1917
Birmingham

N ame?" The woman from the employment exchange waited with pen poised over paper. In Marion's hand her registry of birth quivered. From uncertainty? From excitement that Eddie was with her? From fear that he was with her? Eddie was going to war when he could've been otherwise safely at St. Anne's for another year.

But no, instead that buffoon had snuck off. He'd followed Marion. He'd doctored his papers. He was enlisting for *her*. Heaven help her, Marion smiled at the thought and placed her birth registry before the woman on the pencil-marked table.

"Marion Hoxton," the woman read.

Marion nodded. It was abnormal to see or hear her first name and so-called family name together. The latter had rarely been used throughout her childhood.

"Hoxton," the woman repeated, her gaze traveling from the paper to Marion. The woman's searching eyes remained on her, longer than Marion would've liked.

Marion averted her gaze, and a sense of shame passed through her that her surname didn't originate from loving parents but from

Hoxton Hospital in Hoxton, London, where she'd originally been found. Beside her, Eddie cleared his throat and took her hand.

The woman resumed her task, writing down Marion's name onto the enlistment form. She added Marion's date of birth, overlooking how she was a few days shy of eighteen. Her birthday fell midweek, and it was customary for children to come and go from orphanages on Saturdays.

"Enlisting for the women's army? The navy? The relief corps?"

"The Women's Royal Naval Service," Eddie said, acting as Marion's voice, as he so often did.

"Very well." The woman lifted an eyebrow at Marion. "And you understand this isn't a volunteer job? When you enlist, you are agreeing to serve for a year or until the war ends."

Marion nodded. She'd serve as long as needed to help end the war.

"Very well," the woman said again. "The Wrens must be prepared to be mobile and willing to serve wherever they are sent. Is that understood as well?"

Marion understood, but the idea of being sent *anywhere* was jarring, especially if that anywhere wasn't a location Eddie shared.

"Like on a ship?" Eddie questioned.

The idea of being on water was even more unsettling. She couldn't swim.

The woman shook her head. "The Wrens have the motto 'Never at Sea.' Now, if there are no other questions?" The woman didn't regard them further, and on the paper she wrote down the shorter WRNS abbreviation. There was a page full of questions, but Marion watched as the woman's pen moved from one to the next, skipping questions about Marion's reasoning for joining and the birthplace of her parents. Finally her pen stopped. "Do you have any particular skills, Miss Hoxton?"

Marion internally cringed at hearing that name for the third time in under four minutes, and she hastily handed over Sister Florence's endorsement.

The woman took it, read it, and without a word wrote down *Typist.* "This'll be taken into consideration and will likely put you wherever there's a need for a typist within the Wrens. The women are doing what there are no men to do. It's a real service to our country." She paused. "A real sense of community too. The women are like sisters."

Marion nodded again, unsure how to react. The girls at the orphanages had been friendly enough, for the most part, but never had she considered them family. Caroline had come the closest, for that fleeting amount of time they had been together. But Marion imagined she and the other Wrens would have the shared goal of ending this war. But more importantly she'd have the personal goal of protecting the young man beside her.

"And what about you?" the woman said to Eddie.

"Edward Smith," he said. There was a sense of pride in his voice and a straightness to his back. "Here to serve, ma'am."

And here for me, Marion thought again. How did she get so lucky to have an Edward Smith in her life?

When she'd first learned Eddie's last name, she'd been jealous. *Smith. Jones.* They were surnames often given to orphans because of their commonality. Britain had thousands upon thousands of Smiths. It was a family name passed down and down, derived from metalworking ancestors. The fact there was an abundance of Smiths made it feel richer, like Eddie was part of a big extended family. Whereas Hoxton was a place, a thing. *"You know what Smith means?"* Marion once asked Eddie from their corner.

"What?"

"To smite. To hit. It's a strong name."

He'd smiled. *"Don't worry, Mare, I'd never smite you. But Freddie over there?"* Eddie nodded to an overly large boy who liked everyone to know how big he was. *"He might get smithed."*

Smithed. The wordplay made his name feel even richer and only increased Marion's jealousy.

"King and country are pleased to have you, Mr. Smith," the woman said.

Eddie stated, "We'd like to be kept together in the navy."

The woman considered them, her gaze flicking to their joined hands. "Like I told Miss Hoxton, they assign service based on need. But"—she leaned to the side, peering behind them—"is that your Triumph outside? A 500cc?"

On the other side of the large picture window was their Alli.

Eddie nodded. "Yes, ma'am."

The woman made a note on the form. "The army, air force, and navy . . . they all use dispatch riders."

He parroted, "Dispatch riders?"

"A motorcycle courier. It's safer to deliver messages by hand than through the various electronic communications that can be intercepted by the enemy."

"I've worked as a courier boy," Eddie offered.

The woman made a note of that, saying, "Good. There's a shortage of motorcycles, so if you have the machine, they'll want you using it. I'll make a recommendation for the navy. How about that?"

Eddie smiled at Marion.

She smiled back but couldn't help thinking that Alli was both of theirs, yet he'd claimed her as his own.

The woman went on, "That should keep you on dry land, Mr. Smith. And as I said, Miss Hoxton will stay inland too. If I'm not mistaken, you'll both begin training at the same location."

Hearing this softened Marion, and she had a change of heart, thankful Eddie had Alli.

"After that," the woman added, "how close you'll remain to each other, I cannot guarantee." She put down her pen. "Now all that's left are the physical exams for you both. Right through those doors. Assuming a positive outcome, you'll be asked to report for duty next—"

"Next what?" Eddie cut in. Week? Month? He glanced at Marion. "We were hoping to begin today."

The woman considered them a second time, most likely realizing Marion didn't have a home to return to. Maybe she guessed Eddie was an orphan too. How had Sister Florence not taken into consideration the gap between enlistment and training? Marion swallowed, her throat feeling thick. She appealed to the woman. "Please?"

The woman tapped her pen and said, "Let me see what I can do," before exiting into a back room.

Before the woman returned, Marion and Eddie were called to complete their physical exams, Marion wringing her hands, not at the exam but at once more feeling that her future was in the hands of someone else. She emerged shortly after, her papers stamped to show she was fit. Eddie was waiting for her, a grin on his face. The sight of him eased Marion, and she let her own face mirror his.

"Looks like we're in the Royal Navy now," Eddie said. "And I've just been told we leave within the hour, *Wren Marion*."

CHAPTER 10

EVELYN

June 1940
Wiltshire

After Percy had told Evelyn about the Wrens, and specifically about their motorcycle dispatch riders, the notion of becoming one remained steadfast in her head over the next handful of days.

Put simply, Evelyn felt called to become a Wren. She wanted to go hard and fast. She wanted to do more than sit in sewing circles and see to a victory garden. She wanted to forge her own way, and she needed to do it before her mother tried to ship her off to the Wiltshire Academy to learn how to host dinner parties and be somebody's wife. Not long ago, Evelyn had been Dare D-Evelyn, after all.

Since revealing the motorcycle to her, Percy had done nothing more than speak to Evelyn about how to ride it, never turning over to her the keys. If she heard the word *patience* one more time, he'd truly discover how impatient she was, especially as he was set to return to London that evening. Finally, after nearly three long days, he dropped the keys into Evelyn's palm. With afternoon tea upon them, he agreed to cover for Evelyn with their mothers so she could give his motorbike a whirl.

Evelyn's attempts at riding the motorbike were wobbly at first, yes. But she'd ridden bicycles before, under the careful and watchful eye of her mother. The balance was similar. After momentum came into play, the act of staying upright was relatively easy and was made only a spell harder at a greater speed. She gripped the handlebars more tightly over each ripple of the ground.

But Evelyn stayed on. Her left foot had no bearing on how well she could ride.

She could see herself zipping about London, delivering important messages to important men who would make important decisions regarding the war. What a feeling—a feeling she didn't want to exchange for the mundaneness of her sewing circle. Or worse, the Wiltshire Academy.

At the angle she sat atop the motorcycle, the trunk of her elephant figurine pressed into her leg within her pocket. Perhaps it was time Evelyn made her own luck, jump-starting the coming of something good in her life. The thought prompted an impulsive decision to leave the Harringtons' property and head toward town.

Beside the cinema was a Labor Exchange office.

She hesitated only a moment longer, whispering, "Dare D-Evelyn," to herself before going through the door.

The sunny smile she'd once given Mr. Orwell during her driver's test was now offered to a new person, this time a woman behind a desk.

Evelyn took a seat across from her and greeted the woman with a hello, her name, and her interest in becoming a Wren. The woman's head ticked toward Evelyn at hearing the epithet, but her attention remained on an empty enrollment form.

"Specifically, a motorcycle dispatch rider," Evelyn asserted.

That had the woman looking up. Her face was round with a pointed chin and a thin scar along one of her eyes that disappeared into her hairline. She seemed to study Evelyn before asking, "Date of birth?"

Did she think Evelyn too young? "I turned twenty-one two months ago."

The woman's next words didn't come right away. Her chest rose, then fell. "The actual date, please."

"Right," Evelyn said. She provided the day, month, and year. Then she sat a bit straighter.

How maddening, but the woman once again took her time before continuing, studying Evelyn with too keen an interest. She then asked Evelyn all she needed to know—her height and weight, if she was married, if she had any children dependent on her, if she had any prior convictions—until the woman's pen reached the bottom. "You said you wish to be a dispatch rider?" she asked finally.

Evelyn nodded. "That's right."

"Do you have a driver's license? It's necessary to be a rider."

Evelyn smiled proudly. *Thank you very much, Mr. Orwell.* "Yes, I do."

"Very well," the woman said. She tapped her pen. But what else could there be to think about? The page was filled. "All that's left is the physical."

"Right," Evelyn said again, only this time nerves drew out the word. The initial physical. She was certain most people quickly stood, knowing there was no reason to fail this portion of the enrollment process. But would Evelyn pass?

She walked as evenly as possible as she followed the woman toward a back room. Evelyn's gait wasn't unusual at this pace. She only teetered at anything faster. The woman passed off Evelyn to a male physician. He reminded her of Percy with his dark features. Surely Percy wouldn't have allowed her to come here if he thought the Women's Royal Naval Service would reject her.

Though, to be fair, she hadn't communicated this outing to him. Percy was currently sipping tea as her decoy so she could take his motorcycle for a joyride. But he *had* told her about the Wrens. He'd seen her interest grow with each piece of information he'd dangled, even providing Evelyn the basics of how to drive a motorbike as a dispatch rider would.

He also knew Evelyn to be impulsive and that she could very well be reckless, like the time she'd agreed to his request to send them downhill in her roller chair. After their crash at the bottom, he had begged Evelyn not to tell. She never did, but to his delight she had also suggested they go again. He *had* to have known she'd pursue the Wrens after he'd planted the seed in her head.

In the examination room Evelyn sat on a table, her legs dangling. Evelyn's left leg was noticeably thinner to her, but was it equally obvious to the nurse and physician? She kept her shoes on until the nurse told her to remove them. She still wore stockings. Could they tell her left one was cleverly stuffed? Should Evelyn plainly come out and tell them about her childhood disability?

The room felt too warm. Evelyn resisted the urge to fan herself, a trait no doubt inherited from her mother.

The nurse asked Evelyn to stand to verify her height and weight. Then the physician pointed toward the table again, where she hoisted herself to a sitting position.

Her hair was checked, presumably for lice. The physician continued with questions, asking if she'd ever been sick.

"Nothing of consequence."

If anyone in her family was sick.

"Also nothing of consequence."

He listened to her lungs. Evelyn soon pieced together his main interest was in tuberculosis, which was a large concern in the first war, she recalled from her father's rare stories. The nurse assisted by positioning Evelyn in front of an X-ray machine, Evelyn's back to the physician. The device looked like the frame of a human-height mirror. The nurse unbuttoned Evelyn's shirtwaist dress, then moved the X-ray machine closer behind her to take the necessary pictures of her lungs.

That was when the nurse's gaze dropped to Evelyn's stocking feet, her head tilting. She called the doctor's attention to Evelyn's left foot.

"A *corrected* disability," Evelyn quickly clarified. "I can run. I can jump. I can ride. It's a motorcycle dispatch rider that I hope to be."

The physician studied her, the end of his pen between his teeth. "When you report, you'll need to provide a note from your personal physician." He circled his hand to aid his explanation. "Detailed information about your medical history and such."

Evelyn squeezed her thumb into her palm and nodded.

"Of course," he went on, "there will be physical endurance tests given at training. If you pass those, I don't see why the Wrens would turn you away."

Evelyn let out a slow exhale.

"When should I report?" she asked the physician. He looked to the nurse. She flipped through various sheets of paper. She recited a likely date and how Evelyn would receive official call-up papers and a travel warrant.

Evelyn had one month.

———— ⤝⤞ ————

"Absolutely not, Evelyn."

Evelyn pressed her lips together at her mother's words, projecting a calmness she didn't feel. Inside, Evelyn raged at how her mother's response had cut her off before she had finished explaining about the Wrens.

Evelyn wanted her mother to understand. "I could make a difference, Mother."

Her mother put a gloved hand on her hip. Evelyn had found her in the victory garden. "I forbid you. And your father forbids you. I can't believe this is what you fell into instead of having tea."

"Father hasn't forbidden me. He isn't even part of this conversation to forbid me," Evelyn pointed out, a risky endeavor. "He has no clue I enlisted in the war."

Her mother closed her eyes and waved a hand. It was a small gesture that spoke volumes, as Evelyn's brassed-off mother wasn't one to show emotion. "Do not even use that phrase. There is to be no enlisting. You are enrolled at the Wiltshire Academy. I haven't told you, but . . . there . . . now I have, and you'll begin after the summer holiday." Evelyn's mother opened her eyes but sharply gave Evelyn her back. "In the meantime you'll help me with the garden. This is something useful you are capable of doing."

Did she mean to say Evelyn wasn't physically capable of being a Wren? And *that* was how her mother informed her about finishing school, as if Evelyn had zero say?

No.

Absolutely not.

Her feathers were appropriately ruffled.

Why was it so impossible for her mother to take her aspirations seriously?

Evelyn squared her shoulders, despite the fact her mother couldn't see her do it. "I have passed the initial physicals."

Evelyn's mother shook her head dismissively.

Evelyn pressed, "All I'll need are records from our physician back home."

Her mother dug a trowel into the earth. "Well, that's wonderful news, as you'll never obtain them."

Evelyn crossed her arms. "I'll ask him."

"Sweetheart, Dr. Wilson won't give you what you need. Not after I've instructed him not to."

Evelyn's mouth fell open, only closing again so she could say through gritted teeth, "You cannot stop me. I am of age. By quite a few years, I might add."

Her mother let out an exasperated huff. "Don't remind me of your age, as you are still without a husband. But nevertheless, if you wish to continue to be financially cared for until you do get married— with food on your plate, clothing on your body, and a roof over your head—then you'll go to the Wiltshire Academy as I've planned and you'll forget these silly notions of volunteering for the Royal Navy."

"The *Women's* Royal Navy. The Wrens," Evelyn clarified, hoping the distinction would somehow help.

It did not; her mother more forcefully dug at the soil. The anger in Evelyn only grew deeper as she watched her mother. She recognized her mother's threat. But also she considered that she'd be paid as a Wren. Evelyn would have housing. The Wrens would clothe her, everything except for her undergarments. But she knew saying this would only anger her mother further, and Evelyn wasn't enough of a dodo to bring out that vein in her mother's forehead any more than she already had.

Evelyn's desire to even have the conversation with her mother was out of respect, something her mother didn't have the decency of doing with her when it came to the Wiltshire Academy.

So that was that. Evelyn didn't need her mother's approval. Ironically, her mother's ire had only bolstered Evelyn's desire to serve. She was leaving in a month's time, *before* the semester at the Wiltshire Academy was set to begin, whether her parents liked it or not. The best part: her mother had no clue when she'd be reporting; it was a detail Evelyn was glad she hadn't yet mentioned.

"Really, Evelyn," her mother began again, no doubt wanting the last word, "I cannot believe you even entertained the idea of volunteering in the war. Let us be thankful we are somewhere safe. Let us tend to our garden. Let us pray for the men. And let us forget this conversation ever happened. Enjoy your summer. I'll miss you terribly when you're at the academy. Such a big step for us all."

Evelyn opened her mouth but straightaway closed it. Out of the corner of her eye, she spotted Percy stepping out of the house. She'd let her mother think she had the last word.

Percy held his travel bag, walking with purpose toward his Frazer Nash sports car. He was returning to London. And without a goodbye to her. Evelyn shouldn't let it get under her skin, but he'd also become a bit of a confidant the past few days.

She took after him at a run. Her movements felt stiff, as she hadn't run in quite some time. Percy had a leg in the car when Evelyn called his name. She was good and well out of breath.

"Evie?" he said, half in, half out of his automobile. He stood to his full height. "I almost didn't have a chance to ask. Did you enjoy your ride? It's yours to continue using, if you can get away with it."

"I need your help," Evelyn said, shielding her eyes from the afternoon sun.

A small grin cracked his lips. "Evie, what have you done now?"

"Percy, I'm only getting started."

CHAPTER II

MARION

December 1917

Hampstead

I ntroduce yourself," Marion was told by a woman who'd only just moments ago introduced herself as Section Leader Wren Miller.

Marion was uncertain of the meaning of the woman's ranking, beyond it sounding well earned, or even the various ratings one could be within the Wrens. Everything had happened so quickly after she emerged from the examination room at the employment exchange office. She'd been directed into a lorry. Eddie had followed on their motorbike. They'd driven toward London, arriving at a college campus, vacant on account of the war. Eddie had mere moments to assure Marion they'd see each other that evening before he'd gone one way and she another.

Marion had hastily changed into an ill-fitting uniform. She'd been called a sprogg no short of five times, whatever that meant. And then she'd been thrust into a room with a handful of other women. *"Their initial training began last week,"* Marion had been informed by the woman who had escorted her thus far. *"You have some catching up to do, sprogg."* Without any further ado, her escort had left her with Section Leader Wren Miller.

Now Marion stared at the twelve faces staring back at her. The other recruits had also just told Marion their names, the only name sticking with her being Wren Brown, quite simply because brown was one of her favorite colors—since many books came within a brown leather cover.

It was Marion's turn to provide her name. Except, her condition, as it did in these types of situations, clammed shut her mouth. Her gaze immediately dropped to her footwear, upgraded from her hole-ridden ones to flat-heeled lace-up shoes. An itch overcame her neck, the collar of her shirt uncomfortable, pinned down by a necktie. The itch traveled to the back of her right leg beneath her black stockings.

At least her desire to scratch her leg and neck distracted her from how she stood as a focal point. A "living human curiosity." Marion breathed deeply. She felt her facial muscles relax. She knew that the more quickly this new group learned her name, the faster the attention would be elsewhere.

"Marion," she said in a soft voice. Still, her name echoed in the lecture hall, too big for a handful of women using only a few of the numerous tables.

"And your surname?"

Marion swallowed. "Hoxton."

She wished she could go by Marion. Alas, Wren Miller went on to say, "Welcome, Wren Hoxton. There is a vacant seat beside Wren Brown. We were discussing etiquette and naval tradition."

And that was that. Marion was met with nothing more than smiles. No one scrutinized her. No one tried to coerce curse words from her. Wren Miller simply resumed the afternoon's class.

Wren Brown was more than happy to share her notes with Marion, along with showing her to their sleeping quarters afterward.

A recruit had been dismissed two days prior, opening a space for Marion.

Wren Brown and Marion entered their bedroom as a handful of other women were leaving, each offering a friendly hello. "Sylvia, Ethel, and Ruth," Wren Brown informed Marion, pointing at the backs of the three young women as they giggled down the hall, their arms linked at the elbows. "We're all in the same cabin. You'll note *cabin* and not *bedroom* or *dorm* or *bedchamber* if you're posh like that. Are you?"

Shoulders tense, Marion was quick to shake her head.

"Me neither. The other girls had right fun after I told them I grew up with flocks of birds. My father works in an aviary." Wren Brown shrugged. Marion widened her eyes, at once hoping Wren Brown didn't think she was being dismissive or patronizing. In fact, Marion found Wren Brown's upbringing fascinating, if not unusual. After reading *Robinson Crusoe*, she'd once fantasized for weeks of having her own Poll to sit atop her shoulder as a constant companion.

"I know, it's unconventional," Wren Brown said. "My first sounds mimicked a songbird instead of a human being."

Marion couldn't remember her first words. Nor was there anyone of note to remember for her. She envied Wren Brown, who was watching for Marion's reaction. Customarily Marion would smile a response. A smile was largely interpreted as an agreement, an acceptance, or an understanding. But Wren Brown had been kind to her. Eddie had taught her that not everyone in her life abruptly left. And Marion knew that night she'd lie in bed and daydream of linking arms with the other woman. So Marion urged herself to ease and said, "Charming," as a way to describe Wren Brown's childhood.

Wren Brown laughed. "You don't say much, do you? No fuss.

That's hunky-dory if you're the quiet type. We'll balance each other out." Wren Brown patted Marion's new bed. "We call this a *bunk*. The floor is the *deck*, despite the fact we're clearly not on a ship. It's a *galley*, not a *kitchen*. A *mess hall*, not a *dining hall*. The *head*, not the *loo*. The Royal Navy has their own vocabulary, you see. You'll learn it all soon enough. Speaking of which, it won't be hard to catch up from what you missed the first few days. It was mostly hygiene and how to act womanly in situations, and you're already polished like a diamond."

Sister Florence had insisted on as much. "Cleanliness is next to godliness" had been a cornerstone of her education at St. Anne's.

Marion smiled a response. But then added, "Thank you."

She found her belongings already on her bunk. Marion flapped open her satchel. Jane had safely made the journey with her. It'd be so easy to curl up in her bunk and into those familiar pages. It'd be comforting. But just like at her previous homes, there was a set time to eat, and that time was now. Within her satchel, Marion eyed her chalkboard, realizing Wren Brown had so easily coaxed words from her. The thought warmed her and she closed the satchel.

"As for being here, it could be worse," Wren Brown said as they headed toward the mess hall. "It's my first time away from my home— I'm from Wiltshire—but I've settled in well enough. As for the food, I'm not sure it could be worse." She laughed at her own joke. "But here we are. We usually sit—"

Marion saw Eddie. "Thank you," she made a point to say to Wren Brown, though her eyes never left Eddie. He was on his feet even before she reached the table where his meal and an animated conversation with his tablemates were already under way. His arms wrapped around her. She felt herself relax into him.

When they separated, her eyes fell on an oil mark next to his lips.

Eddie swiftly added more space between them and asked, "How is it so far?"

"It's fine," she said, her thoughts still held up on his response to . . . the idea of her eyes on his lips? Was he worried she'd close the distance and do something so bold as to kiss him?

"You sure, Mare?"

She shook her head and shifted the focus to the rest of him. Eddie's uniform was blue and white, already stained with grease. And there was that mark on his face. "Were you riding Alli so soon?"

"Just for a moment. More of an assessment. I spent most of the afternoon doing teamwork drills." Eddie nodded toward the table of gangly men all similar in age. "The other chaps here are grand."

"The women too," Marion said.

"Oh?" Eddie questioned.

"One of them has taken me under her wing, you could say."

"Like a wren?" Eddie broke a smile as soon as he uttered the words.

"That was a poor joke, even for you."

He laughed good-naturedly. "Go on, point her out."

Marion craned her neck until . . . "There. With the light hair. Her name's Wren Brown."

Being the magnetic force Eddie was, Wren Brown looked their way. Eddie raised a hand in a wave.

"Stop that," Marion snapped. "She'll know we're talking about her."

"Oh, Mare, my Mare. We better eat."

He sat and pulled Marion onto the seat beside him at the long table and moved his plate in front of her. "All yours." He was referencing the corned beef. "I've had my fill."

"Can't stomach the food, can you, Smith?" a tablemate asked

with a slap to Eddie's shoulder. The boy leaned forward to better see Marion. "And who do we have here? You show up late and you have yourself a she-friend already?"

She-friend. They'd heard it before from the whisperings of the other children. But being together like that was something they'd never broached. Marion certainly hadn't pushed for the conversation, not with the chance it could ruin what they had. Having Eddie in any way was enough, even if she sometimes had to remind herself of it. Awkward moments like the one they just shared surely helped her keep her true feelings inside.

"This is Marion," Eddie offered. "We grew up together. She's training to be a Wren."

Marion gave a quick, tight smile. Knowing her well, Eddie didn't engage further but angled himself toward her. "Better eat," he urged. "I'm told there's not much time for it."

Eddie was right. Before Marion knew it, the mess hall was cleared out. Eddie headed one way and Marion another. "See you in the morning," he called.

She found him at the same table. She continued finding him at that table at each of their assigned mealtimes, where they exchanged details from their training. Rope climbs. Toilet scrubbing. Marching. Saluting. Lectures on naval procedures, ranks, and badges.

Laborious, yes. But Marion didn't mind. During lectures, she'd tap her pencil absentmindedly against her lip, then scribble with a flurry when something of import was said.

At the urging of both Wren Brown, who insisted on being called Sara, and Eddie, the two were introduced. Which led to introductions with a chap named Abe whom Eddie had grown chummy with.

A strange feeling it was, to have a small gaggle to pal around with at mealtimes. Otherwise Marion's path rarely crossed with Eddie's. Much of her time was spent with Sara, who was an intuitive type and often spoke for Marion, using *we* with others.

"We'll have the sausage."

"We'll be there in a minute."

"We've completed the assignment."

"We'd like to attend the dance!" Sara proclaimed one evening as they cleared their dishes.

Eddie raised an eyebrow at Marion. The most he'd ever seen her dance was skirting away from a spider.

Sara said, "It'll be the first real moment of fun since being at training. How is it that it feels like I arrived ages ago, yet also in the blink of an eye?"

The sentiment rang true for Marion too. The two-week initial training had concluded that day. Specialty training was set to begin on the morrow. But that night was the dance.

Sara lifted a brow. "Shall we ready ourselves?" With one hand she pulled Abe from the mess hall. With the other she pulled Marion, who then pulled Eddie. And with giddiness in her voice, Sara declared, "Rendezvous in one hour."

Marion's cabin was alive with primping, dabbing, and overall fussing.

What to wear.

How to do their hair.

Red lipstick?

Kohl-lined eyes—or was that considered too daring for the dance? The women were putting on jewelry and letting their hair down, being allowed to break the rule of hair off their collars for one night. Ethel and Ruth made a show of flipping their loose hair, Sylvia laughing on.

Heavens, Marion was in over her head. She also felt included. Sara was applying rouge to Marion's cheeks. "Now," Sara said, "for your lips. The trend is bitten, not painted."

Marion only shrugged, perhaps daftly giving Sara control of her face. Eddie had never seen her wearing cosmetics. She wondered if he would fancy her this way.

"There," Sara said. "I think . . . yes . . . I'm done. My masterpiece. I want to leave your eyes as they are. I didn't realize how long your lashes were until we were nose to nose." Sara smiled, stepped back, and assessed her work. "Perfect. Except for your clothing."

It was all Marion had, besides the uniform she'd been given. The darker cotton of her dress was mended and patched, passed down to her from another girl at St. Anne's.

"I—" Marion began. She self-consciously glanced at Sylvia, Ruth, and Ethel, who were bubbling about the room as they readied for the evening.

"No bother," Sara said. "I'm a wee taller, but we'll make something of mine work for you."

At that Sara kissed Marion's forehead before skipping off to peruse her few hangers. Marion resisted the urge to touch her skin, to relish the sentiment of Sara's genuine care for her, which caused a dampness in her eyes.

Sara's actions felt maternal, despite them being of similar ages. Marion once thought all she needed was an Eddie. But to have a Sara too? Her childhood fears of having her new friend taken away began to bubble to the surface but were snuffed out by Sara announcing, "This'll do!" and holding up a lacy shirtwaist and narrow skirt. She shook her head and said, "I still can't believe this'll all be over tomorrow. Tomorrow will change everything."

Marion hoped that wouldn't be the case. Nor did she like how little control she had over everything changing in this moment too.

But it could be the case.

At least this time Marion knew change was on the horizon. The next day they'd begin their specialty training. Training that could continue at the college or take place elsewhere. What if her new gaggle was separated?

Sara waggled her brows as Marion slipped into the borrowed clothing. "That makes tonight an important one for you and Eddie. If this getup doesn't shake him from treating you merely as a mate, I don't know what will."

Marion's eyes went huge.

"What?" Sara said innocently.

Marion palmed her face, feeling embarrassed. And once more was surprised by Sara's intuitiveness. She hadn't outwardly conveyed to Sara that she wanted to be more with Eddie, but words didn't need to be spoken for Sara to grasp the truth.

Sara grinned. "Now, shall we?"

The girls poured from their cabin, Marion's arm linked in Sara's. She was mere moments away from attending her very first dance. Marion was too gay to obsess over shaking Eddie or to feel the chill in the air, too gay to worry that her only experience with the foxtrot or the grizzly bear, another popular ragtime dance style in the current "animal craze," was Sara hastily showing her a few steps.

"Shall we create an animal dance called the wren?" Sara jested.

In a rare moment of abandon, Marion unlinked her arm, raised her arms, and began to wave them.

Which led to Sara fluttering her own.

Soon the lot of them were doing the wren, making silly birdcalls to accompany their flapping as they headed toward the revelries.

Eddie and Abe would meet the girls at the hall. Their cabins were on the same campus but within different quarters. Hobnobbing in the other sex's building was prohibited. Socializing in an improper manner while in uniform could result in seven days confined to their barracks. Marriage resulted in being released from service. A married woman's place was in a home, not a war.

But marriage wasn't at the forefront of anyone's mind, and Marion was in civilian clothes. Sara skipped the last few steps as a young man held the door for them. Attached again at the arms, Marion and her friends slipped over the threshold like the body of a caterpillar.

Inside Marion's eyes instantly roved for Eddie, as they had on their arrival day, as they did every mealtime. She shouldered off her coat, tossing it over a chair like Sara had done with her own. The dance was well under way, with more bodies than Marion thought existed at their training base. Officers were even in attendance. As a recruit, she was forbidden to speak to an officer first. It was also forbidden to go down the same corridors. A sprogg would have to turn around and find another way to go.

That evening everything felt relaxed.

With the exception of Marion's insides. She searched and searched until she found him, her Eddie. The men still wore their navy blue sailor suits, with low-hanging handkerchiefs around their necks, but they looked more smarting surrounded by so much festivity.

Marion knew the exact moment he saw her in return. His head had been likewise roving. His gaze moved past her, then his eyes came back to her. He slapped Abe on the back before taking eager steps toward her. Abe followed, his destination Sara.

"Mare," Eddie called over the music, coming closer and closer until he was before her. "Is that you?"

It was, and in that moment she thought she'd done it. She'd shaken Eddie. He took her hands, that sentiment not unique, she noted. But when he cupped her hands over his chest, she felt an undeniable thudding of his heart. "You're the picture of Aphrodite."

If her cheeks weren't already rouged, the heat of her skin would surely show her response to his appreciation. She deflected, saying, "Someone's been listening to my book recommendations."

"It's true," Eddie pressed. "You've always been beautiful to me, even the day you walked into St. Anne's when you were thirteen years old with your beat-up shoes and without any of that powder and lip stuff."

Marion swallowed hard, feeling jittery, but managed the retort: "Fourteen." She recalled how he'd wished they were the same age. Now they were, at Eddie's doing. The notion replaced some of her nervousness about dancing with Eddie with a second apprehension that he was there at all.

If he noticed her unease, he didn't let on. "Dance?" he asked her, and placed one of Marion's palms on his shoulder. He extended their other hands to shoulder height.

Sara and Abe, already dancing, took one step and another toward them. As they moved, Sara reminded Marion of the steps, mouthing, *Slow—quick-quick-slow—quick-quick.*

Eddie took a step forward. Instinctively Marion retreated a step. It appeared Eddie had practiced too. Abe's handiwork?

Soon Marion relaxed into the fun, repeating the rhythm, ingraining the beat in her head. Every time Eddie licked his lips, deep in concentration, Marion couldn't help wanting to fall into them. She let her gaze linger there. She licked hers back, hoping he'd notice her unspoken desire.

If he did, he once more didn't let on.

Instead, they smiled. They stumbled. They laughed. He animatedly turned their direction when encountering another couple, a table, a wall. Hours passed in the blink of an eye.

"I'll make a gigglemug out of you yet," he said. "My new wish, now that we're here together, is to forever keep a smile on your face. Didn't I tell you we'd dance?"

Marion's brows scrunched.

"Back when we enlisted, I said we'd be dancing. Though I didn't say well. But here we are."

Here they were. Dancing, yes. But then her brain took a step, too, pirouetting from enjoying herself in the here and now to worrying about what was to come with the war.

Eddie dipped to level his face with hers. "What is it, Mare? Where did you just go?"

"This war—" she began, then shook her head.

"Will be over soon."

Perhaps. Perhaps not.

"I don't want to think about that, though," Eddie said.

"Then what?" Marion asked, her brain once more two-stepped, her attention jumping again to his flushed cheeks and his mouth. She caught herself, lifting her gaze, and Eddie was staring intently at her.

"You. Me." She watched his Adam's apple bob in his throat. "Us."

"Us?"

Eddie's chest rose, just as Sara and Abe swooped in.

Sara said, "Everyone's calling it for the night. Party's over."

Marion hadn't noticed that the music had stopped. People were heading toward the door. The exterior held a soft glow. Daybreak couldn't be far off.

Outside Sara proclaimed in a singsong voice, "I don't want the night to end."

Neither did Marion. Eddie's words were a jolt to her system, still dancing through her head.

Sara spread her arms and twirled in a circle. Her coat spun around her, making her look as if she could take flight.

As they walked toward their quarters, Abe and Sara nestled together. Marion was on Eddie's arm as much for warmth as for not wanting to let go, wishing she could yank him somewhere private and pepper him with questions about what exactly he'd meant by *us*.

She'd shaken him. She was sure of that. If she'd known it'd take a foxy dress and a dab of rouge for him to shift his impression of her from girl to woman, she'd have figured out how to implement these tactics long ago.

There was only one last thing, one last step she ached to take before the night's end.

A kiss.

"I propose," Sara began, "a nightcap of debauchery. I'll retire to Abe's cabin, and Eddie will make himself scarce elsewhere." Sara winked at Marion, whose mouth fell open, despite having the similar thought of sneaking off with Eddie only moments ago.

Sara bumped Marion's shoulder, diverting their path away from the men. There, she whispered, "Never fear, my doe-eyed friend, there won't be any funny business, as the Yanks say. Wren Miller's talks of venereal disease will forever be drilled into my head." Sara released a playful shudder, then held up a finger to say, "However, our good Lord sees nothing wrong with a fair amount of necking."

The night had seemed lawless, and Marion wanted nothing more than more time with Eddie, but she still couldn't help asking, "What if we're caught?" It wasn't as if Marion had a fallback plan if the Wrens released her.

"What if we're struck by lightning?" Sara posed. "All you can do is take caution during a storm. Seek shelter. But if you can't, do not stand under the tallest tree." Sara smirked then. "Truly, I only want some more time with Abe. In a few hours everything will change. We'll get our badges. Abe could be moved somewhere else for training, which will only delay the inevitability of him embarking on a king's ship."

Marion squeezed her friend's arm, even as relief flooded her that her Alli would keep Eddie on dry land as a dispatch rider. But what if Eddie's assignment kept him on dry land, but land on a different base or even a different continent? "Fine, but let us not be under the tallest trees," she said, endorsing her friend's plan, her mind already slipping back to Eddie's side.

Soon her mind and body were one again, and Eddie's arm was strung around her waist. They were on the cusp of more, and Marion welcomed it with every fiber in her being.

Sara and Abe began four-stepping away toward the men's barracks. "Eddie," Sara called. "Before you turn in, be a dear and give a *slow—quick-quick-slow—quick-quick* on Abe's door."

With that, Abe rotated Sara in a circle, and they were lost to the receding night.

"Alone at last," Eddie said. Was that nerves in his voice? At St. Anne's they'd spent every allowable moment together. During training they'd stolen quick touches and words at mealtimes. Now some spins around the dance floor had transformed them—or at least Eddie's words had felt they were going in that direction. What if this was her last opportunity to act upon it?

She laced her fingers with his—and ran.

"Mare," he burst.

"Shh."

Marion did her best to guide them through the night, the blackout in effect in this part of England as well. "We mustn't stand under the tallest tree."

He laughed. "What?"

Marion chuckled, too, slowing their pace. Sara wasn't the only one with thoughts of sneaking off with a sweetheart. Shadowed couples were canoodling on benches, beneath trees, and right smack on the footpath.

Marion took the lead and circled them around an occupied man and woman. Up ahead was her destination: a courtyard she'd tucked herself away in to read one afternoon, reminiscent of St. Anne's with an ivy-covered wall and flower beds.

But best of all, privacy—something that wouldn't be afforded to her in her cabin if Sylvia, Ethel, or Ruth had turned in for the night. The courtyard, with its off-the-path location, would be private, the perfect spot to continue their conversation from the dance. She knew if people were to be caught tonight, they'd be detected before her and Eddie. All those other couples should've looked for a better tree.

"Now," Marion said, "what was it you were saying before?" With a final tug on Eddie's arm, she pulled him beneath and through an arbor. He took an awkward step, and Marion huffed out a laugh. "Did you just dodge a crack?"

"You know this about me, Mare. Why risk it? I may not know my mother, but I don't want her back cracking. And there was that one kid who told me if I stepped on a crack, I'd marry a rat."

"That doesn't even rhyme."

He shrugged. "Still not risking it. What? Don't laugh at me."

Marion only laughed harder, muffling the noise into her hands. Though the moment was filled with humor, it was also laced with electricity. Eddie's eyes lit up. He let out a soft, playful growl, and with his hands on Marion's hips, he backpedaled her toward a brick wall.

When she stumbled from their quickened pace, he scooped her up, holding her under her thighs. Marion's arms wrapped around his neck and her back met the wall a moment before Eddie's mouth found hers. They were better kissers than dancers, instantly moving to the same rhythm as if they'd been kissing all along.

The cadence slowed, and Eddie looked into her eyes. "Does that answer your question?"

He let his lips brush hers, once, twice.

Marion leaned into him, his body keeping hers warm. "It does." She marveled at how the boy before her had been a stranger, then her friend, and now so much more. "Though if this was one of your wishes, you sure hid it well."

"I didn't dare wish it," Eddie said. "I was too afraid it wouldn't come true. Being with you, by you, near you . . . It was all I could hope for. You didn't exactly give me a clear sign you wanted me to kiss you until, well, tonight."

"I'm a woman of few words," Marion said coyly, and the way Eddie looked at her was so reverent, so tender, that *I love you, I love you, I love you* pulsed in Marion's mind fiercely, consumingly.

She knew she loved Eddie, but the feeling had never been so overwhelming. It filled *every fiber of her being.*

"I love you too, Marion," Eddie said, half his mouth ticked into a smile.

"How did you—"

Traveling voices interrupted their secret garden. Far-off reprimands floated through the still, cold air.

They had to go, the evening Marion never wanted to end coming to a close. And now that they'd begun kissing, now that Eddie had told her that he loved her, she wanted to stay in that night and that moment forevermore. It'd be torture not being able to kiss him whenever she wanted. *One year or until the war is over,* she reminded herself. Then she and Eddie could be together however and whenever they pleased.

CHAPTER 12

EVELYN

June 1940
Wiltshire

I'm leaving in a month," Evelyn told Percy.

They stood outside his automobile, Evelyn having only just caught him before his return to London. He had removed his tweed walking hat but put it back on. "To go where? Don't tell me you're actually running away."

Evelyn had to swallow once, but she said it. "Not exactly. I've enlisted in the war."

Percy startled. "You've enlisted?"

She nodded. "In the Wrens. I took your advice. I'm hoping to be a dispatch rider."

Now he rubbed his brow, his hand knocking up the brim of his hat. "That wasn't exactly advice, Evie. I was merely telling you about the women riders. I thought they would be of interest to you."

"Great interest, in fact," Evelyn said. She was enjoying Percy's unease; she couldn't help it.

"But women do more than ride motorcycles. There are a great many roles including radio operators, meteorologists, bomb markers and plotters, code breakers . . . And, Lord, I don't know why I'm wording it this way. It'll only encourage you, when I mean to say you don't know where you'll be assigned."

Curiously, Percy knew more about the Wrens than he'd originally let on. The other roles sounded intriguing too. Still, she said, "I think I'll ride. Surely my experience on the tracks will be an appeal."

Percy's chin dropped to his chest. "Your mother is going to have my head on a pike, especially as you haven't yet told me how you need my help." He looked at Evelyn again, a cringe on his handsome face. "I feel myself being pulled into your scheming web."

Evelyn smiled her agreement. "Fully intertwined, I hope. You see, I passed the initial medical exams, but I have to provide my full medical history upon arrival."

Percy's eyes narrowed, no doubt trying to figure out where Evelyn was leading.

"Well," Evelyn went on, "my mother said she's going to tell Dr. Wilson not to give me my records."

"And you wish for me to provide a report." He didn't even say it as a question. Smart man.

"You were there for it all," she pointed out. "If I remember correctly, you took a keen interest in my surgeries and recovery."

Percy blushed, but Evelyn hadn't meant it in an accusatory manner. Percy was intrigued by medicine from the earliest of ages. She actually envied his long-held fascination, along with his parents' enthusiasm in his interests. Evelyn placed a hand on his arm, saying, "I'm up a creek without your help, Percy. And I feel as if I'll burst if I stay here, after a glimpse of what I could be out there."

"You'll report in a month, you say?"

Evelyn nodded fiercely.

"I'll surely regret this, but I'll do what I can. I'll ring for you when I have news. Not a word to our mothers."

THE CALL OF THE WRENS

Evelyn chortled. Revealing their newfound partnership was not even within the realm of possibilities. Then, excitedly, Evelyn kissed his cheek. She quickly withdrew, the gesture embarrassing them both.

⬤

Percy kept his word. He soon telephoned with news. "Records will be arriving by post next week."

Evelyn resisted a squeal.

Percy had spoken with Dr. Wilson, who, in a fortunate turn of events, hadn't heard a peep from Evelyn's mother.

"Oh really?" Evelyn replied to the revelation. So her mother's threat to contact Dr. Wilson had been phony, nothing but an intimidation tactic. Or perhaps Caroline Fairchild had deemed it unnecessary to contact him. This realization meant her mother, once more, didn't take Evelyn seriously.

It stung, yet again.

And hardened Evelyn's decision to report to London in less than a month, her records in hand, and with her mother none the wiser, thinking she had had the last word.

Either the timing of Evelyn joining up couldn't have been better—or it couldn't have been worse in regard to her safety.

The prime minister had declared the Battle of France to be over after France surrendered to Germany, and thus Mr. Churchill warned that the Battle of Britain was on the brink.

"Upon this battle depends the survival of Christian civilization. Upon it depends our own British life, and the long continuity of our institutions and our Empire. The whole fury and might of the enemy must very soon be turned on us. Hitler knows that he will have to break us in this Island

or lose the war. If we can stand up to him, all Europe may be free and the life of the world may move forward . . ."

While Evelyn's mother had shrunk at Mr. Churchill's words, Evelyn felt assured in her decision. Thrusting herself into Adolf Hitler's warpath would be dangerous, yes. And that knowledge didn't pass without the eruption of gooseflesh on Evelyn's skin. But she also felt certain she could help make a difference as a Wren. Specifically as a motorcycle dispatch rider. Oh, Evelyn liked the sound of that.

Mother, Father, she'd one day reveal to them, *I did that. I rode that. I accomplished that.*

The final *that* was to be determined.

But whatever the scenario, she hoped her parents would finally see her as an accomplished woman. A capable single woman who would marry if and when she decided to. In either case she'd be out from under their thumbs. She found herself nodding.

"Thank you, Percy," she said to him over the telephone. She leaned toward the side to better see down the entry hall, happy to see no one was there to overhear.

Penelope ran by, squealing, Mrs. Taylor on her heels playfully chasing her with the broom.

Seeing the two of them filled Evelyn with happiness.

"Don't make me regret this, Dare D-Evelyn," he said with a sportiveness that made Evelyn chuckle her goodbyes. But as she was replacing the telephone to the cradle, she thought she heard a more solemn, "Please be careful, Evie."

It made her thoughts catch on Percy's initial reaction to her becoming a Wren. He'd supported her. Never once had he mentioned her past disability. Nor had he said her medical records would be a hindrance to her riding as a dispatch rider.

It was encouraging. But for good measure she'd covertly practice her bum off and become an ace on Percy's motorcycle. She assumed he would allow her to take it when she reported to training. Evelyn hadn't asked. She'd been given a travel warrant to arrive via the train, but she'd rather have her own machine, even if it wasn't actually hers. She mused it was better to assume Percy wouldn't mind her taking his motorbike and feign an honest mistake.

She clapped her hands once, energized, and with a careful look over her shoulder, proceeded toward the outbuilding where the motorcycle was kept. She had some practicing to do.

CHAPTER 13

MARION

January 1918
Hampstead

S *low—quick-quick-slow—quick-quick.*
The rhythm rapped on Marion's cabin door. One of the other women groaned and muttered something unintelligible. Sleepily, Marion cracked a smile, wagering her friend was playing the comic by using the melody upon her return. Sara entered, then tiptoed toward her bunk, stopping for a brief moment to stroke Marion's hair.

Marion lazily fell back asleep, waking a few hours later with a sense of urgency. The girls quickly dressed and reported. Sara had said the morning would bring about change, when they received their badges and new training locations, and she wasn't wrong. To Sara's dismay, Abe would be continuing training elsewhere. To Marion's joy, Eddie would stay on at the college, same as her.

On her right sleeve, midway between her shoulder and elbow, Marion now wore a blue patch with crossed quill pens, denoting she'd been placed in the Clerical and Accountant Branch. She'd be a typist, just as Sister Florence had recommended.

Sara was given the badge of an arrow crossed by a lightning flash, indicating her induction into the Signal Branch. She would be starting a three-month training program to become a wireless telegraphist.

Sylvia received the same badge as Sara and would remain at the college, though Marion did not know her specialty. Ethel wore crossed hammers and Ruth a scallop shell.

"Now," Wren Miller said to Marion and the other women, "some of us will be remaining and others will be completing their training elsewhere." Sara squeezed Marion's hand in relief. They'd both remain at the college, despite being reassigned to different cabins. "After your specialty training, some may be sent to Dover, others to Southampton or Folkestone, some to France, even some to places undisclosed for your safety." Wren Miller paused, offering each woman a smile. "But wherever we are, we are all Wrens. A sisterhood." Wren Miller looked from Sara to Marion, and then her gaze passed over the other young women. Sara squeezed Marion's hand again. Wren Miller concluded by saying, "Each of you is a daughter of this service. Even after this war is over."

Daughter.

Marion's mind remained fixed on that word.

Never before had she been called a daughter. A foundling, yes. An orphan. A waif. Even a stray. But not until the Wrens had she ever been called a daughter.

Marion looked again at the blue badge on her sleeve. A sense of pride filled her. St. Anne's had not had a logogram that depicted her as theirs. There, her clothing had been ordinary, generic.

But now she was a part of something, and anyone who looked at her could see it, from the badge down to their matching shoes. The notion of it all—of belonging—made Marion eager to continue.

The first week of her six-week course was smooth sailing, made easier by the fact she was already an efficient typist. It was only the short-hand she needed to commit to memory.

Ruth and Ethel were training within the Household Branch and the Technical Workers Branch in new locations at the college. Marion saw Sara at mealtimes. Sara had also taken to secretly sharing Marion's cabin, preferring to stay together. The girls pealed with mutual laughter every time they tapped their melody, which they did liberally, the intended meaning embellished to any old knock.

Marion lived for mealtimes, with Sara on one side and Eddie on the other. Marion always asked about his training, and he animatedly and enviably described that day's motorbike skills or circuit. It sounded more enticing than remembering how one squiggly mark differed from a curvy line from a rounded notation. And in the evening's spare moments, Eddie would drive Marion around the streets outside the college, or he'd watch as Marion mastered the driving skills he'd spoken of over their meals.

What fun to move so quickly.

What a sensation to have both fear and exhilaration share space in her brain simultaneously. She could fall off. Or she could hold on and successfully make the turn.

She was getting quite good.

One supper Eddie remarked, "That friend of yours, Sylvia, took a whupping this afternoon. She's too timid of a thing and fell off her motorcycle. Hard. Last I heard, she'll be in the infirmary for days."

Marion cringed yet found her interest piqued. "Sylvia is a dispatch rider?"

Eddie guffawed. "That's all you heard out of all of that?"

Sara shook her head playfully while Marion pressed, "The Wrens have dispatch riders?"

"Why, yes, Mare," Eddie said. "Sylvia should make a full recovery."

Of course she hoped Sylvia would. But this information was eye-opening. Wouldn't she rather sit on a motorcycle than behind a desk?

The thought remained with her, even after her training was fulfilled and she'd been given her first assigned location.

Dover.

Marion was now a real typist in the Royal Navy.

Sara still had weeks of training left, so Marion sadly had to say her goodbyes, crossing her fingers Sara's assignment would reunite them, but Marion's greatest wish thus far had been granted: after making requests for the same port, Eddie had also been assigned to Dover.

Before Marion's work began, there were a few magical moments of walking down Maison Dieu Road, passing the grand Burlington Hotel, setting her eyes on the seafront for the very first time, and experiencing the sights, smells, and commotion of the Promenade Pier. All with Eddie at her side.

The HMS *Lynx* was currently in port in the icy waters, the worse for the wear. Marion later learned from the plumbers, which was a clever name for the Royal Navy's engineers, that in the three years of being commissioned, the HMS *Lynx* had been struck by gunfire, hit by German shells, and flooded. She was thankful for the Wrens' "Never at Sea" motto. And she was once again thankful for Alli.

Marion's assignment was within the captain's office, in a small, doorless cupboard. It was there in Dover where embarkment began to France and thus where the sick and wounded returned before being placed on trains to various hospitals, where German refugees fled, where supplies for the army were shipped abroad, and where signals via flags and lights were sent and received.

In Dover the fighting of the war felt removed, even with the impact overflowing the Channel and with bombers attacking London and other eastern towns. It felt different because in Dover nothing resembled the war film Marion had seen.

Still, the captain's office was a whirlwind of activity. There was the captain and the section leader, Wren Sullivan. She was responsible for logging every piece of paper that came into the office before it went to the captain. That left Marion and two other Wrens—Helen and Margaret. They worked a printing machine. Marion was on the typewriter.

The cupboard where Marion worked was small, barely large enough to fit the various piles of files, the typewriter, and Marion herself. But she worked diligently, though with a touch of claustrophobia. As Marion had at St. Anne's, she found the typing rhythmic. She enjoyed the punching sounds, followed by the *ding* of a forthcoming blank line. She imagined each advancement of the typewriter as a tiny progression toward the war's end. She realized they didn't actually go hand in hand, but Marion liked that she aided in the war efforts.

Eddie and Marion both did.

Eddie often rushed into the office where Marion worked throughout the accumulating days, always slightly short-winded from taking the stairs two at a time. And while Marion understood the need for her role and mostly enjoyed it in practice, a pang of jealousy swept into the office with Eddie's arrival that he was literally going places while she sat hunched within a cupboard.

Each time, at the sound of his booming footsteps, Helen and Margaret paused, expectant of his handsome smile, and Marion resisted the urge to glare at them. They were otherwise lovely, and they knew nothing of Eddie and Marion's recent coupling. It was carefully guarded information, considering relationships made the higher-ups nervous that marriage could follow. As a rule, Wrens couldn't marry.

Only Sara, with whom Marion exchanged letters, knew their secret.

"Hello, chapettes," Eddie habitually said as he bounded into the captain's office. "What do you have for me this time?"

Helen would give him messages to hand-deliver, and off he'd go, dispatched to another port, to the headquarters at Dover Castle, or to the various training camps. Sylvia had been assigned to Dover, too, and her less enthusiastic retrieval of messages could only be described as ghostlike, as if she were an apparition that would suddenly and quietly appear at the office's threshold, rather than a booming presence. She'd fully recovered from her fall, yet each day she was earning a new bump or scrape from being unable to handle her motorcycle. Marion felt for her, the fear tangible on Sylvia's face.

"Can you ask her why she keeps on? We've been at Dover for nearly a month now," Marion said to Eddie one evening as they stole time together. Marion's cabinmate routinely took a smoke break before bed, giving Eddie a chance to climb through the first-floor window of Marion's hostel and spend an hour with her. "Surely there's a less dangerous role for Sylvia within the Wrens. She could have mine, in fact."

He did ask Sylvia, and Marion's feelings of sympathy only mounted. Sylvia's father was a mechanic and had taught her the intricate workings of the machine. But riding a motorcycle had proved to be a challenge. And botheration, the woman didn't seem to improve. Sylvia's discomfort as a rider increased on a daily basis.

Whereas, Marion had to admit, her aversion to remaining within her cupboard and in front of a typewriter and without a trace of grease beneath her nails only grew stronger. She was pleased to be useful, but she wished her contributions also included fresh air and the same thrills she felt while riding Alli, and even the alertness of avoiding potholes and ruts as opposed to pressing a wrong key. Marion often found herself studying the locations on a map of where Eddie and Sylvia rode during their stunts, envisioning herself as the one delivering messages.

"I'm here," Marion heard behind her. She turned abruptly and her knee banged on the doorjamb. Sylvia's arrival was once again apparitional. Helen put a hand to her chest and chastised, "Sylvia, darling, you need to stop sneaking in here like a cat robber."

The windows were open that day, letting in the springtime air, along with the noise of the port's ships, horns, and sailors. Marion viewed them all as a tease, knowing she'd have many hours more of being indoors while Eddie roved with Alli.

Sylvia was hesitant to step farther into the office. Poor thing, she knew once she did, she'd be given an assignment and off she'd have to go on her motorbike. Beneath her trifold hat, Sylvia's skin tone had taken on a ghostly pallor.

Marion almost asked her if she was quite all right.

Marion almost asked her if there was anything she could do to help.

The words were on the tip of her tongue.

She remembered the anxiety of knowing there was only one night before moving to a new orphanage, then one morning, then one carriage ride. Then she'd be standing vulnerable in front of a new group of children. Was that how Sylvia felt about her next dispatch and standing before Marion, Margaret, and Helen?

"I'll go for you," Marion said.

Both Helen and Margaret froze at the seldom-heard voice, reserved only for niceties, as Marion otherwise felt no need to talk with them like she did with Sara.

"Can you do that?" Helen asked.

Marion's offer originated from both compassion and altruistic purposes. She wanted to help Sylvia. She'd rather be a dispatch rider.

In either case her eyes fell on the report in Helen's hand. What she was about to do was risky, but Marion didn't allow herself the time to think on the consequences of taking another Wren's assignment. She snatched the message from Helen, passed Sylvia in the doorway, and jogged down the stairs toward Sylvia's awaiting motorcycle.

CHAPTER 14

EVELYN

July 1940
Wiltshire

P ercy's single-cylinder Norton 490cc side-valve engine machine was arguably more fun to drive than her V12 Delage race car.

She'd once watched the men and women roar around the Brooklands's track on their motorcycles with fascination and awe. But never with a vocalization that she'd like to try one herself, as her mother would've promptly said, *"Be serious, Evelyn."*

Oh, Evelyn was seriously committed to being a motorcycle dispatch rider. Over the past few weeks she snuck onto her Norton every stolen chance she found. In the evenings she squirreled away in her room reading the manual to learn the motorcycle's ins and outs. Percy had a model that'd make people whistle. Heavy-duty front girder forks. Strengthened rebound springs. Top-of-the-line sports tires. Steel footpegs. And a ground clearance of five and three-fourths inches. She was a beaut. Minus the olive-colored paint.

Evelyn imagined her mother's reaction to the coloring. "How drab. Couldn't they have done a blue?"

Like one of the colors of the Women's Royal Naval Service.

She could hardly contain her anticipation as the days edged

closer and closer. Then the time had finally come to report. It was a Wednesday, as an old naval tradition dictated that incoming and outgoing drafts occurred on that particular day.

Evelyn didn't leave a note. It wasn't a decision that came lightly. But in the end she determined it was wisest to contact her parents after she'd arrived and after she'd put her signature on the contractual agreement. London was nearly one hundred miles away. Even going a substantial speed and not having to incur any stops because of the nearly four-gallon petrol tank, a ring on the telephone would undoubtedly be quicker. She couldn't have Mrs. Taylor waking, seeing Evelyn's parting note, and alerting her parents. The whole of the New Scotland Yard would be awaiting Evelyn's arrival in London otherwise.

That wouldn't do.

While Evelyn enjoyed fanfare, it wasn't the time nor the place for it.

Within hours, Evelyn was approaching the central training and drafting depot in Greenwich, positioned along the River Thames. On her way she had ached to peek in on the Brooklands, but it would've required more petrol than her tank held.

And what mattered was that she'd made it. She'd pulled off the biggest ruse of her life. Not the dutiful daughter bound for Wiltshire Academy, but Evelyn the daring—if not deceptive—young woman off to do great things.

She was in London. By herself, she might add. Wasn't that a first? A marvelous and adrenaline-pumping first. A bit nerve inducing, too, if she was being completely outright about it.

Evelyn allowed herself a few seconds to revel in her independence and let her pulse calm, then took it all in.

A bustle of men and women moved about outside a grouping of buildings in a parklike setting. Two of the buildings were mirror images of each other with white stone, pillars, and domes over the entrances. Various paths and courtyards cut between the buildings.

Evelyn paused on a path, not sure if her motorbike should even be on such a pathway, judging by the curious looks she received.

"Brilliant, isn't it?" Evelyn heard, but barely, over the rumble of her engine. "The grounds of the naval college."

Evelyn cut the engine. "Truly."

A young woman went on, "I'm told the Queen's House behind us was the birthplace of Henry the eighth, Mary the first, and Caroline the first. Back then it was called the Palace of Placentia, then Greenwich Palace. Later the grounds became the Greenwich Hospital for injured seamen. Now it's ours to put a stop to Adolf Hitler." The girl smiled, clearly quite the talker. "I'm Holly, and yes, I was born near the Christmas holiday."

Evelyn laughed. "I wasn't going to presume."

"Most do." Holly shrugged. "And you are?"

Evelyn extended her hand. "Evelyn Fairchild."

"Nice to meet you, Evelyn," Holly said cheerily. "I see you brought your own ride?"

Evelyn did appear to be the only one straddling a motorcycle. She quickly corrected the situation, stepping off. "I'm hoping to be placed as a dispatch rider."

"Well, you look the part, minus the sundress. I attended university at Oxford, I possess a photographic memory, and I can speak various languages. I'm likely to be placed in Intelligence. I'll prove those Land Army girls wrong who say the Wrens are only here looking for holiday overseas."

Evelyn widened her eyes. No part of Holly's delivery came across as conceited, but Evelyn couldn't help feeling a bit outmatched—and by the very first person she'd met. She swallowed, examining the others who spoke in small groups and a few girls walking by themselves who looked as intimidated as Evelyn was beginning to feel.

Now that she was there, it fully sank in that Evelyn—and all the others idly waiting for training to begin—had pitched herself into a war.

"If you're looking for others like you," Holly offered, "there are a few women doing very dangerous-looking things on motorcycles in the training paddock toward the back of the grounds."

Evelyn craned her neck to see around Holly. "Oh?"

"Mm-hmm. That way," Holly said, pointing. With that, Holly called a greeting to another girl she must've already known—a girl more intellectually stimulating, Evelyn was sure.

She began walking her bike in the direction Holly suggested and heard the engines before she saw them. In fact, a small circle of men and women had formed. Evelyn propped her own motorbike, then approached. Being long and lean, she peered over the heads and saw three women on motorcycles. She had found her people. In fact, she thought she recognized one as a racer from the Brooklands.

Evelyn smiled; finally she was in the right place. She racked her brain for the woman's name, hoping to introduce herself once the hoopla died down.

Theresa, she considered.

That sounded familiar.

The circle grew then, allowing Theresa more room. She rode back and forth a total of four times before, on the fifth pass, she drove while *standing* on her seat, her own sundress catching the wind.

Impressive.

The feat was more daring than anything Evelyn had ever attempted to do. Her experience was mostly on four wheels, yet this girl clearly had had a lot of practice on two.

If Holly intimidated her, Theresa took the cake. Outmatched and now outperformed. She took a deep, steadying breath. It wasn't as if she'd be required to do tricks while delivering dispatches.

Yes, the reminder was a good one.

Still, it wouldn't be good for her nerves to continue watching. Evelyn turned, only to recognize another face in the small audience.

"Rose!" Evelyn called, delighted to see someone else she knew. "I didn't know you'd be here!"

It was a silly thing to say. Evelyn hadn't grown especially close with Rose while they were both at the Brooklands; certainly not enough to have the knowledge of Rose's happenings. Wilkes was her mechanic, not Rose. Still, she and Rose were together when the war was announced over the radio. And here they were, together again.

Only, Rose didn't seem to share the same glad response. "Hello, Miss Fairchild."

"Evelyn," she insisted with a friendly smile.

Rose kept her lips pinched.

Just then, a siren sounded. At first Evelyn startled, but she soon realized from others' reactions and chatter that the sound only meant training was set to begin.

"Here we go," Evelyn said to Rose, another attempt at camaraderie.

Without a word, Rose walked off.

Evelyn couldn't think what she'd done to receive Rose's cold shoulder. But no matter, it was beginning. Evelyn was about to become a motorcycle dispatch rider.

CHAPTER 15

MARION

March 1918
Dover

Marion and Sylvia sat side by side, their stockinged knees touching, their hands in their laps.

They were in the midst of being disciplined. Marion's endeavors had come a cropper. Truly, she hadn't thought of the consequences of taking Sylvia's assignment. She'd only been focused on the lure of being a dispatch rider. Even now, her thoughts felt too much like a runaway train to focus on what Section Leader Wren Sullivan was saying. Naturally, fear coursed through her at the idea of being discharged from service, ripped away from Eddie, and having no income or place to live. Yet exhilaration still swept her senses at what she'd done.

Because she had completed the mission; she'd accomplished Sylvia's stunt without a single hiccup.

From riding Alli, she handled the motorcycle well.

From studying the maps she knew her way.

From Eddie's stories she knew the procedure. She'd handed over her missive; she'd waited for a receipt. It was the returning of that receipt that led to her outing herself and subsequently squirming like an eel in front of her section leader.

Wren Sullivan turned her head away from Marion and Sylvia and rubbed her lips together. After her deliberation, she focused again on the two young women.

How would Marion tell Eddie? She closed her eyes and briefly waited for her ruling.

"We have received a letter from Wren Brown, with whom I know you are both acquainted."

Marion's eyes flew open at the unexpected words and mention of Sara.

In unison Marion and Sylvia replied, "Yes, ma'am."

"While her telegraphist training was set to complete in April, it's been realized her talents could be better used. Her father owns an aviary, providing Wren Brown unique and rare knowledge of birds. Her efforts were needed at a pigeon loft in Flanders."

In France? Marion thought. But that wasn't removed from the war. That location *was* the war. It explained why Marion hadn't heard from Sara in some time, Sara not likely having time to write during her transfer nor while she began her work with the pigeons. Marion felt immediate concern for her friend.

"In Wren Brown's correspondence she noted the need for a dispatch rider to help with the transport of the birds. She requested Wren Pole." Marion glanced at Sylvia, and Wren Sullivan paused with a curt nod of her head. "But in light of Wren Pole's reluctance to ride and Wren Hoxton's misplaced yet obvious enthusiasm and proven skill set for the role, I've decided to recommend Wren Hoxton for the transfer instead. Wren Pole, we'll find you a new role here at Dover."

"I can type. Quickly. Proficiently."

The response came so quickly from Sylvia that it took Marion by surprise. As it was, Marion's brain was still deciphering what Wren Sullivan had just said.

Marion was to become a dispatch rider? Sylvia would be staying. Marion would be going. Not only would Marion be leaving, but she'd be off to France. She would be reunited with Sara. Yet her new path would tear her from Eddie.

Wren Sullivan and Sylvia exchanged words. Marion was at a loss for her own, having nothing to do with her mutism but rather from being separated from Eddie. Finally she opened her mouth . . . to object . . . to suggest an alternative . . .

"This is the solution I'm offering, Wren Hoxton, in response to your transgression. Unless you wish for me to share this event with the deputy divisional director? She may have an interest in knowing about this intentional breach in conduct. I'm fond of your work ethic and wish to spare you the embarrassment and also any other unfortunate outcomes."

Marion understood the consequences of refusing the transfer. Removal from the Wrens meant a loss of income, housing, clothing. It was no small thing, despite knowing Eddie would try to care for her, might even risk stowing her away in his own lodgings. But removal from the Wrens also meant a loss of purpose, which Marion had grown fond of. Never before had she felt like she belonged in such a way. Never before had she contributed to something greater than herself.

Yet the biggest draw of all . . . How could she stop aiding in a war that involved the man she loved, and all because he'd followed her into it? With Eddie in this war, Marion would do everything within her power to work toward its end. In France her impact could be even greater.

But how would she tell Eddie that her new role as a motorcycle dispatch rider would be taking her away? To a far and dangerous place?

Marion had little idea.

Telling him she was off to France, the very place where footage for the war film was captured, would be considerably harder than telling him she was leaving St. Anne's. Back then, he hadn't responded well. Marion had felt abandoned while he processed her going without him. She had twisted her hands endlessly then.

After being dismissed to her cabin, she continued to twist her hands.

Marion's cabinmate, Virginia, had left only seconds ago for her smoke. Eddie would be outside, waiting for Virginia to leave the building. He'd climb through her window, as he had numerous times before, only this time Marion would shatter him.

A mop of wavy orange hair poked through first. Shoulders, torso, then the remainder of him. Eddie always managed to land on his feet, silently, as if he wore only socks instead of his commissioned boots.

"One day," he said, smiling a greeting at Marion, "I'll enter *our* home through a normal entrance."

Their home, where they'd live as man and wife? While marriage felt like a natural course for them—friendship, sweethearts, marriage—they'd spoken nothing of it. It wasn't even something to entertain, not with Marion being unable to wed while she was enlisted as a Wren.

He framed Marion's face with his hands, kissing her. When he pulled away, she brought them back together for another, an urgency in this second kiss.

"Miss Hoxton," Eddie chided playfully at her assertiveness.

"I have to tell you something," Marion blurted.

She'd been planning on waiting until later in his visit. She'd hear about the in-betweens of Eddie's day. He'd tell her something foolish one of the other men had said. She'd remark on any insight she'd gleaned from the missives she typed. A spring offensive by the Germans was feared and rumored, as one such example.

But what she had to tell him was too important to sit on. She wouldn't recklessly throw the words at him like she'd done before, causing Eddie to retreat from her. That had hurt them both.

Eddie's hands slid down her arms until finding her hands. "What is it, Mare?"

"I took Sylvia's stunt today."

Eddie's head cocked, revealing his confusion, and she explained, telling him of completing Sylvia's assignment. In fact, she emphasized the fulfillment it brought her. When she eventually broke the news of her transfer, she hoped he'd recognize how she'd be doing something gratifying.

But that didn't happen.

She told him.

He lost all pallor.

"You're being sent to the front?"

Marion shook her head briskly. "No, not there. Not exactly. The pigeons I'll be helping Sara with are kept a distance away."

His head shook more slowly in disbelief. Eddie's eyes were on Marion, but she doubted he saw her. Instead, he likely envisioned the war film.

"Becoming a Wren and working out of a cupboard is one thing, Mare. But France? That's not where you're meant to be. If I'd known that, I'd go back in time to St. Anne's and insist you go into domestic work."

"Then it would've been me who followed you once you were conscripted. I'm here until this war is over. For you, Eddie."

"Fine," Eddie said, though his tone spoke volumes otherwise. "Then stay here. Help here. Turn down the transfer."

Marion frowned. "Eddie, this isn't something a 'No, thank you' can resolve. There are consequences. They'll make me leave the Wrens if I don't go."

"Which you should've thought of first," Eddie snapped.

"Too loud," she scolded at a similar volume. When he said no more, a silence fell between them.

Eddie sank to Marion's bunk. She gingerly sat beside him.

Finally Marion whispered, "You aren't wrong." She bolstered her voice, yet still kept it quiet. "But I will be glad to have a larger role in ending this war for you. For us."

He wouldn't look at her.

"Look at me," Marion insisted.

Eddie's Adam's apple rose and fell with a rough swallow. "If you must go—"

"Oh, Eddie, please don't scheme like you did before. This is what it is."

Marion's ears pricked at a cluster of voices in the hallway. Marion went still, her eyes on her doorknob.

Marion didn't know what Virginia would do if she walked in and saw Eddie. Marion had told herself they would never be caught. Gloriously, the voices faded, and she began again at a whisper, "I don't wish to be apart from you. But I have no choice in the matter. I'll go help Sara with her birds. The godforsaken war will end. I'll return to—"

"If you must go," Eddie repeated, "I'd like for you to go as my wife."

Marion startled. She hadn't been expecting a proposal. But it wasn't a proposal, exactly. It was more of a statement. She questioned, irritation in her voice, "Do you hope by making me your wife the Wrens will no longer have me?"

"No," he said, his tone beginning hard but softening as he

continued, "by making you my wife we'll forever be joined, no matter what happens."

"No matter what," Marion parroted, also softening.

"Another of our secrets," Eddie added, a mischievous grin slowly forming.

Marion found herself nodding, tears in her eyes.

"So it's a yes? Marion Jane Elinor Hoxton, will you marry me?"

She choked out a laugh. "Jane Elinor?"

Eddie smiled. "All the names you should've been given from a parent and the church. Inspired by your love of reading. I'll be honored to add my name too."

Smith.

Hadn't Marion once been jealous of his surname and how it meant he was part of something larger? Now with a single yes, she'd be part of that robust family too. A name given to her intentionally, with love.

Emotion nearly stamped out her words, but Marion managed, "Yes. Of course I'll secretly marry you."

CHAPTER 16

EVELYN

July 1940
London

Evelyn was the only ninny standing in line to check in at training with a motorbike.

Theresa and the other two women had left theirs in the paddock, it seemed.

At her turn to check in, she wheeled her motorcycle to the table. The woman did a double take, then snapped for another woman. The second woman promptly freed Evelyn of her machine. "I'll just bring this to the paddock area for safekeeping."

Evelyn was caught between relief and reluctance at Percy's motorbike being taken away. But she had little choice in the matter. And already she'd become an unwanted spectacle, singled out.

Evelyn cleared her throat, smoothed her hair, and presented her medical records. They were taken with little acknowledgment from the woman behind the table, who only asked, "Name?"

"Evelyn P. Fairchild."

"Very well," the woman said while flipping through a stack of envelopes. She pulled one free. "In here is your cabin number, training schedule, pertinent information, et cetera." From the ground she plucked a bag from a teetering stack. "And in here is your probationer uniform. At the end of fourteen days, you have the option to leave. And we have the option to release you. If you remain, you'll begin specific training and receive your official uniform. I'll make a note of your motorcycle. I assume they'll want to put you and it to good use. Welcome to the Women's Royal Naval Service."

The next in line stepped forward, but Evelyn remained. "Could you tell me where I can send a telegram?"

The woman tapped Evelyn's envelope. "Pertinent information." She then focused on the next recruit. "Name?"

Evelyn nodded and backpedaled, clutching her new bag along with the one she'd brought with odds and ends: a photograph of her parents, a catchpenny brooch Mrs. Taylor had taken to pinning to Evelyn's nightgown for a splash of polish as she recovered from surgeries, spare undergarments, toiletries, her good luck elephant from Percy, and extra wool socks. The last was for hiding her impairment. Thinking of the socks brought a pang of homesickness. Mrs. Taylor had stitched them for Evelyn after one of her surgeries.

Evelyn inhaled deeply, then she smiled warmly at a passing girl, who gave Evelyn more reassurance than she knew when she smiled in return. Evelyn repositioned her bags and opened her envelope.

Her room, termed a cabin, was in Queen Anne Court, not to be confused with Queen Mary Court. There was also King William Court and King Charles Court. There was little hope of her not confusing the buildings.

The map, however, denoted Queen Anne Court as being located straight ahead.

After passing through an archway, she found herself within a courtyard, then navigated her way to her room.

Her *cabin*, rather.

At the sound of voices inside, Evelyn considered knocking, then chastised herself for having such a thought when entering her own cabin.

This was all new for Evelyn. Being away from home. Being on her own. Frankly, being with other women. Sharing a room with those women. The most experience she had with other females was while at the Brooklands, and apparently she hadn't done a bang-up job considering Rose's poor reaction to seeing her.

Evelyn rubbed her hands together, gathering her nerve, then turned the knob. Her gaze immediately fell on Rose.

Their reactions mirrored each other: mouth ajar, body stiff.

Evelyn broke their standstill to take in the others, who to her delight included Theresa, along with another girl.

"Evelyn, right?" Theresa said, stepping forward. She had changed from her sundress into their assigned blue overalls. It appeared Rose had, too, along with the remaining girl. "I remember you from the tracks," Theresa said. "It took you a few years to work your way toward the top of the leaderboard, no? Shame this war happened before you got there."

"Dare D-Evelyn," Rose said under her breath.

Evelyn made a point to ignore the . . . what was it . . . a jab? She couldn't understand how her racing moniker had a negative connotation. Sure, she hadn't overtaken Doreen in her last race, and she barely had surpassed the Baroness, but she'd worked hard to climb the ranks. She mentally shook Rose's put-down from her head. "Yes, and you're Theresa. I remember you, too, from the Brooklands."

Theresa nodded. "I think that's why we're all in the same room, coming from the same area and all. I see you found a place for your motorbike. I thought you were going to roll it straight in here. Only have four bunks, though."

"No," Evelyn said, faking a laugh while gripping the strap of her bag too tightly. "She's getting settled in the paddock."

Theresa nodded again. "Were you recruited like us?"

"Recruited?" Evelyn questioned.

"Yes, Rose and I first heard of the Wrens from the Brooklands. They were after women with a knowledge of motorbikes. There are a few of us competition riders from local motorcycle race circuits. I reckoned that's how you came to be here as well."

"Not exactly," Evelyn began timidly. "I've been in Wiltshire with my family since the onset of the war. I learned of the Wrens there."

"I see," Theresa said slowly, though not unkindly.

Evelyn risked a glance at Rose, who was giving a measured shake of her head. So far Evelyn's final bunkmate hadn't uttered a thing. She looked mighty uncomfortable, her gaze trained on her shoes.

"I got a quick glimpse of your motorbike," Theresa went on. "Looks like it had some bells and whistles added on. Where'd you come by it?"

"A friend," Evelyn said vaguely.

At that, Theresa and Rose exchanged another look. Evelyn almost questioned what it meant, but she bit her tongue, focusing again on her fourth bunkmate, with whom she hopefully would have a more pleasant greeting. "Hi, I'm Evelyn."

"Mary."

"Pleasure to meet you, Mary. So you're from Weybridge then too?"

"Sweetie," Theresa said, cutting in, "none of us are from Weybridge. Surrey, sure. But not Weybridge."

"Oh."

How on earth was she supposed to respond to that? It wasn't made better by the fact that Rose had said exactly one thing—a mocking comment, no less—ever since Evelyn entered the room, though

Rose clearly had said more than a thing or two about Evelyn prior to her arrival. Fortunately Evelyn had scoured the day's itinerary and it was nearly time for a tour of the grounds.

She said as much and quickly deposited her bags on her bunk and reached for her blue overalls to change into. As she did, her finger grazed her elephant. She could use some of its luck right about now. Evelyn gave it a final squeeze, then said, "I just have to first send a telegraph, so I'll . . ." She trailed off. Evelyn didn't think they cared and was relieved when they left so she could change her clothing privately, without the risk of any of her bunkmates eyeing her left foot. Considering her not-so-warm welcome, Evelyn wouldn't put it past them to try to get her booted by telling a superior that she wasn't fit to be there.

Evelyn was already certain her parents would share in the sentiment of her being unfit to be a Wren. She was thankful for the telegram's twenty-five-word limit, which included not only the message but also her name and address and her parents' names and address in Wiltshire.

ARRIVED SAFELY AT WRENS
TRAINING AND HOPE

Scratch that.

AND ENDEAVOR TO MAKE YOU PROUD

Now to follow through. The news would be shocking to her father and infuriating to her mother.

Evelyn hadn't known about the two-week probationary period, and she cringed at the thought of waking up tomorrow to her mother pulling back her bedsheets, that vein popping in her forehead. There was little doubt in Evelyn's mind that her mother would demand she leave. It was a battle she'd gladly fight.

The welcome tour was set to begin. Evelyn located her group under one of the colonnades, all matching in a sea of blue overalls, and to her relief, it didn't include any of her bunkmates.

She found herself relaxing and enjoying the truly magnificent architecture and history.

In 1694 King William III, honoring the wishes of his wife, Queen Mary II, had issued a Royal Warrant to turn the site into a Royal Hospital for those who had served in the Royal Navy. It was meant to rival the army's Royal Hospital Chelsea.

"Ironically enough," Evelyn's group was told by a prim and proper Wren Monroe in full uniform, "the man responsible for the transformation was none other than Sir Christopher Wren."

The women giggled at the coincidence of names. Later, they reacted with the proper nods of their heads upon learning that the site had been purposely split into four quadrants so Queen Mary II still had an unobstructed view of the River Thames from the Queen's House. And how the Queen Mary Court and the King William Court buildings each had a tower with a clockface, though only one told time. The second clockface marked the points of a compass and was linked to a weather vane on the roof.

Evelyn and her group entered one of the buildings—she wasn't sure which it was at this point—and soon found themselves standing in an ornate hall.

"Rome may have the Sistine Chapel, but London has *this*," Wren Monroe gushed. "The Painted Hall, with over forty-three thousand square feet of art in a baroque style, depicting our naval successes, cultural achievements, and our country's political advancements. The completion of this great hall took over nineteen years and was rumored to have left the posture of the artist, Sir James Thornhill, permanently affected. Be certain to offer him a thanks when you take your seat here for your next meal, for surely you will be dining in style."

Wren Monroe smiled, and Evelyn and the other women responded in kind.

Beneath them was the King William Undercroft, which to Evelyn's surprise included a room once used to keep the royal bees. After passing through the Ripley Tunnel that connected the twin buildings underground, she was even more surprised to find that the Queen Mary Undercroft included a bowling alley.

"In your downtime," Wren Monroe said, "which will include three hours of shore leave your first week, more time accumulating as we go, please feel free to have a game. The Victorian Skittle Alley dates back to the nineteenth century. You'll have to be your own pinsetter, though."

More laughter from the women.

Their tour concluded in the Chapel of St. Peter and St. Paul, which was designed in a neoclassical style. Very opulent, with detailed marble floors, an ornate ceiling, decorative features galore, and a grand organ.

"I hope you all enjoyed a look at the buildings where you'll be spending your time the next two weeks, perhaps longer if your specialty training will continue here. As knowledge is a great source of hunger, I'd like to invite you all to a luncheon in the Painted Hall. Be sure to eat your fill because we'll begin physical endurance tests this afternoon."

Wren Monroe gave her final smile.

Evelyn's own faltered. She felt capable. She *was* capable. But she also didn't know what such fitness tests would include. To think she could fail even before she'd truly begun.

CHAPTER 17

MARION

March 1918
Dover

She'd said yes. She and Eddie were to be married. Doing so in secret felt scandalous. Excitement had gotten the better of her. So had her love for the man. But was it wise?

Before she could falter, Eddie had dipped to her height and said, *"Leave everything to me."* He'd kissed the tip of Marion's nose. He'd begun to pull back, then kissed her lips, her forehead. *"I'll go now. See who I can talk to. See what can be done. Come hell or high water, we'll be married tomorrow. You won't be shipped off yet?"* Eddie had run a hand through his hair. *"Right?"*

"I have two days," Marion had replied in a solemn voice. It'd been a contradiction to how her insides felt because, in truth, the idea had made her feel alive, jubilant.

The feelings hadn't dissipated that night in her sleep, nor did they fade as she went about her final day of duties as a typist. She widened her eyes expectantly at Eddie when he retrieved a message from her office, only to receive a whispered, *"Soon,"* and now she waited for him to claim the seat beside her at dinner.

She was to be married.

Eddie was to be her husband.

She would be Eddie's wife.

He would belong to her and she would belong to him. For the rest of their lives.

Marion felt as if the sentiments were written on her face for everyone to see, and someone would somehow know to question why she carried her registry of birth with her the entirety of the day, even though it was tucked away unseen within her pocket. Having someone discover their secret plans would be a travesty, especially now that the idea of becoming Eddie's wife had been seeded in her head and watered with every thought of her day. She'd be crushed if their marriage didn't come to fruition.

It wasn't very long ago when the consent of a parent or guardian was needed for any persons under the age of twenty-one to marry. Marion had seen it in her novels. Lydia Bennet married at sixteen. Catherine Morland was engaged at seventeen. Marianne and Elinor Dashwood and Fanny Price also accepted proposals as teenaged girls. They all needed their guardians to agree. What would Marion have done if the law hadn't been lifted? She had no such parent or guardian. She couldn't have asked Wren Sullivan for permission. Would she have lied about her age?

At any rate, these extraneous questions only served to work up Marion, fueled undoubtedly by her nerves. Even while swept up into the notion of marrying Eddie, Marion suspected there'd always be a level of restlessness before going up the aisle, especially as a girl who hadn't spent her days fantasizing about being wed. Marion snorted to herself, thinking how she'd been in the marriage market, much like the Bennet sisters, without even realizing it.

"Thinking about marrying me?" Eddie whispered into her ear, suddenly beside her. "I see your smile."

Marion quickly assessed her surroundings. Another woman had left the supper table and she hadn't so much as noticed. She asked Eddie, "Did you work it all out?"

He blew out a whistle.

Marion's eyes widened. "No? Or are you toying with me, Edward Michael James Smith?"

If he'd given her a full name, she'd bestow the same upon him.

The animation from Eddie's face smoothed away, leaving only tenderness in his green eyes. "You're something, Mare. I'm going to be the luckiest man alive . . . but only if we hurry."

"Hurry?"

Eddie pulled Marion to her feet. "He said he'd only wait for a few minutes."

"Who—" she began, but abandoned the question to point out her left-behind plate. They were already halfway across the room.

"Leave it," Eddie said. "What's one more infraction?"

Marion laughed. Marrying in secret when she could very well be expelled from the Wrens felt much larger than an infraction. This was forever. In mere moments Marion's life would be irrevocably altered.

"How is this happening so quickly?" Marion asked, their exertion and her excitement stealing her breath. They were walking at a clip. Where, Marion wasn't certain, until Eddie revealed their destination was the registrar's office. The man had agreed to remain an extra hour. Eddie apologized they wouldn't be wed at a chapel, but finding a priest was an extra and timely step. Usually a marriage notice was submitted weeks in advance and placed on public display. Marion had cringed at that dodged detail. But how had he managed it?

Eddie explained, "Exceptions are made only for exceptional circumstances. Like when the woman you love is leaving for France."

"Let's not focus on that," Marion soothed. She smoothed down a portion of his wavy hair that tended to have a mind of its own. From her pocket she removed the brooch she was found with and attached it to her uniform. The piece of jewelry wasn't worth much monetarily, but Marion sometimes allowed herself to think it held an inkling of sentimental value if her birth mother thought to leave it with her. It was the one glimmer of hope that her mother's abandonment was more complicated than simply not wanting her.

At the sight of the office, Marion surveyed their surroundings, feeling as if she were canvassing the street before committing a burglary.

"All's clear," Eddie said, fully knowing any consequences would affect Marion and Marion alone. Conscription for married men had begun two years prior.

Hand in hand, they all but spilled into the office.

In the end, Marion and Eddie married in their uniforms, witnessed by temporary faces, with only four words softly spoken between them. How fitting it was with their unconventional upbringings.

Marion woke, Eddie's cabin still dark, and circled a finger around where her wedding band would be if she could wear one. Eddie promised it'd be their first task after Germany surrendered. Lazily she turned her head, marveling at the man beside her. How had she become so lucky to be given Eddie, when his magnetism surely could've landed him any woman on the face of the planet? How would she ever leave him?

Eddie stirred beside her. A sudden realization hit her that this could be the one and only time they'd meet the day together in this way, drowsy from sleep, languid from lovemaking, cocooned in their shared bliss.

"Morning, Mrs. Smith," Eddie said, his voice raspy.

Marion shifted closer, fitting herself beneath his chin, tangling their legs together, realizing a new soreness to her body. "Let's pretend it's not morning yet."

That Eddie didn't have to begin his day soon.

That Marion wasn't set to begin her transfer to France.

That Eddie's cabinmate, whom Eddie had bribed to stay away last night, wouldn't return at any moment and catch Marion in a state of undress. No amount of money would restrain a man from gossip if he caught Marion in Eddie's bed. Ironically, it'd likely cost Marion more if Eddie's cabinmate knew it to be a wedding bed.

She couldn't risk it. Grudgingly, she began to detangle herself from her husband.

"Wait," Eddie said. "I thought we were pretending."

Marion kissed him sweetly. "Trust me, I'll be pretending daily we aren't apart and praying we'll be together again soon."

She began to climb from their bed and Eddie lunged for her hand. "No matter where we are, we're still together, Mrs. Smith."

There was that name again. And it was hers.

CHAPTER 18

EVELYN

July 1940
London

E velyn had been right to fear the fitness tests. She now knew intimately what they held in store for her.

Curl-ups. And push-ups. Lots of them. As many as Evelyn could do in two minutes, to be exact. Resting was permitted. However, during the push-ups, Evelyn could only pause in the up position, which frankly didn't feel like resting, as her left foot ached, her arms shook, and her body threatened to collapse. And Lord help her, Wren Philips seemed to watch her knees more than the other girls' as she lowered her body to the ground.

At the end of her two minutes, Evelyn's arms made good on their threat, and she collapsed. With her cheek in the dirt, she noticed many of the other girls had taken the same position. Rose and Theresa, too, bringing Evelyn satisfaction—and also relief.

Someone clapped her back. She rolled to see Wren Philips. "Not bad," she told Evelyn. "I reckon all the wrestling of a steering wheel has strengthened your shoulders and arms more than expected."

"I reckon so," Evelyn said, instinctively rubbing one of her throbbing arms while relishing the fact Wren Philips already knew of her background as a racer.

"Now let's see if that smile stays on your face during the timed run."

At that, Evelyn's megawatt smile did indeed dim. Her clubfoot went unnoticed during the curl-ups and push-ups, but during the run would she be able to conceal it?

Wren Philips was already walking on, calling out to the group of women, "The one-and-a-half-mile run consists of that: one and a half miles. You can run, you can walk, or you can do any combination of the two. However, keep in mind, your scores from the curl-ups and push-ups will be added to your run score. The average of the three will be your final score, which needs to be greater than a 'Good (Low)' rating if you wish to remain here as a Wren. May I suggest you don't walk?"

That was met with a few soft groans, at which Wren Philips narrowed her eyes. The culprits went undiscovered.

Soon the girls were at the starting line. Evelyn flexed her ankle outward, up, then down. So much of her youth had been spent doing such exercises, and in a way, she felt like they had led to this very moment. The preparation didn't make her any less nervous, though. She could run, but could she cover such a distance with no practice? How long before she felt it in her foot? In her entire body? She stretched again outward, up, down. She crossed her arms in front of her body and over her head.

Evelyn felt eyes on her. It came as little surprise the penetrating glare originated from Rose, who maintained perfect balance while holding a quad stretch. Truly, Evelyn didn't understand the other girl's animosity. Was it simply because Evelyn's family lived in a wealthy corner of Weybridge?

It wasn't the time to decode Rose's attitude. Wren Philips gave them their starting cues.

Within their first steps, the women jostled for position. Evelyn took an elbow to the ribs. She shot the girl a menacing look, then decided to throw her own elbow back.

The girls were in such a cluster that Evelyn didn't think anyone would take notice of her, but then the girls began breaking away, leaving her in the dust. Many of the trainees sped on ahead, Evelyn soon finding herself at the back of the pack, where her unusual, wobbly gait was easily spotted.

She felt her cheeks heating, though it easily could have been from exertion too. The effort stretched her lungs. She already felt the novel movements of running such a distance in her legs. The only saving grace was that Rose was long gone, unable to witness Evelyn in such a moment. Theresa was ahead as well, her arms pumping in a rhythmic motion.

Evelyn tried to do the same, hoping an even swing to her arms would somehow counteract the rest of her wobble.

By the halfway point her left foot was screaming at her. Her brain screamed at her to stop, too, just for a moment. She could walk. She saw others walking. She'd just passed one of those girls. But no, she wouldn't slow. She didn't think worse of anyone who did. But she feared that if she walked, her body wouldn't let her increase her pace again. Furthermore, she wouldn't allow herself to slow down, not when the words of her mother rang in her head from when she first told her mother she was joining the service: *"Help me with the garden. This is something useful you are capable of doing."*

In that moment Evelyn had known her mother didn't think she was physically capable of doing much in this world, let alone being a Wren.

For a few rapid beats of her heart, with the throb of her foot so strong she could think of little else, she almost believed her. But

Evelyn wasn't a stranger to that throb. Pushing through pain was something her mother forced upon Evelyn time and time again during the surgeries and subsequent therapies.

"Thank you, Mother," Evelyn said to herself between gulps of air.

She pressed on, her confidence ebbing and flowing, until she neared the finish line. Her heart dropped. Evelyn didn't consider that everyone who'd finished ahead of her would now be staring at her. She didn't have the strength to meet Rose's eyes.

She prayed everyone would simply assume she'd twisted an ankle. Would Wren Philips realize she had a clubfoot and be waiting at the finish line, not seeing the need for Evelyn to finish the probationary period?

She should've waited to telegram her parents.

Head down, Evelyn could at least finish. A chorus of women cheered her on.

"Come on, Fairchild!" she heard one voice shout louder than the rest.

But it wasn't the voice of Wren Philips or one of the other girls. In fact, it was a familiar, if not entirely out of place, voice.

Percy?

She found him standing off to the side, in a suit, his arms crossed, looking every part the leading man there to rescue her.

Evelyn did her best to ignore his presence—the other women surely weren't—and she crossed the finish line. Her time wasn't good, she knew that, but she hoped the average of all three of her fitness scores would be enough.

A few girls offered her a kind "Well done." A few asked if she was hurt. In between gulps of air, she smiled and waved them off.

She heard women cheering for other girls coming in. At least she hadn't been last.

Wren Philips kept her distance, seemingly content in watching Evelyn with a twist of her lips.

Evelyn remained steadfast in her avoidance of Rose. She would've done the same to Percy, but he shouted her name again, causing the gaze of the other recruits to stick to her like glue. And how would Wren Philips react to Percy calling out her name a third time?

The only way she reasoned to unstick herself was to talk quickly with him. She walked as swiftly as she could toward him. "Percy," she seethed, her breath still labored. "What are you doing here? You're making a spectacle of me. I don't need you here cheering me on."

He held up his palms. "I'm only here to relay a message. It didn't seem like it could wait."

"A message? From who?"

Creases cut deep between Percy's eyes. "Your parents, Evie."

Her knees nearly gave way. "My parents contacted you?"

He braced her forearm. "They telephoned me at the clinic. It seems they received your telegram."

"Don't look at me like that, Percy Harrington."

"Like what?"

"Like I've done something wrong."

Percy sighed. "Evelyn, you didn't tell them you were leaving."

"Just tell me what they said, will you?"

He nodded, but it didn't seem like he actually wanted to tell her. "They're upset. I spoke with your father, but your mother was in the background doing most of the talking. She said she warned you that if you joined they were going to—"

"They're cutting me off?"

Percy cast his eyes toward his shoes.

Evelyn felt a pang in her chest. "But they can't be serious. They're only angry, right? I'm their daughter. Their *only* child. They wouldn't dare do such a thing."

"I'm quite sorry, I really am. I don't know. But you're here now. This is where you want to be, so try to take your parents out of the equation. Can you do that?"

"I don't know." Evelyn wouldn't cry. Tears threatened, but she wouldn't give in to the emotion. Not in front of Percy. Not in front of the entire bloody group of recruits. "I'm just hurt."

Percy nodded. "I know. I mean, I can't presume to know how you feel, but I can't imagine it's swell." He squeezed her arm, only letting go when his head ticked toward their audience. "I wish I knew what to say. All I can think is that you have the Wrens, right? Maybe it's time to embrace leaving the nest."

If he meant it as a pun, Evelyn wasn't in the mood to laugh. Yes, she had the Wrens, but for how long? She was living on borrowed time. Unless she proved her worth to the Wrens in the next two weeks, she'd lose everything and have nothing.

CHAPTER 19

MARION

March 1918
Saint-Tricat

W ith so much at risk while there was a war on, Marion knew
she had to make the most of her time in France. Her journey
had begun via ferry across the Channel. Once in France, she'd continued by train from Calais. She ended on foot outside a small village
where locals and soldiers milled about.

How strange it was to be walking by herself down a winding lane
along the scented, poppy-flowered hills, knowing the war wasn't far
off. How far, she wasn't yet certain, and perhaps she preferred her
current ignorance. Marion had been given little information about
her destination and assignment.

The loft, she'd been told, was within a barn outside the village to
reduce the amount of commotion for the homing pigeons. She was to
find the barn by a mill and maize field. Marion's knowledge of farming
consisted only of small mentions within her books, and this journey
had been the first time she'd ever seen wide-open expanses outside
her mind's eye. But she assumed it'd be too early in the season to spot
an actual field of maize.

Fortunately Marion recognized her friend at the top of the hill. A smile sprang to Marion's face and she quickened her pace toward Sara, who was conversing outside the barn with a soldier on a motorbike. Despite how Marion's stomach wrenched at being torn from Eddie, excitement grew that she'd soon receive her own motorbike. In fact, the soldier promptly left on foot, leaving the bike behind. Was it to be hers?

Sara retreated inside the barn.

Marion arrived, pressing a hand into the stitch that had formed in her side. She had planned to go straight through to surprise her friend, but instead a sly smile spread across her face. She knocked their melody: *slow—quick-quick-slow—quick-quick*.

The door was heaved open.

"Oh, Mare!" Sara embraced her, and it struck Marion that Sara had adopted the nickname Eddie had for her. She liked it. She liked their friendship. "I'm both so pleased and sorry you're here! Your company is very welcome, but I've been sick with guilt that I'm the reason you're not still in England."

With Eddie. The words had been so booming within Marion's head that she wasn't certain if she'd spoken them aloud. But Sara didn't skip a beat, continuing, "I didn't feel gay about requesting Sylvia, but I also thought she'd be more comfortable working with a friend. But then the reply I received said you'd be coming in her place. How on earth did that transpire? What have I missed? Who's been doing your talking for you?"

Marion gave a quiet laugh. "There wasn't much need to talk when my job was to type other people's words. I sure missed you though, Sare."

Marion tried out the mirroring moniker.

"Mare and Sare," Sara said, grabbing Marion's hands. "I adore that. Now what else? Tell me everything I've missed."

A slow smile spread on Marion's face. "Well, something of note did happen."

Sara's eyes widened. "Must I pull it out of you?"

Marion tried to hold it in, but she was bursting at the seams to tell her friend. "Eddie and I married." She instinctively held up her ring finger, as if the proof were there. Though it was not.

Sara glanced briefly at Marion's ringless hand, then her astonished face focused again on Marion's, until she promptly clasped a hand over her open mouth, speaking through her fingers. "You mean to say I not only pulled you away from a safer location but I also took you away from your new husband? I'm wretched."

Marion took back her friend's hands, squeezing them. "You are no such thing. How would you have known this would all transpire? I took Sylvia's stunt, proving I was willing and able. That's why I'm here. It was decided I'm more suited for the role. Besides, I'm glad to be here, doing something more crucial to end this war. Though you know I know nothing about birds. I fear I'll be deadweight."

Sara waved her off. "Nonsense. You'll be a quick study. Even I had to do a cram course on how the pigeons are being used during a war. Here, come meet the gang."

Marion hadn't yet said hello to her motorcycle, but she dutifully followed her friend into the barn. Her eyes went wide. "There are so many of them. Hundreds!"

Some sat roosting, while others head-bobbed in various directions.

Sara laughed. "Organized chaos. Much more organized since I arrived, if I can toot my own horn. You'll get used to the noise. It all becomes one long, overlapping *coo*. Very docile creatures, so they don't flutter all around the barn. Being monogamous, they tend to be content to sit about with their mate or hunt for food together. Not overly smelly either."

Sara led Marion deeper into the barn, which looked and smelled to Marion like she expected any normal barn would, with an open space upon entry and a hayloft above. Sara began pointing in various directions. "I have the empty baskets lined up along that wall."

"So many of them too," Marion observed. Stacks upon stacks of large square baskets.

"When you're delivering the birds, you'll wear the basket on your back."

Docile or not, Marion could only think of the pigeons pecking at her head through the bars. She shuddered.

Sara continued, "Nest bowls are over here. These young ones will spend up to twenty-three days in a bowl. They're called *squeakers* at this point. After that they'll join the flock, but it'll take time to train them and also until they're strong enough to make a flight. I work with the army in these parts, and they want the birds to go at least ten miles, but ideally up to fifty. It takes about three months to get the birds ready. I'm working on training my first batch now while I also breed the older females. See there," Sara said, pointing at a tag, "each bird has a number so we can track them."

"And how many birds do we currently have?"

"Two hundred and seven adults. I have thirty-three in the bowls. More are on their way. Usually takes eight to twelve days to lay eggs after mating. Each female lays one to three eggs. Generally two, which'll take eighteen days to hatch. I've hit the ground running with the birds."

"I'd say so," Marion remarked, feeling a bit overwhelmed.

"You'll hit the ground running too. Trust me," Sara said with a mischievous smile.

Marion didn't like that grin. "What's expected of me?"

"Well, for starters, there are lofts all over. All the services are working together. Combined operations. I'll need you to take out your motorcycle to map the nearby lofts, especially the French civvy lofts, and figure out where we'll later need to replenish birds."

Marion's heart fluttered. "I can do that."

"Splendid. I'll also"—Sara paused, that grin appearing again on her handsome heart-shaped face—"need your help with the birds."

"How?"

Sara grinned.

"Sara . . ."

Laughing, Sara said, "Why don't I show you? One thing I do is exercise the birds twice a day."

"You exercise the birds?" Marion asked, confounded by the idea.

Sara laughed again as she widened the barn door and began shooing birds outside. Marion quickly sidestepped, backstepped. Swung her arms like she was doing the wren. She would've done any dance step to get out of the path of the fleeing birds.

They took flight, dashing across the sky in varying directions.

Marion followed Sara outside. "Aren't you afraid they'll fly away?"

"Not if they want their next meal. I always make sure they have enough water, but I feed them just enough so they're always a wee bit hungry. They *always* come back." As if one of the pigeons understood the word *hungry*, he made a beeline to an opening at the top of the barn and disappeared back inside to his food source.

Sara sighed. "I bet you my pillow that's number 87. Laziest one I've got. Let me go fetch him. Will you keep the others active? If you see a pigeon who isn't on his wing but sitting about, give him a nudge."

Marion's mouth fell open. She'd have to touch the creatures? A few were on the ground. She approached one and compromised with a soft prodding with her foot, quickly yanking back her leg and knocking herself off-balance.

"Mare," Sara chastised, holding 87 securely in one hand. "You look ridiculous. They don't bite. Pigeons are harmless. Now, if we were training ostriches, that'd be a different story."

"Small blessings," Marion said, taking it all in. She'd never in her life seen so many birds in a single place. Most were in flight, but she saw a couple more she'd need to get back in the sky.

"I'm glad you turned up today," Sara went on. That grin still hadn't left Sara's face.

"What else is expected of me? Dare I even ask?"

"Well, with the birds kept indoors and out of the elements, I bathe the flock once a week."

"And?" Marion said, her mind firmly rooted to Sara's use of *I*.

Sara's smile morphed into a smirk. "Today's the day."

Neither the pigeons nor Marion enjoyed the bathing endeavor. However, Marion otherwise enjoyed the training once she overcame her distaste of touching the birds.

Soon Marion had it down. She'd scoop beneath a bird, its legs going between her fingers. Then she'd wrap a thumb around its wings. They never tried to flap or peck at her hand like she had feared. They were docile. Sara insisted they were dependable too.

A week later they were putting the latter quality to the test.

On her back Sara carried the two-foot basket with two birds inside. They passed the village, where many army soldiers were billeted, one of the soldiers calling out, "Hello, Jennies."

It was a nickname given to the Wrens, Sara explained to Marion, saying, "It's not uncommon for a female bird to be called a Jenny. But wrens have earned the name Jenny Wren because you can always pick out the females. Wrens, by nature, are songbirds, amazingly loud songbirds considering their smaller size. And the females become *very* vocal when they have a new brood and someone comes near. The name Jenny Wren has stuck, I suppose, and now that we're called Wrens, we also get the Jenny nickname. Ironic considering you're not even a little bit loud, Mare."

Marion snorted a laugh. Though, if truth be told, she enjoyed the idea of having a moniker with meaning. Marion was perfectly suited as a Jenny Wren, with her history of following directives, with her one-word answers to superiors, with her easy acceptance of being alone in the countryside with only Sara and a flock of birds. In fact, Marion and Sara had given up their own billets in the village, both preferring to sleep in the barn. Marion had never felt more fulfilled, more than she ever had while working in her cupboard. Her contentedness could have been improved only by Eddie's presence. She missed him fiercely. However, she'd never wish France upon him.

Sara waved back with trilling fingers to the soldier. "Bet he's happy to be in the reserves instead of called to the front," Sara asserted. "Though I'm not too sure how much longer that'll be. I'm getting pressure to get the birds trained. New lofts are going up. Some lofts are going mobile. More and more army men are being brought in. The men in the village say the Germans are getting close to Paris. Meanwhile we have the battle here in northern France. Those cannons of theirs, the ones called Big Berthas, are said to be able to shoot eighty miles."

Sara quickened her pace, and Marion matched her strides. So the rumors that Germany had been planning an offensive had been true. Now the rumors were that the United States was going to throw their weight in to help stop the Huns, who were gaining ground along the four hundred–plus miles of the front line.

Marion only hoped Eddie didn't know how close she actually was to it all. She'd written him after she'd arrived, explaining how she was stationed outside a small commune in the Hauts-de-France region and how she'd begun riding to the various lofts to map their locations.

At first she hadn't known the distance to the trenches, but now Marion guessed she'd be able to ride to them in under two hours. She hadn't tested the theory, nor did she want to, but she'd come close enough to hear distant shelling and explosions. While visiting another loft, she'd ducked and protectively used her arms to cover her head at a rather close-sounding boom. The loftman had assured her that the sound traveled, especially as the day was getting long.

She, however, didn't feel reassured when the loftman had spoken of how the bombardment of trenches often started hours and sometimes *days* before an attack, the barrage of German gunfire and cannons pummeling a depth of up to four miles. The men were stuck in their dugouts until the firing ceased. Then the men were expected to emerge from their holes and fend off the Germans, who'd go over the top of their dugouts and onto French soil. If the Germans were successful, British troops would retreat deeper into France. And over the past few days, that had been the case. The loftman said this particular battle stretched some forty miles. It'd begun the day after Marion's arrival, less than one hundred miles away. Within days, the distance had been shortened by a likely ten miles.

Marion pressed forward with Sara, on their way to train the birds. But she couldn't help but remember how each trip out she'd taken on her motorcycle the past few days had been an education and, oftentimes, a fright. The first came upon stopping at an estaminet. Marion had been in desperate need of coffee, exhausted from an onslaught of rain that left her sliding, skidding, and struggling on her motorcycle.

There, a dispatch rider from the army had recognized her as another rider. Initially, pride flooded her at being identified and acknowledged. But then what he had to say sent chills up her spine.

"*Was just assigned a new stunt,*" the rider had said. "*I'm to rope in men, officers even, who are deserting. I'm told to shoot them if they don't go back.*" The man had shaken his head. "*Shoot our own soldiers, unbelievable.*"

Unfathomable.

Marion had left the estaminet after that, her emotions frayed, when two planes were suddenly atop her in the sky. A soldier gripped her arm, keeping her on her feet. "*Easy now,*" he'd said. "*It's an aerial dogfight. Two battle planes. They'll be focused on each other, not us fools down here. It's a Hun's observation plane by its lonesome that should send your belly to the latrines. Those devils like to set loose their shrapnel and drop their explosives for the fun of it to make us dance down on the ground. We lost twelve men that way one day, four of them stretcher bearers.*"

Marion had been all too happy to return to her loft and Sara and even their pigeons.

"We'll start from a mile out today," Sara told her and slipped the large basket from her back. "The weather is finally clear and suitable. Now when you're doing this on your own, be sure to grab two birds of the same gender."

"Why the same gender?"

Sara said simply, "It's how it's done. I've got two males with us."

"And what do we hope happens?" Marion asked.

"That they'll fly straight back to the loft. Remember, the trap lets the birds in but not out. And they'll want in again so they can eat. After this first run, we'll increase the distance farther and farther. Pigeons are smart and instinctual. They'll observe their path, finding their way back to their food again even after they've been tossed from a different location. Or at least that's what we want to happen. When the birds are moved closer to the front, they'll train there too. They'll eventually be delivered to the trenches so the men can attach messages to the birds and send urgent updates to headquarters."

Marion had assumed as much about the purpose of the birds, but Sara had never spelled it out so clearly for her before. She may not have been overly fond of the birds, but she felt poorly for the creatures having to be in the midst of battles. Marion was also thankful for them, if it meant headquarters was able to make time-sensitive decisions that could save lives.

Even with Eddie safely in England, he fluttered again to the forefront of Marion's mind. Maybe it was because he hadn't yet responded to her letter. She reminded herself it'd only been a week, and all outgoing posts were read over for censoring purposes.

"Now pay close attention," Sara said. "Pigeon tossing will be your job from here on out."

Marion nodded, watching as Sara retrieved the pigeons, holding one in each hand, and literally tossed them above her head, whistling as she did so. The birds darted into the sky, flying side by side.

"Easy, right?" Sara said.

"Seems so," Marion agreed.

"Now let's go see if they made it home."

They had.

Marion took the same two birds farther the next day, then farther still the day after. Soon she had a basket full of unruly birds on her back and she'd taken them ten miles from the loft.

Sara asked her to see how long it'd take for the birds to complete the flight at that distance. She checked her wristwatch, having agreed to release them at the top of the hour.

When the second hand indicated it was time, she began tossing birds two at a time like a madwoman. Then Marion leapt onto her idling motorcycle, heeled the prop stand back, and lurched forward with her eyes on the sky as the pigeons flew away above her.

Sara had told her that well-trained pigeons could fly close to ninety miles per hour. Marion's motorcycle could only go fifty, and she'd never taken it that fast before.

Marion's eyes alternated between the sky and the road, watching for potholes, branches, and innocent bystanders. The French women she encountered, still working on their farms and in the estaminets, already gave her disparaging glares, falsely assuming Marion was simply a camp follower sent out to "comfort" the troops. She bumped over a rut and, a thrill passing through her, regained her balance. She flashed a glance at her watch. Two minutes. The final batches of birds were in sight. The first ones she'd tossed were long gone.

The birds were required to get back in seven minutes—at most. Marion willed them on. She willed herself to remain steady on her bike.

Five minutes. Six. The birds were able to take a straighter route, and Marion slipped farther behind at her slower speed, but she still saw the specks of birds approaching the barn.

Marion slowed, anticipating a turn, but nonetheless she took it too sharply. She skidded out, her motorcycle slipping from beneath her. Marion landed with a *thud*, scraping into the tall grass.

She scampered to her feet, one of her ankles and her shoulder twinging in pain, and held up her uninjured arm so her wristwatch aligned with the fading birds. A smile spread across her face as she just made out the final two birds disappearing through the opening in the loft.

They'd done it.

The oddest sense of pride filled Marion. She'd done that. She'd trained the creatures. And in that moment, those creatures seemed less creature-like. Dare she say, she was even starting to like her obedient birds.

Marion limped to her bike. It took a few tries, but it thankfully started up.

Back at the loft, Sara was waiting. She called, "Well done, you." But then she noticed Marion's ginger dismount, her torn clothing, the dirt streaked down her right side. "Oh no, did you crack up?"

"I'll be fine," Marion said, removing her helmet. She retrieved her assigned cap she'd left on a post. "I was racing the pigeons." She couldn't help a laugh at herself. "Landed mostly in the grass."

Sara shook her head. "You knew I was timing them too. You didn't have to rush back. It's endearing, though, that you wanted to see how they'd do."

Marion shrugged, a mistake as pain shot into her shoulder and down her arm.

"Come on," Sara said. "There'll be a doctor in the village who can look you over. Let's take care of that scraped knee."

Marion was about to refuse, but from behind her a man's voice stole her words. She turned ever so slowly.

Her mind must've been playing tricks on her. First fabricating the voice, then the likeness of the person she most longed for.

Eddie was here? In France?

At first Marion was certain he was a phantom, a figment of her imagination. Perhaps she had struck her head when she fell off her bike and was now hallucinating from a head contusion.

She blinked, but he still stood there. Gone was his navy uniform, replaced by the khaki the army wore. She concluded she wasn't seeing things, but perhaps she was projecting. Did Marion yearn for her husband so badly she'd confused a ginger-haired soldier for Eddie?

But no, it *was* Eddie, in the getup of the British Army.

Eddie chuckled at Marion's perplexed expression. "Surprise, Mare. I'm in the army now."

"You're in the what?" She turned to Sara, needing more proof that she hadn't bumped her head. But Sara looked as astonished as Marion.

Eddie was in the army. He was in France. Not only that, he was at her loft. A sob escaped Marion and she ran for him. Eddie caught her, her legs going around his waist, her arms around his neck.

She kissed him, but then she smacked his arm. "You fool! You joined the army?"

Marion kissed him again, followed by another *thud* against his arm.

"I'm here, Mare. I told you before that where you go, I go. I meant it."

"But how?"

"I walked up from the village so my engine wouldn't give me away."

She smacked him a final time. "You know that's not what I mean."

Eddie's face changed as he noticed the dirt on her cheek. "Did you take a spill?"

Sara spoke up then, saying, "I'll just give the two of you lovebirds a moment to say your hellos," and then Marion heard the barn door sliding along its rails.

"Yes, I took a turn too sharply, but I'm fine. Why are you here, Eddie?"

Smoothly he lowered Marion to the packed earth. She winced when her ankle smarted. She held up a hand, beating his reaction. "I'll be fine. Promise. It's you I'm worried about it. Did you scheme your way to France? Is this why you didn't answer my letter?"

Eddie appraised her, no doubt looking for other injuries. When their eyes met again, he said, "I knew you'd be angry if I told you ahead of time."

"Like the dickens."

Marion's head still rocked slowly back and forth. She closed her eyes, giving one last quick shake of her head, catching her cap before it fell from her head. "Tell me you're still a dispatch rider and you're not about to be sent to the front? Things are happening around here."

"I know they are. It's likely why my request to transfer to this region was approved. The army needs every man it can get right now. The Royal Navy was willing to give me up."

"As a dispatch rider?" Marion asked again.

He nodded.

Marion rubbed her lips together. She wasn't happy Eddie was in France. She wasn't exactly unhappy either. But she was wholly relieved he wouldn't be one of the Tommies she saw in the war film going over the top into no-man's-land. From time to time in the film, she'd seen a dispatch rider zip across the frame, but if his role was to be like hers, then she'd relish the idea of them being together again.

"Are you stationed down in the village?"

Wouldn't that be something? Not to mention convenient.

"No," Eddie said. "I'm about twenty miles south. My officer commander told me to get myself familiar with the roads and regiments I'd be delivering to. I took the opportunity to ask after any Wrens. Fortunately there aren't too many women here, and most seem to be with the Women's Corps." Eddie pointed toward the village. "One chap made mention of a foxy dame who goes by on her motorcycle. By jove, I thought my heart stopped when he said that, knowing it had to be you. I had to laugh when the chap wished me luck, saying you were working out of the barn up the hill but not to get my hopes up if I was hoping to make any progress with you."

Marion cocked her head. "And do you? Hope to make progress with me?"

Eddie moved quickly, cupping her cheeks, pressing his lips to hers. "More than you know." He groaned. "But I'm due back soon. There's a café I passed about halfway between here and where I'll be stationed. Meet me for dinner?"

"Of course," Marion said.

"Are you happy, Mrs. Smith?"

Mrs. Smith. Not a name she'd heard since her wedding day. One she would rarely hear until this war was over and they could live as man and wife. Marion pushed the thought from her head and nodded, not trusting her words. She was glad to touch him, glad for the slight balm of Eddie remaining a dispatch rider, but also ill at ease from his presence in Flanders. With the Germans having weapons like Big Bertha, Marion wasn't sure any of them were truly safe. She'd come to France with an urgency to help end this war for Eddie's sake. That urgency had become immediacy.

CHAPTER 20

EVELYN

July 1940
London

T alk about being aghast. Evelyn had once been impressed with the gigantic size of the Painted Hall; now she silently growled at its magnitude. It looked even larger down on her hands and knees as she scrubbed.

The morning had begun with lessons about routine and discipline. Then Wren Monroe put the principles to practice.

Evelyn and the other girls received their assignments: clean the cutlery, de-clinker the boiler, heave buckets of coal to the furnaces and cookers, clean the glass of seemingly unreachable windows, polish a very long corridor, which was already gleaming, and scrub the decks, which were not in the same condition as the corridor.

The last one was Evelyn's current task.

And for crying out loud, the recruits hadn't been tidy with their meals. Her arms ached. Though, to be fair, they ached prior to scrubbing. Her whole body screamed at her after yesterday's fitness exercises. Worse, however, was Evelyn's left foot. It had swelled up like a balloon and was the color of a burnt biscuit. She'd seen the discoloration before but usually after a surgery, when nothing had been expected of her besides lying about.

The only consolation now was she didn't need her foot to complete her task. Evelyn had wrapped it tightly with an extra stocking and now crawled from spot to spot. She blew a loose strand from in front of her face. It puffed up and resettled on her damp skin.

Marvelous. Evelyn tried again with her shoulder and arm to no avail. She wouldn't dare touch her face with her gloved hands. She growled to herself, defeated by the strand.

Yet on the outside, Evelyn held a smile. It hadn't left her face since she'd begun. She hoped Wren Monroe and Wren Philips took note of her enthusiasm for becoming a Wren.

Evelyn didn't yet know how she fared from the fitness tests. She knew the number of curl-ups and push-ups she'd done and she knew how long the run had taken her, but Wren Philips hadn't disclosed where her numbers fell on the scale. Evelyn could only hope she had achieved a high enough rating to stay.

She scrubbed harder.

"Missed a spot, Wren Fairchild," she heard.

She knew it was Rose without even looking up. Evelyn debated pretending she hadn't heard her, but with a sigh, she rotated onto her bum, moving her foot carefully. Rose's gaze flashed there, where Evelyn hadn't fully tied her shoe. She wasn't able to.

From countless go-arounds with her mother, Evelyn knew she wasn't one for confrontation, unless necessary. This moment felt necessary. Evelyn's fear of her injury being discovered was a stronger pull than her desire to keep the peace. She was quick to draw the attention away from her foot, saying, "If you think you can do better—"

"Oh, you'd like me to do your work too?" Rose needled, quite literally speaking down to Evelyn. "Perhaps you'd like to dangle from a windowsill instead to clean the windows, though I doubt you could. You are just a slip of a girl, barely used to folding your own pajamas."

Evelyn clenched her jaw. On second thought this confrontation may've been a mistake; she couldn't let Rose pull her into a verbal tussle, especially not with Wren Monroe across the room. Evelyn dunked her brush in her soapy bucket, intent on returning to her original plan: ignore Rose.

But then she let the brush sink. Evelyn's mother liked to nip things in the bud. Evelyn had been on the receiving end of her mother's sharp tongue time and again. Evelyn could try to appeal to Rose in her own way. "I want us to be friends," Evelyn tried. Even to her it didn't sound convincing. She added more warmth to her voice. "Please tell me what I did wrong."

"That's just it," Rose barked. She glanced in the direction of Wren Monroe, who was focused on writing in a book. "You didn't *do* anything. Theresa raced at the Brooklands to help support her family. I was there to do the same. You were there for what? A thrill? You decided you wanted to race and—voilà—your daddy buys you a race car. Theresa had to work for hers. I'm *still* working to pay off mine. It's privileged girls like you who'll give the rest of us Wrens a bad name. And what about that dishy man who showed up here yesterday to cheer you on?" Rose huffed. "Bet he's the friend who gave you your fancy bike, huh? Bet you're only here because you were bored in your safe country home."

Evelyn looked away.

Rose bent, leaned closer. "The Land Army broads already say that the Wrens are silly debs who are only here because we have the prettiest uniforms or because their daddys and uncles are in the Admiralty and got them a cushy position so they can feel good about themselves. Right now, you're not proving them wrong."

"I'm not here for a cushy position," Evelyn snapped. There were only a few other recruits in the Hall, but they caught wind of Evelyn's sharp tone. So did Wren Monroe. Evelyn put on a fake smile.

Rose did the same. "Then why are you here?"

Evelyn wasn't going to answer that, not to Rose, who wouldn't hear a word of it. Or who'd likely reply with a snarky response. It was too personal, anyway. Instead, Evelyn chose to dunk her hand into the dirty water to find her dang brush. Rose could go dangle from another window.

She resumed cleaning.

Rose waited only a few beats more before walking off. She had no idea of Evelyn's upbringing. Yes, that upbringing was posh, but not without hardships. Evelyn grew up mostly alone. Rose may've been from a smaller village, but she likely had spent her days surrounded by siblings and friends. She probably attended a school with all those siblings and friends. She had to have learned that cattiness of hers from somewhere, after all.

Evelyn felt a rawness building in her throat.

She shifted her aching foot.

Tears filled her eyes.

There, her arm could reach, and she wiped away the emotion.

———— ∞∞∞ ————

Day two continued with lectures on naval procedure, ranks, and badges, then was followed by marching and drills. And more drills. And learning the proper naval salute.

Evelyn tried, but she could think of little else other than how her foot throbbed.

After retiring to her cabin after dinner, Evelyn lay on her side on her bunk, back to the room. She had pinned her brooch to her blouse. She pressed a hand over it and squeezed her eyes shut.

Everything was going horribly wrong. So much so that she was tempted to leave. She'd chop off her swollen, bruised foot. Then she'd be done with it all.

Her chest heaved with a cry she wouldn't release in front of her bunkmates.

They talked among themselves, but she didn't bother listening. Instead she lay in her own misery. Evelyn knew she should go to the infirmary, but she'd be putting a spotlight on herself. They would see her as unfit. They could dismiss her before the probationary period ended.

Then what would she do? Where would she go? Desperation climbed up her throat, and she felt her chest tighten. How would she ever overcome feeling like such an utter failure?

Part of her wanted to call her mother and beg forgiveness, but a larger part of her didn't want to give her mother that victory. She was homesick, though; she couldn't help herself. She'd put on the brooch and also the wool socks that Mrs. Taylor had knitted, despite it being July. Evelyn would even take another humiliating visit from Percy.

Percy . . .

Who was in London *and* a physician. She pushed onto her elbow, an idea forming. How had she not already thought of him? His medicine could be the cork jacket that she needed to stay afloat.

There was a strict curfew. But if Evelyn was careful . . .

And desperate enough . . .

She surely knew she was already desperate.

"I have to use the loo," she mumbled to anyone listening. She didn't wait to see if Rose, Theresa, or Mary reacted. Discreetly, she put on her shoes, not able to tighten the laces.

In the hall she made as if she were going toward the loo but went right past it.

At a limp, she made her way outside in fits and starts, pausing at corners to conceal her exit. It was raining. Of course it was raining. But the weather and the late hour, just past curfew, also meant she didn't see a soul other than a lone guard. When he turned his back, Evelyn made her move. Soon she had located her motorbike in the paddock.

Riding was heaven.

Her hands and her right foot did most of the work. Her left foot was only a shifter and she mainly kept it on the peg.

Evelyn's many trips to London had given her a knowledge of the roads but never roads this darkened. On account of the blackout she kept her headlight off, but white squares had been painted on the curbs of many roads to help nighttime driving. While she'd arrive at Percy's doorstep looking like a wet dog, she was grateful for the rain's reflections to better see.

While she drove, she imagined herself with a pivotal missive tucked into a shoulder bag. A missive she'd deliver that could make a difference in the Battle of Britain. She felt it looming, just as Mr. Churchill had said. But she could do her bit. She could. Evelyn was more than everyone said she was or could be.

But she needed Percy's help to get there.

It wasn't until she knocked on his clinic that she thought he may've already gone home to the townhouse. But if she knew Percy . . .

He opened the door, deep lines instantly forming between his tired eyes.

"Evie? What on earth?"

"Could I trouble you to come in out of the rain?"

Percy laughed at the nicety. Inside he quickly fetched her a towel and said over his shoulder, "I haven't heard anything more from your parents, if that's why you've come." He paused. "I won't believe you if you tell me you left the Wrens already."

"I haven't," Evelyn said, feeling more determined to remain on after her ride. She dropped into a chair in the entrance room, the back rooms of the clinic already dim. Only his office light had been left on.

Evelyn began to remove her shoe, her socks, then uncoiled the stocking she'd used around her foot. "I'm sorry for my temper yesterday. This hasn't been the easiest for me."

Percy said nothing, only gathered Evelyn's wet hair into his hands and into the towel. The act was one of familiarity and it gave Evelyn pause. It was definitely something Percy the Man would do, not the boy.

When Percy got a glimpse of Evelyn's foot, his cheeks puffed out. "Oh, Evie. I can see that."

"Can you help?" she asked in a small voice.

"Rest is the best medicine."

"And if that's not an option?"

"Let me see . . ." Percy carefully took her ankle in his hands, and Evelyn reacted to the coldness of his skin. "Sorry." He examined her foot. "Well, it's hard to tell due to the inflammation. I'd like to do an X-ray. But I don't think you've done any real damage."

"Tell that to my foot."

Percy opened his mouth. Evelyn held up a hand. "Stop, please don't actually talk to my foot."

He chuckled, again examining her. "You had the right idea with compression, but I'll give you something better to use. How about something for the pain too? I know it may hurt, but I'd suggest movement exercises, otherwise you'll likely get too stiff for your daily drills. I assume you will be keeping up with those?"

Evelyn nodded.

Percy gave her a prolonged look.

"What?" she questioned.

"I've been thinking, and I wonder if your parents' threat was an empty one, if they figured you'd immediately run back to them. An attempt at reverse psychology."

"My mother is nothing if not direct."

Percy shrugged.

"Regardless, I want to be a Wren."

He nodded. "You'll make a swell one too. How long is the probationary period?"

"Two weeks. Only twelve days to go," Evelyn said with an impish rise of her fist.

"Do you think you'll be assigned as a dispatch rider?"

"Most likely. I arrived with—"

"My motorcycle," he finished.

Evelyn grimaced. "Are you quite angry?"

"I expected as much from you, Wren Fairchild. Stubborn and determined, just like your mother. Now let's get you patched up and on your way."

Evelyn was reluctant to leave Percy and return to her less-than-welcoming bunkmates. On her ride back she mused they likely thought she had the trots with how long she'd taken to return.

The thought actually made Evelyn chuckle. Let them give her a wide berth.

After arriving back at the naval college, Evelyn stored her motorcycle again in the paddock. *No one the wiser*, she assured herself.

She felt lighter. It was well worth the risk to visit Percy. Not to mention the pain medicine he'd given her. Mercifully, it had kicked in. She concentrated on walking with a normal gait as he had suggested. Favoring it would likely aggravate surrounding muscles and tendons, he'd also advised her.

It was late, and although the rain had stopped, she didn't see anyone else besides the same lone guard as she snuck back toward her building. She slipped inside.

"Wren Fairchild," a voice boomed.

CHAPTER 21

MARION

April 1918
Saint-Tricat

T he surprise of Eddie being in France still hadn't worn off, even days later, and Marion was befuddled by the fact that her husband sat across from her.

Befuddled and unnerved, if she were being honest.

The estaminet he'd suggested they meet at served sirloin of sumptuous tender beef, spring cabbage, spuds, and carrots. For dessert: pudding. Marion licked her spoon, anticipating the arousal that would come alive in Eddie's eyes.

Before the war, newlyweds often held their bridal tours in London hotels. Marion and Eddie did theirs mere miles from a battleground.

The estaminet had become their almost-nightly routine, Sara joining them occasionally. On the nights she did not, dinner was followed by clandestine trysts among the growing maize stalks. On one such occasion Marion covered a laugh when Eddie had shown her his paybook. Within it, the secretary of state for war had included a message for the soldiers.

In this new experience you may find temptations both in wine and women. You must entirely resist both.

"There's simply no resisting you," Eddie had said, his fingertips pressing possessively into her soft skin. *"My wife."*

"Shh," Marion had implored him, touching a finger to his lips. *"Someone could hear you."* And if their secret was discovered and she was sent away, Eddie's following her to France would all have been for naught.

As it was, more men seemed to be called to active duty each day. The regiment at the nearby village had been one of those regiments engaged.

Marion had seen them leave with her own eyes, but other learnings were overheard. Half of the estaminet served as the mess for signal officers, and it was from that half of the room that Eddie and Marion often gleaned snippets of news that came in from the signal office.

One night they heard an exchange, the first man saying, "The Huns got Merville."

The second man: "Good God, where we got our service caps made?"

"That's the place. Word is they walked right through. The line's even closer now."

"I don't want to put money on it, but my guess is we'll have to pack up in the middle of the night one of these days."

The first man: "Don't you even go saying it aloud."

The second: "Too late. I'll tell you what, I'm getting beaten down by it all. There's some places that I'm not sure are worth fighting over." The man gulped his drink. "Three and a half years. We've been trying all that time with little to show for it."

Their callousness shocked Marion. She openly stared—glared, rather—not caring if they saw she was listening. She knew and appreciated how they were risking their lives, but she also viewed their dedication as a direct correlation to Eddie's safety. She wanted to shake a finger at them, tell them to do their duties, doggone it.

Eddie drew her attention back to him, whispering, "You could get out, too, you know."

"I can do what?"

"You don't need to be in this war, Mare. Let's tell them we've married. You can go somewhere safe."

"Go where, Eddie?" Marion said in an exasperated tone. "My family's estate?"

He ignored her sarcasm, saying, "We could figure it out. I can send money to you."

Marion dabbed her mouth with her napkin. "You'll do no such thing, Edward Smith. Nor will I." Marion raised her chin. "If you're here, I'm here."

Eddie grumbled to himself, but he didn't press it, not yet anyhow. She was safe, relatively, but her leaving became an unspoken point of contention between them. Marion was always at the ready to remind him that the front line near the loft hadn't been pushed more than a few miles closer than it was upon her March arrival. It was the other locations, like the one the men had vexed about, that had been walked all over by the Huns. In some areas word was the Germans had moved the line over thirty miles by early April, if what the men were saying wasn't an exaggeration. Even men on the front often lived by speculations and hastily written reports.

In May battles were fought near Paris and at Cantigny. In June at Château-Thierry and at Belleau Wood. It was after the Wood that Marion blessedly heard officers boasting of a German retreat.

The news had been grand. "See," Marion said to Eddie. "No reason for me to go anywhere." She even insisted they split two bottles of champagne at fifteen francs each.

On account of the libations, her ride back to the barn was more precarious than she would've liked, especially since she couldn't use her headlights. But Marion felt unfettered from the spirits and the lingering effects of Eddie's touch. For a moment she even allowed herself to believe the war would soon be coming to an end.

She nearly toppled her motorcycle on her dismount, giggling to herself as she tiptoed into the barn, trying not to incite the pigeons. Marion and Sara had bunks they'd cordoned off from the birds with makeshift walls. A soft snore rose from Sara. Their feathered friends would wake her early. On Marion's pillow Sara had left a note, and Marion lit a lantern.

An assignment came in.

Marion gripped her orders, a heavy feeling settling in her stomach. The orders dictated that she replenish the stock of birds closer to the front. She was told to bring her gas mask, as she may need it. Marion was also informed to wear an army-issued tin hat instead of her soft Wren's trifold.

She was to leave by six in the morning.

Marion swallowed, rereading the portion about needing a gas mask and more protective headgear. What was she riding into?

Marion stumbled to her feet. She barely made it outside into the balmy night before emptying her stomach of her fifteen-franc champagne.

The morning brought an ache in Marion's head and a pit in her stomach. Outside the barn she held the lantern over her map, studying her path, too jittery to yawn despite a restless night.

Afraid she'd oversleep, her body instinctually had woken her again and again. She dragged her finger over her map, determining her route. The directive said she was to go first to Abeele, then Reningelst, before meeting with an officer commander in Boeschepe to arrange an exchange with various brigades. She'd never been to any of those villages before.

Marion tapped her fingernail. If she had a lorry, she could load enough birds to make a single trip there and back. But her twenty-eight-inch basket was only able to fit up to twenty tightly packed and agitated birds, not enough pigeons for all her stops.

Two hours to Abeele, two hours back. Two hours to Reningelst, two hours back. That was already an eight-hour day—more, with the in-betweens of packing and unpacking birds. Then there was the meeting with the OC: another drive of two hours, along with however long the exchange took.

And Eddie wouldn't know where she was. He had his own stunts throughout the mornings and afternoons. She only ever saw him as a nightcap to her day. He'd be expecting her that night for dinner. When she didn't show, he'd worry.

But he'd go to the barn, she reassured herself. Sara would tell him she was on a stunt. Marion hoped Sara didn't tell him where. If she did, the unspoken point of contention between them would rapidly escalate to spoken.

Marion quickly gathered what she'd need: tools for her bike, a tin hat, and a gasbag with a gas mask inside. She prayed she wouldn't need it.

Marion checked the petrol levels in her gas tank. She paused, wiping her hands down her skirt, ready to begin. Except, she realized, she'd forgotten to pack her birds.

The whole reason for the stunt.

At a clip, she entered the barn and went about choosing the birds.

She marked their numbers in Sara's book, apologizing to the animals as she stuffed them in the too-small basket and feeling a bit sad for them that she'd be taking them from the safety of the barn to the dangers of the front. But it was their job.

It was her job.

"You'll be out of this little basket soon," Marion assured them, glancing a final time at the corner they had made into a makeshift cabin.

Sara hadn't yet stirred, but she would soon. Beams of light began to seep through the cracks of the barn. It was six. Marion wanted to wait, to tell Sara goodbye, but she couldn't dally, especially with the rain the night before, the roar of thunder having sounded too close and like explosives. The roads were likely thick with mud.

Marion's assumptions proved to be right.

She drove slowly, navigating the darker portions of the road denoting mud.

Even with a mud guard, her arms, legs, and face were speckled in brown.

The pigeons grunted, a sound she hadn't heard from them before. But it'd make sense if they were distressed, packed tightly like sardines. It was the first time Marion had ridden with so many. Fortunately, with no space for them to do more than a slight fan of their wings, their weight remained balanced. A relief, as riding in general required great stamina and concentration. Even such a trivial thing as a small animal darting across the road could send a rider airborne if the creature was hit right.

She reached Abeele only slightly late, her arms rattled, her fingers stiff, and her eyes dry. There wasn't another human being in sight, the area resembling a deserted medieval village with the weed-grown look that must've crept in quickly from neglect. The road was cobbled, lined on each side by buildings of varying heights. Some, Marion noticed, had holes in their red-tiled roofs. The fireplaces in a number of the homes were crumbled and half lying in the road. The road itself was littered with shell holes that had been crudely filled in. One hole stretched nearly the entire width of the road, a sight Marion wouldn't soon forget as she imagined the explosive that had caused such damage. Gone were the days of circumventing harmless potholes.

Marion didn't know exactly where she was to go in town, but the sounds of her engine brought a lone man outside. "Aren't you a sight for sore eyes, even with all that muck covering you," the loftman said in greeting and offered her a cup of coffee before she even had the birds off her back. No sooner had she accepted the mug than the man began to remove her basket. Marion juggled her coffee to slip her arms from the straps. Without a word, he set off, Marion following. She couldn't leave without a receipt.

His loft was set within a brewery, an overwhelming earthy smell hitting Marion's senses as soon as she walked in.

"I'll get them breeding straightaway."

"I selected ones likely to lay eggs within the week," Marion offered. "But they're also fully trained."

"You're a smart one, aren't you? I'll be honest, when I got the communication that a Wren would be bringing the birds, I had myself a laugh at a bird bringing birds." His gaze passed over Marion, taking in her skirt, her stockings. "Never before saw a woman do such work."

Marion raised an eyebrow.

"Though," the man went on, "with it being so quiet around here now, it would've been fine if a Martian came knocking. Anyone but a Hun."

Marion sipped her coffee, too tired to determine if what he said was an insult. "My receipt?" she prompted.

"Of course, of course," the loftman said, yet he didn't make a move. "We used to have lots of commotion here, with us being the main supply route to Ypres. But with the battle back in April, the civvies were cleared out. We had shells in the gardens, shells outside our bedrooms, shrapnel on our roofs. Then the Fritz started sending over gas. For two days and two nights we were in the cellar with gas masks on. Lord, it was horrifying. Hasn't been anyone here since, save for three lofts. You'll go to the one in Reningelst next, that right?"

Marion shook her head.

"No?" he questioned.

Marion realized her mistake, that her head shake wasn't an answer for him but her internal reaction to not wanting to go to Reningelst. She didn't want to be in Abeele either. But she corrected her error with a nod.

"Well, good luck to you, miss. That there was a stopover for many soldiers on their way to or from the front. The Huns took an interest in it. Too many new recruits with no sense. They die because they can't grasp the difference between shrapnel and high explosives. They stand there, listening and watching the big bombs fall, and I'll tell you, those ones take their time. Thirty seconds to scatter, yet the men stand there like sheep, and then the shrapnel goes off, the bullets fanning out in a way the men should've."

The man finished with a sad shake of his head, then gave Marion her receipt. Before she left, she asked him, "Why are you still here?"

"It was a sheer folly to stay on. I bet that's what you're thinking, huh? But I'm here for the birds," he said with a weak smile. "Some lofts need to be in reserve in case of another retreat. I'm here to breed them, train them. If pigeons are needed again, we'll be ready." The man bobbed his head, as if reassuring himself. "But you be careful, you hear? Being on that there motorcycle, you especially need to keep an eye on the sky. Folks on foot can get anywhere to take cover, but on wheels, you have to keep to the road."

"I'll be careful, thank you."

Marion left, wishing her stunt was complete. But it wasn't.

Sara was exercising the birds when Marion returned to restock. She would've done anything to be prodding birds with her toes to keep them on their wings, that first day seeming ages ago, not months.

"How was it?" Sara asked her.

Marion shuddered. "You'll tell Eddie where I am if I'm not back until late?"

"Of course, Mare."

Evelyn dreaded arriving in Reningelst, which was even closer to what people were calling the Second Battle of the Somme, and the loftman from Abeele wasn't wrong. It had been hit harder. Instinctively she touched the gas mask bag that hung around her neck. After delivering the birds, she hastily put the village in her rearview, only to shudder after she had restocked and was once again headed toward the front line and where the OC would be waiting for her in Boeschepe.

The officer commander was a tall man, a dandy, his uniform exacting. The only tell of his exhaustion came from dark circles beneath his eyes. Otherwise he was young and quite handsome.

She met him and his dispatch rider in a large hut within a camp, a map unrolled on a table. Red, blue, and green lines noted battalion and brigade areas, along with the Germans' lines, which appeared astonishingly close, a matter of miles.

"Thanks for making the trip," the OC said to Marion, as if she had a choice. But even if she could've declined, one look at the other dispatch rider filled Marion with a sense of duty. That man and Eddie could be interchangeable. And that man looked worse for the wear. His overalls were caked in grease and mud. A head wound, not yet healed, stretched from temple to ear. He leaned forward on the table, both arms supporting him, as they studied the map.

"We've got brigades here, here, and here," the OC said to Marion, pointing out each on the map, his vowels coming out prolonged, his cadence slow. His tone felt antithetical to the seriousness of the situation. "I need you to get to Mont Vidaigne, which is a good central place for all of them."

The dispatch rider traced his finger along the map. "Can't go this way. Nor this way. Germans have it under observation. But earlier I was able to get through along here."

The path he noted would take Marion down the line. It put the wind up Marion, and behind her back she clenched her already fisted hands.

The OC nodded. "There's a French civilian nearby who has been raising birds. You can take yours for acclimation to his loft and take baskets of trained ones for our brigades. Point out those locations, Donavant."

The dispatch rider did, and Marion made a mental note of where she'd need to go.

"You'll lodge at our camp for the night and go in the morning. We have a lorry you can use."

"Yes, sir," Marion replied, even as her stomach sank. She should have considered that the stunt could take more than the day, but she hadn't. For any other soldier it mattered little where they rested their body. But it mattered to Marion, when her secret husband would be walking circles until she returned.

"You'd do best to keep a keen eye out for unexploded shells,"

Donavant said. "Shells in general. The Huns take to barraging us relentlessly before an attack. It pushes our men down into their holes and keeps them there until the Huns are ready to come for us. At the moment, they've been firing shells at random, a not-so-friendly hello. They have their observation planes out too."

At once Marion remembered what a soldier had told her. Battle planes weren't a reason for concern. It was the observation planes. They'd use their artillery on her if they saw her on the ground.

She clenched her teeth as she swallowed. Marion had been trained as a typist. And while she could ride a motorcycle, she'd never received formal training for being in a war zone. She never sat through lessons on what to do if an incendiary bomb was suddenly falling from the sky toward her. Earlier the loftman had told her it was not knowing the difference between a high explosive and shrapnel that resulted in so many deaths.

She'd received a great deal of insight over the past few weeks, yet in this moment all it did was shine a spotlight on how ill-prepared she truly was.

The OC considered her. "First time this close?"

"Yes, sir."

He nodded to the gasbag slung over Marion's neck. "Mind the gas alarm siren, keep your wits about you, and when in doubt . . . run. You'll be fine."

From his lips to God's ears. She prayed he was right.

In the morning Marion grudgingly left her motorcycle at the camp and climbed behind the steering wheel of a lorry. The OC had assumed she knew how to drive one and she had no mind to correct him. But she'd figure it out. Hadn't she once helped Eddie put Alli back together and learned to ride her?

It felt novel to have a roof and doors. As the skies began to spit, she also felt gratitude. Marion made a clucking noise as she studied the pedals and levers. She quickly identified the clutch, gas, brake pedal. She eyed the gear shift.

"A lorry can do more than sit there," a voice said, suddenly at her window.

Internally, Marion grumbled at the stranger's statement. Many soldiers assumed she was a nurse. But for those who recognized her as a dispatch rider, she sometimes received disapproving looks, as if she had no business doing what she was doing or as if she were putting her propriety "at risk." To Marion, the latter seemed to be a problem created by the men themselves.

Marion did as she always did: she smiled politely.

"I'd be happy to help," the man offered, gesturing to the controls.

All Marion wanted to do was complete this stunt. "Very well," she said. "How's it done?"

The soldier chuckled at her directness. His instructions were less direct and involved him hovering in her personal space, but she soon was free of him and choppily making her way toward the French civilian's pigeon loft, her gaze jumping between the ground, looking for any undetonated bombs, and the sky, watching for any falling from the clouds.

She already felt exhausted by the time she arrived at the loft, which appeared to have been an addition to the outside of the man's home, with screens added on three sides and a tin roof on top. With the rain increasing, rivets of water poured from the roof.

Marion slammed the lorry's door, alerting the Frenchman to her arrival. When he exited his home with a gun pointed at her, she stumbled backward, her hands hitting the steel door of the lorry.

"I'm with the British Royal Naval Service," she proclaimed, adding, "helping the British Army. I have pigeons for your loft, and the officer commander gave me orders to leave with baskets of birds for his men."

It may've been the most she'd ever said to a stranger. She'd also never had anyone point a gun at her.

"Pigeons," she reiterated and gestured toward his loft. The man remained motionless, the gun still on her, his hat shielding his eyes.

The little French she'd picked up in the four months she'd been in France—*café, monsieur, oui, non*—would do little to help her now. How had she never learned the word for pigeons?

Marion was left to pantomime.

She flapped her arms. She mimicked holding a large basket and presenting it to the Frenchman. She pointed to the loft. She acted as if she was receiving birds from him. She mimicked turning a wheel.

Was her playacting even working? Marion stopped, feeling ridiculous, and wiped rain from her eyes. "*S'il vous plaît,*" she said, the phrase coming to her. Her pantomime also made her recall being at training with Sara, when she and the other girls had pretended to be flying wrens. A pang of longing hit her.

The Frenchman slightly lowered his gun. "For army?" he questioned.

"*Oui! Oui!*"

He waved her toward his loft, Marion's shoulders relaxing. Still wary of his gun, she kept an eye on him while she retrieved her basket of birds. He accepted it, and it was as if she let the air out from a balloon with how the man relaxed. Fortunately he had a stack of baskets. Together they filled the lorry with his birds.

"*Merci beaucoup*," Marion said before quickly climbing into the driver's seat. She waited until she was around a bend before she stopped to study the map, raindrops still dripping from her nose. The routes Donavant said not to take would be considerably faster, preferable with how she shivered, but Marion erred on the side of caution.

She drove as quickly as possible, both liking and disliking how the roof didn't provide her a clear view of the sky. At a distance, Marion eyed the observation balloons. What a fright it must be, to be so high in the air, open to an attack. But then she remembered their purpose: intelligence gathering. The men in the balloons were observing the British and the French so the Germans could mount their own attack.

At any moment Marion expected to hear a shell, and she knew she wouldn't know the difference between a high explosive and shrapnel. All she knew to do was scatter, to not be a sheep. Her foot never left the accelerator, even as she stole glances at her map. She'd only look occasionally, too worried about keeping her focus on the dirt road for any undetonated bombs or shell holes. She glanced again, second-guessing herself, horrified she'd take one of the many small turnings and drive straight into the Huns. If the OC's maps were correct, the Germans were only one or two miles away.

A farmhouse she passed was nothing but ruins.

Barbed wire, still coiled in rolls, sat waiting at the edge of a maize field.

Movement caused her to jump, until she recognized the khaki of the men. The Germans wore a light gray-green, she'd been told.

Within the human-high stalks of maize, it appeared the men were constructing trenches. A Frenchwoman looked on, noticeably bereaved, wet to the bone. To think the fields were once used for her food. Perhaps to sell to support her family.

Marion soldiered herself with a breath just as a loud *boom* filled the sky, the lorry's cabin, her head. She ducked, squeezing her eyes closed, not knowing if shrapnel would be able to pierce through the sides of the lorry. Finally she risked looking. The soldiers in the field were pointing far off. As if nothing had happened, they began working again.

Marion continued driving.

The songbirds perched on trees seemed unfazed. Her pigeons too. Sara once made a comment about how pigeons became easily acclimated to loud noises. Such foolish animals; at least Marion recognized the danger she was driving into.

Ahead, a line of lorries sat waiting, tucked beneath rows of camouflage strung across the road like streaming banners. She stopped behind the final lorry and exited into the rain. She worked quickly to unload the baskets, satisfied to leave the pigeons and go. An awaiting soldier greeted her. Baskets disappeared as quickly as she put them down. Marion continued unloading, focused on her task, failing to notice a whistling sound amid the commotion. She was reaching for the final basket when suddenly a soldier tackled her to the ground.

Down the road, where Marion had been not more than a minute ago, bits of earth splattered to the ground as pink dust rose.

"All right?" the soldier asked, still shielding her body with his.

Marion nodded, or at least she thought she did. A moment later she was on her feet, the man having heaved her up. Within another few moments, she was in her lorry, the soldier in the driver's seat.

"You look poorly, ma'am," he said, urgency in his voice.

Had they left the birds?

Marion checked the mirror—no, the pigeons had been moved to the lorries—just as another bomb hit the road behind them. A high explosive, she assumed, the detonation not coming until it met the ground.

Hurry, she screamed in her head. But they could only go as fast as the lorries in front of them, and they were the last in line, the others spitting dirt, their windscreens nearly covered. Sara's words rang in Marion's head: *"Do not stand under the tallest tree."*

It wasn't wise to be in the final lorry.

As if reading her mind, Marion's rescuer bumped them into a field, cutting the corner toward a different road. Like a broken record, he willed them not to get stuck. They careened back onto a new road.

The soldier didn't slow down until they were back at camp. Forgetting any trace of manners that she should thank him for saving her life, Marion all but fell from the lorry and went straight for her motorcycle.

The men had the birds. Her job was done.

"Hoxton," she heard. Marion almost didn't recognize her name, but then Donavant was turning her around. "What do you think you're doing?"

"Leaving."

He simply shook his head. "Not today you're not. It's too wet. Your belt will slip."

"No," Marion protested, even while knowing he was likely more knowledgeable about motorbikes than she. Marion had fixed a puncture. She'd fiddled with battery connector cables. But her belt slipping? She wasn't sure if it would, and if it did, she didn't know how to correct it. When she was training the birds, she always waited for favorable conditions.

"Be reasonable," Donavant said.

Heaven help her, she was trying to be reasonable, and reason told her to get far away from the falling bombs that had just nearly killed her. She wiped a wet strand of hair from her face. She was soaked through.

"Let's get you out of the rain. Something dry to wear. Something to eat. Let your nerves settle. You'll be on your way again as soon as you're right as rain."

He smirked at his weather-related pun.

Marion did not. She wanted to protest again, but she found herself being led by the arm. And after she was given too-large men's fatigues and after she'd forced down a few bites of food, she next found herself in a large hut where a concert was being put on. Donavant insisted it'd be good for her spirits.

The concert was to be a farewell for a captain who was returning to England. Marion at once envied him. Sitting on long benches, the men passed around large mugs of beer scooped from even larger buckets. A friendly-enough-looking man patted the bench beside him. She obliged him, but not the mug he offered to her. Marion passed it along.

The men were having themselves a good old time, rarely a moment when a song wasn't being sung.

Over the hill lived a girl from America
She rode her bicycle down and back all day
One summer night she hollered how her name was Danica
The moon shone bright and the glowworms were all that were on display

The man beside Marion elbowed her and pointed to the singer. The similarities between Marion and the girl from the song were flimsy at best. Their gender. The fact they both rode something two-wheeled. Still, she smiled. That was, until the final lines:

Until she hit a rut and it all went askew
I saw her red and white, and her blue too

Despite this song having nothing to do with her, Marion's cheeks heated. The men roared with laughter and applause. The soldier beside her paused long enough to say, "He wrote that one himself."

"You don't say," Marion responded, making to stand. "If you'll ex—"

"Stay for one more," the man prodded. "For the captain."

Oh, was it? Marion sighed, resolving to sit through one more song.

Another man took the makeshift stage constructed of crates, but Marion was fairly certain his balance wouldn't keep him there for long, especially after he called up a second fellow to join him in a skit. With eyes rolling, they began singing, both with surprisingly pleasant voices.

After the last performance, she dared to let herself listen to the words.

If you were the only girl in the world and I were the only boy
Nothin' else would matter in the world today
We would go on lovin' in the same old way
A Garden of Eden, just made for two with nothing to mar our joy
I would say such wonderful things to you . . .

Perhaps it was the exhausting and eye-opening past two days. Perhaps it was coming so close to the Germans and experiencing the damage they could do. But Marion found herself discreetly dabbing her eyes. And thinking of Eddie. And a garden of Eden built for two. With nothing to mar their joy.

CHAPTER 22

EVELYN

July 1940
London

E velyn's heart sank. She'd been caught.

"*Wren Fairchild*," the voice had boomed. Wren Philips stood in full uniform with her arms crossed. "It is well past curfew. Do tell me why you are not in your cabin? While you're at it, do tell me why you shouldn't be immediately dismissed?"

Evelyn's mouth fell open but nothing came out. She had saluted Wren Philips but wasn't certain if it was correct procedure. She searched her brain for an answer, unsure of what to do or how to act. What could she say that would save her? Would Wren Philips take pity on her if Evelyn said she had nowhere else to go if the Wrens spit her out?

But wasn't seeking pity and advantages exactly what Rose had been saying was the problem with girls like Evelyn?

She wrung her hands together, feeling like whatever she uttered would be wrong. So she let honest emotion bubble out of her, saying, "I don't want to fail, ma'am."

Wren Philips's voice echoed in the empty entrance hall. "How does that explain why you are out of your bunk after curfew, with an untidy appearance, no less? Only this morning, did we not speak of how we must present ourselves?"

"Yes, ma'am," Evelyn said in a small voice. How could she explain? She smoothed a palm down her hip. All Evelyn could think was to come clean. "All of this is in the records I submitted, ma'am, but I had a clubfoot as a child. It's corrected now." Evelyn swallowed her pride and bunched up the leg fabric of her overalls to reveal the elastic brace on her foot and lower leg. "However, the vigor of the past two days has been a lot for me. I understand physical fitness and drills are important to my training, and I have every intention of continuing. That was why I left tonight, to seek treatment from a physician so I could carry on." Evelyn took a breath and forced out, "But I understand if my behavior and any deficiencies must result in my removal from the Wrens."

Wren Philips twisted her lips, much as she had while Evelyn finished the timed run. "I do not see you as deficient, Wren Fairchild. I'd like to begin there. I naturally noticed your unusual gait, and I reviewed your medical records. I see nothing in either that should prohibit you from continuing your training to be a Wren. Your fitness results were above average, in fact. The problem lies in whether you will be able to continue due to your injury. And then there's your behavior. You left your cabin after curfew. Not only that, but you sought your own treatment. You are aware we have an infirmary here?"

"Yes, ma'am."

"You'll begin using it. You will no longer hide your injuries."

Evelyn's mouth fell open again. So she could stay? She didn't dare interrupt. She bit her lip to hide a relieved smile.

"Report to the infirmary in the morning. In between treatments you are to clean every inch of the hospital wing. It'll likely take all day. I will allow up to two days of this 'rest.'" Wren Philips gestured finger quotations around the word. "Any lecture notes you miss will need to be made up in the evening and on my desk the morning after. This infraction will be recorded. There will not be another."

It was a gift, Evelyn knew. She wouldn't waste it.

Dismissed, she stood to attention and saluted.

Evelyn knew her absence over the next few days would be noticed by the other recruits. It wouldn't help the impression Rose and any others had of her. At least they didn't witness her in the infirmary, where Evelyn was instructed to do more resting than cleaning. The doctor informed her that her body needed at least forty-eight hours for the swelling to go down. Ideally, longer.

"I've been allowed two days," Evelyn said.

"We'll use every minute we can," the doctor responded.

At the end of the first day, Evelyn walked slower than necessary, even more than her injured foot required, when she returned to her cabin, dreading having to see her bunkmates. Primarily Rose.

Last night the other girls had been asleep when she'd returned from her outing to Percy's. Evelyn had made sure to leave again before they'd awoken. Now, though, she couldn't avoid them. Evelyn needed their notes from the day's lectures. She debated hunting down the sharp girl, Holly, she'd met first when she'd arrived. Her note-taking was probably unrivaled. But Evelyn didn't know what cabin she was in. So she was left with asking her own bunkmates for help.

Oh, she felt so inadequate interacting with her peers, especially those giving her the cold shoulder. She was simply unpracticed. With her schooling held privately in her home and with her activities severely limited, who had there been to truly be a child with? Who had there even been to get into quarrels with?

Percy?

He was so good-natured.

Mrs. Taylor?

She doted on Evelyn.

Her father?

He left most matters to her mother.

So, her mother. And Evelyn had always picked her confrontations wisely.

She turned the knob into her cabin.

Evelyn could've done a jig. Only Mary was in the room, stretched flat on her bunk. "Hello," she said to the woman, really not more than a girl. She only noticed then that Mary wore a sad expression.

"Is everything all right?" Evelyn asked her.

"Missing home, is all."

Evelyn eyed a photograph Mary had beside her bunk on a small table. She swallowed roughly. Her own family photograph was never unpacked. But Evelyn could've fit right in with Mary's family with the red tones of their hair and freckles. "You have a lot to miss. You have quite the large family."

"Jimmy, Tommy, and Michael are with the Royal Navy too. I volunteered because of them, especially Michael. We're twins. He's over in the King Charles Court. Anything to get him and my other brothers home more quickly. The other three are my younger sisters. I'll do what I can to help end the war before they're old enough to volunteer."

"I'm sure your family is very proud of you," Evelyn said, a tightness in her chest.

Mary smiled. "They say as much. Doesn't make it any easier being away, though. But how are you? I heard you were in the infirmary for your . . ."

Evelyn bobbed her head, trying for carefree. "My foot." So people were talking. "It'll be fine. I was actually wondering if I can see your notes from today. Wren Philips asked me to have my own copy on her desk by the morning since I wasn't able to attend in person."

"Of course," Mary said, sitting up to reach her notebook on her bedside table. "I reckon you already know most of it, all about—"

Rose came in.

"Um," Mary went on, momentarily distracted, "it was about proper etiquette and acting like a lady in all situations."

"Oh?" Rose said. "Are you talking about the lecture Evelyn missed?"

"Yes," Evelyn said pointedly. "I am making up the work."

"Will you be dropping to the deck next and making up the curl-ups and push-ups? Perhaps you'll run the grounds before bed? We did that today too."

Evelyn rubbed her lips together, considering a response. Would telling them she'd been told by the doctor to stay off her foot make them more amenable to her? Not likely. "Just the notes for now. Thank you, Mary." She took them and proceeded to her bunk.

"Of course," Rose muttered.

Evelyn turned, feeling a twinge in her foot, and decided she'd had enough of Rose's ire. "I didn't *ask* for special treatment. I only asked to stay, to be given the chance to prove that I deserve to be here. But do you know what else I didn't ask for?" Evelyn didn't wait for Rose to respond; she bulled on, almost afraid to stop or else she'd lose her nerve. "I didn't ask to have an operation when I was four hours old. Nor did I ask for countless more. I didn't ask for my left foot to be two sizes smaller than my right." She watched as Rose's and Mary's gazes dropped to her shoe. "I didn't ask to be tutored at home. I didn't ask for my mother to treat me like a porcelain doll who may break at any moment. Believe me, I didn't ask for my parents to accompany me *everywhere*. This is the *very* first time I've ever been away from them. And you know how that's possible? I ran away. And that man you saw during the fitness test? He's my only friend. My *only* friend."

Evelyn glanced at her good luck elephant and the brooch she'd placed on her bedside table. Never before had she exposed herself in such a way to anyone outside her family, Mrs. Taylor, and Percy. Her voice grew softer as she said, "Yes, I grew up with buckets of money. Yes, my parents bought me my race car. Yes, my friend gave me his motorcycle. Well, in truth I took it without asking. I'm not saying any of this for pity. I'm saying all of this because I just want you to understand that being here is important to me."

A silence fell between the women.

Rose ever so slowly nodded. "All right, Evelyn Fairchild. I'll give you a chance. Prove that you deserve to be here."

CHAPTER 23

MARION

July 1918
Saint-Tricat

M arion returned from her grueling stunt near the front lines exhausted, rattled, but oddly satisfied. Eddie unsurprisingly was at the loft when she arrived, his own relief evident on his face. His arms wrapped tightly around her.

She chastised him, reminding him he should be completing whatever stunt had been assigned to him that day.

Eddie didn't care.

Skirting his duties was grounds for disciplinary action. Wouldn't his own discharge be an interesting turn of events? But if that were the case, he'd surely demand Marion leave the war with him. And while she'd be ecstatic about Eddie returning to England, Marion knew she didn't want to go. She wanted to stay.

She'd spent so much of her life drifting, yet with the Wrens, in this war, she felt grounded. Being a Wren was about more than Eddie now and hoping to end the war for his sake. She was a Wren for herself, too, and she felt as if she was accomplishing something worthwhile by training the birds and delivering them to the various lofts and battalions, as if she truly had a hand in the war's outcome.

As it turned out, the next large battle had not occurred where Marion had restocked the birds. Battles had been fought farther away, south in Soissons.

Still, Marion felt an immense amount of pride for what she'd accomplished. And even if the battle hadn't been fought where she was sent, the Germans were undeniably there. Perhaps the Germans in their observation balloons saw the preparation Marion had aided in? Or maybe a local counteroffensive was still bubbling to the surface near Ypres?

Marion knew only a sliver of the war's happenings, but as horrifying as it'd been to be so close to the Huns, she believed her actions had been beneficial; the soldiers were proclaiming the Battle of Soissons a turning point, in fact. The objective had been to cut both the main road and main railroad that ran south from Soissons to Château-Thierry. By doing so, the Germans' ability to resupply their armies was greatly inhibited.

Hurrah!

Hourra!

The remaining French civvies appeared just as pleased as the English.

And Marion was pleased to return to training her birds. She'd grown particularly fond of number 486, who head-bobbed around the barn on Marion's heels endearingly, as if he were a puppy. Sara joked 486 had imprinted on Marion and saw her as his mate. Eddie jested he was competing with a bird. She assured him that he was not; though, when no one was looking, she secretly doted on the bird, giving him an extra handful of food.

Eddie's stunts began calling him farther south, but then one day he delivered a missive to Marion and Sara.

"For you," he said with a bow, removing his hat to reveal his overgrown orange hair. Trimmed or shaggy, Eddie always looked handsome.

Marion rose a playful eyebrow at his antics. "Do you deliver all your dispatches in such a manner? I'll grow jealous."

He chuckled but was also quick to say, "Read it to me?"

Dispatch riders delivered anything from directives to intelligence briefs to weather reports and even reconnaissance film and photographs. They were expected to destroy the message, by swallowing or burning, if captured by the enemy. Some were instructed to memorize their messages, so if they escaped, they could still deliver their message. In some cases, if a rider didn't return within a set time, a second rider was sent in his place. But the messages Marion and Sara received were never of such import.

Marion joked, "You didn't read it? Was all my teaching for naught?"

Eddie sighed. "I'll confess to being too nervous. If it's another dangerous stunt, then—"

Marion stopped him with a raised hand, feeling disappointed his playfulness had flipped to the same argument they always had. She knew how he would've continued: if it was another dangerous stunt, then he'd really like her to hang up her uniform. And she didn't want to battle with him. She wanted this war to be over *for* him. But it was a point he refused to see or try to understand.

Marion decided to read the message to herself first, wiping her hands on her skirt before opening the dispatch.

"Well, what's it say?" Eddie asked.

She knew he'd eventually see it, unless she swallowed the dang thing, so she said, "Both Sara and I are needed."

"Sara?" he questioned.

They both knew this request was abnormal, as Sara never had been called away from the barn.

"They need both of us and all our birds. Mobile lofts will transfer the pigeons. We're to report to the main camp in the Amiens sector." She felt the rebuttal rising in Eddie. "Please don't fight me on this. You know it's my duty, Eddie."

He sighed. "And what about the influenza outbreaks in those camps?"

"Our loft will be kept at a distance, just as it is here."

Marion could tell Eddie wanted to question her further. It was written plainly across his face. But because he said nothing more, she kissed him and then reassured him, "The tides are turning, remember?"

"But they can turn again, just as quickly. I really don't want you going, Mare."

"Well, it's not up to you."

She hadn't meant for it to come out harshly, but there was an edge to her voice. The last thing she wanted was for either of their feathers to be truly ruffled. She brushed Eddie's hair from his face, saying in a more cheerful voice, "Where is my optimistic husband? The one who makes wishes and talks of our future?"

"I'd be happy to talk of our future, Mare. Shall I tell everyone we're married so you can get started on it?"

Marion rolled her eyes. "Soon, Eddie. Soon. I'll say it one *last* time. I want to see out the rest of this war. I will have a hand in its end." She tried again to brush the hair from his face, a stubborn strand having fallen back out of place. "Then, after the war is over, I'll tell everyone far and wide that Edward Michael James Smith is my husband. We'll start our married life together, our real married life."

Marion kissed him again, her eyes wet with moisture. She so badly ached for that day.

"I'd still rather you not be involved with the war."

"I know," Marion said, allowing him this final gripe, "just as I wish you weren't involved."

"But only one of us is conscripted to be here."

"Eddie," she warned. He knew she'd signed the same contract he had.

A wise man, he said nothing more. Eddie only sighed, then agreed, "Fine. Soon. And what does this future look like to you?"

Marion opened her mouth, expecting the words to tumble out, but she only closed it again. Before, she'd never put voice to a future due to the uncertainty of orphan life. And now, uncertainty still hovered over her. Them. The only constant had been Eddie's presence in whatever awaited her.

"You," she said simply. "My future is you. Us."

Eddie smiled, a genuine one that allowed Marion's shoulders to ease. "I see you working with books. Me? Something with my hands. We'll have our own place. Finally. Without any birds. Unless you want birds."

Marion chuckled. "Pigeons only. They have wormed their way into my heart."

"And children?" he asked. "Should we have those too?"

"Our children. Adopted children," Marion said with a nod. "A family for lots of children, Eddie. And yes, I'll work with books. And at night I'll read to the little ones."

Marion instinctively placed a hand on her stomach. Her womb was empty, but she would dream of the day it wouldn't be. Being a mother wasn't something she'd ever actively seen for herself, unable to fully picture what a mother was. But she could see it now. She saw kissing foreheads and caring for scraped knees. She saw loving her children so immensely she'd croon *I love you, I love you, I love you* over and over to them. Marion smiled.

Eddie kissed her. "We'll have them, Mare. A girl first, the spitting image of you."

"Equal parts of us both," she offered.

She liked this future for them. But now that Marion voiced it, she feared not ever having it.

"It's ours," Eddie assured her then.

And he assured her again after he received his own directive a few days later. He was to report to Amiens too. Many of the regiments would be making the same journey south. And hypocritical or not, Marion's own optimism began to fade at both of them being called to the front. She replaced it with pluck.

Marion and Sara traveled to their new camp like thieves in the middle of the night. At first, following her new orders was easy enough for Marion: continue to train her birds. She could do that.

Notices had been posted outside the mess hut, outside a dressing station, outside the baths that all said the same:

KEEP YOUR MOUTH SHUT

Marion could do that too.

Secrecy was of the utmost importance for anyone who was within the Amiens sector, though no one knew exactly what they were keeping a secret. Marion only knew with certainty that with each new morning, the camps had grown with British and Canadian and French and Australian soldiers, who arrived under the cover of night like she had. Eddie finally joined them, bunking close by.

They all camped in the woods, Sara and Marion sharing a tent with nurses and women from the Land Army. They speculated about their purposes in Amiens. The nurses were there presumably to treat injured men, yet the men who currently lived in the mile-and-a-half trenches hadn't received any orders, that were known, and no additional men had been moved up from the reserves to join them.

"If we're befuddled, it bodes well that the Germans would be too," Sara had joked one night in their tent. Marion agreed, especially after Eddie had learned from one of his dispatches that bogus radio communications were being sent out for the Germans to overhear saying that the British Army was weakening its numbers, when it was in fact doing the opposite.

Did it make the Germans think an offensive wasn't coming? *Was* an attack coming? Marion didn't know. Usually before an offensive, a barrage of artillery was unleashed for days to suppress the enemy's movements. The Germans had done it. The British Army had done it. But no such bombardment was happening, by either side.

In July the Australians performed a small trench raid on Germany's side of no-man's-land, returning with prisoners.

A month later, the Germans retaliated north of the Somme, penetrating a few thousand feet before retreating to where they'd begun.

A few days had passed, and since then, the Huns had only made their presence sporadically known, firing shells with eleven-inch diameters at the city of Amiens. Marion was so near the front-line trenches that she heard the missiles whizz over her head on their warpath to the city. The men called the cannon the Germans were firing the Amiens Gun, so large that it was mounted into a railway wagon. One soldier often boasted that he'd be the one to dismantle it.

But how did he expect to get his hands on it? Did he know something the women did not? All Marion knew for certain was that there was electricity in the air foretelling that *something* was about to happen.

In her tent she crossed her arms over her stomach as the women theorized. They sat on what were unaffectionately known as their biscuits—their mattresses, which were two very hard straw pieces, held together by a bedsheet, that would inevitably separate by morning, leaving Marion with her bum on the ground and with a sore back.

The women spoke in whispers, not only because they didn't want to be overheard from anyone passing closely to their tent but also because a few of the other women were already asleep. The remaining four—Marion, Sara, Beverly, and Betty—had grown close and often stayed up late talking, Betty sharing nursing anecdotes and Beverly telling of her day. On that particular day she had helped erect a dressing station.

"Marion," Beverly asked, "what do you see when you're training the pigeons?"

"Nothing of note," Marion said, yet she imagined somewhere in the woods there were field guns, tanks, and aircrafts hidden under camouflage, ready to be moved into position. The mobile lofts—five of them to fit their birds—were also on wheels, resembling a train car but with mesh sides and a double door on the back. Currently the lofts were close to camp, but as the army progressed, the mobile lofts could move with them—if the army was to attempt an advance.

Marion added as an afterthought, "And I train all over. When I'm tossing the birds to familiarize them with the area, I use different roads every day in case the Huns are watching. There are some roads I can't go on because it'll kick up too much dust."

"In case they're watching," Beverly repeated softly, almost to herself.

"Think they are?" Sara whispered.

Betty shuddered.

Marion repositioned on her biscuit, uncomfortable, and tried to focus on their conversation. But it was difficult. There were so many secrets.

Beverly scratched her head aggressively. "I better not have head lice."

Betty snorted. "I'll check you tomorrow. Anyone else?"

Sara threw up her hands. "Might as well check me too. I'm itchy."

"Marion?" Betty asked.

Marion shook her head. "I spend more time with birds than humans."

Sara waved a finger. "Birds can get lice too."

Beverly laughed as Betty remained focused on Marion. "I'm here if there's anything else you need. You know we're all good at keeping secrets."

Sara cocked her head, as if she thought it a peculiar thing to say to Marion.

But Marion didn't think it was peculiar. In fact, she thought Betty was a very perceptive nurse.

Marion had only just made the discovery herself that she was likely with child. She hadn't been given much from her mother except for regular monthlies.

She hadn't told Eddie. She hadn't told Sara. She hadn't told Beverly or Betty. But Betty, whom she'd known for only a matter of days, had somehow looked at Marion and known her secret.

Marion had all the usual signs her monthly was coming: puffiness in her lower belly, tenderness in her breasts, a general sense of noticeable irritation. But then those symptoms hadn't subsided.

They'd continued, without her courses following. She was eight days late.

Still, Marion thought it could be the weight of the war taking its toll on her body. She'd heard of such things happening, until Betty had strengthened Marion's own suspicions last night. If only there was a way to medically put it to the proof so she'd know with more certainty.

Marion stroked a hand down the back of 486.

At the idea of carrying Eddie's child, a joy filled Marion. But the emotion wasn't unfettered. This child was indubitably, indisputably, and undoubtedly wanted by Marion. There'd be unquestionable gaiety from Eddie too. She pictured how he'd twirl her around and whoop with joy. But then, when he set her back down, she knew the initial veil of excitement would lift as he realized he'd whirled Marion and their unborn child atop a potential battleground.

She knew what his reaction would be. His adamance for Marion to leave the Wrens would double. She was beginning to question if maybe she should go. She had their unborn child to think of now too. But her thoughts kept circling back to how she and Eddie had been at war for nearly a year. She had many months before their child came. Marion wished to spend that time aiding in the war's end, not being removed to a place she couldn't yet picture. Life after the war simply didn't exist yet. A life for her child wasn't safe yet.

So she'd wait to tell Eddie. So she'd continue with her birds.

Both Marion and the pigeons were ready. When she was called upon, she'd deliver them where they needed to go. Her guess: to the front for the soldiers to use. The birds would be delivered with tubes attached to their backs. Any important messages would be rolled inside and the birds tossed, flying straight back to Marion—in reality, back to their food—at the loft. From there the messages would be retrieved and promptly driven to the commander, who'd initiate an action or decision.

What if that decision had a hand in ending the war?

A year or until the war ends.

They could be back in England, the war over, months before their child was even born.

"Marion?"

She startled at Sara's voice but recovered with the same forced smile she'd worn her whole life.

"You spoil him," Sara said of 486.

Marion was still absently stroking his feathers. She put him into the loft with the others. "He deserves it. I'll be delivering them . . . soon."

Sara twisted her lips. "Is that why Betty asked if you were well last night? Are you nervous?"

Marion resisted touching her stomach. "Eager, actually."

Sara began divvying out food for the pigeons. "Yeah?" She didn't sound convinced, even though what Marion said was true.

"Betty's a nurse," Marion added simply, focusing on the water troughs. "I imagine she's always on the hunt for symptoms to mend."

"But the secrets portion, Mare. Something is going on with you. You'd tell me, right? You know I can keep a secret. No one knows about you and Eddie. No one. And just the other day Betty asked me if you and Eddie were sneaking around together."

Marion's hand froze on the water trough, Betty's guess at her pregnancy making more sense. "She asked that?"

"She did. And now she's talking about keeping secrets. And, Mare, you and I have been hip-to-hip for some time now. But last week I was the only one"—Sara lowered her voice—"on the rag."

Marion faced her friend. Sara towered over her, but there was nothing formidable about how she looked in that moment. The curves of her face showed concern.

"Mare . . ."

"You can't tell anyone, Sare," Marion pleaded, taking her friend's hands. She glanced at the soldiers who milled about around them, going about their various duties in the shadows of the trees, but none paid them any mind. They were simply the Jenny Wrens with the birds.

Sara said, "You know I won't utter a word."

"Not even to Eddie," Marion insisted, feeling a pang of guilt that the circle of those who knew grew, yet none were the father of the child.

Sara opened her mouth, closed it, began, "But . . ." Sara stopped and leaned closer, whispering, "You're having a baby. Oh, Marion, if I wasn't horrible before, I'm without a doubt the worst now. It was bad enough you came in Sylvia's place, then Eddie followed you. Both have weighed on me. But now, a child? You can't stay here. Go to Wiltshire. My parents would have you, and I'd send you ridiculously detailed notes about everything Eddie does. Even how long he brushes his teeth."

"You're the very best, Sare, but if Eddie's here, I'm here. Women have been riding in carriages and on horses for ages while with child. A motorcycle is hardly any different."

"Until you fall off," Sara admonished.

"I'll be careful, even more so now."

"Oh, Marion." The way Sara said it wasn't disapproving; it was laced with her own guilt and understanding. "Your secret is safe with me."

Marion was called to the officer commander's hut.

She saluted. Eddie was already in the room. Her stomach turned over at the sight of him, so handsome in his uniform, yet the khaki was a reminder of why she must remain in France and do her part.

"Wren Hoxton," the OC said in greeting.

Smith, Marion corrected silently. By the look in Eddie's eye, he'd done the same. Emotion filled her. She couldn't look at him again. Not with how guilt flooded her that he didn't yet know about her growing secret. Not with how her love for him also grew, knowing he'd be a wonderful father. She was experiencing too many feelings that could be written across her face for the OC to see.

He asked her, "The pigeons are ready?"

"Yes, sir."

"Good." The OC was a man of few words and used those few words to explain what would be needed of Marion, relying on a map to do most of the talking for him. The British Corps was in position north of the Somme, the Australian Corps to the south of the river, and the Canadian Corps to the south of the Australians. Marion noted each location on the map. She was to deliver a basket of pigeons to each. She was free to use a lorry if she wanted, but Marion said, "That's not necessary, sir."

The lorry would mean one trip, but she'd prefer to do the back-and-forth on her motorcycle. If Marion was targeted, she'd rather only have a single basket of birds with her as opposed to an entire lorry of pigeons that could be lost. But more importantly, Marion wanted to be able to see the sky more easily. Keeping the pigeons safe was one thing, but keeping Eddie's child safe was paramount.

"Very well," the OC said. "Any questions?"

Oh, she had questions, but the OC had told her all the information she was going to receive. "No, sir."

Eddie hadn't been addressed yet, and to Marion's surprise they were both dismissed before the OC spoke to him.

"Why were you there?" Marion whispered to Eddie once they were outside the OC's hut.

"I met with him first and asked to stay," Eddie said.

"What do you know?"

Eddie playfully punched a passing soldier on the shoulder and said a hello.

"Eddie," Marion pressed quietly.

"Just wait, Mare."

She realized they were walking toward her tent. Eddie looked over his shoulder one way and then the other. When the coast was clear, he grabbed her and pulled her inside. His lips were on hers before the flap even closed.

Marion laughed into his mouth. "What was that for?"

Eddie smiled, the freckles on his cheeks even more pronounced from the sun. They were mixed with flecks of mud. He'd been out riding.

"You're glowing today, Mare. It was nearly impossible not to touch you in the OC's hut."

"Sweet talker," she said, unable to help her own grin. He was a charmer, all right, but the fact that he was to be a father made him even more enticing, more handsome. She knew he'd be overjoyed when the time came for her to tell him why she was glowing. But Marion couldn't do it yet, she reminded herself, especially now that she had orders to fulfill. And, it seemed, Eddie had more information. She asked him, "Where'd you ride today?"

"All over. It's all happening, beginning tomorrow. The pigeons are one of the final steps. The men are all in place, as the OC said."

"And what will happen? A barrage?"

Eddie shook his head. "A raid. A surprise attack. They won't know we're coming. Planes will lay smoke screens over the battlefield. A heavy mist that'll eat up all of no-man's-land. Then at exactly four twenty in the morning, we'll open fire with nine hundred guns. It'll happen all at once, with the artillery at the zero hour, right ahead of the men charging toward the German trenches. Tanks will follow. The Huns won't know what hit them." Eddie spoke with such excitement it was contagious. Marion found herself on her tiptoes, a protective hand across her stomach. "And the best part," he went on, "is that you'll be far away from it all. You'll deliver the birds today, but then your part is done."

Marion half laughed. "You never give up, do you?"

"Not when it comes to you, Marion."

Oh, how she loved this man. "Do you think this'll be it, Eddie?"

"It'll be something, Mare. I feel it. This battle is going to change everything."

Marion kissed him. It was quick. They were alone, but never truly alone with so many troops around—though many of the men had already advanced. Men whom Marion had been tasked with delivering birds to. They'd be relying on her.

This battle was going to change everything. What if this was *the* battle to end the war? What if on the heels of victory Marion revealed the happy news of their child to Eddie? What a day that would be. But first, the birds.

CHAPTER 24

EVELYN

July 1940
London

E ach day with the Wrens, Evelyn woke with the birds. At 5:30 a.m.
it was customary for sailors to walk the halls and shout, "Wakey,
wakey, rise and shine!" to stir the recruits. But Evelyn had something
to prove, and that morning she had beaten the birds and the sailors.
She was already awake and at the infirmary.

When breakfast hit the table in the Painted Hall, she was there,
hands around a strong morning tea.

At morning drills she marched, her heavy, laced-up shoes feeling
especially cumbersome. But as the keep-fit continued, so did Evelyn.

During the lectures, she sat with her foot raised, listening to how
the Wrens should protect themselves in an emergency and what to do
during a gas attack.

Evelyn felt Wren Philips's eyes on her. Evelyn had politely
requested to rejoin the recruits rather than continuing on at the infirmary. *"As you wish,"* Wren Philips had said, a hint of pride in her voice.

At night Evelyn collapsed in her bunk, too tired and sore and
bruised to even see eight thirty. Rose never acknowledged Evelyn, a
fine alternative to her treating her like a cow.

Saturday afternoon Evelyn and the other recruits were *finally* given their first three hours of leave time. Evelyn lay on her bunk. How comical was the use of *finally* when they'd only arrived on Wednesday. Still, training was the hardest situation many of them had ever been in, and the enthusiasm to be doing something, anything different was palpable. Excited voices carried down the halls and seeped through the walls, some suggesting a film show, others going on about a dance, and others organizing a bowling game in the Queen Mary Undercroft.

Arms behind her cradling her head, Evelyn had no intention of going anywhere. During her many recoveries as a child, Mrs. Taylor had often encouraged Evelyn to read, needlepoint, paint, write letters—to whom she wasn't ever certain—or partake in a variety of other games or activities she could do while lying or sitting. Sometimes she had. But mostly Evelyn had been content to wallow.

She had no desire to do any such thing now. Rose, in her own way, had pushed Evelyn to not simply comply with the path provided for her but to forge forward on her own accord—as much forging as a person who had to follow a rigorous routine could do, anyway. And while she had no intention of staying in and feeling sorry for herself, she very much wanted to simply and purely *sleep*.

Rose and Theresa were first to leave. Eyes closed, Evelyn listened to them go. Moments later, Mary's footsteps began, then paused. She'd said earlier that she'd be meeting her twin brother. She'd even suggested Evelyn should join them and went as far as to say that Michael would likely fancy her. It was a nice gesture and sentiment. To think, there *could* be other fish in the sea for Evelyn. "I'll be fine, Mary. You go on. Clock's ticking."

Mary hesitated, but left.

But then, not even a minute later, Evelyn heard the door again.

Without opening her eyes, Evelyn said, "Don't make me chase you away. I assure you I'll be unconscious in only a matter of time."

"I hope not before a quick cuppa."

Evelyn shot to a sitting position so quickly her head spun. "Percy, what are you doing here?" She looked around her room, making sure Wren Philips or Wren Monroe wasn't hiding in the corner, ready to pounce. "You'll get me in trouble."

Percy looked animatedly over his shoulder. A girl and boy ran by, holding hands. "Not for the next few hours, I don't think."

"How'd you know I'd have leave?"

"Lucky guess," he said with a shrug. "First weekend and all that."

"And how'd you know I'd be here and not traipsing about?"

"Educated guess." This time he smirked, one of his dimples showing. Then he held up a thermos.

"Tea? From a thermos?"

"Do let me know when you're out of questions, Evie," he said as he pulled two small teacups from within his inner jacket, as if he were a magician.

Evelyn hid a smile and repositioned to sit with her legs crossed. She wore a pajama trouser and blouse set, nothing he hadn't seen her in before from the many holidays their families had spent together when they were children. But in the privacy and intimacy of her cabin, and considering Evelyn was no longer a little girl, she found her stomach fluttering with the novelty of the situation. The flutter accelerated to hummingbird wings when Percy's eyes lingered on her, then he held out the two cups.

She kept them steady as he poured. Steam rose, a pleasant surprise as she doubted the thermos could rival a kettle, and she brought a cup to her nose. "Mm, lavender."

Evelyn caught a tender expression on his face as he placed the thermos on her bedside, right next to the elephant he'd given her.

He didn't comment on it, but his eyes lingered there as he said, "I added the apple pieces like Mrs. Taylor does before bed."

"I miss her." Evelyn glanced at her brooch. "But you'll do as a fill-in."

Percy laughed. "Big shoes to fill." He sipped, then placed his cup on the floor beside her bed. "Mind if I check the patient?"

Evelyn motioned agreeably toward her foot, hiding yet another smile behind her cup as he rubbed his hands together to warm his skin.

"I expected worse," Percy observed after removing the elastic brace. "Quite bruised still, but that'll take time to fade. The swelling is considerably better. Does it hurt very much now?"

"It's tolerable. Almost as if my foot has called a truce with me. It'll do its bit if I take care of it after."

One of Percy's eyebrows rose. "Look who's talking to her foot now."

Evelyn sipped, studying the sharp curves of his cheekbones, the dark stubble beneath, his lips anchoring it all. How normal it felt to banter with that face. How easy it'd be, Evelyn realized, to lean forward and close the distance between them.

Well, hello. That wasn't a thought she'd ever had before. Evelyn mused how during their earlier years, he'd always been her entertainer or her partner in crime. Of late, Percy had morphed into the man Evelyn's mother deemed as her only option. But removed from her mother's reach, Evelyn dared to let herself think of Percy differently. Could he be doing the same? He'd come to see her, after all, bringing Evelyn her favorite evening tea.

"I'll have you know, I almost joined one of my bunkmates tonight," Evelyn began, wondering after his reaction to what she'd say next. "Mary said she wanted to introduce me to her brother, who'd likely fancy me."

She watched Percy's face. Was she hoping for a spark of jealousy? Would the thought of Percy dating women turn her into a green-eyed monster? Botheration, it would. But Evelyn had chosen poor timing to test Percy's reaction because his physician brain was soundly on her foot, bending and turning it.

Distractedly he said, "You would've missed out on some excellent thermos tea."

And you, Evelyn thought. She would've missed out on seeing him. Only the two of them, greatly removed from their parents' expectations.

She sipped her tea, the taste growing on her and unexpectedly not too far from excellent. She only had to stretch her mind, a slight shift in her perspective. It certainly had potential.

It was the final endurance test of Evelyn's training. Mary held Evelyn's legs while she curled from the ground to her bent knees again and again and again, Mary's mouth silently moving as she counted each repetition.

Evelyn had never appreciated how long two minutes felt until she was in the midst of seemingly endless curl-ups and push-ups.

At least the push-ups portion was complete. What an atrocious exercise, likely devised by the devil himself. Each time her chest grazed the ground, she fought the urge to give in and lie there. Resting *was* permitted, but only in the up position. Evelyn didn't call that rest. She called it another torturous exercise, this time invented by Joseph Pilates or Royal H. Burpee.

When Wren Philips blasted the horn after two minutes, Evelyn had collapsed to her stomach.

"Thirty-four," Mary had told her. "Jolly good, Evelyn."

She snorted. Evelyn hadn't felt jolly good, but it'd been better than her initial push-up test nearly two weeks ago. Much improved, in fact.

Now she was mid-curl. She'd lost track of how many she'd done, but Mary was barely blinking while she held Evelyn's feet and counted.

With each curl, Evelyn watched the faces of the other girls. Their expressions were rightfully a mix of pain and anguish. She reckoned some of the anguish was from more than simply the fitness test, however. Mr. Churchill had warned that the Battle of Britain would soon begin. And it had.

Only days ago, German bombers and fighters began attacking British ships in the Channel. Were they testing the waters, so to say? Adolf Hitler had conquered most of Europe, including France. The only major country left to fight back was Great Britain.

Their island.

After the attack happened two hours southeast of London, Evelyn saw the ghostlike faces of the other girls. She heard some say how they wouldn't stay on as a Wren; they were too shaken. They justified that they had every right to leave since there was no conscription for women and they hadn't yet been officially accepted as a Wren.

They weren't wrong. Any of them could leave during the probationary period. And they had every right to be shaken. Evelyn knew staying on meant thrusting herself into Adolf Hitler's warpath. But she'd undoubtedly stay on. That was, if the Wrens would have her.

She curled with gusto.

Her breath came ragged.

In the final seconds Mary began counting out loud: "Fifty-eight, fifty-nine, sixty, sixty-one . . ."

The horn sounded.

"Should I count it?" Mary asked. "You were all the way up, right?"

"Count it," Evelyn heard from behind her. She twisted to find Rose. But before Evelyn could say anything more, Rose was on her feet, walking toward the start line for the concluding leg of their fitness test: the run.

The swelling in Evelyn's foot had gone down. There was a dull ache, but in all honesty, there wasn't a place on Evelyn's body that wasn't sore. It was comical, really, how every muscle—even muscles Evelyn hadn't known she had—throbbed.

Wren Philips signaled for the run to begin, and they were off.

Promptly, the women jostled for space.

Evelyn looked for an opening, an opportunity to perform an overtaking maneuver as she'd done on the racetrack.

In Evelyn's peripheral vision a girl tripped. Like she was roadkill, the girl was leapt over by the girl behind her. Evelyn stumbled, too, caught up in someone else's feet.

A hand caught Evelyn's elbow.

"Thank you," she muttered, then noticed who her savior had been. "Rose."

"See you at the finish line, Fairchild."

Rose increased her pace, and Evelyn fixed her eyes on Rose's back. She set her arms at a ninety-degree angle and pumped, feeling the effects of each and every push-up she'd done. With each unsteady step, her focus narrowed. Evelyn told herself she was one foot closer to becoming an official Wren, one foot closer to finding her place and proving that wherever she ended up, Evelyn was exactly where she belonged.

CHAPTER 25

MARION

August 1918
Amiens

Marion had thought it before and now she thought it again: *This battle is going to change everything.* She felt it in her bones.

The battle would be won.

She'd tell Eddie about their child.

They'd plan their future.

She was giddy for it all. Marion was ready for the battle to begin.

The pigeons she had delivered to each of the corps the night before had been recorded and tagged. It was something Sara and Marion always did before giving out birds. But this time the birds' tags would be of the utmost importance because the birds would be returning to Marion and Sara from the front line with crucial information for Sir Henry Rawlinson.

As the promise of dawn hummed in the August air, the women lay awake on their biscuits. Marion had slept little. The night had been especially dark, on account of their usual blackout but also because there was a new moon. She wondered if the lack of moonlight had been a factor in deciding the date of the morning's raid. She hoped every consideration had been taken.

A thrill coursed through her at what was to begin . . . in mere minutes.

Her wristwatch was difficult to read, but she saw it had turned four. She'd done her part. The birds were trained and in the hands of the men. Now to wait patiently. An impossibility.

Marion had to get up, to move, to do something other than lie there and speculate and daydream about this particular battle being *the one*. She ran a hand over her flat stomach, her child likely no larger than a poppy seed. She liked to think of her child in such a manner. Poppies were a common sight throughout France, and Marion smiled to think that something so precious as a child would come from this war.

Poppy, she mused to herself. Right from the start, Marion wanted to think of her child by name. She couldn't wait for Eddie to learn of their Poppy.

She stood from her biscuit, tiptoeing toward Sara.

"I'm awake," Marion heard before reaching her.

"Me too," Beverly said.

"So am I," Betty said.

The remaining women chimed in as well. They'd all received their orders. Betty and the other nurses would report to dressing stations. Beverly had said she'd been given instructions to sort through the letters the soldiers had written to their families in the hours before they'd traverse into, through, and beyond no-man's-land. Marion had no letter to write. Everyone she loved was here with her.

Already in uniform and with the latrines but steps away, Marion and Sara were at their mobile loft within minutes. They idly ate biscuits as hard as their mattresses and stared at the dark sky through the trees.

A fog hovered above the ground, and Marion couldn't help

thinking that the lack of moonlight as well as the mist would help reduce the Huns' visibility during the attack.

Marion scratched her head beneath her hat. "I think the lice have found me."

Sara snorted. "Let that be the worst this war does to us."

How true. Marion's chest rose and fell in anticipation, her heartbeat greatly outpacing the ticking of her wristwatch.

The night was eerily silent.

Until the roar of planes reached them.

"It's beginning," Sara said at a whisper.

Within no-man's-land, the Royal Air Force was likely releasing smoke at that very moment, further concealing the battlefield. An unfathomable number of aircrafts—eight hundred—were to participate throughout the length of the battle.

At exactly twenty past four, just as Eddie had said would happen, the sounds of gunfire filled the air. Nine hundred guns and cannons, Marion remembered Eddie saying. She covered her ears, not more than four miles from the mayhem.

The front line cut through various woods, and Marion envisioned the men winding through the trees to reach the Germans and their first line of machine guns. Just shy of four hundred tanks would follow, and Marion knew they'd struggle in the boggy terrain. She herself had to heed caution when she'd been on her rides.

All Marion and Sara could do was wait for the birds to return. And for Eddie to arrive to do his part. The loft wasn't far from the commander's headquarters, but as soon as a pigeon returned, carrying news of a completed or failed objective, Eddie would zoom the missive to HQ on his motorcycle.

Nearly three hand-twisting hours later, Eddie arrived with the first of the day's sunlight. There was no hello. He greeted them instead with a pronouncement, hollering louder than the deafening sounds of the battle that it took the Germans a full five minutes to find their wits and return fire.

He looked jubilant. The news was so promising Marion almost told him right then and there about their Poppy. But she didn't want to cause any distractions from their responsibilities during the battle, especially as she spotted the first of their pigeons returning.

"The Australians," Marion called, recognizing the color of the marker on the bird's leg. The pigeon flew straight through the trap as he'd been trained.

Sara dove into the loft and retrieved the rolled missive from the bird's back, the animal already eating the food that had lured him home. Eddie sat waiting on his motorbike, the engine roaring, when Sara delivered the note to Marion, who passed it to him.

Anticipation coursed through Marion. "What's it say?"

Sara now held her pigeon log, prepared to check in the returned pigeon, her pen raised above the paper, also waiting to hear the news.

Eddie shifted his weight, reading, then blurted, "Australian units have reached their first and second objectives! They've advanced over four miles."

Marion found herself jumping. When had she ever jumped in such a manner before? Never. She didn't even know the particulars of the Australians' objectives, but she didn't care. They had been successful. The amount of earth they captured felt astounding. She checked her wristwatch: a few minutes past seven thirty. When she looked up, Eddie was on his way. He blew Marion a kiss before re-gripping his handlebars with determination.

"Be safe," she whispered. Her breath hitched when she could no longer see the tan of Eddie's uniform through the trees.

She watched the minute hand, ticking forward ten times, until he appeared again. Marion cheered and Eddie chortled at her reaction to his return.

Together, they searched the war-torn skies for the next bird. Within an hour, another appeared, flying straight and true back to the loft.

The Australians again! Their fourth and fifth divisions had passed through the initial breach in the German line.

With haste, Eddie set out again on Alli to deliver the news. It wasn't another five minutes before another pigeon returned, this update from the Canadians, who'd also passed through the breach. Remarkable!

This second missive couldn't wait to be delivered to headquarters, and Eddie hadn't come back yet. "I'll take it," Marion told Sara.

"Be careful," Sara pleaded.

Marion palmed her tin hat atop her head. "Always."

"Exceptionally careful," Sara implored of her friend, her gaze dipping to Marion's middle.

Marion bowed her head, then set off. Even knowing the battle had advanced miles away, her heart was in her throat. More than once, Marion reminded herself to breathe, especially when the road left the cover of trees.

So many aircrafts. So much smoke. Such noise. Not a soul in sight, the most bizarre feeling when the sounds of thousands and thousands of fighting men felt all-encompassing. With each turn, she expected to come between gunfire, but she pressed on, accelerating, hunching herself closer to her handlebars. She risked slowing, maneuvering around an alarmingly large and fresh shell hole. Marion shuddered; to think artillery of this size was exchanged again and again and again.

At HQ, Marion's missive was received with nothing more than

a nod and a scribbled signature, and she was back on her motorbike. Her eyes searched for Eddie as much as they did for explosives, but she never laid eyes on him on her return ride. It wasn't to say he wasn't on a different route, Marion assured herself, and her relief came out as a sob when she saw his tall, willowy frame outside the loft with Sara.

His reaction matched her own, and Eddie all but tore Marion from her bike to place her again on solid ground.

"Your part in the battle was supposed to be done, Marion."

"I know," she said. "But I couldn't let the message just sit here."

He sighed, pulling her into an embrace. "You did the right thing."

Marion's eyes widened at his unexpected acceptance of her actions. "But hopefully I can take it from here. It's a fright out there," Eddie murmured into her neck.

"I can't imagine being in the thick of it," Marion replied in earnest. "But riding to HQ is okay. I can do that."

He kissed the tip of her nose, his lips lingering as Sara called out, "Incoming bird!"

Excitement surged in Marion again.

Eddie delivered the dispatch that told of the Canadians pushing the line another three miles.

The next pigeon came in before Eddie's return, and Marion again took it upon herself to complete the delivery. The Australians had matched the distance with their own advance.

Still, there was nothing from the British Army. It was nearly eleven. The raid had begun seven hours back.

Sara posed the question first. "Think our army is in trouble?"

Eddie rubbed his lips together. "They're north of the river, where the Huns did that small invasion two days ago. I wonder if the attack unsettled things more than was let on. Only a single tank battalion was assigned to them. The terrain there is rougher too."

Marion nodded. "I saw the ridges when I delivered their birds." Then a worry flashed in her mind. "What if the birds are casualties?"

What if they hadn't received word of the British Army's progress because there weren't any surviving birds to deliver the missives? She'd heard of birds becoming casualties before. The idea of losing any of her birds nearly sickened Marion, having grown close to the animals. She hadn't included 486 in any of the baskets for that very reason.

"Think we should restock?" Eddie suggested.

"I don't know," Marion answered. Thinking of delivering the birds to the front during a battle made her knees noticeably weak. "We haven't been given orders to restock."

Eddie removed his hat and ran a hand through his sweat-dampened hair, making it appear more red than orange. "But what if the commander is blind to what's happening north of the Somme? If they need pigeons . . ."

His words swayed Sara, who began packing a basket with a message book, pencil, and clips. She then moved on to the birds. When Sara marked 486 in her book, Marion almost reached out to stop her. But there wasn't time to argue. And her bird was well trained.

Marion swallowed her unease and took the basket of birds from Sara. She had one arm through the straps when Sara proclaimed, "No," and Eddie demanded, "What do you think you're doing, Mare?"

She marched toward her motorcycle. "I'm taking the birds."

Eddie's eyes were large. "You are not. I'll go instead."

Marion threw a leg over her motorbike. "You're in this war because of me. And this is *my* job. I took them before; I can take them again." She kicked the bike's prop stand as Eddie took hold of her handlebar.

"I'm a grown man, Marion," he barked, making an attempt to grab the basket with his free hand. "I made my own decision to enlist."

A grown man. Marion almost scoffed but refrained from a

reaction that'd only add fuel to his fire. He was little more than a young man. But no, she countered to herself. He was a man. And he'd soon be a father. It didn't mean she wanted him to go, though. If she'd been a schemer, she'd have thought to turn in his doctored papers ages ago and have him removed. Why hadn't she had that thought before now? Instead she said, "I'm going, Eddie. As I said, the birds are my responsibility. I know which roads to take. You don't. I'm just as, if not more, capable."

Tears filled Eddie's eyes and his voice was softer as he said, "It has nothing to do with being capable. I know you are. It's about me needing you to be okay more than I need myself to be okay."

"You don't think I feel the same—"

"Stop!" Sara yelled.

Marion and Eddie both startled.

"Marion," she said. "You *cannot* go. Be sensible."

Marion clenched her teeth together. Sara's words hadn't exposed her secret, but Eddie was poring over Marion's ruffled reaction and it was clear it gave him pause.

"Marion, look at me. What does Sara mean by that? Are you hurt?"

"I'm not hurt," she said, meeting his eyes. She wondered if Poppy's irises would be the same shade of green. Or would Poppy inherit her brown? And she knew . . . she knew she must tell him. It was wrong to keep her pregnancy from Eddie. She also knew it'd be reckless for her to go on such a dangerous stunt when it was more than her own life she was risking. But accepting she shouldn't go meant putting Eddie in the line of fire. "I'm not hurt," she repeated slowly, edging herself off her bike. "I'm carrying our child."

Eddie's mouth parted in surprise.

"I only just found out," she added rapidly as she began to remove the basket from her back. "Sara guessed my condition."

Perhaps it was the fact that Marion had conceded to not completing the stunt that allowed Eddie's smile to start slow, then grow and turn into a purely joyous response. Marion would forever be thankful for that small blessing.

As she had previously imagined, Eddie swooped her into the air and twirled her around. His words came so quickly that she couldn't decipher them. But then he said, "I'll be back soon. I promise. Then we'll celebrate. I'll ride like the dickens. I may even float. This war is ending, Mare. I know it, and then . . . a child."

"Poppy," Marion said. A tear tracked down her cheek. "I've taken to calling her Poppy."

Eddie's kiss was passionate. It acted as another promise of his safe return and their future together. Marion watched him ride away, both hands pressed over her stomach. He'd be back soon, then their future would truly begin.

CHAPTER 26

EVELYN

July 1940
London

E velyn had done it. She'd conquered the last hurdle and had officially become a Wren.

Not only that, she'd been assigned the role of a dispatch rider. She
"owned" a motorcycle, after all.

She lay in her bunk, exhausted, foot raised, and completely jolly.
If only she'd felt half as chipper about writing her parents with the
news. It wasn't that she wasn't proud to shout her accomplishment.
Her hesitance was that her parents wouldn't share in her excitement.

Dear Mother and Father . . .

That was all she'd managed so far. The pen and paper lay
beside her.

Evelyn had received her appointment and official uniform only
hours ago. She immediately sewed a badge, depicting an arrow crossed
by a lightning flash, onto her jacket sleeve, feeling pride in each and
every stitch. Gosh, did it feel more rewarding than the needlework
she'd done in the sewing circle. And tomorrow she'd begin her new
training program in the Signal division.

No more scrubbing the floors.

Hallelujah.

In the meantime the other women were buzzing about, talking about who'd be staying, who'd be moving on to finish their training elsewhere, who'd been assigned to which role.

It wasn't a surprise that Rose and Theresa would also be motorcycle dispatch riders. Mary would be completing her training at Mill Hill, if Evelyn remembered correctly.

Evelyn sighed, felt for her pen, and bit it between her teeth.

All the new Wrens were encouraged to write home, not only to share the good news of surviving the probationary qualifying period but also to request that their families turn in all available aluminum to the Ministry of Aircraft Production. Pots and pans would become fighter planes like Spitfires and Hurricanes.

Evelyn sat up and readied her pen to write. Where to begin?

I am well.

Despite her parents remaining true to their threat, Evelyn had to believe they cared about her welfare. They always had.

Today I pledged myself to the Wrens after successfully completing a probationary period.

She tapped her pen against her bottom lip.

While I know you don't support me in this decision, and I do not intend to try to persuade you otherwise, I hope you'll further support this war.

She explained the need for aluminum, even mentioning how the Brooklands was involved in the production of aircrafts. That last part would appeal to her father. She only hoped her mother wouldn't snub the war efforts on account of Evelyn's involvement in them. Or that her mother wouldn't be scared into denial of the war's happenings. Evelyn remembered how her mother had shrunk at Mr. Churchill's warning words.

Letter completed, she sighed a final time just as Rose entered their cabin, largely hidden behind a ridiculously large bouquet of flowers.

"Suits you," Evelyn said with an earnest laugh.

Rose deposited the flowers onto Evelyn's bedside table. "They're not for me."

Rose's tone wasn't unkind. Still, Evelyn cringed. That monstrosity wouldn't help Rose's impression of her.

"Go on," Rose said. "Who are they from? Your parents?"

"I won't hold my breath," Evelyn said flatly. "My mother isn't the forgiving type."

"Then it appears you have even more backbone than I gave you credit for, Dare D-Evelyn."

Before, Rose essentially spat Evelyn's nickname at her. This time felt different. Friendly, even.

Evelyn almost didn't say it, but she did. "You're being awfully nice to me. Usually you treat me like a daft cow."

"Well," Rose began, her weight shifting from one side to the other, "I realize I've been unfair to you. Preconceived notions and all that. Back at the Brooklands, Wilkes told me you weren't just a silly deb. I see that now." A smile passed between them before Rose quickly added, "So who is the mystery sender then?"

Evelyn twisted her lips; she had an idea who the flowers could be from. But to be wrong and let down . . . "Will you read it for me?"

Rose wasted no time plucking the small card from within the peonies and roses.

She read aloud, "'I knew you could do it. P.'"

Rose wasn't the type of girl to gush and shimmy her shoulders. However, her eyebrow did rise to the heavens. "And who is this *P* who's congratulating you on becoming a Wren?"

"The owner of my motorcycle."

"I see," Rose said slowly. "And what do these flowers mean coming from the motorcycle owner?"

Evelyn laughed. "How should I know?"

"Isn't there a whole language of flowers?" Rose gave her an unbelieving look. "You're telling me you weren't taught such things at a posh finishing school?"

"*This* is my finishing school." And boy, did Evelyn feel proud saying it.

"Roses, though," Rose suggested. "Everyone knows they mean love."

"You were certainly misnamed then."

Rose's mouth fell open, and Evelyn covered her laugh. What an unexpected scenario: there she was jesting with her onetime rival and contemplating the symbolism behind roses from Percy. To think she almost missed this strange moment. She almost *was* sent to a finishing school. "I'm only joking. But I think roses suggest romance when red," Evelyn said, surprised to feel a profound disappointment. "I have no clue what white roses mean."

"Well, whatever they mean, what do you plan to do?"

Evelyn aimlessly arranged the flowers in the vase. She bent to smell them, rising again with a smile. "What do you mean?"

"I mean, aren't you going to reply?"

"Should I?"

"I'd think so. Even I was taught to say thank you when given a gift."

"Okay," Evelyn said, her pulse quickening. "I could telephone him."

Rose shook her head. "Or you could do it in person. How is it I'm better at this than you are?"

Evelyn laughed. "I really am out of practice. Actually I've had no practice."

Could the flowers mean something of greater significance? He'd called on her and brought her tea. Now flowers.

"Go," Rose said and nudged Evelyn toward the door.

"You mean I should thank him right now? It's a Wednesday evening."

"We have leave for the rest of the night. Why not?"

Evelyn bobbed her head. She'd shown up unexpectedly before. She supposed she could do it again.

❦

She debated going to Percy's clinic, but his townhome was closer. She'd try there first. It was logical, especially as the day was becoming later. What wasn't adding up was Evelyn's nerves. Percy had sent her flowers. Still, she climbed the three steps, then abruptly stopped outside his door, arm raised, a knock away from doing the polite thing and thanking him for the lovely gesture.

But was a simple thank-you enough? Somehow she spoke multiple languages, yet she felt completely uneducated in both the language of flowers and the language of love. Lord, she felt ridiculous even thinking it: *the language of love.*

Should she have brought a gift in return? If the tea and now the flowers were Percy's way of showing his growing interest in her, then should she have put more effort into her appearance? Rose had rushed her out the door, so she hadn't had any time to gussy herself up, but at least Evelyn had on one of her better dresses. And in a pale green too. Percy liked green.

She shimmied her shoulders, trying to loosen up, but she only felt annoyance with herself. Enough at least to complete the knock. The Fairchild in her made her follow it with two firmer raps.

Percy didn't keep her waiting long.

"Evie?" he proclaimed upon opening the door. "What a surprise."

"A good one, I hope."

"Of course," Percy said, but he also ran a hand through his Cary Grant hair. "Are you hurt?"

"No, not any more spoiled than usual." She tried for a calming smile. "I came to thank you for the flowers but also for the sentiment. On the note," she quickly added. "Your words. They meant a great deal to me."

Percy smiled easily at that. "I meant every one of them. I believe in you, Evie. And now look at you, a motorcycle dispatch rider. Quite the spiffy machine too." ·

Evelyn looked over her shoulder at the motorbike. "Some fellow gave it to me."

"Gave it to you, huh?"

They stood grinning at each other a moment, Percy still propping the door open with his hand, but then he cleared his throat. "Where are my manners? I'd invite you in, but . . ."

"You're on your way out, aren't you? And I've kept you," Evelyn said, instinctively retreating a step on his stoop.

Percy reached for her and for a heartbeat Evelyn gazed at where his hand met her elbow. "I'm glad you came by. It's always good to see you, Evie. But yes, I'm afraid I have a prior engagement."

She nodded, not trusting her disappointment not to shine through in her words.

"But soon?" Percy asked. "How about bowling or the film your mother was so keen on us going to together? I hear *Ask a Policeman* is good. Folks in the services get free tickets to the cinema, I've been told."

And suddenly Evelyn felt lighter again. "She was rather keen on us having an outing, wasn't she?"

"The delicate nudgings of a mother," he teased.

"I'd call it something other than delicate."

"Careful, your mother will hear you all the way from Wiltshire."

Evelyn thought to correct him; that no, given her mother's last message through Percy, she doubted her mother cared much for her at the moment. But she didn't want to voice it, and judging by how Percy shifted his weight and studied the pavement, he regretted the mention of Evelyn's mother.

"Soon, then," Percy said, a quickness to his voice.

"Soon," Evelyn agreed.

A future with the Wrens and a future date with Percy. There was much to look forward to, it seemed.

CHAPTER 27

MARION

August 1918
Amiens

Marion stared through the trees of the forest at Amiens, antici-pating Eddie's return, imagining their future as a family that would truly begin after the war concluded.

"Everything's going to be okay," Sara said.

Marion sighed, her head slowly shaking. "Remember your anal-ogy from all those years ago? That all we can do is take caution during a storm. And if we can't find shelter, we can at least not stand under the tallest tree." Marion closed her eyes, not wanting to finish the thought. "It feels like the front line is nothing but tall trees."

Sara didn't respond. Moments passed. Finally she said, "Try to rest. We could get a pigeon at any time. We need to be ready to do our part. That's the best way we can help Eddie and all the other men out there."

Marion nodded. The Australians sent updates seemingly every hour, and thankfully it was nothing but positive news. She sat on an overturned log. Immediately her hands found her middle again.

It still felt astonishing to think a child was slowly growing and forming inside her. Marion tilted her head back, a beam of light catching her face between the trees. Her stomach growled. When had she last eaten? How long would it take for Eddie to come back? How long until another bird returned with news?

She exhaled and stood to go in search of food. A pigeon caught her eye.

"Sare!" she called.

Sara was poking around the loft, most likely making sure the birds weren't overeating.

Marion cupped her eyes. She squinted, her vision focusing on the arriving bird. However, the pigeon wasn't flying straight and true. Normally not even throwing a stick at a pigeon would make it duck or weave. But this pigeon was wobbling. It was hurt.

As it got closer, her hand flew to her chest. She recognized the tag and the bird's markings. It was 486.

"Sara!" she called again.

"I see him!"

Marion willed him home. Once he was back inside the loft, they could tend to his injury. Her heart beat wildly as she recognized other pigeons, all with similar tags, trailing 486. Others also struggled to fly.

Marion's knees buckled and she reached for a tree trunk to hold herself up. The only way the birds would return in such a manner—too quickly, all at once, some wounded—was if something had gone horribly wrong.

Marion mentally coaxed 486 through the trap door. Sara was already hunched inside the mobile unit to receive him. "He's been hit," she yelled.

Marion knew Sara was referring to 486, but she could only think of Eddie. She collapsed against the tree, her mind traveling at what seemed like a million miles per hour. What she really needed to be doing was traveling toward Eddie.

She took a stumbling step in the direction of her motorcycle.

"Marion, no," Sara called from within the small loft, unable to fully stand.

"I have to go after him," Marion insisted.

"No."

Marion shuffled forward, the edges of her vision darkening. "I have to. The birds . . ."

"I know, Mare. But you can't go after him. It's not safe for Poppy."

The name nearly dissolved the trance Marion felt caught in. Still she reached for her handlebars. Suddenly Sara was beside her. "I'll go. Let me. Please, Marion. I'll go."

Marion shook her head and mounted the motorcycle. "You can't ride. You don't know the way." She reached for the key already in the ignition hole, and Sara grabbed the fabric of her skirt.

At her yank, Marion tumbled off the motorcycle, taking the key with her. Her arm swung and caught Sara across the face, leaving a streak of blood that disappeared into her hairline.

Sara let out a yelp but held tight to Marion, pulling her farther from the bike. "As God is my witness, I will lock you in the loft, Marion. You aren't going. But I will. I'll go. There will be people to help me find him."

Marion's smaller frame was no match for Sara's. She was taller, stronger. There was simply more of her, and Marion knew it was a physical battle she wouldn't win. But even more than that, she knew their standoff was wasting time.

"Fine! Go. Go, Sara. Please. Find him."

July 1940
West Devon

Marion softly uttered the same words she'd said twenty years earlier: "Go. Go, Sara."

However, now she meant for Sara to simply leave her be. She'd showed up on Marion's doorstep last evening and asked her to return to the Wrens. Of all the coldhearted things to do, as if she hadn't pulled Marion deeper into the war once. As if that action hadn't set in motion everything that happened that day at Amiens.

Sara had gotten help from soldiers at a dressing station to go in search of Eddie. Miraculously, he'd been found alive.

Marion later learned that Eddie had made it past the British dugouts, through no-man's-land, and beyond Germany's three lines of abandoned trenches. The British Army had been held up at Chipilly Spur, a seventy-five-foot-high ridge. There, gunfire was being exchanged. Eddie had been approaching the battlegrounds when he'd been spotted by the Germans.

The bullets came quickly.

Eddie lost control of his motorbike.

The impact broke the basket and freed the pigeons, who did what they knew to do: return to the loft. It was because of her beloved 486 that Marion had been able to see Eddie one last time.

Marion had arrived at the dressing station, where Eddie still lay on a stretcher, no need to switch him to a bed. In the glow of the moonlight, she draped herself over him. Her tears came swiftly, and she remembered—Marion remembered the children's book, the sand fairy, and the wishes. She remembered how Eddie had once asked her what she'd wish for.

"To be wanted," Marion had told him honestly all those years ago.

"*You are,*" he'd said as a child, his cheeks reddening beneath his freckles.

It felt like forever ago. She wiped the blood from his cheeks, her tears wetting his skin. Eddie's eyes were closed, but his chest slowly moved.

She was reminded of the first time she read to Eddie, when he hadn't woken up until after she'd started whispering words to him. She'd been afraid that if she gifted that portion of herself to him, he'd be taken from her.

And he would be.

It was happening in that very moment.

"*You made me feel so wanted,*" Marion struggled to say. "*So wanted,*" she went on, her mind progressing. "*I am so angry you got your wish.*"

Marion had felt a dangling sense of worry at his outlandish desire to stay with her after she'd left St. Anne's, and she had feared a disastrous result would follow. And what could be more disastrous than being wanted by a man she'd spend the rest of her life without?

"*I'm so angry, Eddie,*" Marion whimpered into his chest, her own eyes closed. "*And I'm so sorry. I promise to do right by our Poppy.*"

Marion had been torn away by strong hands, telling her she was too close to the battle, insisting there was nothing else she could do.

Eddie was gone.

He was buried with countless others, forever on a battlefield. The men dug each grave, but the filling in and tidying had been done by the Land Army women.

"*I'll take care of him,*" Beverly had assured Marion. It'd been a small comfort to have a friend take a personal interest in his burial. The sound of a trumpet's bugle calls, however, which were sounded at military funerals, left Marion shaking with grief.

They were too loud.

And they were played too routinely, not only for deaths but also to mark the end of each day's activities.

Day after day, the trumpet sounds had taken Marion back to Eddie's death.

Again and again and again.

Yes, it'd been a lot. Yes, it'd been taxing. But she'd carried on, stifling a cry when Alli had been given to a new dispatch rider, accepting whatever stunts were asked of her with her birds, determined to see the war to its end for Eddie.

For their Poppy, she allowed food to pass her lips.

Marion didn't need Sara to intervene. She'd already done enough. She was the reason Eddie had been in France in the first place. But Sara stuck her nose in. She applied on Marion's behalf, behind Marion's back, for a compassionate discharge.

Sara revealed Marion was a widow.

Sara revealed Marion was in a family way.

The Wrens granted Marion's release, the war no place for her.

And it nearly broke her.

Germany had retreated two days after Eddie's death. The war itself endured only a hundred days more.

A hundred days more.

Yet Marion hadn't been there to see its end, leaving only a few weeks before Germany surrendered. She hadn't been there for Eddie.

He'd been right about the war soon ending. Marion, too, had been correct. The battle at Amiens changed everything.

Every single thing.

After her discharge, Marion once again didn't have a say in when or where she'd go.

She was taken to Sara's home in Wiltshire.

Without a purpose to her days.

Feeling again like a foundling, an orphan, a waif—no longer a daughter of the Wrens.

No longer did she wear an arrow crossed by a lightning flash on her sleeve. She'd traded her uniform for the clothes she'd worn the day she'd been forced to leave St. Anne's, though the waist needed to be let out, her belly rounding by the day.

Of course Sara intervened again. *"There's a family,"* she began, *"who can't have a child of their own."*

They wanted Marion's.

They wanted the only piece of Eddie that Marion had left.

For the sake of her Poppy, she agreed. Marion had promised Eddie she'd do right by their child, and Marion knew that meant she couldn't keep their baby. Not when she envisioned a family of three instead of two for Poppy. Not when she didn't have the means. Not when she didn't trust herself to care for another human life, as she could barely care for her own.

Marion had failed again.

Sara had brought 486 to Marion after nursing him back to health. If the woman expected it to fix all she'd done, she'd be wrong. Very wrong. But he'd be all Marion had left after Poppy was born.

Sara saw to the arrangements of Poppy's birth. All the expenses would be covered. Marion's care before and after would be seen to.

Then, when the time had come, Marion had woken from a twilight sleep, her womb empty of her child and her hand firmly clenched around the brooch she'd once been found with.

"Poppy? Where's my baby?" Marion had croaked through slitted eyes.

A nurse entered the dimly lit room. *"It's a girl,"* she had said.

"Poppy," Marion said in a raspy voice, her head lolling on the pillow. Her Poppy was a girl, just as she'd pictured her to be.

"There's a contract beside the bed."

Marion lazily turned to see a document. She knew what it said already; she'd agreed to it prior to the birth. The contract forbade Marion from ever speaking of the child's adoption.

"They will allow you to meet the child, but only for a moment. They have decided to continue with the adoption."

In the haziness of Marion's mind, she noted it was a peculiar thing to say.

The nurse had then asked, *"Do you wish to see the child?"*

Marion had squeezed the brooch before placing it atop the contract, then whispered a no.

Now, in the quiet of her bedroom, Sara only a stone's throw away in the other room, Marion whispered no again, the word not a refusal but a regret, a denial, a renouncement of all that happened in the wake of Eddie's death. She once had a purpose. She once had a future. Now . . .

Marion only wished for sleep but knew it wouldn't come. Hadn't Charlotte Brontë once said "a ruffled mind makes a restless pillow"? Marion felt it keenly.

Outside the rooster crowed. Marion's head rolled on her pillow toward her door. Sara, the harbinger of unwanted memories, would soon awake, if she wasn't already lying in wait for Marion to emerge.

Marion suspected there was something more Sara had wanted to say after asking her to enlist again. And while Marion was fine letting her curiosity fade and die out like the last embers of a fire, she knew Sara wouldn't leave until she said what she'd come to say. Until she had once more intervened.

It came as no surprise that foot-shaped shadows lingered in the space beneath her door. Marion grumbled, "Just come in and say it so you can leave."

The door slowly creaked open. Sara perched herself at the foot of the bed. Feeling old beyond her years, Marion shifted to lean against her headboard.

"Go on, spit it out."

Sara inhaled and brushed hair from her face. It pulled Marion's attention to Sara's scar.

Sara said quietly, "The Germans are already on French soil. Jonathan is there." Sara spoke of her husband, whom Marion had never met. All Marion knew of him was his last name, the same as Sara's maternal name, leaving Sara a Brown even after they wed.

Sara leaned closer. "They'll be coming for our island next."

Marion cringed internally. *France.* On the outside she remained stoic. Yet Marion felt nothing but unsteady, as if she were back on the battlefield, the earth shaking beneath her. And she couldn't help it. Anger rose in Marion that Sara would leave her children and run off to another war. What if her husband didn't return? What if Sara didn't? Marion couldn't remember the ages of Sara's children, let alone their names, but they couldn't yet be double digits.

Marion uttered, "Go home to the children you are fortunate enough to have. They are already without a father." She wished for the sentence to sound hard-bitten, but her resurfaced memories infused a forlornness into her already deep-toned voice.

Sara insisted, "I must go back to the Wrens. You more than anyone understand duty. None of this is easy for me."

"It never is," Marion said, deadpan.

"I don't *want* to bring you into another war. I haven't forgiven myself for what happened in the first one."

Good, Marion thought. She hadn't forgiven Sara either. "Yet trying to bring me into a war is exactly what you are here to do."

Sara sighed. "You were one of the best. Your presence could be of great value."

Marion shook her head. She wondered if Sara had been sent to ask her to return or if she'd come on her own accord. Most likely the latter, considering the circumstances of her leaving the Wrens.

"It's not only about the war. You should return for another reason too, Mare."

Mare.

There'd only been two people on the face of the earth who had called Marion by that name. For that reason she was willing to hear Sara out. "What reason?"

"Poppy."

Sara dangled the name, barely more than a whisper. Just that one singular word.

"Why?" Marion said, emotion in her voice. Her body took on so much weight she felt pinned to the bed. "Why would you mention her to me?"

Sara tried to edge closer, but Marion raised a shaky hand to stop her.

"I don't want to hurt you any more than I have, Mare. But . . ." Sara stopped. She pressed her lips together. Then she began again. "But I think I met her. No, I'm positive it was her. I wouldn't be telling you otherwise."

Marion closed her eyes, but Sara's words kept coming, relentless, little slices of a knife. "I volunteered at the Labor Exchange. A girl came in, eager to sign up. She looked so much like . . ." Sara trailed off again. "Her last name was Fairchild."

Marion shook her head, eyes still closed. "That's it? Because the girl shares the same last name as the family who adopted our Poppy? It's a common name. And it could be her married name, for Pete's sake."

"She's not married. She has no children. And her birth date, Marion. It's the same. And she was hell-bent on being a motorcycle dispatch rider, as if it's in her blood. It can't all be a coincidence."

Marion shuddered a breath.

No. No, it couldn't.

The same surname. The same birth date.

"What is the child's first name? I'm assuming they named her as they wanted."

"Evelyn."

Marion repeated the name aloud in her deep voice; it sounded foreign, unfamiliar. This child wasn't their Poppy. She was someone's Evelyn. She wasn't even a child. She'd be twenty-one now, older than Eddie was when he died.

What a strange thought . . . thinking about time. Wasn't it supposed to heal all wounds?

Who had said it?

Certainly a fool. Probably a poet.

Well, that felt unnecessarily cruel. Marion liked poetry. She enjoyed literature of any kind. She was only feeling sorry for herself.

"But," Sara continued, yanking Marion from her digressive thoughts, "Evelyn also listed a middle initial of *P*."

Marion felt a rise in emotion. She swallowed roughly. That middle initial felt less incidental and more purposeful. Marion had referred to the baby as Poppy in front of the Fairchilds. Could they have honored Marion? Did Evelyn know from where the name could have originated? Or rather, from whom it originated?

Marion shook her head. Evelyn couldn't know, she reconciled. The Fairchilds were insistent the child never know she was adopted.

"She's tall, thin," Sara said, letting a twinge of excitement creep into her voice. "Her hair is auburn, the perfect combination of you and . . ."

"Eddie," Marion whispered. She averted her gaze to the rolling hills outside the window. The hills that reminded her so much of France. Now there was another war, and Evelyn was to be a part of it as a Wren. Of all the services, a Wren.

Sara squeezed Marion's leg beneath her bedsheets and stood. "I'll go, now that you know about Poppy. I'll be going to London, and I hope you'll consider joining the Wrens again too. We need someone with experience to lead the new riders. I have to imagine leading a group of women will be marginally easier than managing hundreds of birds."

Sara tried for a smile, and for a moment Marion almost returned it. Following the call to enlist . . . being a daughter of the Wrens . . . training her birds . . . being on her motorbike . . . It had given Marion life. The purpose, the satisfaction had been greater than the dangers of the war when it'd been only Marion's life at stake.

It'd been a long time since Marion felt like she was living.

But to leave her home? To once again enter a war? To have the opportunity to meet her Poppy and risk caring for someone else again?

Sara's smile morphed into a twist of her lips, then a sigh. "I know we both have many regrets from before. Hard choices had to be made. But I really think it could be good for you, *Wren Smith*."

Sara began to leave. She made it all of two steps before Marion blurted out, "I'll go."

Marion had entered the other war as Wren Hoxton, but she hadn't had the opportunity to finish it as Wren Smith. This could be her second chance to honor Eddie in that way. He had followed her into a war, and now she'd follow their child, the last piece of Eddie she had left. And this time she wouldn't fail at keeping what she held dearest safe.

CHAPTER 28

EVELYN

August 1940
London

The woman who stood before Evelyn was diminutive in size and nature. Her uniform was pristine, her posture stiff. Evelyn noted how the new petty officer didn't wear a wedding band but was well past the age when society usually called for marriage. Did she elect not to get married? Was she so different from Evelyn, unsure if she ever wanted to take on the weight of being a wife? Or was she widowed and simply no longer wore a ring? Mysteries for another day.

Wren Philips had introduced the woman as Wren Smith. Since then, Wren Smith hadn't made a peep, and her eyes remained trained on a dirtied chewing gum spot only inches in front of the black leather shoes of Evelyn and the other girls.

The silence and idleness gave Evelyn the fidgets, and she readjusted her feet, causing Wren Smith's gaze to jump to Evelyn. Just as quickly, Wren Smith's attention returned to the pavement, and Evelyn cursed herself for becoming restless.

She'd officially become a Wren two weeks prior. Since then, she'd completed two weeks of motorcycle training, improving her riding skills along with ensuring she could care for her bike. Things such as checking oil and tire pressure, changing flats, repairing and replacing chains. This morning she'd arrived at her new home in Notting Hill, part of a block of flats they referred to as their Wrennery.

Now there Evelyn stood, in a queue of newly trained dispatch riders outside a brick office building in Victoria. Behind the girls, their motorcycles were also neatly lined.

In her peripheral vision Evelyn saw Rose mouth something, but she couldn't make it out, and she gave a small shrug in return. She'd ask her later. She was glad she'd have the chance. Despite their friendship's rocky beginnings, they'd grown close during training, the two of them rising to the top of their recruitment class. Theresa was a close third. She, however, had been sent overseas to a secret location, one where her family could only contact her through a PO Box address.

At least other girls had family who wanted to do such things. This time, Evelyn hadn't bothered to write her parents of her new location. She had a sneaking suspicion Percy was doing so on her behalf. She had a mind to ask him and *almost* did when they'd gone to see *Ask a Policeman* the weekend prior, but she hadn't wanted to spoil their fun.

The film was a true comic gem, with hilarious one-line gags. The film just wasn't . . . romantic.

Evelyn and Percy laughed, they bantered, there'd been subtle glances—ones Evelyn hoped were cast with similar intentions—but the night ended with a chaste kiss on her cheek and a cordial *"We should do this again soon."*

It was the type of thing she'd say to anyone, with the exception of her dentist.

But Percy Harrington shouldn't be stealing her thoughts. They should be steadfast on the woman before her. However, that'd be significantly easier if Wren Smith would actually address them. Could the idleness be an extraneous part of their training? A test of their composure?

Challenge accepted.

It wouldn't be her first. The rider training at the academy had been daunting yet exhilarating. Racing an automobile at the Brooklands involved circling a relatively flat track, save for the incline at each bend. But the hills and obstacles of the motorbike training had been a thrill. So had mastering the inner workings of her motorbike. It was something Evelyn's father would've enjoyed hearing about, a thought she let the wind whip away. Why let regret bog her down when she was soaring forward at seventy miles per hour?

Evelyn ached to receive her first assignment. The office building they'd work out of was designated for combined ops, where various services would be working together. A mixture of pride and elation had filled her earlier when she'd signed Evelyn P. Fairchild on the Official Secrets Act and as she imagined the covert information she'd be carrying on her shoulders.

If only Wren Smith would give her an assignment.

Evelyn remained poised.

Her arm throbbed with a dull pain, the result of various inoculations. Evelyn, Rose, and a few of the other girls wore red ribbons on their jackets to signal their arms were quite sore. But she was thankful for the science that would protect her, and she wasn't going to let a little discomfort stand in her way.

Finally Wren Smith's chest rose with what Evelyn guessed to be a fortifying breath, and then Wren Smith lifted her chin. Her eyes passed from girl to girl, lingering on Evelyn longer than the rest. It'd been enough to give her the fidgets again, which, of course, Wren Smith noticed. Drat.

The woman was diminutive in size and nature, Evelyn thought

again, but hawkeyed. And her voice deep toned. Evelyn hadn't been expecting a baritone from Wren Smith, but there it was when she said, "Hello."

The word hung in the air for a moment, and Evelyn suspected the woman would be short with commands, until she began again, saying, "I will be honest that it is not easy to stand before you. I have been at war before. I have been a Wren. With it came great loss and many emotions, one of which was great pride. I was once told that being a Wren means you are part of a sisterhood. And you'll remain as such even after we end this war. And end it we will, hopefully before anyone else we love comes to harm." Wren Smith exhaled slowly. "This is new for me. I don't have a lot of experience leading a group of women. I worked with pigeons last time, and they never stopped moving or making a commotion. I hope you'll all follow directions more sharply."

Evelyn smiled, and Wren Smith's breath hitched. "We'll . . . we'll begin by practicing our routes and gaining a familiarity with the streets. I want you so familiar you'd be able to complete the stunt with your eyes closed."

Evelyn nodded. She wanted to shout, *So let's begin then!* but her patience had grown from the girl who impulsively showed up at the Labor Exchange office a few months prior. To think she'd already accomplished so much in such a short amount of time.

Still, she felt like she was only just beginning. Evelyn could feel her heart pounding in anticipation, so similar to before a race, as Wren Smith began calling out names and assigning routes to rehearse. Rose would practice driving to a place called Bletchley Park, some fifty miles north. The other girls had longer routes to Dover, Portsmouth, and even Plymouth. Some had shorter ones to locations along the River Thames and other spots within London where the Admiralty, command posts, and embassies were located.

And while they were only honing their routes at this point, Evelyn was ready for the challenge of her first real stunt. The responsibility would be hers to deliver critical messages: Important supply-chain information. Classified battle memos. Letters between generals, embassies, and the Admiralty. She could make a real difference.

At long last, Wren Smith focused her attention on Evelyn, the woman's gaze passing over her red ribbon, and called Evelyn's name.

"I'd like you to practice the route to the Baker Street offices."

"Yes, ma'am," Evelyn said, keeping her back ramrod straight, despite the fact it made her tower over her petty officer. She accepted the paper with the drawn path, and Evelyn's heart all but sank.

Rose would be driving for over an hour, but Evelyn guessed her route would take all of ten minutes. Fifteen, tops.

"If your route is of a shorter distance," Wren Smith told them, "please repeat the route for the duration of the afternoon. You'll have the advantage of knowing the roads thoroughly. I'll be driving around, too, with a watchful eye."

At that, they were dismissed. The girls began putting on helmets, fastening their goggles, tightening their laces, studying their maps, walking toward their motorcycles.

Evelyn made a beeline toward Rose, who was already swinging a leg over her machine. "Care to switch?"

Rose laughed. "Not a chance. Better get a move on. Your route looks daunting."

"Very funny."

Engines started. Girls began to peel off. Wren Smith stood watching. With a sigh, Evelyn began.

Within seconds, the sigh was forgotten and replaced with a smile. She couldn't help it. This was how she would spend her days? Evelyn could pinch herself. She no longer felt displaced. She was a Wren, with a duty and a purpose.

Even if that current purpose consisted of completing a route that had exactly four turns. Evelyn allowed everything else to fall away except the task at hand. Her mind narrowed. She was in the zone, focused on nothing else until she was outside 64 Baker Street, where she eyed the stone six-story building. Satisfied she'd made it, Evelyn circled her bike around and drove the four turns back. She circled around again.

Evelyn already could do this with her eyes closed.

As she was approaching the Baker Street location a third time, a man was exiting. A man who looked startlingly like Percy. It couldn't be. Could it? Evelyn wasn't near his clinic or his townhome. And he didn't make house calls. Except for her— a thought that made her smile. Yet here was a man with the same dark features, the same tall build.

It *was* Percy. She'd bet her bottom dollar it was him. What on earth was he doing at this very building, where she'd soon be delivering covert war information?

That man had some explaining to do.

CHAPTER 29

MARION

August 1940
London

M arion felt comically like an operative, keeping an inconspicuous distance as she trailed Evelyn. She told herself she would keep a watchful eye on all the girls assigned to the routes in London and not focus her attention solely on Evelyn's movements.

She'd also told herself she wouldn't become wordless while standing in front of her new unit.

She now knew she needed to give herself grace.

On a motorcycle, she followed Evelyn. Her riding skills were rusty. But within minutes, it all came back to her, and the same exhilaration and alarm she first felt as a young woman filled her once more. If only panic didn't dampen the emotions, her heart palpating at the speed Evelyn took rounding a corner. Visions danced before her eyes of when Marion herself had lost control and fallen off her bike. Fortunately, there weren't many turns on the shorter route Marion had assigned to her daughter.

Her daughter.

Being able to see and touch her daughter would overwhelm Marion if she allowed her mind to dwell on it. Before her introductions, she had watched from inside the office building as the girls arrived and gathered outside. She'd taken in her daughter's appearance from a distance, examining her every feature and movement.

Marion owed it all to Sara, she admitted, something that went a long way in bridging the divide that had existed between the two women for the past two decades. And when Sara slipped an arm through Marion's as they stood in front of the window, Marion hadn't pulled away.

A sisterhood, that was what they were. Sara hadn't forgotten it, even if Marion had. But being back in uniform, being among other Wrens, had filled Marion with a warmth she hadn't expected and that she hadn't allowed herself to feel.

Since Eddie, Marion had felt so little.

But he'd want her to feel, and lately she'd been experiencing many emotions, especially when it came to their Poppy.

Marion had shamelessly pored over Evelyn's application and her medical reports during the downtime of her own officer training. The mention of a corrected clubfoot had sent Marion into an emotional spiral and to a library. She pored over literature to learn about the condition, the knot in her stomach growing tighter and heavier at how pediatric clubfoot was potentially both genetic and environmental. Had the birth defect run in Marion's family? In Eddie's? Neither knew anything about their family history. Or perhaps the position in which Marion had carried Evelyn within her womb had affected their daughter?

How was Marion to know? She'd felt physically sick to think Evelyn began her life in such a manner. And suddenly it had made sense, the comment the nurse had made to Marion only minutes after she had woken from her twilight sleep.

"They have decided to continue with the adoption."

The Fairchilds hadn't been expecting a child with a birth defect. They easily could've changed their minds. And where would that have left Evelyn? Marion hadn't been fit to be a mother; she'd been too broken, and she wouldn't have had the means to see to the care that Evelyn needed.

But the Fairchilds had embraced her. They had given Evelyn the extensive care she needed, no doubt with the finest London doctors and surgeons. They had given Evelyn their name. Fairchild was a strong name, one with generations of success attached to it. It would take her a lot further than Smith or Hoxton. It already had.

And Evelyn Fairchild had grown up beautifully.

She was beautiful.

Her auburn hair, the wave to it, her milky skin, the smattering of freckles across her nose, her height and slim figure . . . it all reminded Marion so much of Eddie. Not to mention Evelyn's eyes. Marion had envisioned her countless times, contributing little of herself to Poppy's possible characteristics but much of Eddie, beginning with his green eyes. Eyes she'd once likened as a child to the Loch Ness Monster. How silly. Yet there Evelyn was, the spitting image of her father.

While watching from the window, Marion had needed to sit. She pressed a hand to the yellowed adoption document she always kept pocketed. To this day, she'd never spoken of Evelyn's birth. Doing so, revealing her secret, was a punishable offense. But more so, Marion wouldn't dare open Pandora's box on Evelyn's life. Or even on her own.

Marion had shared all of herself with Eddie, only for him to be ripped away. She'd let Sara into her life, only to feel betrayed. The idea of making herself vulnerable to losing Evelyn again was too much.

Sara rubbed her back, both a comforting and an unsettling reminder that returning to the Wrens with her was a step toward allowing Sara back in. *"Still our secret, Mare. If it helps, think of yourself as a mother figure to all the girls, not only to Evelyn."*

A mother figure. Could she be such a thing? Marion had little in the way of an example of such a role, having relied mostly on her books. She recalled that Jane Eyre had various mother figures—first Bessie, then Miss Temple. Jane later went on to have a maternal influence over Adèle. She shared her skills with Adèle. She showed Adèle compassion. Could Marion do that for these young women?

Sara had said gently, *"The girls are waiting. Remember your breaths. Talk when you're ready. You'll do wonderfully."*

Once Marion stood in front of the girls, it hadn't begun wonderfully. The many pairs of eyes on her had taken her back to childhood, and her ability to speak was initially lost to her. Eventually she'd been able to settle herself and find her voice.

She hadn't expected to talk as much as she had. She thought she'd say hello and dispense assignments. But Marion found herself caught up in the nostalgia of being a Wren again. She even allowed herself a moment of joy, making a joke. And when Evelyn smiled, Marion's heart was squeezed and air rushed from her lungs. It was as if Eddie had been smiling at her.

What a gift it'd been.

What a gift it still was to be close to their daughter in this way, even if Marion could only ever be Wren Smith to Evelyn.

Now she watched and followed unobserved as Evelyn drove a third time toward the Baker Street offices. Evelyn really was quite comfortable on a motorcycle. The notes regarding her training had mentioned she was at the top of her class. Marion imagined Eddie's pride but also his fear that their daughter would also experience a war against Germany. She suspected official stunts would begin any day, even any minute or hour.

Yesterday the Battle of Britain shifted. The Germans had been focusing their attacks within the Channel. But the raids had moved inland along the coast. Manston, Lympne, and Hawkinge. Their aerodromes had all been targeted. And in Kent and Sussex, and on the Isle of Wight, radar installations had been wrecked.

The circulated intel said that all the airfields were serviceable again, and most radar stations had been mended and were now back on-air, but Marion shivered at the thought of the Germans creeping closer and wreaking such havoc. She knew it was only a matter of time before Hitler set his sights on London. History was too keen on repeating itself, a notion Marion knew wouldn't allow her to sleep at night, vowing to keep Evelyn safe, no matter the cost.

Marion slowed, matching Evelyn's deceleration. She'd be circling again, dutifully following orders and returning to their headquarters.

But then Evelyn planted her feet. She called out something, a name perhaps, and a dark-haired man responded. He went still, cupping a hand over his eyes, his expression one of great surprise. But then a smile not only formed, it took over his face, punctuated by two perfectly symmetrical dimples. Evelyn remained on her bike, and he leaned forward to kiss her cheek in a friendly greeting.

Who was this man? He didn't wear a uniform, but he wouldn't. He'd come out of the offices where Marion knew a secret operation was stationed. As with the first war, Marion was only told what she needed to know. So how was Evelyn familiar with him, because clearly he knew her and was quite pleased to see her?

A protectiveness swept over Marion. *Oh, Eddie, what are we in for?*

She watched Evelyn animatedly talk to the man, unable to see more than her back. What she'd give to be a little birdie privy to their conversation; the distance was too great, and their engines were too loud to hear anything that passed between Evelyn and the man . . . who'd just spotted Marion.

She startled at the man's fixed gaze on her.

Quickly Marion yanked her handlebars in a new direction. She was about to lift her feet when she saw the man bring Evelyn's focus to her.

Evelyn startled much like Marion had before quickly facing the man again. Marion was inclined to flee, having been caught lurking. But then Evelyn turned off her bike, kicked her prop stand into place, and began walking slowly toward Marion, her goggles hanging loosely around her neck.

Marion's heart beat wildly. She reminded herself she was of higher rank and had done nothing untoward. In fact, Marion had even communicated to the girls that she'd be driving about to keep a watchful eye.

However, in that moment Marion felt more like a spying mother than a supervising petty officer. In all the uncomfortable situations she'd been in, and there had been many, she felt completely at a loss for how to handle herself.

"Wren Smith," Evelyn began, stopping only steps away. At Marion's ranking, Evelyn wasn't required to salute, and she held her arms stiff at her sides.

"Wren Fairchild," Marion replied and quieted her own engine so they could more easily converse. With any other Wren in her unit, Marion would've been inclined to let the girl talk first, to which Marion would've replied that the infraction was barely even an infraction. Not to worry. To carry on. But Marion couldn't help the question that fell from her mouth. "Who was that you were speaking with?"

"I'm sorry for deviating from orders. I only planned to stop for a moment. I was surprised to see someone I know."

Marion slowly bobbed her head. She knew so little of Evelyn's life, only privy to what was in her application: where she was from; that she was unmarried and without children; that she had never been arrested. The last one a relief, to be sure.

But her family life? Her friends? Her hobbies? What—or who—made her laugh? It was all a twenty-one-year-old mystery she craved to unravel. She asked, "A friend?"

"Yes, ma'am. A family friend."

"I understand," Marion said, but the response only sparked more unknowns about how Evelyn spent her leisure time, and if she spent a lot of it with that particular man. He currently walked slowly down the pavement, discreetly looking back every few steps. Did he care about Evelyn? The swarming questions in Marion's mind resulted in a prolonged silence between them.

"He's a doctor," Evelyn said, perhaps feeling the need to fill the awkward quiet, "so I hadn't been expecting to see him . . ."

At the mention of a doctor, Marion's gaze instinctively fell to Evelyn's foot. She caught herself too late, and when her eyes met Evelyn's again, the girl's lip was between her teeth, uncomfortable or perhaps frustrated. Her hands had balled into loose fists at her sides as well. In a soft yet determined voice Evelyn said, "I passed the physical exams like everyone else."

Marion was so overcome with emotion that she hid behind a stoic expression, well trained from her own past. Had Evelyn spent her whole life explaining or cloaking—or perhaps contending with another action Marion couldn't comprehend because she never experienced it firsthand?

"I apologize," Marion said in a cracked voice. "I saw in your medical history you suffered from a birth de—" She stopped, the term *defect* feeling insensitive and cold. Evelyn had been an innocent child, a baby, who had no say in how she was born or who she was born to. It felt all too similar. Evelyn's clubfoot didn't make her inferior, just like Marion's selective mutism didn't make her deficient. She felt compelled to try again, feeling that she needed to fill another awkward gap she'd created, but her words came out clumsily. "I saw that your treatments were extensive." Marion quickly added, "But successful."

Evelyn swallowed roughly. "Yes, I had my last surgery when I was sixteen."

"So much of your life." Marion hadn't meant to say it aloud, but her inhibitions had been exhausted.

Evelyn stood like a statue. Marion hated herself for the trajectory of the conversation. How had she managed to bungle nearly every moment of it? Yet Marion had let her tongue run free. How ironic. She tightened her grip on the handlebars. "I'll let you carry on, then."

"Yes, ma'am," Evelyn said, and she all but fled from Marion.

CHAPTER 30

EVELYN

August 1940
London

Tears welled in Evelyn's eyes. Splendid, she'd fog her goggles, and for what reason? She wasn't entirely sure why she felt on the verge of crying. Perhaps it was because the exchange with Wren Smith felt personal. Too personal.

An inquisition.

And one Evelyn didn't feel she deserved.

She'd spoken with Percy for less than a minute. Her engine had remained on. She hadn't even gotten off her bike!

Evelyn sighed, gripping her handlebars too tightly. Still, it wasn't the impression she had wanted to make on her first day, nor was that the first real interaction she wanted to have with her superior.

She sighed again, trying to push the awfulness of it all out of her mind. What she wanted to think about was Percy.

Percy!

That sly fox.

He'd sure gobsmacked her.

Before, she had questioned him about the war, asking him if he'd enlist. He'd said, *"If I'm required."*

What he should've said was, *I already joined up, Evie. But it's all very clandestine.*

What's more, he shouldn't have made Evelyn feel bad for sneaking off to London without telling her parents when he'd done worse. He'd snuck off *and* still hadn't told his parents a thing.

When Evelyn had pressed and pushed and implored him to tell what group or service he was in as they stood on the street, Percy folded and responded coyly, "*We call ourselves the Baker Street Irregulars.*"

Evelyn wasn't upset at his deception. If anything, she felt even more of a kinship with Percy. His parents thought his work as a doctor exempted him from the war, which it did, but little did they know what he was really up to.

Oh, he was sly, all right.

And crafty.

And roguish.

And the way his face lit up when he saw her. He could've kept his caper going, but he hadn't. He had been willing to break the rules and confide in her, as if he wanted to impress her, like he had as children and now even as adults. As if he fully trusted her.

Evelyn approached her headquarters; her intrigue with Percy had eclipsed her irritation with Wren Smith. Without delay she began another loop of her route.

The next day, however, it was hopeless to keep her irritation at bay. Wren Smith assigned new routes, and it took an immense amount of patience for Evelyn not to question why she was once again given a shorter route. Shorter even than the distance to Baker Street. Evelyn was certain it was the shortest route of any of the girls.

She no longer wore a red ribbon from her inoculation, so it

couldn't be because of that. Besides, Rose had worn one, too, when her arm had been sore, and her route had been one of the longer ones.

Could it be an unspoken punishment for yesterday? Or maybe Wren Smith didn't believe in her talents as a rider.

What hogwash.

Evelyn felt like she'd been proving herself since the first hours of her life. Proving her body could work like any other's. Proving her independence. Proving her worth. Proving her abilities.

And hadn't she proven herself to Wren Philips, Wren Monroe, and even won over Rose, who likely was the biggest naysayer of them all?

"It's still an important route, no?" Rose had said after they'd been given their assignments. Her words betrayed the cringe on her face, even as Rose added, *"It's Mr. Churchill's current residence, I believe."*

Sure, Admiralty House wasn't a destination at which to turn up one's nose, and Evelyn knew the route would be used frequently, with Mr. Churchill being such an important figure. But Evelyn still couldn't shake the feeling that Wren Smith purposely gave Evelyn the shortest route again, though she tried to convince herself Wren Smith was simply alternating who did each route, picking from a hat, perhaps.

"My route is in London today," Rose pointed out.

That was true.

But then that evening Wren Smith stood before them, her tricorn hat firmly on her head, and announced the first real stunt.

It was given to Rose, who ended training with an identical score to Evelyn's.

Irked and frustrated, Evelyn watched Rose switch her cap for her helmet, mount her motorbike, and leave, a satchel slung over her shoulder. Evelyn and the other girls were dismissed back to the Wrennery, curfew set to begin immediately following dinner.

Evelyn barely tasted her food. In the cabin she shared with Rose, she studied the route maps and city map, her finger slowly rubbing beneath her nose in an attempt to concentrate. But it was of no use. She'd rather brood about not being selected to complete the stunt. Why Rose? They'd both been top of their class.

God bless Percy. Her thoughts once more shifted to him and away from feeling sorry for herself. There was more she wanted to ask him: How long ago had he joined up? What role did he play in the war? Was this how he had known so much about the war and the Wrens? Evelyn *had* wondered.

But she was tired of wondering, and she didn't know when she'd see him again. She'd snuck out before—from a guarded academy, no less—and their Wrennery was just a block of flats. This time she wouldn't be caught.

She quickly changed from her uniform and tiptoed across the parquet floors, her low heels dangling from her fingertips, and down the shared hallway. She was outside in the spitting rain in no time, balancing on one foot, then the other, to put on her shoes. She'd nip straight there on the tube, the underground entrance nearly at Percy's doorstep.

⁂

"Evie?" he proclaimed upon opening the door. "What a surprise."

It was what he'd said the last time she showed up unannounced. But this time he didn't hesitate to invite her in. His townhome was exactly as she remembered it, exactly as his mother had decorated it, heavy with floral prints and nature-inspired decor.

"I like what you've done with the place," she poked.

He smiled, running a hand through his hair. "I've been busy."

Evelyn perched herself on the arm of the sofa. "You don't say. I hope you've turned over all your pots and pans."

"That I had time for." A snifter of scotch already sat on the side table. "Can I offer you a drink?"

"Oh, but, Percy, I'm a lady."

Her comment brought out a dimple. "How could I forget?"

"But best top off yours. This lady is dying to uncover all your secrets. I barely got anything out of you before you caught Wren Smith spying on me. You'd think she was the one in a secret organization."

Percy snorted and sank into a wing-back armchair, gesturing for her to become more comfortable on the sofa. She did. But she'd be even more comfortable with him beside her. That kind of thinking was still so novel to her. How was it that she was falling for Percy J. Harrington? She almost didn't want to for the sole reason of not giving her mother what she wanted.

Percy sipped from his snifter.

Internally, she snorted. He was ever the proper, wealthy doctor, safe from conscription. Yet there he was, volunteering to put his life in jeopardy. "Tell me, how long have you been with these Baker Street Boys?"

"Baker Street Irregulars."

Evelyn cocked her head. "The alliteration works better, no?"

One of his eyebrows rose higher than the other. "You beguile me, Evie."

She'd seen this expression before but never known it was one of beguilement. The word *beguile* itself could be translated in different ways. She wasn't trying to hoodwink him. But enchant him? Maybe she *was* hoping to do that.

"We became official only last month, a directive from Mr. Churchill. Prior, I worked underground with the army. I still attend to my clinic, a splendid cover for my Baker Street work."

"If your mother only knew."

"Without a doubt, I'd be cut off just like you."

Evelyn laughed. She felt herself leaning forward on the sofa. But then she remembered the need to ask him about his allegiances. "I don't mean this as an accusation, but merely a curiosity."

Percy held up a finger, took a gulp of his scotch.

She shook her head, amused. "You've been in continued contact with them, haven't you?"

"Your parents?"

Evelyn nodded.

He snorted. "It appears my undercover skills could use some spiffing up. Are you very upset?"

"Relieved," she said, realizing she actually was. "I suppose I've derailed everything my mother had planned for me. Finishing school and marrying are quite different from delivering messages in a potential war zone. I'm glad to know she truly hasn't given up on me."

"She'll come around," Percy said.

"Until she does, I suppose that means you're stuck with me." Her eyes scrunched. "I must ask, though, did you tell them about our outing to the cinema?"

He snorted again. "I most certainly did not. They'd be on us like wolves." Percy paused then, his gaze averting, before he said, "Evie, there is something I must tell you."

"Uh-oh, this sounds serious."

"Yes, well—"

A siren began to wail. The red warning. An attack was in progress or imminent.

Evelyn jumped to her feet, needing to steady herself on the arm of the chair. Percy reached for her, already moving toward the door. "The tube is the closest shelter," he said over the deafening noise.

He held her hand, leading her down his stoop and into the throngs of other people pouring onto the pavement and street.

CHAPTER 31

MARION

August 1940
London

The siren felt like it was all around her, the signal rising and falling. Marion looked to the ceiling of her flat, then stood so hastily her chair upturned. Sara stood quickly, too, their game of chess forgotten.

The Royal Observer Corps had caught enemy aircrafts on their radar.

"Let's go," Sara said, as if it actually needed to be said.

"Wait," Marion called out. She rushed across the room and returned with 486 within his birdcage. Together the women hurried from their shared flat. In the dimly lit halls Marion spotted girls from her unit. "Hurry," she said, the siren swallowing her words.

The Germans were on their way. But to London? Intelligence implied London wasn't supposed to be a target unless the orders came from the Luftwaffe chief himself, from instruction direct from Adolf Hitler.

Had those orders come? Could a bomb come crashing through the roof at any second? It'd set the building ablaze. It'd knock down walls, entrapping them. It'd take their lives.

Making his discontent known, 486 fluttered his wings, his left wing lifting at an odd angle.

"Shh, it's okay. Good boy," Marion spoke softly. "You'll be okay. I'll make sure you're okay."

She'd do the same for Evelyn. As the red warning screamed around her, Marion searched for her daughter's face among the other men and women funneling down the staircase toward the bomb shelter. Marion saw Evelyn's roommate on a lower flight of stairs, but Evelyn wasn't with Wren McMasters.

Marion continued outside into the darkness and to the adjacent alley, where their bomb shelter was located. The brick structure, half set into the ground, was their designated air-raid location.

It was where Evelyn should be. But Marion didn't see her inside the shelter either. She walked the entire length of it, nearly one hundred feet, passing each crude hanging light, and noted each ashen face on the two rows of seats.

Panic clawed at Marion. She approached Wren McMasters, demanding, "Where is Evelyn?"

Unblinking, she waited for a response.

"I don't know, Wren Smith," Wren McMasters answered. She paused as if not wanting to reveal what she said next. "She wasn't in our cabin when I returned."

So where was she?

It was beyond curfew. Where could she be? Marion twisted her hands together. A heat rose in her body. The sirens continued to wail.

CHAPTER 32

EVELYN

August 1940
London

The all clear finally sounded.

Evelyn's knee had bounced the entire time she and Percy had been in the underground. It bounced while he navigated his Frazer Nash sports car through the darkened streets to bring Evelyn back to the Wrennery.

"Good luck," he said, squeezing her hand.

She'd need it. There was no way Wren Smith hadn't noticed her absence with her hawk eyes. Evelyn would go straight to her petty officer's flat and face her fate. She'd fall on Wren Smith's mercy. She'd pray that Wren Smith would allow her to remain as a Wren.

If she didn't, where would Evelyn go? What would she do to support herself?

But even more important, what could she do that would give her the same level of fulfillment?

She cursed herself for breaking the rules. She'd impulsively, and she'd admit obstinately, run off to see Percy—on a night when the sirens sounded, no less.

Fortunately, the German planes never came.

Percy had stated in an indifferent tone that the sirens had likely been a false alarm, but his demeanor suggested otherwise. While they cowered in the tube, he'd been nervous, his own knee bobbing, and Evelyn suspected his words were spoken to calm anyone within earshot. It was why she hadn't asked him how close he thought the Germans actually came to London.

As she pulled open the door to her building, she also realized she never asked him what he had started to tell her. Not *wanted* to tell her, which could have been something lovely, like *I wanted to tell you that you look smashing this evening.* But no, Percy had said he *must* tell her something.

She rolled her shoulders, tension collecting between her blades, and opened the door to her building before passing through the still-dark lobby and through another door. It wasn't until then she experienced any type of light.

Wren Smith's flat was on the third floor. She hesitated, then knocked, half hoping her superior wouldn't answer and she could slink off to bed.

Evelyn wasn't that lucky. Her heart pounded as Wren Smith appeared, still dressed in her uniform.

"Evelyn," the woman breathed, her hand twitching toward her. "Where have you been?"

"I came straightaway after the all clear," Evelyn said, hoping this small fact would sway Wren Smith toward charity. The woman's lips were pressed together in a stern line, yet worry lines stretched across her forehead. Evelyn tried for honesty, explaining herself.

To which Wren Smith recapped, "You skirted curfew to meet up with the gentleman from yesterday?"

Behind Wren Smith, Evelyn noticed Wren Brown at a table, the radio on at a low volume.

"Yes, ma'am. And I greatly understand it was wrong of me. I will accept whatever punishment you feel is fair." Evelyn squeezed one hand into the other. "For what it's worth, I will do anything to remain a Wren."

Wren Smith didn't respond. She didn't move. She stood there, perfectly poised in her double-breasted jacket, white poplin shirt, black tie, navy skirt, black stockings, and black leather shoes, and stared at Evelyn, the moment making Evelyn's neck prick with heat. Again, it felt too intimate.

Finally, Wren Smith said, "Report in the morning."

Evelyn repeated "Thank you" no short of three times before she began down the hallway and toward the stairs.

Rose was in her cabin when Evelyn burst into the room, giddy with relief.

"There you are!" Rose put down the issue of *Picturegoer* she'd been reading. "Wren Smith asked me where you were. I told her I didn't know, but she stared at me so intensely I gave up the fact you hadn't been here. I'm sorry."

"It's okay," Evelyn said, slumping down next to Rose on the couch. "I told her the truth of it all."

"Which is?"

"I visited Percy. But I'll have you know, if you were home, I likely wouldn't have gone and broken curfew, so this is partly your fault."

"You are too much."

Evelyn smiled. "I am joking, of course. Somehow I think I'm in the clear with Wren Smith." She sighed. "Though I wager I'll be assigned to even lesser tasks now."

"What? You expect special treatment?"

Rose said it facetiously, with no ill intent, and Evelyn felt the impulse to stick out her tongue at her friend. She knew it was a childish response, but she'd also missed out on such simple comebacks during her childhood. She'd never dream of doing such a thing to her mother. Even with Rose she refrained, mostly because her thoughts had already steered elsewhere. "It's peculiar," she began, "but I do feel like Wren Smith treats me differently. Beyond giving me the shortest routes because she thinks I'm incapable, I mean. It's hard to explain, and it's only been two days, but she always seems to have her eye on me. Of all of us she could've been watching on our first day, it had to be me she trailed? Why? I will say, the way she interacts with me, it feels too personal. And tonight, while I'm overjoyed she didn't kick me out, I *did* get off easy."

Rose shrugged and returned her attention to her magazine. "You should be counting your blessings."

"You're right," Evelyn conceded. "I'm being silly."

"Though," Rose said, a drum of her fingers on Greta Garbo's face, "now that I think back on it, when Wren Smith asked me where you were, she didn't call you Wren Fairchild. She said Evelyn. She hasn't called anyone else by their first name."

Evelyn's mouth parted. She absentmindedly rubbed a finger beneath her nose as her own brain thought back. "She called me Evelyn when she answered the door tonight."

"Maybe she does have an eye on you. Your very own Mother Wren."

"Stop." Evelyn groaned.

Rose laughed and teased, "Better be on your best behavior. I heard reprimands are given out for things as silly as a lost uniform cap."

"Dear me," Evelyn said. But then she thought, *Where on earth is my cap?*

CHAPTER 33

MARION

August 1940
London

M arion had told Evelyn to report in the morning. It was clear
Evelyn feared being dismissed from the Wrens.

Marion sat again with Sara at the table, the radio still playing at a
soft volume, and immediately began kneading one hand into the other.

"You know," Marion began, "training and tossing pigeons was a
great deal easier. They never spoke back. They followed instructions
a great deal better. Of course, they were fueled by food."

Sara laughed. "Perhaps you could try enticing Evelyn with a biscuit. It's what I do with my own children."

Marion smiled, then faltered. She knew almost nothing about
Sara's family. "Tell me about your children."

"Oh," Sara said, caught off guard. "Where to start? Helen, she's
ten now. All arms and legs, faster than all the boys. Henry is eight and
the spitting image of his father."

"You glow when you talk about them," Marion observed. "They
must miss you terribly."

"And I them. They think Jonathan and I are ancient; they couldn't
understand why we weren't too old to be in the war."

"I wish Evelyn was too young."

Sara rubbed her neck. "I'm sorry. I do too. Is this too difficult a topic?"

There was a time it would've been. Marion purposely never thought about Sara's family. Sara had sent her an invitation to her wedding. During her visits throughout the years, she had mentioned her children. But Marion had just as quickly extracted Sara's words from her head. She had been too bitter to retain any of Sara's happily ever after, after hers had been taken away.

"I'll be honest," Marion said. "I thought about reporting her."

Sara knew she meant Evelyn. She frowned. "You wouldn't do that."

"No," Marion said. "I couldn't."

If it had been any of the other girls, she likely would have. And the thought had quite temptingly crossed her mind to report Evelyn to their section leader. Her disciplinary discrepancies—both of them, the first occurring during Evelyn's probationary period—likely would have resulted in her demobilization from the Wrens. Evelyn would be free to return to Weybridge, which was listed as her residence on her application. Or better yet to Wiltshire, where Sara said she'd enlisted Evelyn. Marion suspected Evelyn had evacuated and had been staying with friends, as it was marked as a reception area and was definitely a safer location. It was where Sara's own children were.

But Marion couldn't report Evelyn with the purpose of having her removed. How could she when she'd warred with Eddie when he'd wanted to do the same thing to her? Though, if Marion was being honest, it wasn't the only reason she chose to look the other way regarding Evelyn's infractions. And it wasn't solely for Evelyn's happiness, though Evelyn was most likely joyful to remain.

Marion decided not to report Evelyn for purely selfish reasons.

Evelyn's leaving would've put an end to discovering what made Evelyn *Evelyn*, like how she rubbed a finger beneath her nose while deep in thought or how she balled her hands when frustrated or uncomfortable. Many others shared the mannerisms, no doubt, but Marion liked how Evelyn also tightened and wrung her hands when feeling uneasy.

Marion was doing it in that very moment.

"She reminds me of myself at times," Marion remarked aloud.

Sara looked up from the radio. "She has your eyes. Not the color of them, but the shape. Your long lashes too. I hadn't noticed at first because I saw so much of Eddie."

Sara's gaze dropped, Eddie's name seldom spoken between them. With Marion's return to the Wrens, their friendship had begun to knit itself together, but it felt delicate, with still so much left unsaid.

Marion touched the corner of her eye. She'd never thought of her eyes as having a shape. But she liked that her daughter shared it with her. "Thank you," she said. "I wouldn't have noticed such a resemblance. What I meant, though, is how we seem of like mind."

"Stubborn?" Sara said, humor in her voice.

Marion narrowed her eyes. "No."

Sara chuckled. "I know what you mean. I heard it, too, when Evelyn said she'd do anything to remain a Wren."

"Yes. That," Marion said. "And it terrifies me. Did I just make a mistake by not reporting her? If I hadn't been so fixated on being a Wren—"

"Mare, you need to stop punishing yourself."

It was a charitable thing to say. Sara easily could've said, *You need to stop punishing me.* Marion had been. She'd been punishing them both. Though perhaps Marion had begun to accept that Sara's actions hadn't been betrayals but what had been best for Marion at the time.

Evelyn's life was what it was because of Sara, after all. But Marion wasn't ready to forgive herself for all the little moments and decisions that culminated in Eddie's death.

Sara reached across the table, leaving her palm upturned for Marion's hand. Marion accepted her friend's kindness.

Kind was all Sara had ever been, and Marion had treated her horribly over the past two decades. "I'm sorry, Sare. I've blamed you for so long. I blamed you in part for Eddie's death, as one of the dominoes that brought him to France. And after France, I blamed you for having the life I should've been happily living. A marriage. Children. A family. But all of that anger was misplaced. It wasn't fair of me, and I know Eddie wasn't your fault. You had no way of knowing he'd finagle his way from the navy to the army. You didn't assign him to Amiens. You weren't even the one to tell him I was pregnant."

Sara's shoulders rose, then fell. "I told them about you being a widow, about Evelyn."

Marion sighed, the response meant for herself, not for Sara. "But you also told me to leave the war after you discovered I was pregnant. If I had listened, maybe things would've gone differently. With Eddie. With Evelyn." Marion shook her head. "I don't know. I'll never know. But I do know now that I made the right decision to give up Evelyn, which you put in motion, taking care of every piece of the adoption for me. It took coming here to see that. I mean, look at Evelyn. She's flourishing." Marion released a sharp breath. "She wouldn't have flourished with me. Not with the state I was in twenty years ago. Back then I felt so much anger and guilt, but I placed it all on you. I'm so sincerely sorry, Sare."

"You're human, Mare. You were grieving."

"I was horrid, and still you didn't give up on me. You kept coming to visit me. All those years."

Sara stretched out her arms and began flapping. "How could I ever give up on the girl who created the wren?"

Marion dropped her forehead into her hand. "That dance move. The dance itself. Your strangely logical tallest-tree metaphor. All of it." She met her friend's eyes. "You know you were my first real friend, besides Eddie, don't you?"

Sara nodded. "Mine too. Birds don't count. Sorry, 486."

Both women laughed. And for the first time in a long time, Marion felt lighter.

If only the feeling would've lasted.

From the radio, Marion's ears perked at the mention of Birmingham. It had suffered a heavy bombing.

Marion felt like the wind was knocked out of her. Birmingham may've been two hours northwest of London, but it was close in her heart: the location of St. Anne's, where Eddie first came into her life.

And now Hitler and his Luftwaffe aimed to batter it relentlessly. She felt a pull toward the city, to protect it in some way, though she didn't know how beyond continuing to lead the girls. Much to her dismay, the bombings continued in Birmingham every day, without fail.

What would be left of it?

The thought was crippling, but Marion couldn't focus solely on Birmingham. Over the next few days, much of England—the midlands, the south, the north—began to be bombed, the air raids targeting airfields and aircraft factories. To destroy Britain's air force and prepare for an invasion.

That was Marion's guess. It felt all too similar to the first time she'd gone to war. Before an attack hadn't the Germans relentlessly launched bombs over no-man's-land and into the British trenches, destroying the dugouts and incapacitating the Tommies?

The only blessing: she'd heard no whispers of London becoming a target. She prayed they'd never come. She prayed the attacks elsewhere would cease. But it wasn't so.

Throughout the following week, Marion's girls worked tirelessly to hand-deliver crucial messages. Her eight-hour shift during the day was followed by another at night that Sara oversaw. Marion did everything she could to limit Evelyn's involvement, but her hand was forced with the harefooted frequency at which intel was being exchanged and at which the girls were dispatched. Still, she kept Evelyn's routes confined to London, away from the midlands, the south, the north.

Evelyn's agitation with her assignments was visible in her exaggerated inhales and exhales. The terseness of her voice when she'd say, "Yes, ma'am." But Marion cared little for how her daughter reacted.

If she could, Marion wouldn't have sent any of her girls to the more harrowing locations. Already, Evelyn's bunkmate, Wren McMasters, was recovering at a base near Plymouth after cresting a hill and being struck head-on by a lorry that was evading an undetonated bomb. McMasters was launched through the windscreen but, thank the Lord, would recover. The account had almost cemented Marion's eyes shut. To think she gave the assignment. Marion had expected Evelyn to shrink at the news of her friend's injuries, but it only hardened Evelyn's resolve to take on more stunts.

"I'll go," Evelyn offered.

"I can go," she suggested another time.

"I will take it," she said of yet another dispatch.

Marion internally cursed her daughter's relentlessness. In some instances she was able to assign another girl. In others Marion had no official ground to deny Evelyn the stunt.

After nearly a week, the strikes lessened across England, both sides at a stalemate. Another day passed, then another, and another. The lull allowed the British forces to regroup and reestablish themselves. Meetings and conferences were being held. But it wasn't lost on Marion that Germany was allotted the same amount of time to recover and plan.

The thought terrified her, though exhaustion was the greater of her two mental states. She yawned as she entered their headquarters for a new day, relieving Sara from her shift. Sounds of typewriting, chatter, and street noise filtered through the room. Sara informed her which girl was where and for how long they'd be dispatched. "The telegraph room just informed me a rider is needed at the Baker Street offices too," Sara said, pressing her fingertips into her forehead.

Marion had a similar dull ache. She blinked, running the names of the available girls through her head.

Evelyn stepped forward. "I can go. I've practiced that route extensively."

Marion opened her mouth. She hadn't even known Evelyn was within earshot. But it shouldn't have come as a surprise. Nor should the fact that Evelyn had implemented the same tactic that had worked in her favor previously. Marion's emotions felt stretched like a taut elastic, ready to snap. She reluctantly gave Evelyn the go-ahead.

CHAPTER 34

EVELYN

August 1940
London

Evelyn slipped her gas mask bag over one shoulder and a satchel over the other, the straps crossing over her chest. She adjusted her helmet, positioned her goggles—and she was off.

The ride to Baker Street would take all of ten minutes, but she would be happy for every second of it. There, she'd receive her orders, which could have her retracing her drive back to headquarters or elsewhere with a dispatch.

She hoped for elsewhere, to prolong her stunt.

Evelyn reveled in how her new tactic had been working. She'd simply volunteered for dispatches every chance she got.

So far, so good.

The weather was even cooperating. The past few days had left much to be desired with either clouds and showers or brutal wind and rain. But today the clouds gave way. The sun shined.

It could drizzle; wasn't there always the chance of that? But Evelyn was content to be zooming across the earth.

It reminded her of her days at the Brooklands, her first foray into feeling that she was finally and actually living. She cherished her days.

She cherished the Brooklands, and she would forever be grateful for her time at the tracks. Truly, the Brooklands had felt like a gateway to her current role.

While the last few days had been quieter, Germany was still poking, as if to assess for holes and any weaknesses. Gunfire could be heard and far-off dogfight vapor trails could be seen from London; however, elsewhere in England, the fighting was more than distantly seen and heard.

Birmingham continued to be blitzed, something that seemingly unzipped the usually stoic Wren Smith and brought a hand to her heart.

A railway booking office was hit southwest of London.

Estuaries in Tilbury, Purfleet, and Northfleet were targeted.

Night bombings continued to strike ports and harbors.

Explosives were dropped at Harrow, less than an hour from London. It was horrifying to think those bombs landed on cinemas, a dance hall, a bank, homes. Miraculously, nobody lost their lives.

But what really shook Evelyn was an aerodrome in Croydon.

Croydon was in Surrey.

The Brooklands was in Surrey.

The Brooklands had its own aerodrome.

The Brooklands, with all its importance for Evelyn.

The connection felt too close, the literal distance of only twenty or thirty miles.

It fueled her. So did Rose's accident. Some of the other girls acted timid in response to Rose's sudden encounter with a lorry and the idea of undetonated bombs. But both situations only made Evelyn more eager to go on dispatches.

She accelerated. Baker Street was a turn away. Evelyn navigated the corner and saw a man out front, most likely with her orders. She'd admit her heart dropped a little that it wasn't Percy.

Percy rarely left her mind. Who'd have thought? Seeing Percy in a new way was yet another perk of forging her own path. She'd conjure him right now into her path if she could.

Maybe then they could continue their last conversation that'd been so abruptly interrupted by the red warning. What had that mysterious man felt compelled to tell her?

The intelligence officer met her at the curb. She planted her feet, and he extended a small envelope and mouthed off a destination. Evelyn nodded, already picturing the route in her head. Excitedly at that. She had studied her maps extensively, and this ride would take some time, traversing the heart of London and along the River Thames.

She was being dispatched to a vital airfield in Hornchurch, one where the pilots were dispatched themselves to protect the London Docks, the Thames and its estuary, and also factories in Dagenham and Tilbury.

Evelyn rode swiftly and confidently away from Baker Street. Comparatively to before the war, London was quieter, but the weekend put more people on the streets. Heads turned as Evelyn whizzed by in her uniform. Seeing a woman do war work was a spectacle, and she enjoyed the attention. It was easy to let her mind slip to the Brooklands, imagining that the people were track spectators and she was in the midst of a race.

She'd only gone a block or two when her gaze jerked toward the pavement. At first she didn't trust her eyes. Hadn't she just thought she'd conjure Percy if she could?

But there he was, walking in her direction, and he wasn't alone. Blimey, his fingers were interlaced with a woman's. A beautiful one. They were deep in conversation, their heads tilted toward each other, creating a picture of intimacy that made Evelyn's throat thick with emotion.

Who was she? What was she to Percy? What was *Evelyn* to him? He'd been the one to bring her tea, to send her flowers, to suggest they go see a film. Percy had made her see him in a whole new way, not as her childhood playmate but as something more adult.

Oh, she felt so foolish.

This woman clung to his arm, a visible and learned intimacy. Yet at the cinema Evelyn had urged her courage to do something so dinky as to share their armrest.

The street traffic suddenly halted and Evelyn hastily braked, barely planting her feet in time. The quickness pulled Percy's attention, and the unusual rigidness of his body made it clear he saw Evelyn, recognizing her despite her helmet and goggles. Though she supposed not many women went about London dressed in such a getup.

The woman he was with surely didn't dress in a similar manner. She was prim, proper. She was everything his mother would expect.

His mouth opened, but no words came out. Not like she'd hear him over the din, nor did she want to hear him out if he tried. Traffic may've been at a standstill, but Evelyn could blessedly maneuver her motorbike through the cracks and escape.

She did just that, her hands tight on the handlebars.

Evelyn had a job to do, one that didn't involve Percy and his woman friend. Like she did on her other rides, she'd concentrate fully on her task. "Focus," she told herself, and she arrived at the airfield in what felt like record time. Evelyn handed over the message, received her receipt, and turned toward headquarters.

Orders complete, her betraying brain returned to Percy.

The sun was at her back. It warmed her already heated mood. Mostly she was huffy for allowing herself to fall for him. And why had she? Evelyn didn't want to be a physician's wife and host his dinners, not if it limited who she could be in life. But would he have put such restrictions on her? Percy had surprised her lately.

She groaned; what did it matter? Percy was very much with that woman, and he had very much misled Evelyn. She felt utterly betrayed and lied to. He saw her as his childhood friend, nothing more, and if anything, the moment hardened her belief that she didn't want the life her mother wanted for her, not if—

The skies behind her exploded with noise.

She lost control of her motorbike, thumping over a curb, nearly running over a mother and child. Evelyn screeched to a halt, turned around to see if the two were okay, and realized they were not paying her attention but instead their eyes were fixed on the skies.

German aircrafts.

Right over London.

The last time such a thing happened was in 1918 during the Gotha bombing raids of the Great War. Was history repeating itself?

Not even a heartbeat later, the sirens began, a far cry from a warning, as the Luftwaffe was already there.

Evelyn all but fell from her motorcycle, letting it clamor to the ground. She grabbed the woman's arm, using her free hand to push the child forward, and they ran toward cover.

The ground shook.

A rush of heat added to their momentum. Almost losing her footing, Evelyn whirled her head around. A building, not more than a block away, was a cloud of smoke and flames. An incendiary bomb, meant not only to destroy but also to spark a fire to consume even more.

Forward again, breath ragged, Evelyn muscled the woman and child toward a shelter. Running behind a child with inconsistent footfalls wasn't easy. She kept stepping on the child's heels, so she picked her up.

The young mother's face contorted with sobs, a sound lost to the roar of German planes, the wailing sirens, and, most terrifying of all, the crash of another bomb.

Hurry, she willed them.

A public shelter wasn't far.

Outside, a disorderly queue had formed. People pushed, shoved. Eventually Evelyn broke through. She handed the child to her mother, the mother quickly enveloping her daughter in a cocoon, and Evelyn sank into a seat. Her chest was pounding at the realization that the Germans had come to London. It felt profoundly important and disastrous.

She glanced at the mother who soothed her daughter, whispering in her ear, stroking her dark hair. Evelyn was surprised that the child hadn't been evacuated. Perhaps the young woman was unable to part with her. Evelyn had heard of it happening, a family deciding to remain in London together. What would Evelyn's own mother have done, if they hadn't had the means to relocate elsewhere? Evelyn knew her mother wouldn't have sent her away. And she couldn't help it . . . She missed her mother, despite all that had transpired between them these past few months.

At least her mother was far, far away from the bombs. She would be safe, and Evelyn would continue to ride to ensure her parents remained as such. She'd also continue to ride for herself.

CHAPTER 35

MARION

August 1940
London

M arion had almost grown roots at the window, the same place she'd stood the first time she set eyes on Evelyn, and she waited, absently thumbing the adoption document in her pocket.

The all clear had sounded, and so as not to appear too eager, Marion forced herself to watch for Evelyn's return from inside their headquarters as opposed to pacing the street like a madwoman.

How had this happened again, with Evelyn elsewhere while the sirens wailed? Only this time, German planes had truly come, and Marion had no notion where Evelyn's dispatch had taken her.

She wouldn't let herself think about her daughter not returning. It wasn't an option she'd consider. All that was left of Eddie on this earth would be fine. More than fine. Evelyn would thrive. She *was* thriving as a Wren. Marion felt it in herself, too, a spark once again coming alive in her.

A street post danced as Marion's vision blurred from her fixation, but then there was motion, a motorcycle rounding a corner and then the post.

Marion nearly collapsed with relief.

Evelyn was alive and seemingly unharmed.

She drove toward headquarters, stopping short of where the motorbikes were stored along their brick building. Evelyn's head turned in reaction to something.

Marion hadn't noticed the man across the street, who was also apparently waiting for Evelyn's return. She leaned closer to the glass, watching as he approached Evelyn. Was it the same man Evelyn had been talking with outside of Baker Street? Her doctor friend? The man she had snuck off to see? Marion wasn't certain, having only seen him that single time. But he was smartly dressed, tall in height, and dark in hair. Most telling, however, was how Evelyn crossed her arms and pitched her weight to one side, painting a picture of displeasure at seeing the man.

The picture only sharpened as they spoke, Evelyn gesturing demonstratively and the man's expression one of culpability. Even without knowing what was being said, seeing Evelyn stand up for herself filled Marion with pride. Eddie would've been proud too.

Could the fortitude Evelyn displayed have come from Marion? The magnitude of that thought left Marion speechless, her mind snagged on the idea that her daughter could have inherited this trait from her, and she in turn from her own mother. Even all these years later, Marion couldn't help the direction her thoughts took her, to the mother who once abandoned her and to the father who was nothing more than a life-size question mark. Had he even known about Marion?

It gave Marion an odd sense of peace to know that Evelyn didn't question who her parents were. Keeping Evelyn's birth a secret wasn't simple, especially in moments like this when she wanted to charge down to the street and wrap her arms around her daughter while glowering at the man who upset her, but she knew the secret was worth keeping. The truth would disrupt everything Evelyn had ever known.

Evelyn turned on her heels, and Marion ducked away from the window, not wanting to be caught. Marion counted to sixty, waiting for Evelyn to join the other girls in their main room, then she went to address them all, asking after the entire group's welfare.

She was met with nods that, yes, they were all fine.

Good, because they were needed. The reprieve from their duties in the aftermath of London's first attack would be short-lived. Marion's riders were needed right away.

Marion pretended that she didn't hear Evelyn when she volunteered for a dispatch and assigned another girl. The disappointment on Evelyn's face tugged at Marion's heartstrings, yet she felt reassured in her decision as another air-raid siren sounded mere hours later. The Germans had returned, and Evelyn was beside her in a shelter, their shoulders touching, a constant reminder that her daughter was safe for that moment in time.

If only they could remain in their seemingly safe swaddle, but outside, London's East End was on fire and tensions were escalating. The night sky glowed blood red, and fountains of flames billowed from windows. Buildings crumbled. Looting ensued. Innocent civilian lives had been lost. An outraged Winston Churchill ordered for Berlin to be bombed in response, an action that would no doubt outrage both the Luftwaffe chief and Adolf Hitler, who had boasted their capital would never suffer an attack.

Marion knew Germany wouldn't take kindly to the British striking back, and a few days later, Adolf Hitler confirmed her fears during a public speech broadcast over the radio.

"The other night the English had bombed Berlin. So be it. But this is a game at which two can play."

Marion listened to his words from her cabin. The radio sat between her and Sara while the women quietly ate their scones with cream and jam, a rare moment when they were both between shifts. Sara's head shook slowly as she carefully chewed.

"When the British Air Force drops 2,000 or 3,000 or 4,000 kilograms of bombs, then we will drop 150,000; 180,000; 230,000; 300,000; 400,000 kilograms on a single night. When they declare they will attack our cities in great measure, we will eradicate their cities."

Marion pressed her lips together and closed her eyes, leaving the remainder of her scone untouched. His words were spat like poison darts, one after another. And he wasn't finished.

"The hour will come when one of us will break—and it will not be National Socialist Germany!"

Hitler's threat felt tangible, a gauntlet thrown down. And while Marion worried greatly for the safety of the island, the safety of Sara, the safety of her friend's children, it was her fear for Evelyn that resounded the strongest.

Sara took to nibbling on the skin of her thumb, her expression otherwise blank. "This is going to get worse before it gets better. And I brought you into this again. Mare, I'm—"

"You are wonderful, Sare. You always have been. It's war that's ugly."

"And incredibly damaging."

Marion nodded, at first not wanting to verbally respond but then saying aloud, as if making a promise, "We must do all we can to keep the girls safe."

"You know they call you their Mother Wren, don't you?"

Marion snorted. "Their what?"

"A play on mother hen and likely Mother Goose. Isn't there an Old Mother Hubbard too?"

Marion didn't think there was a correlation between the names, but she wasn't keen on the reference to Mother Hubbard. She'd read the nursery rhyme as a child, and while she couldn't remember all the verses, many of which were added over time, she recalled the oldest line.

"Old Mother Hubbard went to the cupboard, to get her poor doggie a bone; but when she came there the cupboard was bare, and so the poor little doggie had none."

And wasn't that what worried her?

What if she was truly Old Mother Hubbard? And the cupboard was the war? The doggie was Eddie—and now Evelyn? And the bone, the bone was safety for the dog. It always came back to keeping those she loved safe. She felt she had failed Eddie in that way. What if she failed Evelyn too?

CHAPTER 36

EVELYN

September 1940
London

E velyn wanted nothing more than to pick up the gauntlet Adolf Hitler had thrown. And her strategy to be assigned to stunts had changed. Improved. Before, she tried to be first to volunteer. Now she'd be the first to learn of the dispatches, finding it more effective to wait in the telegraph room for stunts to come in.

She even planned to skip lunch, much to her stomach's dismay.

At a table behind the telegraph technician, Evelyn's eyes trailed over her map of routes, not only wanting to refresh her brain but also wanting to distract herself because as much as she didn't want to think about Percy, she couldn't help herself.

It was quite maddening.

She'd replayed their argument on the street countless times since it happened.

She hadn't expected to see Percy. More so, she hadn't been ready to see him. Her brain had been largely in a fog from a bomb nearly dropping on her.

To his credit, her safety was the first thing he asked about.

"*Thank God you're okay, Evie,*" he had said, smartly stopping a few steps from her to give her space.

"*Yes, I feel like I dodged a bomb.*"

He hadn't caught her double meaning at first. But as she stared fiercely at him, he realized it wasn't an explosion she was referring to.

"*I tried to tell you. I wasn't hiding Victoria from you.*"

"*No?*"

Percy had licked his lips. "*I started to tell you, but then that air raid happened and we dashed off.*"

Evelyn crossed her arms. "*How convenient.*"

"*No one knows about Victoria. Not even my parents. But, honest, I was going to tell you.*"

"*So tell me. Tell me about your girlfriend. She's quite beautiful.*" Evelyn immediately chastised herself for her pettiness. This Victoria had done nothing wrong. She likely hadn't known about Evelyn either.

"*We've been seeing each other for some time, but like I said, I've kept it a secret. I don't want my parents to pressure me to marry, be it Victoria or any of the other women they're not so subtly forcing on me.*"

"*You mean me. You mean how I was being forced on you?*"

"*That's not what I meant, and it was a poor choice of words.*" Percy had run a hand through his annoyingly perfectly coiffed hair. "*You're very important to me, Evie.*"

She'd ignored the sentiment and instead spat, "*Is spying for my parents the only reason you took an interest in me?*"

"*Of course not. We're friends. I've never not known you as a friend.*"

"*A friend.*" Evelyn had bobbed her head, exasperated. "*I think we're on the same page now.*"

Percy stepped closer, only for Evelyn to retreat a step. "*No, not at all. You've surprised me, Evie. I knew you, but I didn't truly know you until recently.*"

"*And what? You thought you could have both me and Victoria?*"

"*That's not fair. How have I acted in the wrong? I sent you congratulatory flowers. We saw a film. I brought you your favorite tea and checked on your foot as a physician. I never tried to kiss you. I never—*"

"I get it, Percy." Tears had threatened. She held up a palm, stopping any more jabbing words from him. "*I get it.*"

"*Evie,*" Percy had tried. "*Evelyn, please. I didn't mean . . .*"

Evelyn had already turned on her heels but then stopped again at her name. "*What?*" she snapped at Percy.

He'd sighed, looking defeated.

"*Do you have anything else that needs to be said?*"

"No," he said quietly. "*I guess not.*"

Evelyn swallowed roughly. "*Fine. Good. This is done. Nothing left unsaid.*"

But so much hurt.

Even days later, she still felt wounded. Daft too. Evelyn wouldn't say Percy was blameless—oh, she blamed him plenty—but he also wasn't technically wrong; he hadn't treated her as anything more than a friend. And now even that friendship felt ruined. He hadn't stopped her when she walked away a second time.

A flurry of activity at the telegraph desk was a welcome diversion. Wren Smith would likely sniff out how information was being received and come look for herself. Evelyn quickly crossed the room and read over the technician's shoulder.

A radar station had detected enemy aircrafts. London should be on alert. A number of nearby aircraft factories were listed as possible targets. They should be warned of a potential attack.

Evelyn kept reading, scanning. Then her blood ran cold.

Vickers Aircraft Factory at Brooklands.

No, not the Brooklands. Not the place that molded so much of who Evelyn had become. She couldn't bear to think of the Brooklands being bombed.

The intel said to send dispatches immediately to each location and stand by for more updates.

Oh, she'd most definitely go immediately, even without permission. Evelyn had to be the one to warn them. The telegraph technician would call for Wren Smith any second now to give her the news and someone else could be assigned to the stunt.

"I'll take Vickers," Evelyn said to her.

The technician opened her mouth as if to question her, and Evelyn asserted, "I have the Brooklands covered."

The woman's head ticked toward the door, probably hoping Wren Smith would intervene, as she stammered, "But . . ."

It was too late. Evelyn was already slipping out of the telegraph room.

The technician's alarm wasn't unfounded; Evelyn hadn't been assigned the order, so she shouldn't be going anywhere. She didn't have a lick of care.

Evelyn ducked out of headquarters and rode in the direction of Weybridge. Relief surged through her that no one called after her. She'd gotten away unnoticed by anyone. That relief was soon replaced with pure adrenaline for the task at hand. She rode fast, cursing at any automobiles or pedestrians slowing her pace. Once she left London behind, she could go faster on the motorways. She'd be there within the hour if she pushed her motorbike to its limits.

She neared with each minute, only a mile or two more to go, her nerves charged. Would she make it in time?

She risked a look backward, almost losing control, and searched through the towering trees and glowing sunshine for any planes. If they were there, the foliage and sun hid them, and her own engine overpowered any other noise she might have heard.

Her hand twisted the throttle, but Evelyn's motorcycle was already going as fast as it could. She hoped her warning would be in vain and no attack was imminent. Courses could change. Planes could turn back. A dogfight could've cut off the Germans. Radar wasn't always accurate.

That was when Evelyn's senses all fired at once.

A deafening *boom*.

A blinding brightness.

The taste of metal.

The smell of rotten eggs.

She felt air around her, then the sensation of falling.

Evelyn hit the road hard. Her ears rang. She opened and closed her mouth, hoping to relieve an unbearable pressure. Rolling onto her back, she wiped her goggles clean. The planes were already past her. The ground smoked from where the Germans' bomb had struck, not more than a stone's throw away.

Evelyn crawled toward her motorbike, quick to see gas leaking from the tank. Nearby trees sparked with fire.

She had to get away, and quickly.

In the distance the planes continued on, gaining on the Brooklands, but blessedly not traveling straight toward it.

They didn't see Vickers yet.

That must be it.

The factories were camouflaged. Netting and trees disguised the racetrack. The only giveaway would be the railroad tracks. How long until the Germans put the pieces together? Could Evelyn beat them there?

A half mile, that was all that was left for Evelyn to go. She'd traveled this road countless times before, but never with so much at stake. She pushed to her feet, immediately buckling. Her knee felt tender. Her arm felt broken. Still, she began to run.

Outside a hangar, the propellers of planes whirled. Evelyn heard the din from where she was. There was little chance the men loitering about would hear her yell. Or the German planes, which began a big circle in the sky, coming back around.

An air-raid siren hadn't sounded.

It was up to Evelyn. As she ran, she waved her unbroken arm. She screamed despite knowing the engines overpowered her. She prayed she'd catch the attention of the workers. She prayed she'd beat the Germans.

CHAPTER 37

MARION

September 1940
Weybridge

M arion had never felt so tense on a motorcycle. Not when riding
to the front line, not when riding through a bomb-stricken
town, nor when explosives had landed where she'd been only heartbeats before.

But to think that Evelyn was riding into a potential raid . . .

Marion had to go after her.

She should've known her calculating daughter would beat her to
the dispatch. As she'd begun doing to thwart Evelyn's efforts, Marion
had gone to visit the telegraph room. The technician had nearly barreled into her at the door, quick to tell her about Evelyn.

She'd gone to the Brooklands.

Marion knew the location was important to Evelyn. She'd overheard her daughter and Wren McMasters speak of it, trading stories
of races there. The joy she'd seen in Evelyn's eyes was unmistaken. It
was a place her daughter treasured. It worried Marion. Passion often
clouded judgment.

Marion had spat off orders to her girls, dispatching them to the
other locations, then set off toward the Vickers Aircraft Factory

herself. Each second felt like a minute, each minute felt like an hour. But finally she was turning onto St. Peter's Way. She wasn't far now. Marion kept an eye on the skies the best she could while navigating the road. In a break of trees, her breath hitched at the sight of the planes. She rounded another corner. A group of trees was ablaze, and a great pit was in the ground. A motorbike lay discarded on the road.

Evelyn's.

But where was she?

Marion zoomed past, the road straightening, and Marion saw her, running at a limp, her arm flapping wildly. Sara once told Marion how Jenny Wrens became very vocal and protective when someone came near their babies. That was Evelyn in that moment, fanatical about getting to the Brooklands and warning them.

And they saw her! The men standing outside a hangar looked to have caught her notice and her them. But did they understand?

Marion tore her gaze from her daughter and peered again at the skies. At the German planes.

They were almost immediately above.

The men looked.

Evelyn looked.

Bombs began to fall from the underbellies of the planes.

Then Evelyn began to run again, not away from the bombs but toward them and where the men still loitered like sitting ducks.

Time slowed, the explosives falling and falling and falling. Marion knew it would take over thirty seconds for the bombs to make landfall, a statistic she recalled from the Great War. All she could do was continue to ride toward her daughter, screaming her name, her voice rising from the usually deep tone to a frantic shrill.

Marion reached the hangar, hastily dismounting her motorbike. On foot she ran, still screeching Evelyn's name, Evelyn intent on warning the men, oblivious to a falling bomb.

"Evelyn!" Marion called, praying she'd be heard.

Evelyn stopped and turned. A blast rang out. Marion crumpled to the ground as earth and debris and portions of the building rained down.

Ears buzzing, Marion began dragging herself toward her daughter. She let out a sob when Evelyn's head lifted, her auburn hair coated in dust and dirt.

Marion stumbled to her feet, coughing, tears trailing down her cheeks. She knew her daughter would've run straight into the path of the bomb if she hadn't heard her name.

But Evelyn was alive.

The air-raid siren finally sounded.

Gunners began shooting at the planes in the too-bright sky. Marion tried to track the gunfire, tried to see where the planes were now.

That was when she saw another explosive falling straight toward her. Panic seized her and she lost the ability to use her legs. Then warmth was around her. An arm, a body, dragging her from the bomb's path, until the force came and tore Marion from Evelyn.

"Evelyn," she croaked.

It was the second time she'd awoken in a sterile room, asking for her daughter. She tried to sit up, but the ache in her head wouldn't allow it. An IV was stuck into her arm. Gingerly, she touched her cheek, her forehead, both covered in bandages.

She was alive; Evelyn had saved her. But where was her daughter now?

Her pulse quickened just as a nurse entered.

"Oh, Mrs. Smith. Wren Smith," the nurse corrected. "Welcome back. How do you feel?"

"Where is Evelyn?"

"I'm sorry, love. I don't have an Evelyn on my rounds. You're lucky to be alive. Hundreds of men came in after the raid. You're due for more medicine. Let me just . . ." She trailed off as she administered the dose.

Marion was barely aware of the nurse's movements, her head spinning. "Women? Were any other women admitted?"

"You're the only assigned to me from the—"

"How many deaths?"

The nurse paused, frowning before she answered. "Many."

No, she wouldn't accept it. Evelyn had saved her, yet Marion was supposed to be the one protecting her. "Fairchild. Can you please ask about that name?"

The nurse gave her a sad smile. "There was a lot of chaos—"

"Now!" Marion demanded. Her head screamed at her almost as loudly as that single word. She clutched her forehead, saying more kindly, "Please ask. Now. Please."

The nurse nodded subtly.

Left alone, Marion's thoughts dissolved to nothing but Evelyn. Had she survived?

She closed her eyes, squeezed them tightly.

She didn't open them again for some time, the medicine having done what it needed to do.

When she woke a second time, the nurse was with her. Marion opened her mouth, but the nurse held up a hand. "I asked. There was a Fairchild admitted."

Marion tried to sit up. The nurse was quick to lay a hand on her. She gently pushed Marion back down. Her voice was just as gentle when she said, "There's an Evelyn Fairchild. I saw the patch on your uniform. I'm assuming she's one of yours?"

Yes, she was Marion's, in more ways than one.

The nurse tried for a smile, but it only served to unnerve Marion even further. "Her injuries were substantial. Miss Fairchild only recently came out of surgery. She's stable and sleeping now."

The tears came then, the ones she knew would eventually fall. What she didn't know was if they'd begin falling from grief or relief. But Evelyn was okay. She was alive. "I must see her."

"I'm sorry. Only family is able to see Miss Fairchild at this time."

"Her parents?"

"They've been contacted."

Marion smacked her lips. It was likely Caroline and Alfred Fairchild weren't in Weybridge but in Wiltshire, where Evelyn enlisted. What if Evelyn woke before they traveled across England? Evelyn couldn't wake alone. Marion wouldn't allow it. She couldn't bear it.

But Marion could be there. She could be there for her daughter. "My uniform?" Marion asked. "I need something from it."

The nurse began crossing to a small table. "It's just over here."

From the pocket Marion pulled out an aged piece of paper. It'd grown soft from passing from pocket to pocket and from the oils of her skin, touching it again and again as a reminder. While it'd been with her for the past twenty-one years, Marion had never unfolded the document and relived the words.

She opened it now.

CHAPTER 38

EVELYN

September 1940
Weybridge

E velyn dreamed of masked faces whirling above and around her, of concerned eyes, of quickly spoken instructions. She felt a gentle touch, the back of a hand, against her cheek.

It was a touch she knew well, from years of coming out of surgeries.

"Mother?" she said groggily, opening her eyes to see a petite woman, her skin ashen, her eyes moist. "Wren Smith," she uttered instead. Wren Smith also wore a hospital gown, bandages on her face and head, a mobile IV positioned next to her.

Wren Smith withdrew her hand, folding it in her lap, kneading one hand into the other. "There you are," she said in her deep voice, but somehow still delicate and melodic. "How are you feeling?"

Evelyn muttered, "Everything hurts." Much of her felt stiff and immobile, in casts or stitches.

"I can imagine." Wren Smith eyed the chart that'd been left at the end of Evelyn's hospital bed. "You've gone through a great ordeal." Her lips curled into a small smile. "But you're alive, you stubborn thing."

If Evelyn wasn't mistaken, Wren Smith sounded almost proud.

Evelyn gave a half smile. Even that hurt. So did talking, but she felt the need to say, "I had to be the one who went. The Brooklands is special to me."

"I know," Wren Smith said in a low tone.

Evelyn licked her dry lips, noting the setting sun outside. Had the rest of the day already passed? "What came of it? The bombs beat me there, but then what?"

"Not all the bombs. You still gave a warning." Wren Smith sighed. "But I don't know how bad it was. I only woke recently myself. I know one thing for certain, though. I wouldn't be here without you. I'm deeply grateful."

"You saved my life first."

Wren Smith's body seemed racked with emotion. She averted her gaze, a hand pressed over her heart. Her bottom lip trembled, as if she were on the verge of saying something more, but then she stood, crossed to a pitcher of water, and poured a glass.

By the time she returned, moving her IV with each step, Wren Smith's expression had eased.

Evelyn drank through the straw, Wren Smith instructing her to go slowly. After Wren Smith had taken back the cup, she said, "I should go, let you rest."

"Stay?" Evelyn was quick to ask. "I don't want to be alone."

"Your parents will be here shortly."

Evelyn slowly shook her head. "Not likely."

Wren Smith's brows scrunched. "Whyever not?"

"We had a falling out when I joined the war."

"Oh, Evelyn," Wren Smith said, reaching forward to gently pat Evelyn's unbroken arm, one of the few places it seemed that was intact. "They'll come. There's no way they wouldn't be here for you, no matter what has happened in the past."

Evelyn studied Wren Smith's face, one she imagined was once very beautiful but was now aged from time and perhaps experiences. Strands of gray shot through her dark hair. Dark spots dotted her otherwise milky skin. She probably didn't bother to protect her arms, neck, and face from the sun. There was a familiarness to her. And maybe it was the drugs talking, but Evelyn recognized the sadness in Wren Smith's round eyes, accented by thick lashes, so similar to her own. "You don't call the other girls by their first names. Only me."

Wren Smith sat straighter. "Oh?"

Yes, Evelyn thought. Time and time again she believed Wren Smith singled her out. She thought it could've been because of her disability. She thought it could've been due to her background. There was that infraction, or two. But it felt greater than that.

Wren Smith said no more, but Evelyn wanted to question her. Surely there couldn't be a better time than now. They both wore ill-fitting hospital gowns. They had saved each other's lives. In that moment the other woman didn't feel like Wren Smith. Funny, Evelyn didn't know her by another name. Yet Wren Smith knew her as Evelyn.

She'd say it. She'd simply ask. "Why do you treat me differently than the others?"

Wren Smith's expression was unreadable, the way it was the majority of the time. Then her jaw slacked. She rubbed a finger beneath her nose. "Because you are remarkable. That's all I have the ability to say."

Evelyn's head cocked at the peculiar answer, just as two people all but fell into her room.

"Mother? Father?"

Evelyn had never seen her mother move at anything faster than a brisk walk.

THE CALL OF THE WRENS

"Oh, Evie, darling," her mother lamented. Then her gaze fell on the back of Wren Smith's head, waiting for her to turn and introduce herself.

But Wren Smith had gone as white as a ghost. "If you'll excuse me," she said, head down. Wren Smith stood, and Evelyn could sense her unease. Perhaps it was from standing before her parents in a hospital gown. They certainly weren't becoming. Still, Evelyn could help her feel more comfortable. "Mother, Father, this is Wren Smith. I daresay she's the reason I'm alive."

Wren Smith had gone still. Evelyn's mother eyed her an awkwardly long time before she turned to her husband. "Alfred?"

It was rare for her mother to defer to her father. It only happened in moments when her mother was overwhelmed. And in those moments her father's chest would puff out and he'd become high and mighty. That seemed to be exactly what was unfolding now as he demanded, "What is the meaning of this, Mrs. Smith?"

Evelyn's brows rose, royally confused. "Father, you know each other?"

Instantly, Evelyn suspected that Percy wasn't the only one her parents were in cahoots with. Was that why Wren Smith had taken a particular interest in her? She should've known.

"Evelyn, sweetie, it is nothing to concern yourself over. Why don't you get your rest and the adults can talk in the hall?"

"*I'm* an adult," Evelyn protested. Her mother treating her like a child was enough to annoy her, yet she was doubly miffed that her parents came in firing daggers at Wren Smith instead of asking after her well-being. She was nearly just blown up—again. Not to mention they hadn't spoken to her in months. She guessed they didn't need to if they had Percy and Wren Smith doing their bidding. "So you asked Wren Smith to report back to you about me? Is that it?"

Her mother's face puckered. "You mean to tell me Mrs. Smith hasn't told you? I don't believe it."

Wren Smith slowly raised her chin, meeting Evelyn's mother's gaze. "No. I've respected our agreement. I only came because I didn't want Evelyn to wake alone."

"What agreement?" Evelyn said from between her teeth. She turned her ire on Wren Smith. "Did they ask you to sideline me? Is that why you are so resistant to assigning me stunts? Are they paying you?"

"Evelyn, don't be absurd," her mother snapped.

"Then what is it?" Evelyn demanded, groaning at a flash of pain as she tried to sit up. She lay back again. "Tell me!"

"Yes, tell her, Mrs. Smith," Evelyn's mother said with a flap of her arm. "You've gone and ruined everything anyway. Did you recruit her yourself? Are you the one who lured her into this godforsaken war?"

Her father spat, "You better believe we'll be consulting our lawyer."

So many questions from her mother, punctuated with a threat from her father? Evelyn's head felt as if it'd explode. She pressed on her temples, trying to ease the pain, and waited for Wren Smith to clarify. But she didn't. It didn't look as if she could, with how her lips moved ever so subtly but produced no sound. Her gaze remained on the tiled floor until she met Evelyn's eyes.

"Wren Smith," Evelyn said quietly, "can you please tell me what is going on? I don't understand."

Evelyn's father cleared his throat. "We'll be the ones to explain." Her mother made a noise, but he cut her off. "It should come from us, as *we* are Evelyn's parents."

Evelyn flicked her attention from Wren Smith to her parents

and back to Wren Smith. Never would she have guessed the words that would be spoken next, words that would change her life forever, especially as they came from Wren Smith and not from her parents.

CHAPTER 39

MARION

September 1940
Weybridge

E velyn, I'm your biological mother."
There, she'd said it, and at once Marion felt a surge of relief but also fear. She gripped the pole of her IV stand for support as her words seemed to linger in the room, their effects showing differently on each face.

Confusion.

Outrage.

Indignation.

Caroline Fairchild let out a screech. Alfred Fairchild growled again how he'd be speaking to their lawyer.

Marion couldn't pull her eyes away from Evelyn. She was at a loss for how to describe her daughter's reaction after the initial rise of her eyebrows, for Evelyn now gave her nothing. She lay there, her eyes closed, looking exactly as she had when Marion first entered her room when Evelyn was still asleep.

Marion knew the anger would come. Evelyn would likely feel betrayed. She would feel abandoned, an emotion Marion knew all too well. Evelyn could cast blame for her clubfoot. She'd ask questions about her biological father. If he had wanted her. Where he was now.

Oh, Eddie, what had she done?

Marion shouldn't have been the one to tell Evelyn. Not only had she broken legal constraints, but she was responsible for the upheaval of Evelyn's world. Marion hadn't been able to help herself, though. When Alfred Fairchild had said the truth should come from them, her *parents*, something in Marion became possessive. They had barreled into Evelyn's hospital room, yet they seemed more concerned about Marion's presence than Evelyn's welfare. Even now, she felt their gazes burning into her back. Marion refused to look at them, anticipating the same hard-nosed expression Sister Margaret used to wear when displeased.

Evelyn's voice came softly but sternly, her eyes still closed. "I think you should go."

Marion nodded, a lump in her throat, an even larger knot in her stomach. Eyes down on her stocking feet, she turned toward the door, pushing her IV ahead of her.

"Evelyn, darling," Caroline began.

"All of you," Evelyn demanded.

Marion quickened her steps, retreating from Evelyn, escaping from Caroline and Alfred. A shooting pain ran down her back. A new headache was forming. Her body ached all over.

She wanted nothing more than to withdraw and disappear, much as she had the past twenty years.

———— ∞ ————

Naturally, Sara wouldn't stand for that.

Marion knew she'd come, and as expected, Sara arrived the next day. Marion had been in the hospital for a day, likely leaving later that afternoon.

"How have you not given up on me yet?"

"Hello to you too," Sara said lightly in her pixie voice as she entered Marion's hospital room.

"I'm sorry." Marion picked at a thread on her blanket. "I haven't said that as much as I should. Why do you put up with me?"

"Your winning personality?"

Marion gave a half laugh and adjusted her pillow to sit more upright.

"Now where's all this coming from? Should I sit?" Sara smiled as she seated herself on the visitor chair.

"Don't get too comfortable. I'm not ready to talk about it."

"These chairs aren't exactly made for comfort, Mare. But I think you should talk about it, whatever it is. Don't let another twenty years pass with it all locked up. You've come alive these past few weeks."

Marion sighed. It was true. She'd felt more alive. She felt she had a purpose again. But now it all felt lost. "Evelyn knows."

Sara's head tilted at an angle, her one eye squinting. "Knows what?"

"That I'm her biological mother."

Sara's mouth rounded into an O shape before she eventually uttered an "Oh."

"Yeah," Marion assented.

"And?"

Marion instinctively rubbed the back of her neck, squinting at the pain that surged at her touch. "And she asked me to leave her room. Caroline and Alfred too."

"Caroline and Alfred? The Fairchilds were there as well?"

Marion nodded, saying, "Can we talk about something else? No one has told me anything about the Brooklands. How are the other girls? Did they make it back safely? Any other raids? Any news from Wren McMasters in Plymouth?"

Sara placated her friend by not pressing any further about Evelyn. She answered each question in kind. The other girls were fine. News was that Wren McMasters was improving. England suffered various other raids, with casualties at Bristol and Banwell, even more in Liverpool, but Weybridge took the greatest of hits.

By the time the gunners opened fire at the Brooklands, explosives had already fallen. The scene was said to have been one of chaos, the air-raid siren beginning too late. Survivors said the Luftwaffe came and went within three minutes, with unthinkable wreckage in such a short amount of time.

The old racing grandstand had been hit. A second bomb had gone through the roof of a repair hangar and detonated inside. A third directly exploded on an air-raid shelter. While shelters protected from blasts and shrapnel, they weren't built to withstand a direct hit. Close to eighty had lost their lives. Hundreds were injured.

A worker had explained how they never heard or noticed the Germans coming. Approaching planes and aircraft noise were a normal part of their working day.

"But one worker said he saw Evelyn running toward the hangar. He said he was able to clear the hangar before it was hit. Her actions saved a lot of lives."

Marion let those words sink in. "She's something special. I saw her banged-up motorcycle. The trees were on fire. It's likely an explosion knocked her off. Yet there she was running at a limp, calling to the men, waving at them with one of her arms."

"She'll win an award for it."

That she would, but Marion didn't think for a single second that

Evelyn had done it for the accolades. Still, Marion asked Sara, "Will you tell her? About what she did for the Brooklands, I mean."

"You'll tell her, Mare."

"She said I saved her life."

Sara squeezed her friend's hand, no doubt knowing the importance of that for Marion.

Marion shook her head. "But that was before she found out I was her biological mother, before she sent me away. I don't think Evelyn will want to see me again."

"She will," Sara said. "In time. Let's just hope she doesn't keep you waiting for years. Smiths are stubborn creatures."

CHAPTER 40

EVELYN

September 1940
Weybridge

E velyn lost track of how many times she'd awoken and fallen
asleep. Each time it seemed another bouquet of flowers had been
set at her hospital bedside. They were too far out of reach for her to
see who they were from. She doubted her bandaged and cast-ridden
body would cooperate anyway.

The nurse could check a card for the sender; Evelyn had caught
a glimpse of her in her white uniform leaving the room once or twice.
But Evelyn couldn't work up enough enthusiasm to ask her. Her whole
life had been turned upside down and shaken.

Caroline and Alfred Fairchild weren't her biological parents.
Wren Smith was. Wren Smith and some unknown man. How comically unfunny that Evelyn didn't even know her biological mother's
first name.

She should want to know. But she was also content to lie there
under the fluorescent lights and brood.

Actually, she was not. That was the old Evelyn, pre-Wrens, who'd
been reconciled to lay despondent. But Evelyn didn't feel like that girl

anymore. She called for the nurse, who came not a moment later. "Yes, Miss Fairchild?"

Fairchild. The name seized at her chest, but she pushed on. "Could you ask my parents to come in?"

For a few heartbeats she panicked, wondering if her parents were even still at the hospital. They could've run off to do their own brooding. Or to talk to a lawyer. Or even to get away from the dangers of Surrey and London.

"Yes, of course. I'll go fetch them," the nurse said.

Evelyn let out a slow breath.

In came her mother very timidly. A first for her. To explain. To answer questions. To reassure her, possibly.

"Evie," she began softly. "I'm so glad you wanted to see me. You look much improved already. More color in your face."

Or what could be seen of it. Evelyn gently touched along her cheekbone. Thankfully some of the swelling had gone down.

"Where's Father?" Evelyn asked, noting how her voice sounded stronger. "He better not be talking to the lawy—"

Her mother held up a hand. "No, darling. I asked if I could come in alone this time. So much that happened back then was my doing. At my insistence. And I wanted to be the one to explain. May I?" she asked, pointing to a visitor chair.

Evelyn nodded, a bit dumbfounded by her mother's meekness. She sat, straightening her skirt, then crossed her ankles. Her mother ran a hand down her lap a final time. "This all isn't as big of a scandal as it's being made out to be."

Evelyn almost laughed darkly, that rare meekness she'd seen in the formidable Caroline Fairchild dissipating.

"But," her mother said, "like I said, I'd like to explain. You must understand, your father and I very badly wanted a child. We'd been trying for some time, when your father was called away to war. I'll be honest, his leaving felt like a welcome reprieve from feeling so disappointed in myself that I couldn't conceive. Then, only months, maybe even weeks, before the war's conclusion, I was contacted by the Harringtons. It's all very complex, but a friend of theirs, a local aviculturist, if I remember correctly, said his daughter's friend had found herself in a family way, but that she'd be unable to care for the child. A private adoption was suggested." Her mother paused to smile. "It all felt serendipitous."

A word, Evelyn mused, she'd never heard her mother say before.

"I know, I know," her mother granted. "It's fanciful of me. But it truly was. I've never told you this, but I myself was adopted."

Evelyn's mouth parted in surprise. "Why did you keep that a secret?"

"I haven't told a soul, Evelyn, beyond those who already knew. Your father didn't even know until after we were wed. I was adopted by the Pitt family, who hailed from a long line of barons. Though my father was less concerned with titles. He'd chosen to become a—"

"Reverend," Evelyn finished. She'd never met her grandfather, but she'd heard her mother and father speak of "the reverend" over the years.

Her mother nodded. "It was a respected family. I was very fortunate to be adopted by them, especially as I was a child at the time and no longer an infant. And while it was known I wasn't biologically a Pitt, my mother made it clear I should be treated as nothing but a Pitt. It was as if the first years of my life didn't exist, and any talk of my life prior to that time was forbidden. I can't say I even remember any of my time at an orphanage. Multiple orphanages, perhaps. So you see, when the idea of a private adoption was presented to me and your father, I was very agreeable. Eager, even, to give another child—to give *you*—a life you wouldn't otherwise have."

Evelyn picked absently at the white hospital sheet. That was all very fine and well, but, "Why not tell me? Would you ever have told me if this all didn't happen?"

Her mother rubbed her lips together. "It's not likely. No. Your grandmother counseled me not to speak of your adoption. She suggested I do as she had done, to erase any time prior to you becoming a Fairchild. As it was, you were ours from your very first breath. Still, your grandmother recommended a binding agreement, that your adoption would never be spoken of. I saw no reason not to follow her advice. Your father agreed as well. We saw it as a way to protect you and secure a future for you, just as mine had been secured."

A future that had felt very much planned for her. Learn to adequately run a household. Marry. Bring up a family. Hold events for other ladies. It was exactly as her mother had done, orchestrated by her mother before her.

Evelyn felt the need to squirm, to reposition herself, but her injuries wouldn't allow it. So she turned her head away from her mother. Evelyn needed to process, to let her mother's words sink in. She didn't feel that her life had been a lie. She truly was a Fairchild. But it felt like an omission not to let Evelyn know that she could've been . . . what? A Smith?

How different her life would've been with the stoic Wren Smith. Another thought came to her, and she turned her head back toward her mother. "Did you decide to keep me after you saw my condition? Or were you contractually obligated?"

Evelyn's mother lurched forward. She grasped Evelyn's arm, quickly loosening her grip so as not to hurt her. "Oh, Evie. You were certainly wanted by me and your father. By Mrs. Smith too; however, she wasn't in a position to care for you. I never want you to question that."

"But was I a disappointment?"

"Never. You were a remarkable, resilient, and brave child. We knew you'd be the instant you were born, and you've proven it to us time and time again."

Tears came to Evelyn's eyes. "You've never said such things to me before. It was always what I couldn't do or shouldn't do. Or what I must do."

Her mother sighed, but not in an exasperated manner. Her exhalation was rueful. "I've been protective. I'll admit, perhaps to a fault. But it's not as if I've been wrong. You nearly were killed, Evelyn, and it hurts me to see you injured in this way. I'm furious with myself that I was unable to stop you from running off to join the war."

"Mother." Evelyn paused to temper feelings of annoyance. This was an important conversation for them, one they should've had long ago. "My future is my own to decide."

"Of course, darling. Of course. But what is so wrong with the future we've discussed? The life I've built with your father is a wonderful one. I take so much joy from caring for him and you and our home. I've done what my mother did. The Ratcliffes and the Pitts were old family friends. The Pitts and Fairchilds are old family friends. And see, we have the Harringtons."

"Please, Mother, not again with the Harringtons." Evelyn didn't want to think about Percy. So she wouldn't. "I don't regret joining up as a Wren. Not for a second. In fact, I want to stay on."

"You couldn't possibly, Evelyn!" Her mother turned bug-eyed. "Look at you. You could pass for a mummy."

She could. Evelyn wouldn't deny that. But her bones would mend. Her muscles would strengthen again. And as they did, her desire to make a difference in this war would only grow. She wanted to ride again.

Evelyn told her mother as much.

Her mother only harrumphed. "Can't you see that I only want—your father and I only want—what is best for you?"

Evelyn could feel herself getting choked up, but she wouldn't allow it. She pushed out the words. "What if what's best for me is different from what you think it is?"

"Whatever do you mean?"

"I may marry, Mother. I may not. If I do, I may decide to work *and* raise a family."

"Oh, Evelyn—"

"In any scenario I'd like your support. I hope you'd be proud of me regardless."

"We are proud. We are so very proud. What you did, no matter how careless it was, made a difference. I'm told you saved many lives the other day. You accomplished that, sweetheart. I have no doubt you can accomplish whatever it is you set your mind to."

Evelyn's throat grew thick. Her mother's words were ones she'd ached to hear for so long.

But in true Caroline Fairchild fashion, she mucked it up, saying, "But now that you have these Wrens out of your system, it's time to settle down."

Evelyn's heart sank a little. Her mother had gone full circle. She'd once said the same thing about racing. They had thrown her that bone. They had let her chew for a bit. Then her mother had tried to swap the bone for . . . she didn't know . . . the medicine in her body wouldn't let her complete the metaphor. But was this why her parents hadn't bum-rushed her out of London once she contacted them? She could ask, but Evelyn already knew the answer.

To her mother's credit, she also hadn't stormed into London and demanded Evelyn leave the Wrens. Evelyn had been free to do as she wished, with the only interference being Percy spying on her. That was something.

Her mother was a work in progress. So was Evelyn. She was still becoming . . . what, she wasn't sure. But she knew it was with the Wrens. She still felt their call, even though she knew she'd have grounds to be medically discharged if she so wished.

Her mother sighed. Not ruefully this time. "We'll talk more, darling. You need your rest, but first"—she ticked toward the door—"there's someone else who's been waiting patiently to see you."

"Who?"

"Percy."

"Oh no, no," Evelyn said. She'd sit up, shoulders square, back straight—if she could—to add emphasis to her words.

Her mother scolded her. "Darling, don't be rude. Percy has been worried about you. He's been in the waiting room for hours."

Now he stood in the doorway. No, not standing, cowering.

"Percy, please come in. Evelyn is still on medications and doesn't know her own tongue."

Unbelievable. Her mother was more of a work in progress than expected—with her sights still firmly set on Percy. Little did her mother know there was a Victoria.

"Hi, Evie," Percy said timidly. His usually coiffed hair was disheveled. He took her in, his posture void of his usual assuredness, and his expression was soft. Sympathetic? Unsure of himself?

"I'll just give you two a few moments," Evelyn's mother said with a smile. She gave Evelyn a soft peck on her forehead before leaving, squeezing Percy's arm as she passed.

"Hello," he greeted Evelyn again. "Thank you for seeing me."

Evelyn gave a flat "Hello."

"I suppose I deserve the greeting. Things didn't end well between us last time."

"I do believe *end* is the essential word there."

Percy hovered in the space between the door and Evelyn's hospital bed. He covered the distance to her, acting as if he'd sit, but Evelyn shot him a glare. Instead he remained standing, tightly gripping the back of the chair her mother had sat in only moments ago.

"I wish it could've been otherwise, Evie."

Evelyn rattled her head and closed her eyes. "Why are you doing this, Percy? Why are you here?"

"Because I've been a fool."

Evelyn opened her eyes but twisted her lips. "Go on."

"A ninny."

Her expression remained unchanged.

"A dunderhead? A clod? An ignoramus? How about that? Truly, I've been blind to you, Evie."

Evelyn swallowed roughly. He wasn't wrong. She said in a softer voice, "Go on."

He expelled a quick breath. Not quite a chuckle; he probably wouldn't dare do that at the moment. But one eyebrow rose higher than the other, and she saw it again. She beguiled him. Though it seemed Victoria did as well.

"It's over with Victoria," he said, as if knowing Evelyn was thinking of the other woman. "I'll start with that. There is no other woman in my life now. Unless you count my mother." He paused, waiting for his joke to land. "Nothing? I suppose it wasn't my finest. I suppose I haven't been at my finest in general. It's just that you and I have been friends for so long. Then both our mothers put so much pressure on the two of us getting together that it became a deterrent."

He wasn't wrong. Evelyn had felt exactly the same.

"But then," Percy admitted, "our fight and, more importantly, you ending up in hospital put so much into perspective. I don't think I fully embraced the idea of what you and I could've been together. I let myself feel glimpses of it in the past few weeks. But there was Victoria, and it was easy to focus on her. But it's not Victoria I want. It's you I want, Evelyn."

"You're saying I had to almost die in order for you to realize you want to be with me?"

"Like I said, I'm a clod. But to be fair, it wasn't until I told you I was a secret agent that you began to see me differently."

"To be fair, I caught you in the act. It's also not my fault you were previously a bore."

His mouth fell open, knowing she was being funny. But then his expression turned more serious. "I've made a lot of mistakes, Evie. Can you forgive me?"

Could she? The question felt a touch rhetorical. She'd been miserable after her fight with Percy. It'd been eye-opening for her as well. Warmth spread in her. Percy saw her differently. He wanted to give it a go with her. She let that sink in and then said, "Yes, I suppose I do forgive you."

He exhaled. "Splendid. And in the spirit of coming clean, I'll admit to another mistake I made."

"Percy . . . ," Evelyn began, nervous for whatever words he was about to utter next.

"You see, it's a regret of mine that I never *did* try to kiss you."

As much as her heart began to stammer in her chest, Evelyn still fought to keep her composure, saying, "I'm glad you didn't. That wouldn't have been fair to Victoria."

"No, it wouldn't have been. But now . . ." He smirked.

"Percy J. Harrington—if that *is* your real name—our first kiss will not be as I lie in a hospital bed. I will be on my feet. I will not be black and blue. And my hair will be brushed."

"As you wish."

She smiled. "So, to clarify, we're going to try this between us?"

He rounded the chair, finally sitting, finally touching her. His palm slid under hers and he gently rubbed his thumb over her hand. "I'd like that very much."

"Doesn't it feel like we're giving our parents exactly what they want? We could hide it, you know." She wagged her brows the best she could without releasing a wave of pain. "A covert relationship."

He shook his head. "I did that with Victoria. And one of the reasons was because I wasn't sure if Victoria was the one—and I didn't want the pressure from my parents to make her the one."

Evelyn felt warm all over. "But me?"

"For you I'll endure an offensive from our mothers. It'll likely be fiercer than the Germans."

Evelyn laughed, following it with an "Ouch."

Percy lurched forward.

"You'll have to restrain yourself from making me laugh for a few more days." A thought came to her and she bit her lip before saying, "Before we try this, I'd like to go on the record as saying that I don't see myself as the type of wife to host dinner parties. I don't know what I want for my future, not exactly, but I'd like to be free to figure it out."

"I'm not looking for conventional. And I know you, Evie. I know how important the Brooklands was to you. I'm not looking to clip your wings."

She snorted. "Was that another wren joke?"

"Unintentional. But it works, does it not?"

Evelyn shook her head the slightest of bits, careful not to bring on another wave of pain. A thought came to her. "How is the Brooklands? No one has told me."

Percy scooted his chair even closer. "I know you're likely beating yourself up for not getting there sooner than you did, but you got there and you saved a lot of lives, Evie. You made a difference."

She'd made a difference. She let those words settle over her. During her rides, she'd daydreamed she'd do such a thing. And she had. No part of her wanted to stop making a difference.

"The Brooklands wised up too. The Germans came back yesterday, but the Brooklands had put up barrage balloons and the gunners were able to fight them off."

"Foiled," Evelyn said with a smile. "It appears you were more successful today in your own endeavors." She nodded to the flowers beside her bed. "I presume the preposterous number of flowers are from you? Your grand gesture to win me back?"

Percy's head ticked toward the arrangements.

"They're not from me. Not this time."

"Oh?"

He gestured toward a note on one of them. Evelyn nodded.

Percy said, "It appears these flowers are from a Rose. 'Beat you to hospital,' it says."

Evelyn chuckled. She missed her friend. "I suppose that means she's better. She took a spill a few weeks back. And the other arrangements?"

"They don't appear to have notes."

"In that case I wager they're from my mother. 'Oh, Evelyn, darling, the room is too drab. That won't do.'" She smirked, but then her head tilted. "So no grand gesture from you, then? I may've been too hasty in my forgiveness."

He smiled mischievously.

"What?"

"Well . . ."

"Percy?"

"Prior to coming, I asked around. I spoke to a few people."

"To whom?" She let out an amused breath. "Why?"

"To Wren Smith, for starters."

Evelyn stilled at hearing the name. She'd put the woman and her adoption out of mind, unsure what to make of either. Not ready to deal with those emotions. But given how smoothly he said Wren Smith's name—no hesitation, no intonation—Evelyn assumed he didn't yet know Wren Smith was her biological mother. She'd tell him eventually, but she was too curious to interrupt him now. "What did you talk to her about?"

"Your future. If I know you, you won't want to leave the Wrens, even though—"

"You're right. But why would I leave? I just did something good. Really good, Percy. There's no way I'm stopping now."

"The thing is, your mother told me the doctor's prognosis. Your tibia-fibula fracture alone could take six months to heal."

Evelyn's eyes widened. "Six months?"

"They haven't told you, have they?"

She shook her head solemnly. And, if she was being honest, bitterly. Her mother was doing the same song and dance. She may have sway with the doctors, but too bad for her mother; Evelyn's future, whatever it may be, wasn't up to her mother. She raised her chin. "I'll heal. If I know how to do anything, it's that."

Percy circled his thumb over her hand. "It's made you who you are, Evie. Strong. Resilient. The woman capable of saving all those people. But this time may be different. You'll likely need a cane to walk."

Evelyn's heart sank. "You mean forever, don't you?"

Percy's face said it all.

It felt like a cruel joke. She had just done something important for the first time in her life. She hoped to continue riding, continue helping in the war, but how would that be possible now? And if the Wrens couldn't have her as a rider, maybe they wouldn't have her at all. She swallowed roughly, her eyes swimming with tears, and she questioned where that left her now.

Would she ever be Dare D-Evelyn again?

What could she do that would make her feel she had value?

Percy leaned forward and gently tapped the underside of her chin. "None of that now. There's still my grand gesture. I didn't just want to come here and beg for your forgiveness. I wanted to come to you with a possibility. You've spent too much of your life waiting to go and do and be. As I said, I spoke with Wren Smith, who in turn did some digging and had her own conversations, and, well, she found you a new role."

"A new role?" Evelyn felt her spirits lift. "Wren Smith did that?"

Percy gave a nod. "That is, if you're interested. This is your future, after all."

"So you mean to say you came bearing a future for me?"

He laughed. "With the Wrens and with me. How'd I do?"

Evelyn scrunched an eye. "Depends on the role."

"Well, the general thought is that you'd be well suited as a plotter. You'd be much like a croupier at a roulette table."

Evelyn raised a brow. "Come now?"

"You'd manage a large table, with a map of whatever area you're stationed to. Portsmouth was mentioned."

"Portsmouth." Evelyn followed the town's name with a deep sigh. There was nothing like starting a relationship living hours apart, both with few chances for leaves.

Percy nodded. "I'll write you. You'll write me, telling me what you can about your work. I find it quite interesting. I hear it's all underground, as in literally under the ground to protect from attacks. Very secretive. Very crucial work. You'll tire your mind more than your body. That mind of yours has always been powerful, Evie. As I understand it, information will come to you regarding aircrafts— their positions, their heights, their bearings—and you'd use a plotting rod to move the aircrafts around the table. It's hugely crucial when monitoring incoming raids. It's quite the lively table, from what I'm told. You'd have your work cut out for you."

"Sounds thrilling."

"Truly?"

Evelyn nodded. It wasn't a motorcycle. It wasn't racing around a circuit. Plotting wasn't where she'd seen herself a few days ago. It'd be an adjustment, a pivot. But it *did* sound thrilling in its own way. She liked the idea of stretching her brain muscles. And in doing so, she could continue to make a difference. She'd still be Dare D-Evelyn, in a sense, existing in a high-adrenaline situation, working on her toes to thwart any attacks and outmaneuver the Germans to coordinate their own.

But the icing on the cake: it was *her* choice. Evelyn could say no and become something else entirely. But she liked this idea. "I choose to be a plotter, and I choose you, Percy Harrington, even if I'll have to wait until this war is over to fully have you."

"I very badly want to kiss you, Evie." She pointed to her hair, and Percy playfully admonished her with a shake of his head. "I should've thought to bring a hairbrush too."

Evelyn laughed but then grew more serious. "Thank you, Percy."

And as she said it, she realized there was someone else she needed to thank, someone she was finally ready to talk to.

CHAPTER 41

MARION

October 1940
London

Marion stood at the window at headquarters, a mug between her hands. Her heart raced as she kept an eye out for any of her returning girls.

Lord help her, each time a motorcycle approached headquarters, she couldn't resist looking to see if it could be Evelyn, knowing full well her daughter was still recovering—and coming to terms with her new reality. The last Marion had seen or spoken with Evelyn had been when she was asked to leave Evelyn's hospital room, and Marion had respected her wishes. Marion had also been too much of a coward to push for a goodbye or to exchange any other words for that matter. She'd been discharged from the hospital shortly thereafter. And shortly after returning to London, the hellish air raids had begun in earnest in London.

The German planes came during the daytime.

They came during the evening.

They came every day, by the hundreds, waves of bombers, protected by their fighter planes, swelling over the island.

And every day Britain's fighter squadrons had met them. Still, they were not always broken up, and the Germans began targeting more than London docks, factories, and bases. It had become clear, and it had been echoed by Mr. Churchill himself, that Adolf Hitler hoped to terrorize London as a whole, civilians be damned.

The Luftwaffe boasted, even issuing a press notice that they had dropped more than one million kilograms of bombs on London in a twenty-four-hour period.

Marion shuddered and sipped her coffee, needing something stronger than tea. This war . . . these ongoing attacks were ghastly.

Already Hitler had been giving the orders to blitz London for over a month, and Marion doubted that man would ever grow a soul and call an end to it anytime soon.

Day after day, Marion dispatched her girls to London and beyond, praying each would return to headquarters unharmed. With so many raids, getting to a shelter wasn't always a possibility, and the girls were instructed how to quickly dismount their motorcycles and use them as shields in an emergency, hoping the bodies of their machines would block some of the shrapnel and debris. Blessedly, Marion hadn't yet lost a girl.

Wren McMasters had recovered from her prior incident, but instead of returning to London, she'd been restationed in Portsmouth, where she'd begun working as a ship mechanic. Evelyn would begin there, too, after a new round of training, but as a plotter. Dangerous still, yes, but Marion would be pleased to have her daughter removed from the heart of Hitler's current attacks.

It was today, actually, that Evelyn had been released from the hospital. Marion had called the hospital daily to check on Evelyn's progress. She'd only just hung up.

Marion's breath clouded the windowpanes, and she squeezed her mug. The heat seeped into her palms, growing almost too hot to bear. She repositioned her grip to the handle as a vehicle stopped in front of the building. Fewer vehicles roamed the streets. Fewer pedestrians too. Mr. Churchill had said it was a time for everyone to stand together and hold firm.

"Every man and woman will therefore prepare himself to do his duty, whatever it may be, with special pride and care."

Marion knew that meant leading these girls. It also meant doing whatever was asked of her for the entirety of the war. She'd see it through this time, heaven help her.

The driver brought out a wheelchair from the boot and then helped a young woman from the automobile. Marion's heart leapt and her coffee sloshed over the rim of her mug. It was Evelyn.

Truth be told, Marion hadn't known when or if she'd ever lay eyes on her daughter again. She'd already been given a second chance. Who was she to think she deserved a third?

But before she knew it, she was descending the stairs to the first floor, then proceeding to the curb.

Evelyn was thanking her driver before looking up at Marion as she approached. "Wren Smith," she said. The driver righted Evelyn to Marion before stepping away.

Alone with her daughter, Marion breathed deeply. Yes, that was better; she could talk to Evelyn in that way, as Wren Smith. Though the love for her daughter pulsed inside of Marion so fiercely, so consumingly. "Oh, Evelyn," she said impulsively.

But that was all. She didn't know where to go from there.

Evelyn smoothed a wrinkle on her lap, looking equally unsure. She wore her uniform, her sleeve rolled up to allow for her arm cast. The cast of her leg stuck out from beneath her blue skirt. Not a hair was out of place beneath her cap. The swelling and bruises below her eye had mostly vanished. Once again, Marion recognized the shape as her own and knew she had to begin.

"I'd like to apologize for blurting out that I'm your biological mother. In all the times I daydreamed of telling you, I can assure you that was not the way I saw it going."

A smile teased Evelyn's lips. "Is that so?"

"You have your father's humor and his intelligence," Marion said. "I hope that's all right to say."

Evelyn gave a nod. "I'm glad you mentioned him. I spoke more with my parents. Funny, I had to ask them your first name. But I also asked them if they knew anything about my biological father . . ."

Marion had never spoken of him to Caroline and Alfred. "Eddie," she said now. "Edward Smith." She paused to smile, remembering the day he first introduced himself to her. "He was a character. Witty. Caring. Adventurous. Tall, like you. Same red tint to his hair. Same freckles. The first time I saw you smile, I thought my heart would burst at the similarities. He was"—Evelyn swallowed roughly—"my everything. We married in secret, all very scandalous." Marion sighed softly. "Back then, Wrens couldn't marry. It wasn't long before I learned I was pregnant. Your father was overjoyed."

Evelyn asked quietly, "What happened to him?"

Marion ran her tongue over her teeth, gaining composure. "He didn't survive the first war. Almost, though." She cleared her throat. "Eddie died on a battlefield in Amiens. He was a dispatch rider, in fact."

"I'm sorry," Evelyn said.

A sudden roar of an engine came from above. Marion reached for Evelyn, both women watching the skies. This time, no danger followed. The sound of planes had merely traveled miles through the cooler air.

Marion lowered the hand she pressed over her heart. "Thank you. He would've loved to meet you."

Evelyn swallowed roughly. "I would have liked to meet him too. It all feels so unfair, doesn't it? Sometimes I struggle to understand why things happen. So much feels out of our control. But I'm learning all I can do is push and push for the things most important to me, then . . . I don't know . . . see how things break."

Hadn't Marion been fighting for control her whole life? Fighting for something that was impossible to fully achieve? And although it couldn't eradicate twenty years of guilt, she felt lighter hearing her daughter's words. "I'm going to push and push to finish this war in his honor. I didn't finish before . . ." Marion trailed off, hoping Evelyn wouldn't see herself as the reason. But Evelyn did, her face falling, and Marion was quick to say, "But I see leaving the first war as the best decision I've ever made." That admission, too, made her feel lighter, breathe easier. "May I ask you something?"

"Of course," Evelyn said.

"The *P* of your middle name. What does it stand for?"

"Poppy."

Marion pressed her lips together and nodded. "Then that is an example of life breaking beautifully. Someday I must thank your parents. That was what I called you. They didn't need to include it in your name, yet they did."

"I wouldn't give them too much credit. My mother had no intention of telling me. Including Poppy in my name was likely a pat on her own back at the time."

Marion nodded. "Well, it's still there—in your name—and that means something to me. You coming here means something to me as well. Thank you for stopping here and talking with me, Evelyn. I wasn't sure I'd be given this chance."

"I won't say I wasn't mad. And hurt. And a slew of other emotions. But when Percy told me you had worked with him to find me a new assignment, that all fell away. You could've refused to help. You could've had me demobilized. But you somehow knew this was important to me."

"'I am no bird; and no net ensnares me; I am a free human being with an independent will.' One of my favorite authors once said that. It reminds me of you, Evelyn."

"Oh, but I *am* a bird," she said, smiling slyly. "I'm a Wren. Just like my mother."

Marion's eyes filled with tears. The wetness spilled over. What a gift this child was, one she was beginning to feel worthy of.

Evelyn went on, "And what about you? Are you to remain in London as you finish out the war?"

"For now, until I'm needed elsewhere. I am their Mother Wren, after all."

"I didn't know you knew we called you that."

Marion only smiled.

It felt like a natural end to their conversation. But Marion also felt their relationship was only just beginning.

Evelyn looked to her driver, and he approached to help her back into the car. Off she'd go to training as her body finished healing, then off she'd go to Portsmouth. Marion had little doubt her daughter would make a difference—a large one—in the remainder of the war.

Before Evelyn was wheeled away, she outstretched her hand. "May I write you?"

Marion took her daughter's hand. "I'd like that, Evelyn. I'd like that very much."

CHAPTER 42

EVELYN

June 1944
Portsmouth

Dear Marion,

We've done it! We've made it to the shores of France. They say liberation is in sight! I'm bubbling with pure joy because I just know that today's successful invasions are going to change everything.

You were the very first person I thought of to gush to (besides the other Wrens and military folk I work with—everyone was hugging and cheering all throughout the day as updates came in). I've only just returned to my cabin—my brain and body completely exhausted, I might add, after working round-the-clock shifts—but while all that adrenaline is still coursing, I wanted to write you straightaway, even while knowing it'll likely take some time for this to reach you in Italy.

This is the first I've had time to digest all the happenings of the day. So much has gone into it, for months and months. Everything was accounted for, even the tides and moonlight. Today I began early.

Earlier than usual. As I stepped off my bus, the sky
was already brimming with planes and gliders. I'm
getting quite fast with my cane. You should see me!
So I hightailed it down to the plotting room and took
my place at the table. It was already filled with plots.
I didn't even have my headphones on yet to chart the
new ships coming in before I was told it had started.
Operation Overlord, that is. I can finally put those covert
words into a letter.

The beachheads in Normandy have code names
as well. Omaha, Utah, Gold, Juno, and Sword, and
it's where we began the invasion, launching right here
from Portsmouth. I might add the invasion caught the
Germans completely by surprise. You may know these
details by now, but if not, Hitler and Rommel had
their sights set on Dover, just as we wanted them to.
There, our army had thousands of mock tanks in place.
False radio reports and fake radar signals were sent. The
Germans ate up the phantom army with a spoon.

I would've loved to see the faces of the Germans
when, suddenly, they were faced with 3,000 landing
crafts, 2,500 ships, and 500 naval vessels coming across
the Channel. Imagine, over 100,000 troops suddenly
on your shores, over two hundred miles from where you
expected them to be!

Bloody brilliant.

I can finally tell you my location in Portsmouth too.
More than a hundred feet beneath Fort Southwick! It's
become the headquarters for all that's going on, where
all of the forces have been working together. There's a

spiral staircase that leads to a mile of secret tunnels, including one that leads to my (small) plotting room. I've reassured you (many times) in my letters that my location is bombproof. Do you finally believe me now?

It's you I worry about, especially since your recent letters place you all over Italy, so close to all that will be going on. It feels so far, but it also makes me happy to think you are back overseas, back on a motorcycle, back with your birds, back with Wren Brown. There's something poetic in all of that, don't you think? You'll have the chance to finish this war the way you'd wanted to complete the first. Mostly. I know Eddie is not there, and it's probably been very emotional for you. But you'll do it. You'll finish this war for him. I also hope you'll see how you're seeing it through for yourself too. Or at least I hope the past will be reconciled for you.

It'll be onward!

For us all!

Rose gave me a scare earlier today. She's been on the HMS Arethusa, which I saw from our table had suffered a direct hit. I had to put it out of mind and focus on the job, but before writing you, I asked an officer, and thankfully Rose wasn't listed among the casualties.

I heard from my parents recently. Ironically my mother is coming around to me being in this war, just as it is (hopefully) coming to an end. Also, you'll be surprised to hear, there wasn't a single mention of marriage. I remain in shock.

Have you seen Percy? I know you likely haven't.

"Overseas" is a large place. But that's all I know of his location. To think, I haven't seen him since you and I were in the hospital. I told you how we had plans to finally see each other a few months ago. Well, his leave was changed, and we were unable to do so. Soon, I hope.

Before I go, I wanted to express how sorry I am to hear 486 passed away. I know now how special he was to you. I'm glad you had each other all those years. He may've been the longest-living pigeon known to man.

There's a great noise outside I must go investigate. Write me soon. Tell me of Italy. Quote more of your books to me. Tell me tales of your past. Tell me stories of now. I look forward to it all. Maybe, just maybe, by the time I hear from you, this war will be over!

Sending my love,
Your Poppy

Evelyn put down her pen next to her good luck elephant on her desk and stuffed her letter in an envelope, smiling the entire time. Exchanging letters with Marion had become one of her most favorite pastimes, second only to writing to Percy.

Funny how Evelyn and her biological mother had grown closer while being such a great distance apart. Evelyn felt she could express herself freely in writing, more so than she could with spoken words.

In time she had begun signing her letters as Poppy. It just felt right. To the world, she was Evelyn Fairchild. To a few, she was Evie. To Marion, she was Poppy. She would've been the same to Eddie too.

Oh, how she wished she could have known him, met him, seen the pride she knew would've been present in their matching green eyes.

Marion shared story after story, word after word filling the page.

About a motorcycle they'd called Alli.

About joining the war together.

About a first kiss.

Evelyn imagined it couldn't have been easy to write about, and letters had been tearstained on occasion, but she also recognized the flourish in Marion's handwriting, as if she was depicting something that breathed life into her once upon a time, and maybe, just maybe, she was letting herself experience again.

While Marion spoke of the past, she also recounted escapades from her life now that often had Evelyn gripping the paper. At first, Marion's updates came from London, while Germany relentlessly continued to bomb there. The raids had gone on in London and other large cities for nine unfathomable months, leaving much of Britain in ruin. However, it didn't break the British as Adolf Hitler had hoped.

London began to rebuild, and in time Marion had begun working with her birds again, first in London and eventually in Italy, sending letters from Sicily, Delianuova, Cassino, and other locations Evelyn failed to recall offhand.

But she'd never forget the stories Marion's recent letters told of hazardous terrain, horrible conditions, and moments that skyrocketed Evelyn's heart rate, like how Marion nearly missed spotting a wire that'd been set as a booby trap across a road. She had to turn the bike on its side, push it under, then slip beneath herself—all with birds on her back.

Evelyn's head ticked to the hubbub outside. The masses were celebrating. She reached for her cane, intent on joining them. Only now, she wouldn't be hightailing it. She wasn't sure her muscles would even allow it from all the standing she'd done at her plotting table. And for the past few days, she'd stood longer than usual. There'd also been more activity than usual, causing her to move about the plotting table more. To think more. She liked using all of herself in this way.

After seeing what the hubbub was about, she'd take a good soak. Her mind and body would thank her.

She headed outside. The first signs of nighttime showed in the sky. The last update she'd been privy to had come after the lunch hour. Troops advancing from Sword Beach had captured a handful of German strongpoints inland, and thus the men were continuing their advance on Caen.

Hours had since passed, and Evelyn imagined more progress had been made. A champagne bottle was thrust into her hand, Evelyn responding with a laugh. She took a sip. A small one. She couldn't remember when she'd last eaten. Oh, what was one more nip?

A uniformed man raised his fist and cheered. She was greeted with smiles from faces she recognized, waving in return, and faces she'd never set eyes on before; it made little difference. It was a joyous day indeed, and she truly believed what she'd written to Marion: the day's successful invasions would change everything.

London would rebuild.

Portsmouth would rebuild.

Much of Portsmouth had been razed to the ground, on account of the naval shipping and dockyards being there. Evelyn had grown accustomed to watching her step and taking care with where she placed her cane.

It was why she didn't see him approaching.

It was why she had no clue he was there until she heard, "Evie."

Her head snapped up, nearly losing her footing. Not more than a handful of steps away stood a man. Dark hair. Sharp cheekbones.

A day's worth of stubble. A face she'd recognize anywhere, even after three years, seven months, and eighteen days of not seeing him.

"Percy?" she said, bewilderment turning his name into a question. "You're here? I thought you were overseas."

He closed the distance, lifting Evelyn off the ground, holding her close, embracing her, speaking into her ear. "I was. I've been all over. The coordination that went into today is practically mind-blowing. But now I'm here."

Evelyn's feet hit the ground again. "You're here," she parroted, still feeling flabbergasted. Wonderfully flabbergasted. To see him. To touch him. To smell him. To be with him, if even for a short period of time.

Percy made a show of examining her.

Evelyn's brows scrunched. "What is it?"

He smiled cheekily. "You are on your feet. You are not black and blue, save for the blue of your uniform." His smile grew. "And your hair is reasonably tamed. I'd say enough to declare it adequately brushed, despite the hectic day you've likely had. And for that reason . . ."

Percy leaned in and kissed her. Their first kiss, the scruff of his face tickling her chin. The first of many scruffy kisses, if Evelyn had any say in it. And with Percy, it felt like she'd always have a say.

"Somewhere," she said, pulling back, looking into his brown eyes, "our mothers are cheering."

Percy's head fell back as he laughed. "Let them." He brushed his lips against hers again. And again. "This is our relationship, though I've had to remind my mother of that a few times already in my letters."

"We're all eager for this war to end, it seems. I wrote to Marion just now about today's events."

"She'll like hearing from you. Discovering her feels like something good that's come of the war, no?"

Evelyn gave a soft huff. "To think I didn't even know I was look-ing for her. Or you." It was her turn to kiss him. Then once more for good measure. "I'd like to do more good, Percy, even after this is all over." She saw nothing but acceptance in his eyes. She added, "It *will* be over soon, right?"

Evelyn looked to him for that reassurance. For as jolly as she was from the day, fear still niggled at her insides that Marion was likely mere miles from the front line with her birds. The war had yet to be won, and she couldn't shake how Marion had lost Eddie in the last days of the first war.

"We've done all we can," was all he said.

CHAPTER 43

MARION

May 1945
Ferrara

Dearest Evelyn,

As always, it is a relief to hear from you, knowing you are well and thriving. I felt your excitement come through the page as you explained Normandy's D-day and your involvement in it. I'm very proud. However, I'll be honest, your last letter left me paralyzed with fear. I was desperate for updates about D+1, D+2, and each day thereafter. Each seemed promising that the landing could be the beginning of the end. Still, I'd been afraid to have hope.

Before Amiens, Eddie had said something similar to what you put into your letter. You wrote how the invasions were going to change everything. He'd said how the Battle of Amiens was going to change everything.

Uncanny, the likeness of your words, no? I like to think you are an optimist, just like Eddie. Still, you can understand how I've been ill at ease, especially after Herr Hitler retaliated with his doodlebugs on London.

I tell you, those flying bombs are exponentially more terrifying than the Big Bertha guns we faced during the first war. It didn't help that the Nazi propaganda hailed their "wonder weapons" as a way to turn the tide of the war back in Germany's favor. I prayed it wouldn't be true.

Once Paris was liberated, I allowed myself a glimmer of hope. Our success at the Battle of the Bulge and the Americans crossing the Rhine River, though, gave me genuine hopefulness. As you know, Berlin fell soon after and, only days ago, the German forces surrendered where I am here in the Po Valley. Yesterday, Germany as a whole surrendered.

I am so grateful to write those words. I stared at them, willing them to remain on the page. And they do. It's why I can finally respond to your letter. With everything feeling so fragile, fear held me back until now. I'm a silly old woman who imagined I'd somehow jinx the outcome. I hope I haven't caused you very much worry while you waited for my reply.

I'm sure you've also heard the rumors that Herr Hitler took his own life, squirreled away in a bunker beneath Berlin. Time will tell if that is true. There's been much speculation and stories about him in the camps. One that struck me was how Herr Hitler was a dispatch runner during the first war. I don't know the particular battles he fought in along the Western Front, but it's an odd coincidence that Herr Hitler, Eddie, and I all held similar roles. If I allow it, my anger will grow, thinking that Herr Hitler survived while delivering his messages,

yet Eddie did not. I no longer wish to be angry, though.
I no longer feel the insurmountable weight of causing
Eddie's death.

You were right, my Poppy. Being back with my
birds, back with Sara, back on a motorcycle has been
a balm. And now I can say that I've finished a war. A
bookend that gives me such peace, although I feel it's
only natural a piece of me will always mourn the loss of
your father. What I'd give for him to have the chance to
meet you. He'd be immensely proud of the woman you've
become. With still so much ahead of you. Knowing that
also brings me peace. Do you know what will be next
for you?

Sara is delighted to return home and to be reunited
with her husband and children. She's afraid Helen and
Henry won't remember her after all this time. But I've
assured her they'll find their way to each other again.
And one day they'll understand why she wasn't able to
be with them these past few years. She poked fun at me,
questioning my newfound optimism. I believe it comes
from various sources, yourself included, but also from a
trusty friend, Jane Eyre. The novel has ventured with me
from orphanage to orphanage, to a war, to my cottage
in West Devon, and back again to this final war. Last
night my mind whirled after the surrender, and I calmed
myself by reading. I came upon this line once more from
Mr. Rochester, and I read it differently this time.

"What necessity is there to dwell on the Past,
when the Present is so much surer—the Future so much
brighter?"

Funny how each season of life can bring about new perspectives. As I've questioned what's next for me, I've come to the conclusion that I no longer want to live in my past. While I enjoyed my work at the library in the time between these wars, I have no desire to return to my tiny cottage and my tiny existence. I'm told the Wrens will not disband this time, and so I plan to stay on. Perhaps you'll stay on too? It's your decision, of course. Maybe we can even put Percy to work as a naval surgeon. He'd look handsome in blue.

Whatever you decide, wherever you decide to be, I know with absolute certainty your future is bright, Evelyn. I think mine will be too.

With all my love,
Marion

A NOTE FROM THE AUTHOR

I t has been my complete pleasure to write a novel of the little-known yet remarkably brave women of the Women's Royal Naval Service. Upon seeing mention of the Wrens in other literature, I came to the realization that they hadn't yet had a moment all to themselves as heroes within a novel. Thus, *The Call of the Wrens* was born, and I was in for a treat to research and write about this special group of women who participated in both world wars.

At the onset of the Great War in 1914, the only military role viewed as "suitable" for a woman was in the capacity of a nurse. Nineteen thousand women served as nurses and up to one hundred thousand as Voluntary Aid Detachments. No small number, and invaluable to the war efforts. Still, women weren't seen as a viable asset until 1916, when the British realized a large manpower shortage. The Battle of the Somme was devastating to British numbers, and in conjunction with declining recruitment, Britain began conscription for men and was finally considering "radical measures" of allowing women to perform basic military tasks in an official capacity. In 1917 the Women's Army Auxiliary Corps (WAAC) was the first to form under the banner of "Free a Man for the Front," allowing women to serve not only at home but also abroad.

The Royal Navy had already been including women for centuries, fulfilling positions of—again—nurses and also as laundresses in naval hospitals. After the creation of the WAAC, the Admiralty asked Dame Katherine Furse to establish their own women's corps, the WRNS, nicknamed the Wrens and often affectionately referred to as the Jenny Wrens.

The Wrens, adopting their own ethos of "Free a Man for the Fleet," officially began in 1917, and by 1919 was over seven thousand strong, including such positions as cooks and stewards, writers and telephonists, sail makers, coders and cyphers, and my personal favorite: motorcycle dispatch riders. At the conclusion of World War I, the Wrens were no longer seen as necessary, and the service disbanded. Similar women's services followed suit, such as the Women's Royal Air Force. However, on the eve of the Second World War, the Wrens and other disbanded services were re-established.

At its peak in 1944, the number of women who served within the Wrens was nearly seventy-five thousand, with postings all over the world, including South Africa, India, Ceylon (Sri Lanka), Egypt, Malta, Gibraltar, Italy, France, and Belgium. While the Wrens' motto of "Never at Sea" was true in that the women didn't serve in action aboard battleships, they did serve as stokers, boats' crew, and coxswains in dangerous wartime waters.

By the end of World War II, the lives of 303 Wrens had been sadly lost during active duty, of whom almost 100 served as dispatch riders. Unlike after the first war, the Wrens did not disband following the Second World War, and in 1993 the Women's Royal Naval Service was officially integrated into the naval branch of Britain's military.

As mentioned, I took a particular interest in women serving as motorcycle dispatch riders. I watched war film of them zipping across the frames, and I wondered and imagined their larger role in the war. The characters of Marion and Evelyn are fictional, but I've drawn from real-life Wrens and have placed them in situations inspired by real people and events.

Bunty Marshall volunteered at eighteen years old and underwent a week of training before being stationed as a dispatch rider. While completing a stunt, Wren Marshall crested a hill and a truck hit her head-on. She crashed through the windshield. While her days as a dispatch rider were over, she continued to serve until the end of the war.

Third Officer Pamela McGeorge was another Wren carrying an urgent message when the unexpected happened. Wren McGeorge found herself caught in a heavy air raid. A bomb exploded close by, and she wrecked her motorcycle. Undeterred, she ran the remaining distance, bombs falling all around her, to deliver her message, receiving the British Empire Medal for her gallantry.

Third Officer Brenda Heimann's memoir, edited by her daughter, was invaluable to stepping into life as a Wren and breathing life into what Marion and Evelyn likely experienced. I was further influenced by diaries, anecdotes, additional memoirs, letters, films, and documentaries.

During the Battle of the Somme, dispatch rider Oswald Davis dodged gunfire to deliver pigeons and messages to the front-line troops.

The air raid at the Brooklands is a factual moment, as is the fact the Wrens initially used competition riders from local racing circuits for their dispatch riders, wanting women who could not only ride but also maintain their own machines. Many of the racers mentioned within *The Call of the Wrens*—Gwenda Hawkes, Elsie (Gleed) Wisdom, Kay Petre, Doreen Evans, and Baroness Dorothy Dorndorf—were actual lady racers from the Brooklands, though not all would have raced at the same time I've placed Evelyn there.

I'd be remiss not to mention the birds. The use of homing pigeons in wartime efforts is no secret, with the birds utilized in every branch of service to provide secret, fast, and undetectable messages. But I was surprised to learn that the ins and outs of pigeon use were largely unknown, even by those in the military. I enjoyed learning all I could about these ten-ounce unsung heroes. In part, 486 was inspired by pigeons named President Wilson and Cher Ami.

I did my very best to align with historical timelines, battles, and facts and to avoid those sneaky anachronisms. Any mistakes in details or language or inaccuracies while representing the conditions within this book are my own and ones I know I'll kick myself for.

I'm so thankful for the support of the entire Harper Muse team with Amanda Bostic at the helm; my editor, Kimberly Carlton; my agent, Shannon Hassan; and my editorial dream team of Julie Breihan, Jodi Hughes, and all the proofreaders.

This novel never would've come to fruition without the support of my husband and children, without Lindsay Currie reading each chapter as I wrote it, and without the cheerleading of Carolyn Menke, Victoria Schade, Suzanne Baltsar, and Helen Little, along with my wonderful and supportive nonauthor friends who listen to me go on about books. A heartfelt thank-you to all of my fellow authors (at the risk of missing someone and feeling guilty for days, please allow me to blanket your many names), to all my new and longtime readers, and to all the generous book influencers and groups who have helped to champion this book.

Please continue to tell people about these remarkable women who made a difference in the world but who haven't always received the wide acclaim they deserve. Thank you to the Wrens, past and present, for your service. Thank you to the birds too.

DISCUSSION QUESTIONS

1. The cover is an intriguing one. It is haunting to have a single female rider. With the dual point of view and the two strong female narratives, why do you think one woman was shown?

2. Sometimes the most satisfying part of reading a novel is discovering the meaning of the title. *The Call of the Wrens* is a title that could have different meanings within the context of the story. Marion and Evelyn were "called" by the Women's Royal Naval Service to serve. A calling is also a purpose. How do you think the title came about, and how do both meanings come into context throughout the novel?

3. Both Marion and Evelyn have disabilities that defined their childhoods and shaped who they are. How do these women turn their disabilities into strengths?

4. Eddie and Percy play integral roles in Marion's and Evelyn's lives as protectors, childhood friends, and lovers. How do these relationships evolve over time? How do these relationships define the other relationships Marion and Evelyn have?

5. Both women enlist for different reasons. Marion aches to belong. Evelyn strives to prove herself. How does the need to belong and the need to be seen continue as themes throughout the novel?

6. The concept of family is discussed throughout the novel: the feeling of creating a family, duty to family, and the roles our families give us. What role does the Wrens play for the characters? How do our families, both biological and chosen, affect our perspectives and behaviors?

7. Names play an important role in this book. Marion learns her name means "wished for child." Evelyn has a moniker that makes her feel strong. Marion and Eddie bestow full names on each other. Marion and Evelyn are addressed formally by their last names and intimately by nicknames. Think about the meaning behind your various identities. How does the name define the person? How do the names of the characters provide them with a sense of self?

8. Marion finds comfort, friendship, and a sense of escape while reading books. Do you have a book or character that provides you with similar feelings?

9. In the author note Walsh speaks about the inspirations behind the story, her research, and the reasons for some creative liberties. In reading what inspired her, did this change the reading of the novel for you? What piece of research or anecdote surprised you? Did you feel compelled to read more about the time period or the real-life people who inspired the novel?

10. Walsh's previous novels also feature real-life, independent women: Bonnie Parker and Eleanor Dumont. How do you think having a female voice empowers the reader?

Questions written and compiled by Marisa Gothie and Nicholle Thery-Williams from the Bookends and Friends book club.

ABOUT THE AUTHOR

J enni L. Walsh worked for a decade enticing readers as an award-winning advertising copywriter before becoming an author. Her passion lies in transporting readers to another world, be it in historical or contemporary settings. She is a proud graduate of Villanova University and lives in the Philadelphia suburbs with her husband, daughter, son, and various pets.

Jenni is the author of the historical novels *Becoming Bonnie, Side by Side,* and *A Betting Woman.* She also writes books for children, including the nonfiction She Dared series and the historical novels *Hettie and the London Blitz, I Am Defiance, By the Light of Fireflies,* and *Over and Out.* To learn more about Jenni and her books, please visit jennilwalsh.com or @jennilwalsh on social media.